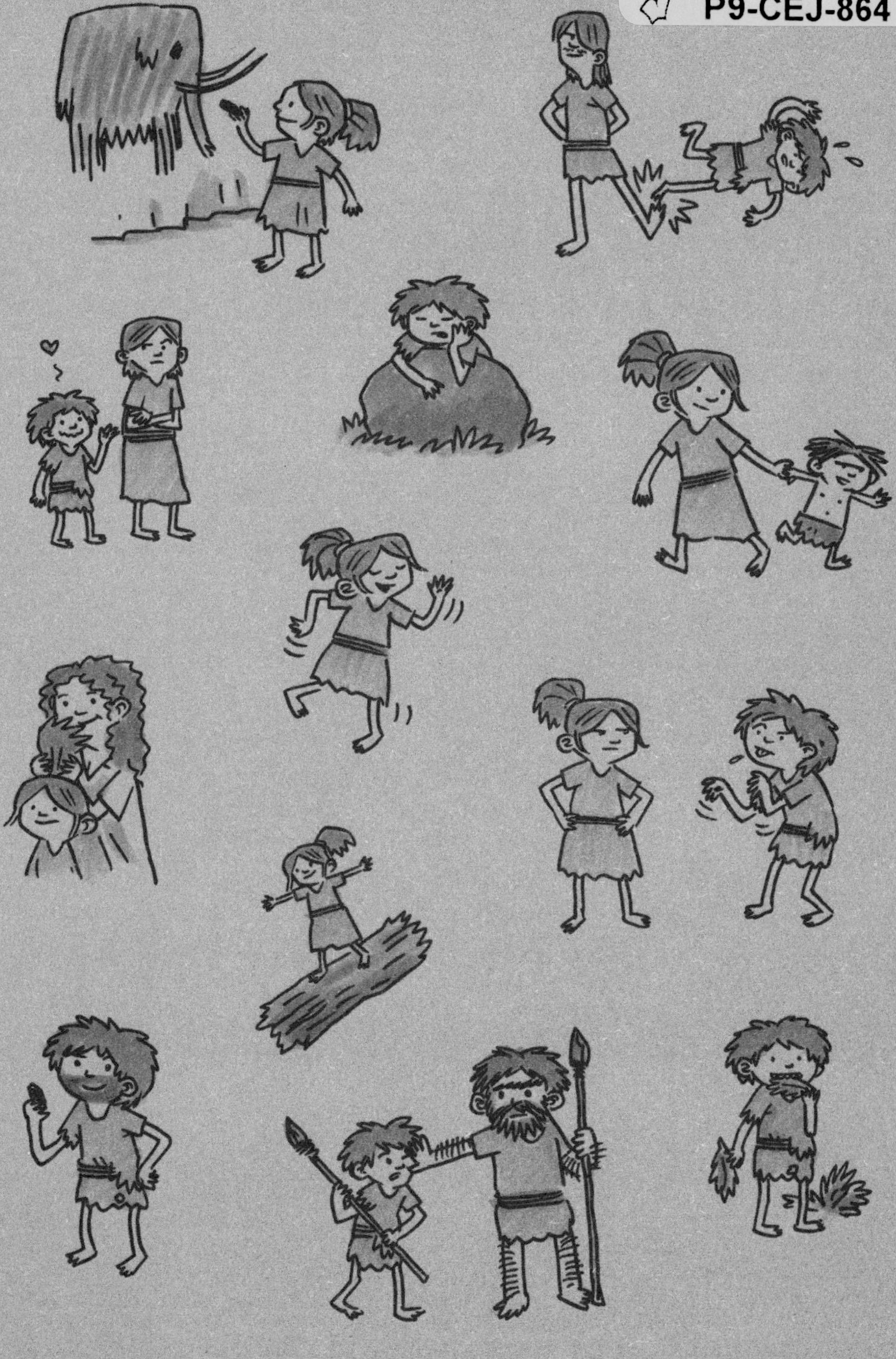

LUCY & ANDY NEANDERTHAL

Also by Jeffrey Brown

LUCY & ANDY NEANDERTHAL: THE STONE COLD AGE

PRAISE FOR

LUCY & ANDY NEANDERTHAL

"Brown's vivacious plotlines are laugh-out-loud funny. . . . This is an auspiciously clever and engaging series opener."
—*Kirkus Reviews*

"Kids will learn a great deal about the Neanderthals while laughing their way through the story. . . . An amusing and enjoyable graphic novel." —*School Library Journal*

"Readers with an interest in fossil discoveries won't be able to put this down." —*Publishers Weekly*

"Brown is particularly adept at drawing out humor in everyday situations, thanks to his spot-on comedic timing. . . . Middle-graders who loved Brown's Jedi Academy series will adore this, too." —*Booklist*

Praise for

STAR WARS: JEDI ACADEMY

★ "With its mix of comics and text, it will also appeal to fans of Jeff Kinney's Diary of a Wimpy Kid and Dav Pilkey's Captain Underpants hybrid books. On a deeper level, this book tackles serious issues like failure, bullying, friendship, determination, and starting a new school in a fun and funny way." —*Booklist*, Starred

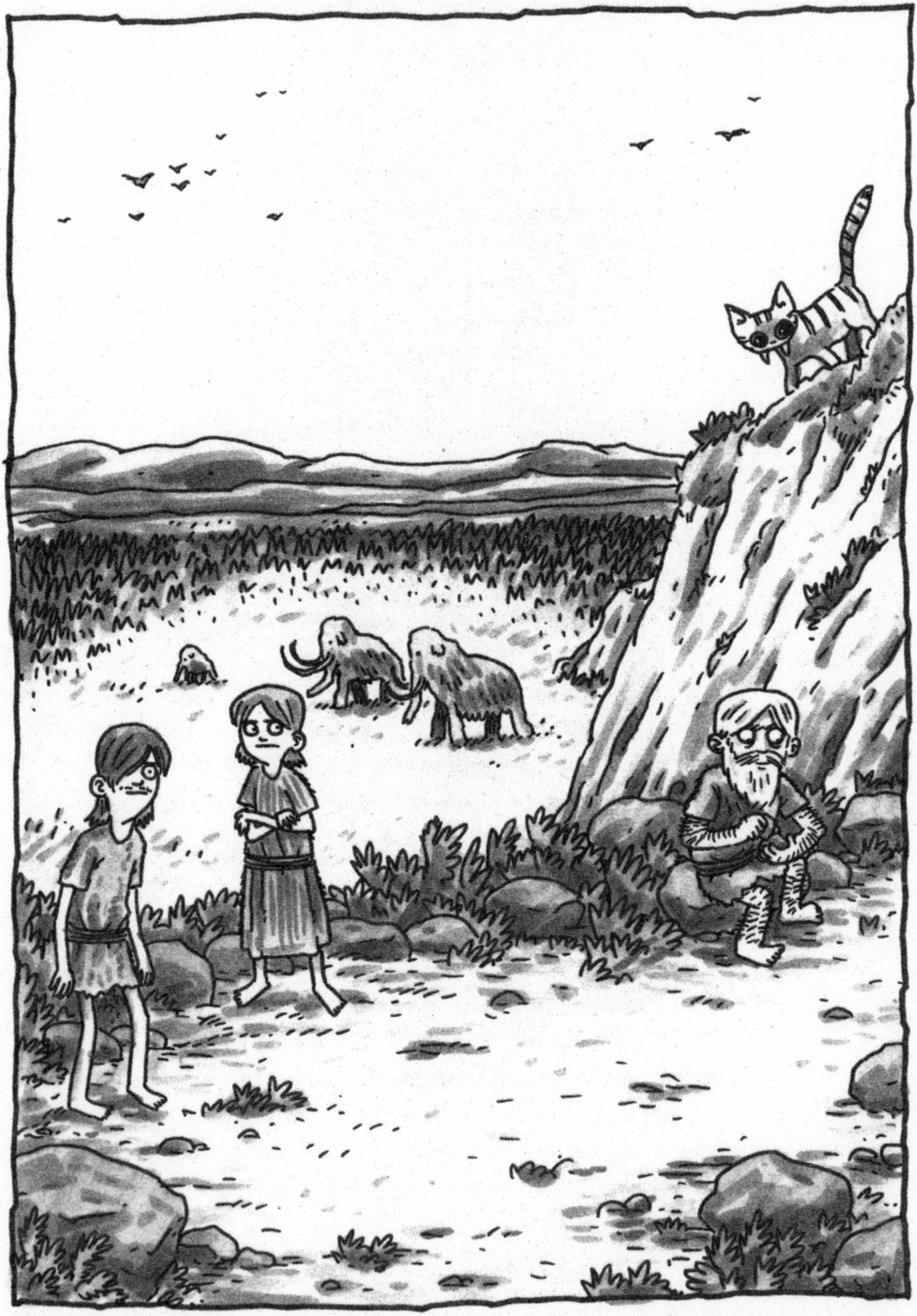

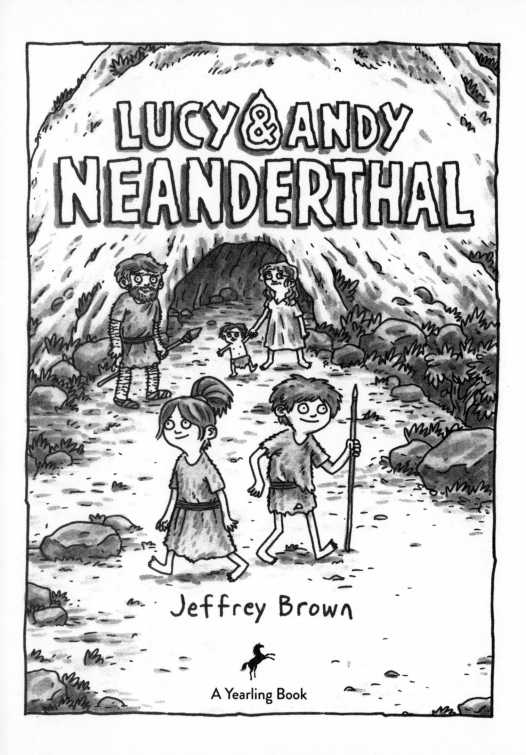

LUCY & ANDY NEANDERTHAL

Jeffrey Brown

A Yearling Book

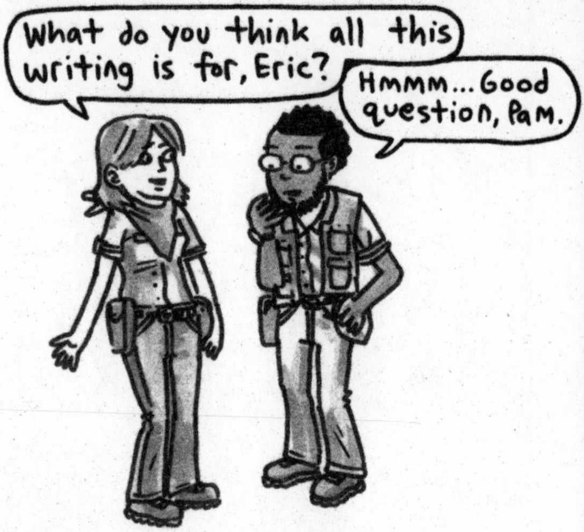
What do you think all this writing is for, Eric?
HMMM... Good question, Pam.

Thank you to my family, friends, publishers, and readers for all of their support. Thanks also to Marc, Phoebe, and everyone at RH for making this book happen. And special thanks to Kevin Lee for giving me the nudge that led to the idea for this book.

For his expert assistance, grateful acknowledgment to Jonathan S. Mitchell, PhD, Evolutionary Biology, and member of the Geological Society of America, Society of Vertebrate Paleontology, and Society for the Study of Evolution.

 Published in the United States by Yearling, an imprint of Random House Children's Books, a division of Penguin Random House LLC, New York. Originally published in hardcover by Crown Books for Young Readers, an imprint of Random House Children's Books, a division of Penguin Random House LLC, New York, in 2016.

Library of Congress Cataloging-in-Publication Data is available upon request.
ISBN 978-0-385-38835-1 (trade) — ISBN 978-0-385-38837-5 (lib. bdg.) — ISBN 978-0-385-38836-8 (ebook) — ISBN 978-0-525-64397-5 (pbk.)

Printed in the United States of America
10 9 8 7 6 5 4 3

First Yearling Edition 2018

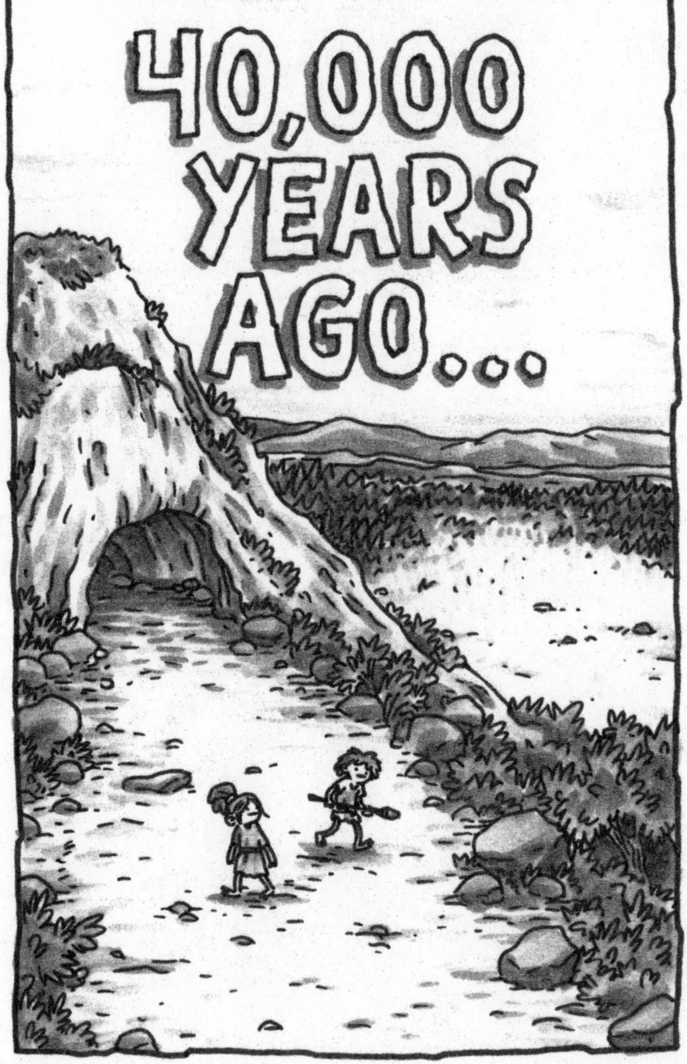
40,000 YEARS AGO...

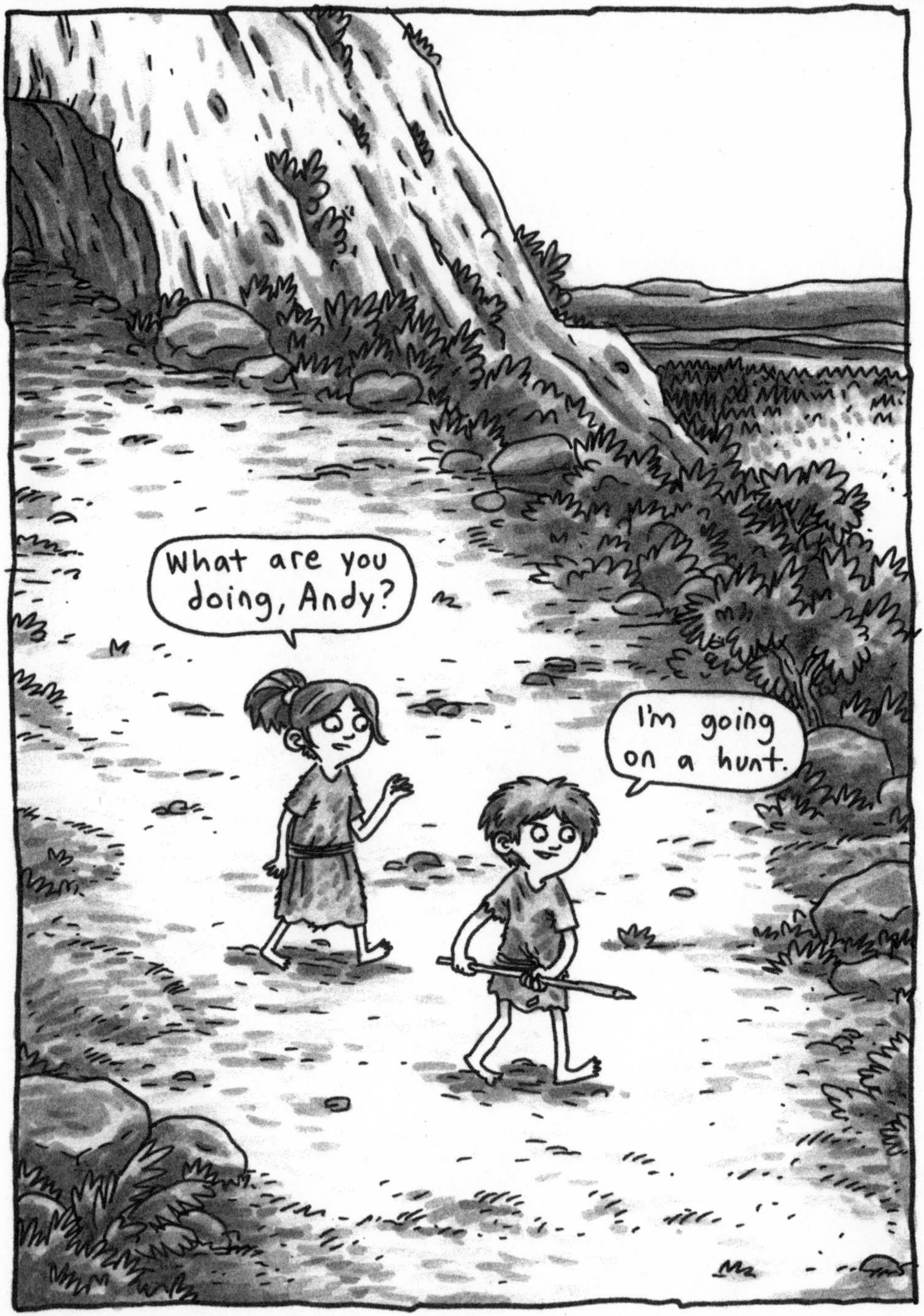
What are you doing, Andy?
I'm going on a hunt.

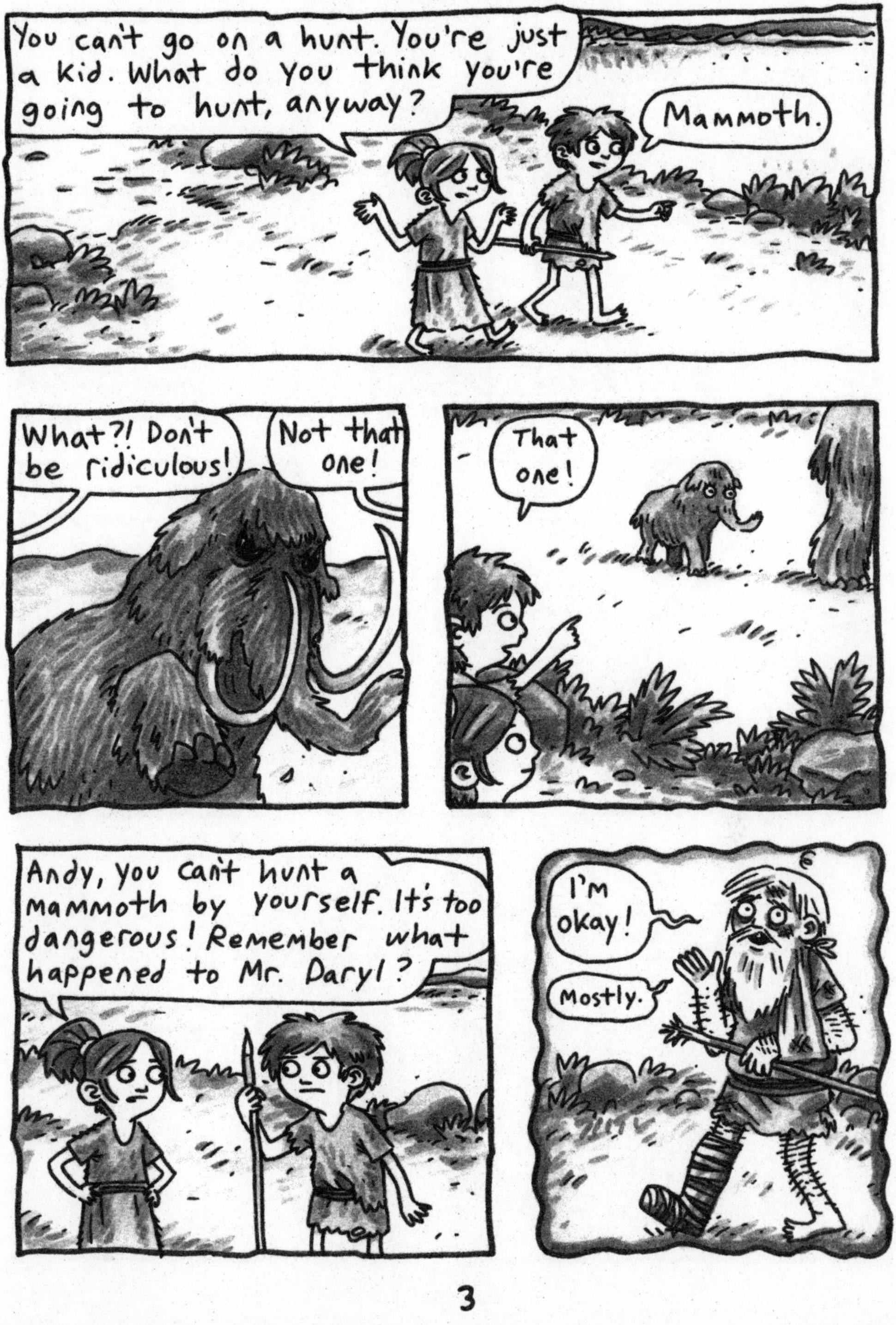
You can't go on a hunt. You're just a kid. What do you think you're going to hunt, anyway?
Mammoth.
What?! Don't be ridiculous!
Not that one!
That one!
Andy, you can't hunt a mammoth by yourself. It's too dangerous! Remember what happened to Mr. Daryl?
I'm okay!
Mostly.

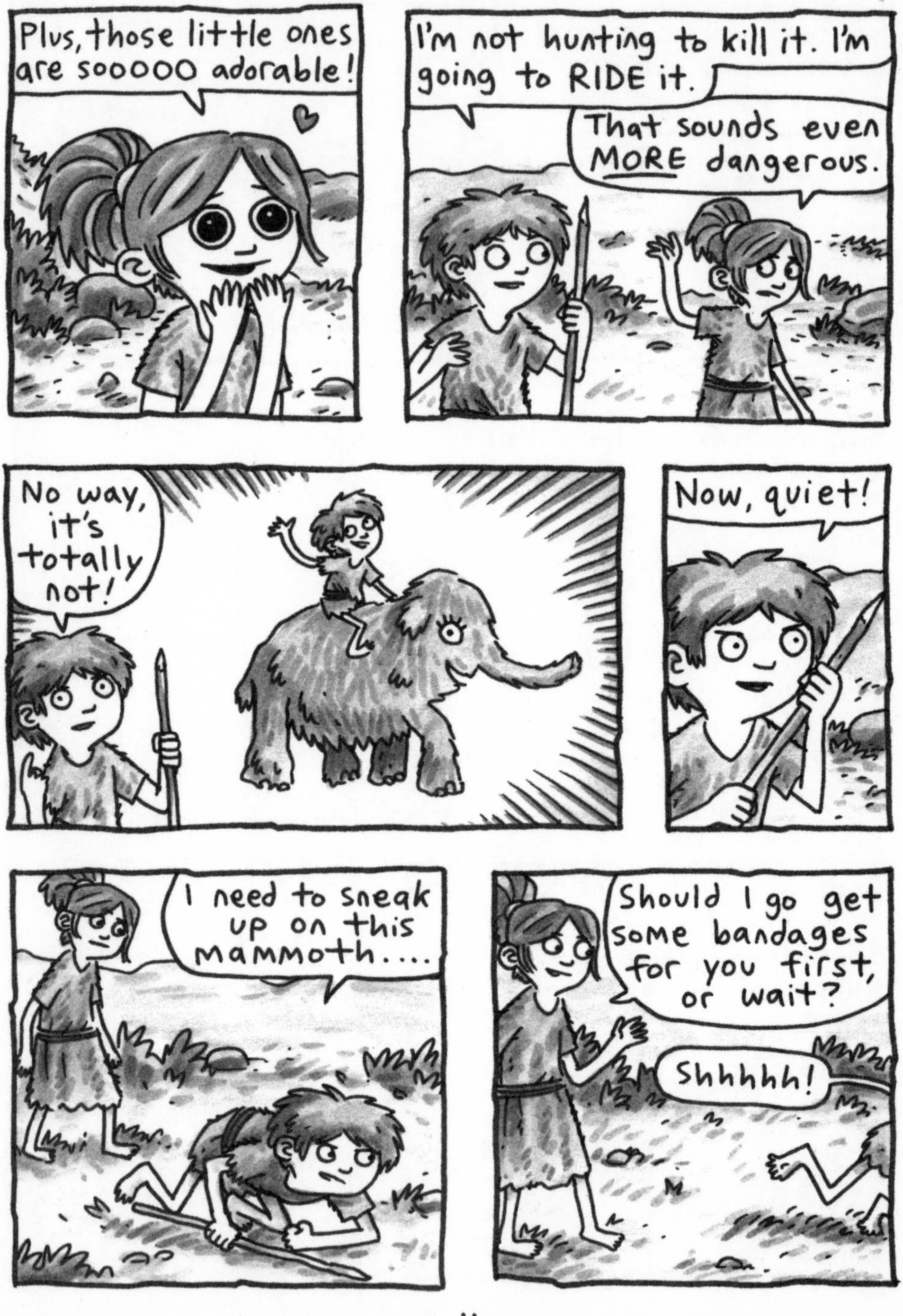
Plus, those little ones are sooooo adorable!
I'm not hunting to kill it. I'm going to RIDE it.
That sounds even MORE dangerous.
No way, it's totally not!
Now, quiet!
I need to sneak up on this mammoth....
Should I go get some bandages for you first, or wait?
Shhhhh!

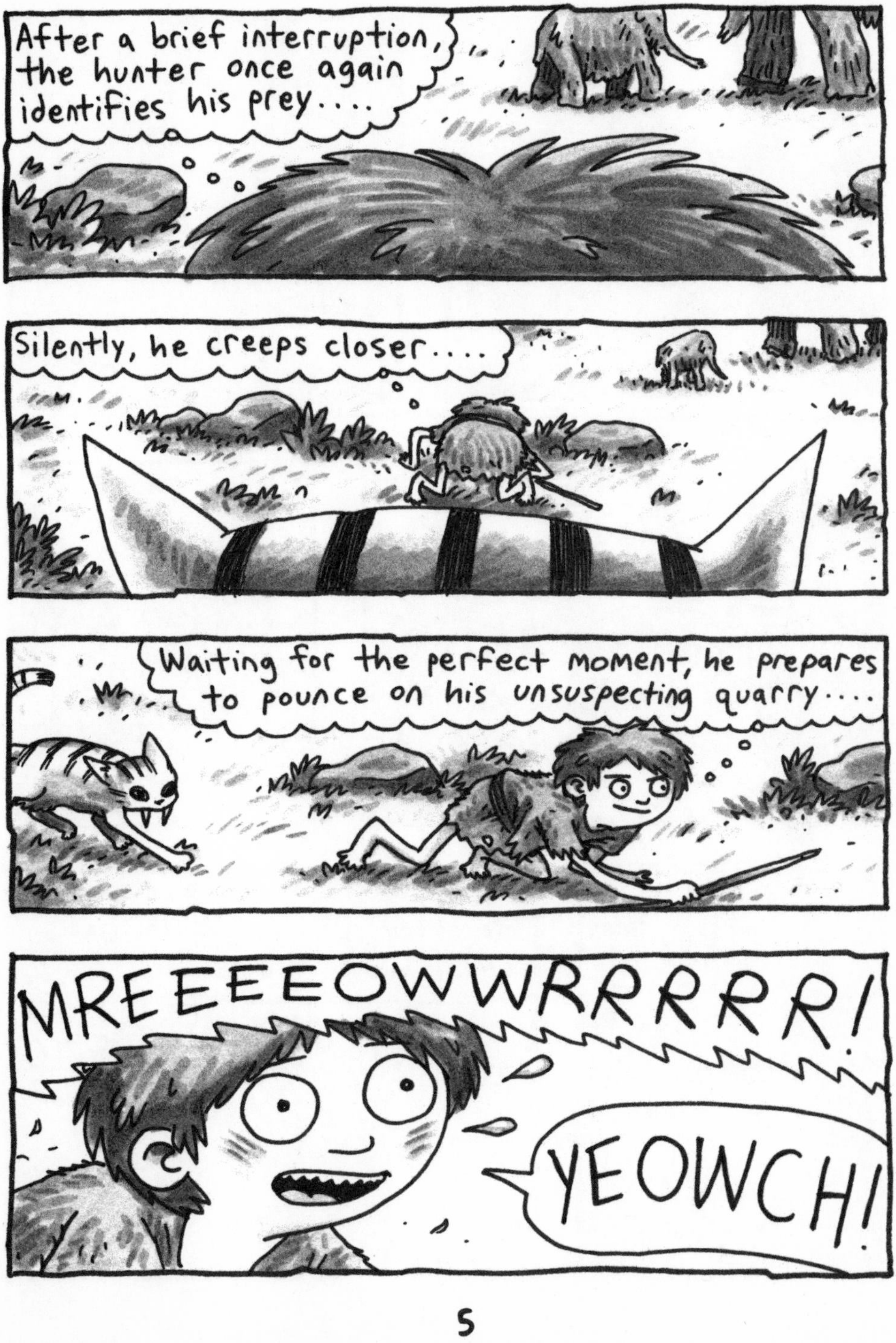
After a brief interruption, the hunter once again identifies his prey....
Silently, he creeps closer....
Waiting for the perfect moment, he prepares to pounce on his unsuspecting quarry....
MREEEEOWWRRRRR!
YEOWCH!

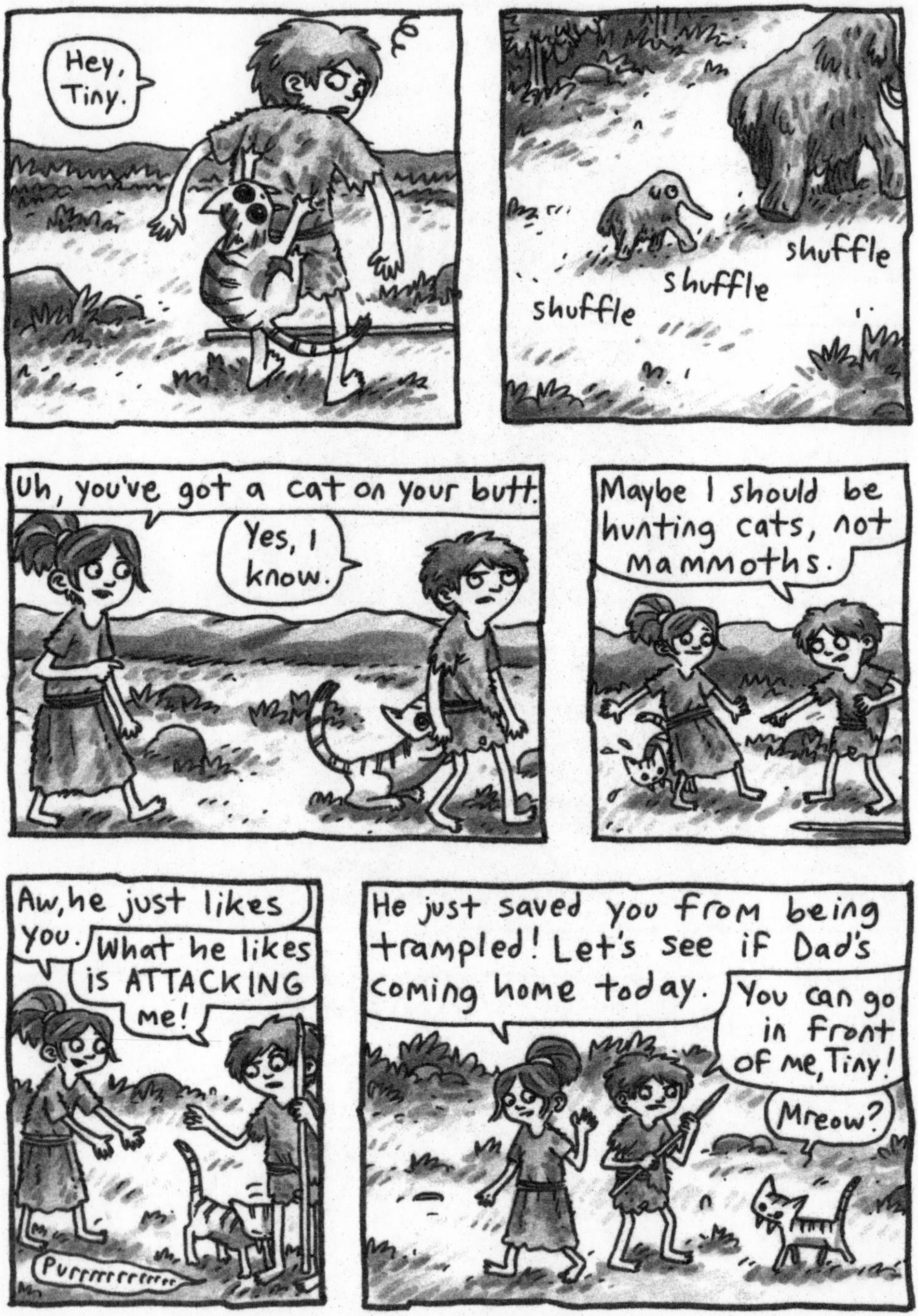
Hey, Tiny.
shuffle
shuffle
shuffle
Uh, you've got a cat on your butt.
Yes, I know.
Maybe I should be hunting cats, not mammoths.
Aw, he just likes you.
What he likes is ATTACKING me!
Purrrrrrrrrr
He just saved you from being trampled! Let's see if Dad's coming home today.
You can go in front of me, Tiny!
Mreow?

ACTUALLY, Neanderthals probably didn't have pet cats, because there were no house cats 40,000 years ago. The cats back then tended to be a lot bigger. Their pounces were much less friendly!

Cave lion

European jaguar

Nice kitties!

Ngandong tiger

The saber-toothed cat Smilodon didn't live in the same places as Neanderthals, but the smaller Homotherium — scimitar cat — did. It wasn't as tiny as a house cat in reality, though.

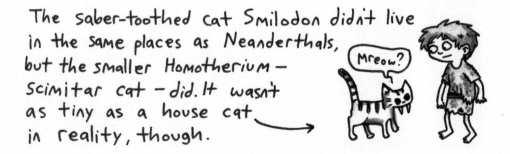

Mreow?

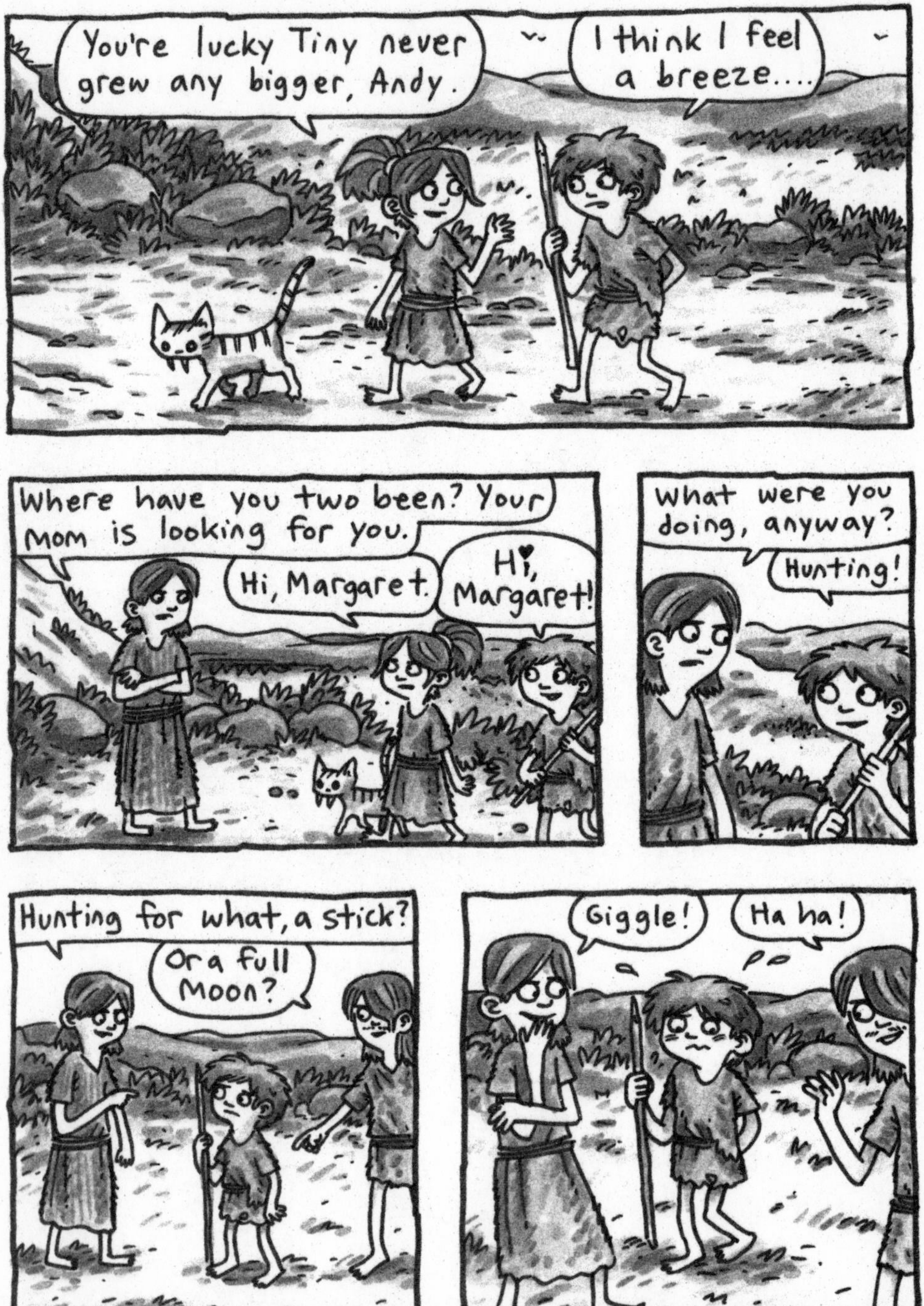
You're lucky Tiny never grew any bigger, Andy.
I think I feel a breeze....
Where have you two been? Your Mom is looking for you.
Hi, Margaret.
Hi, Margaret!
What were you doing, anyway?
Hunting!
Hunting for what, a stick?
Or a full Moon?
Giggle!
Ha ha!

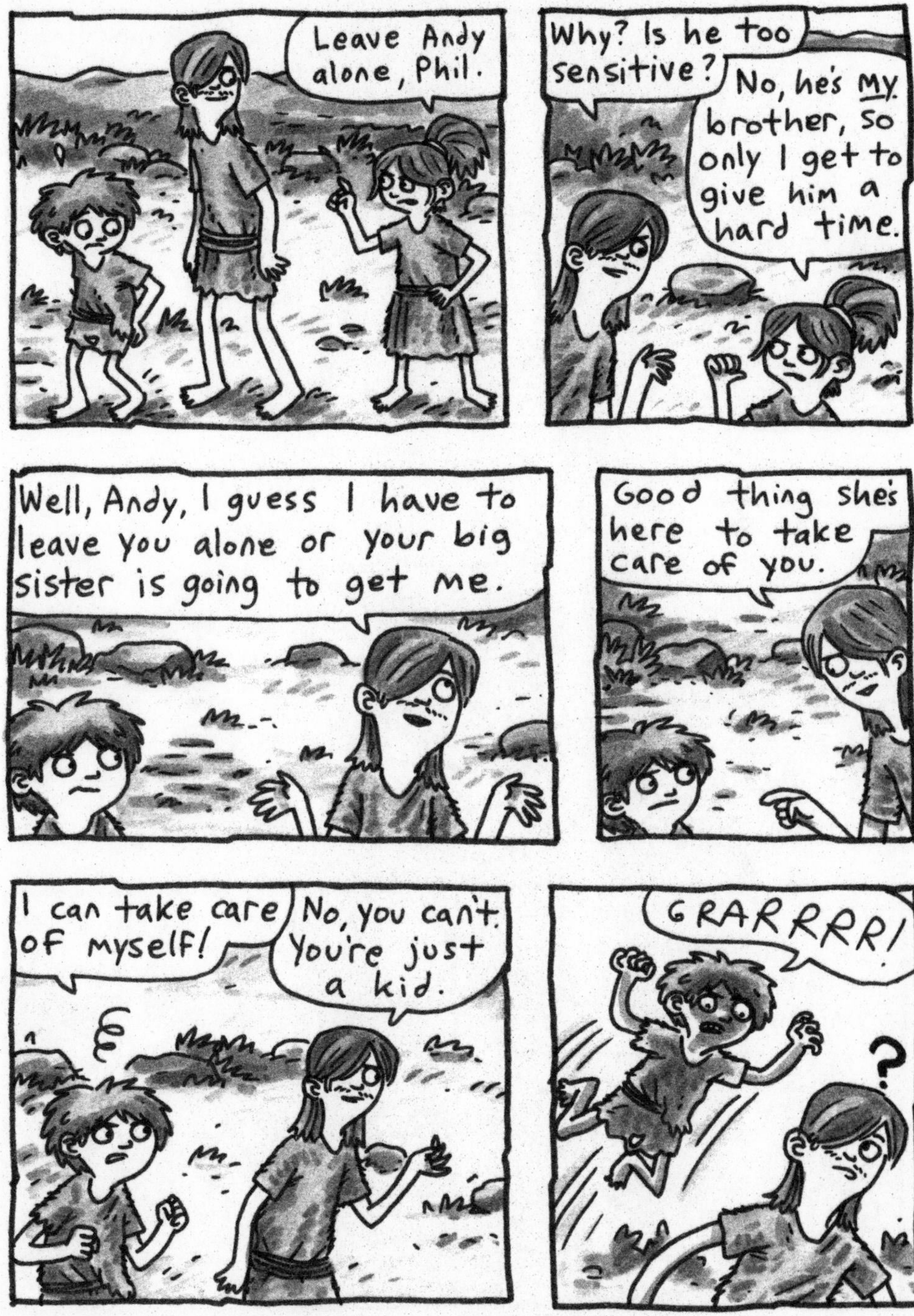

Leave Andy alone, Phil.
Why? Is he too sensitive?
No, he's MY brother, so only I get to give him a hard time.
Well, Andy, I guess I have to leave you alone or your big sister is going to get me.
Good thing she's here to take care of you.
I can take care of myself!
No, you can't. You're just a kid.
GRARRRR!
?

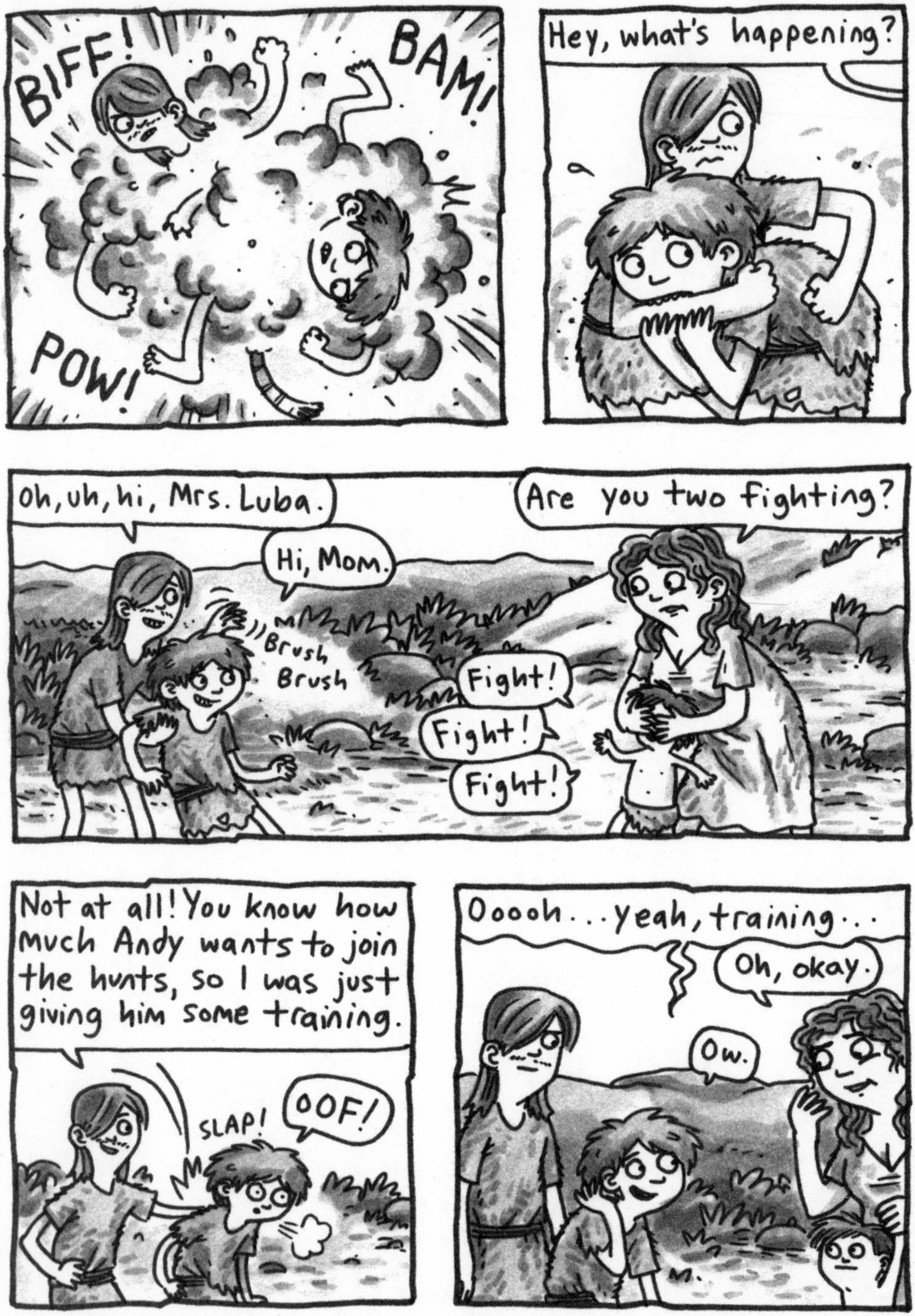
BIFF!
BAM!
POW!
Hey, what's happening?
Oh, uh, hi, Mrs. Luba.
Are you two fighting?
Hi, Mom.
Brush
Brush
Fight!
Fight!
Fight!
Not at all! You know how much Andy wants to join the hunts, so I was just giving him some training.
SLAP!
OOF!
Ooooh...yeah, training...
Oh, okay.
Ow.

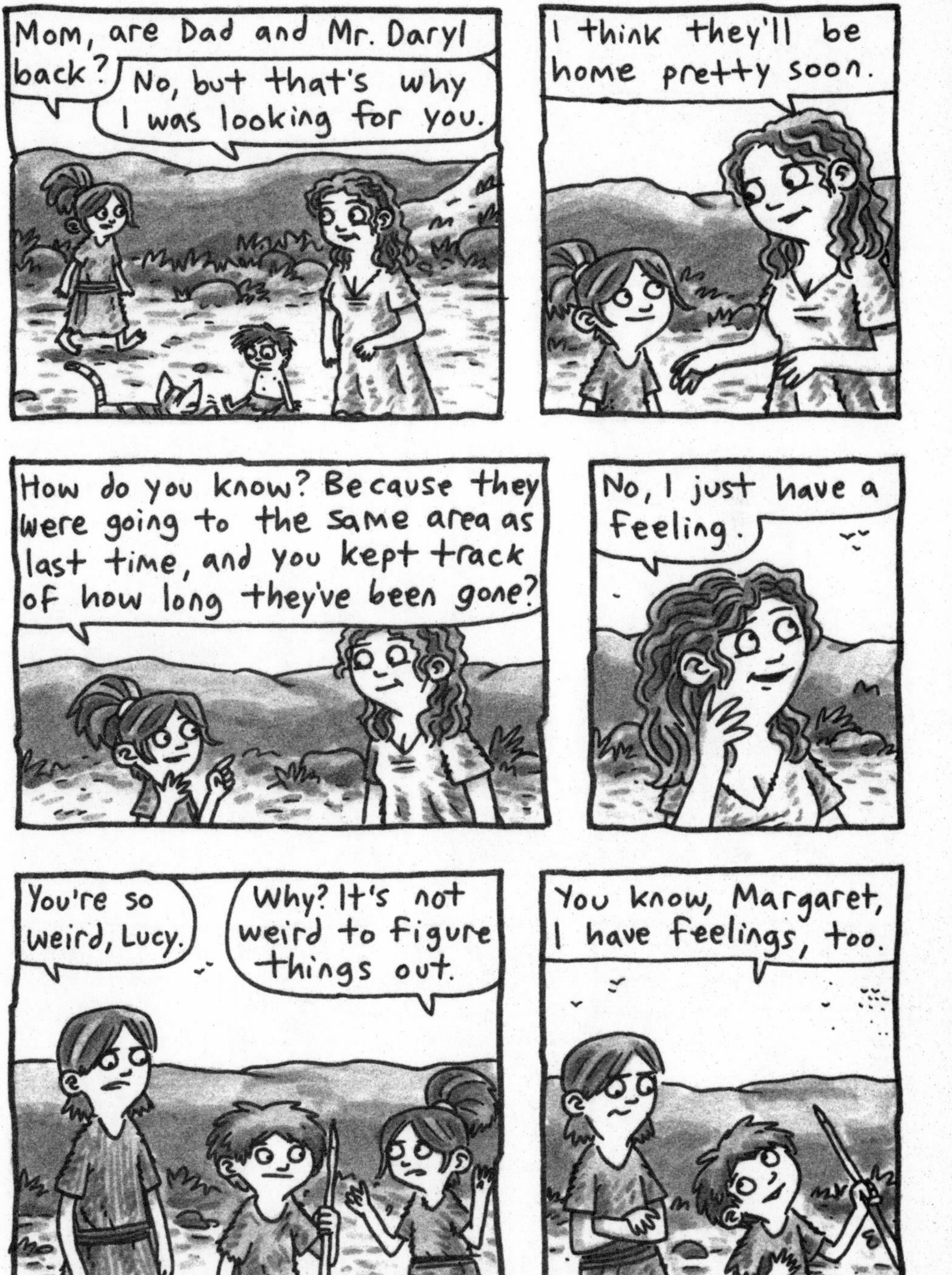
Mom, are Dad and Mr. Daryl back?
No, but that's why I was looking for you.
I think they'll be home pretty soon.
How do you know? Because they were going to the same area as last time, and you kept track of how long they've been gone?
No, I just have a feeling.
You're so weird, Lucy.
Why? It's not weird to figure things out.
You know, Margaret, I have feelings, too.

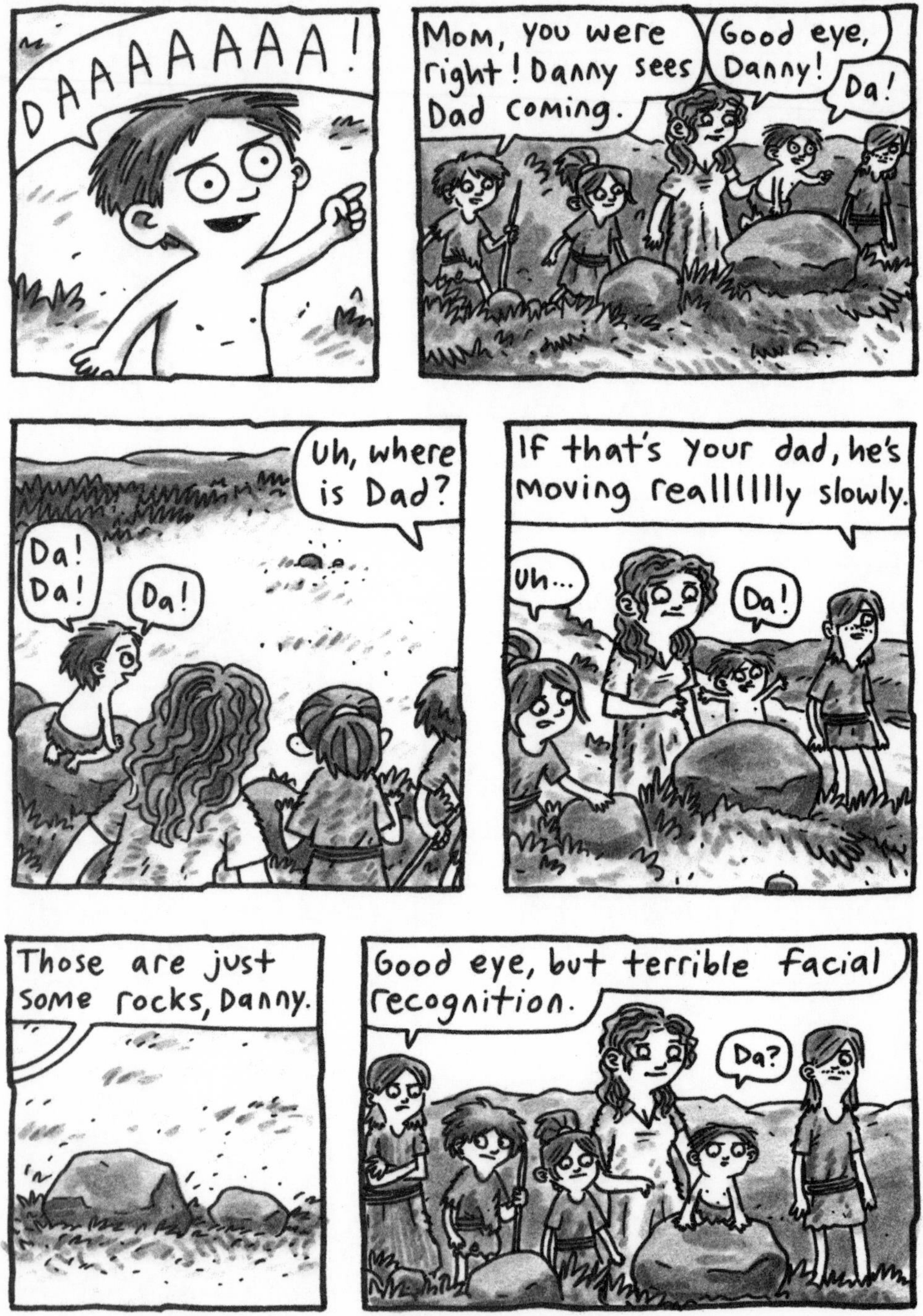
DAAAAAAA!
Mom, you were right! Danny sees Dad coming.
Good eye, Danny!
Da!
Uh, where is Dad?
Da! Da!
Da!
If that's your dad, he's moving reallllllly slowly.
Uh...
Da!
Those are just some rocks, Danny.
Good eye, but terrible facial recognition.
Da?

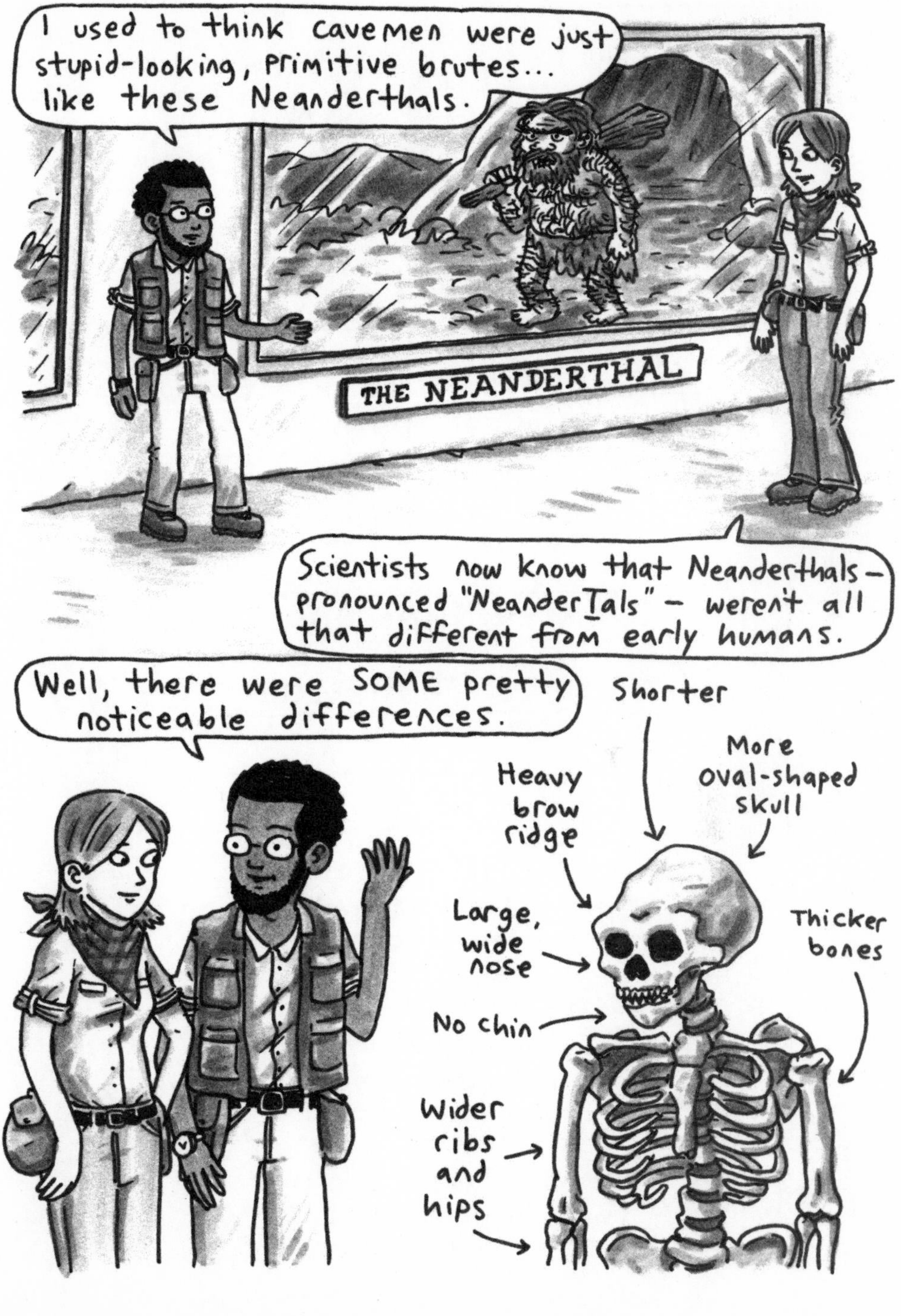
I used to think cavemen were just stupid-looking, primitive brutes... like these Neanderthals.
THE NEANDERTHAL
Scientists now know that Neanderthals—pronounced "NeanderTals"—weren't all that different from early humans.
Well, there were SOME pretty noticeable differences.
Shorter
More oval-shaped skull
Heavy brow ridge
Large, wide nose
No chin
Thicker bones
Wider ribs and hips

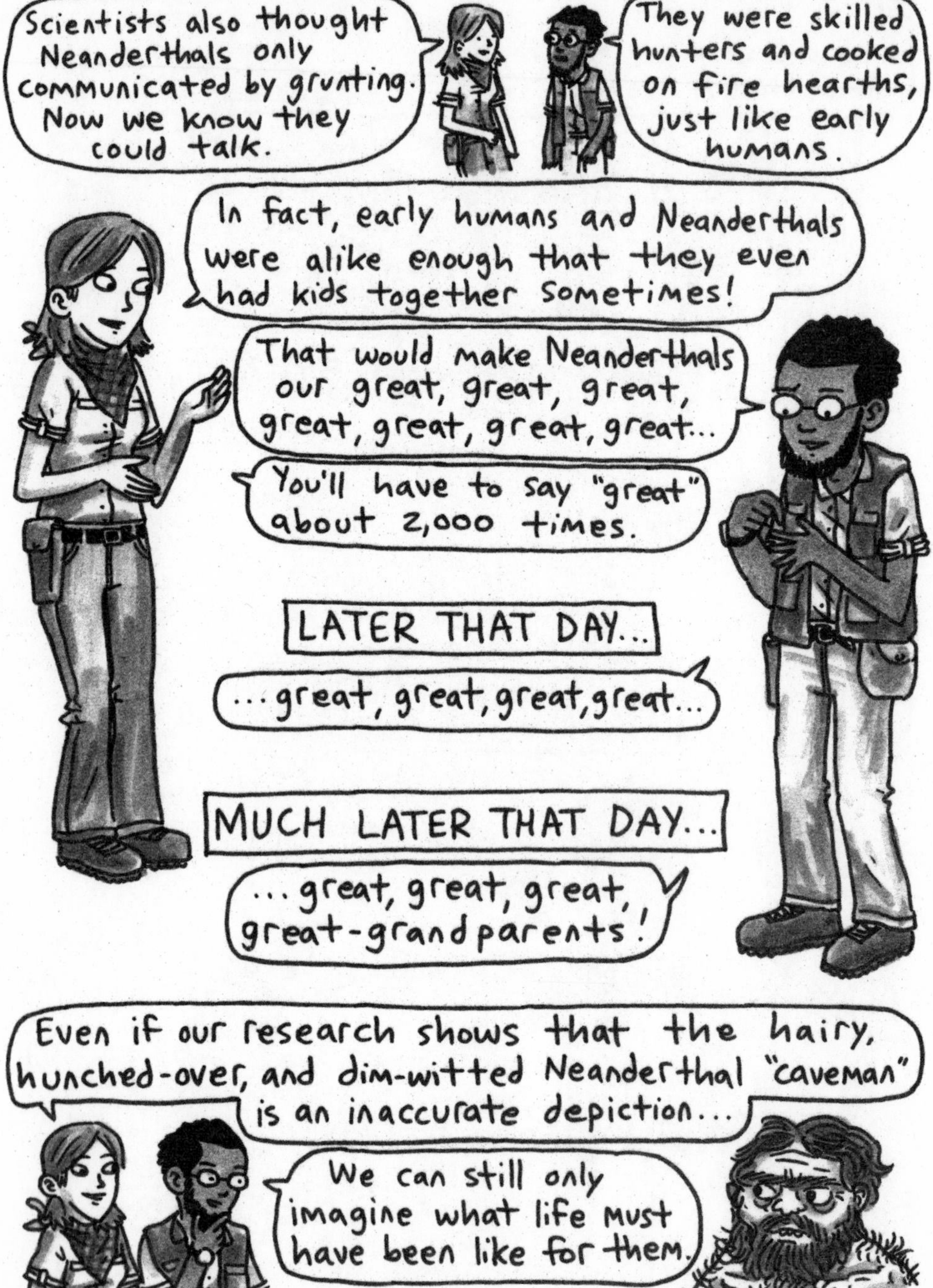
Scientists also thought Neanderthals only communicated by grunting. Now we know they could talk.
They were skilled hunters and cooked on fire hearths, just like early humans.
In fact, early humans and Neanderthals were alike enough that they even had kids together sometimes!
That would make Neanderthals our great, great, great, great, great, great, great...
You'll have to say "great" about 2,000 times.
LATER THAT DAY...
...great, great, great, great...
MUCH LATER THAT DAY...
...great, great, great, great-grandparents!
Even if our research shows that the hairy, hunched-over, and dim-witted Neanderthal "caveman" is an inaccurate depiction...
We can still only imagine what life must have been like for them.

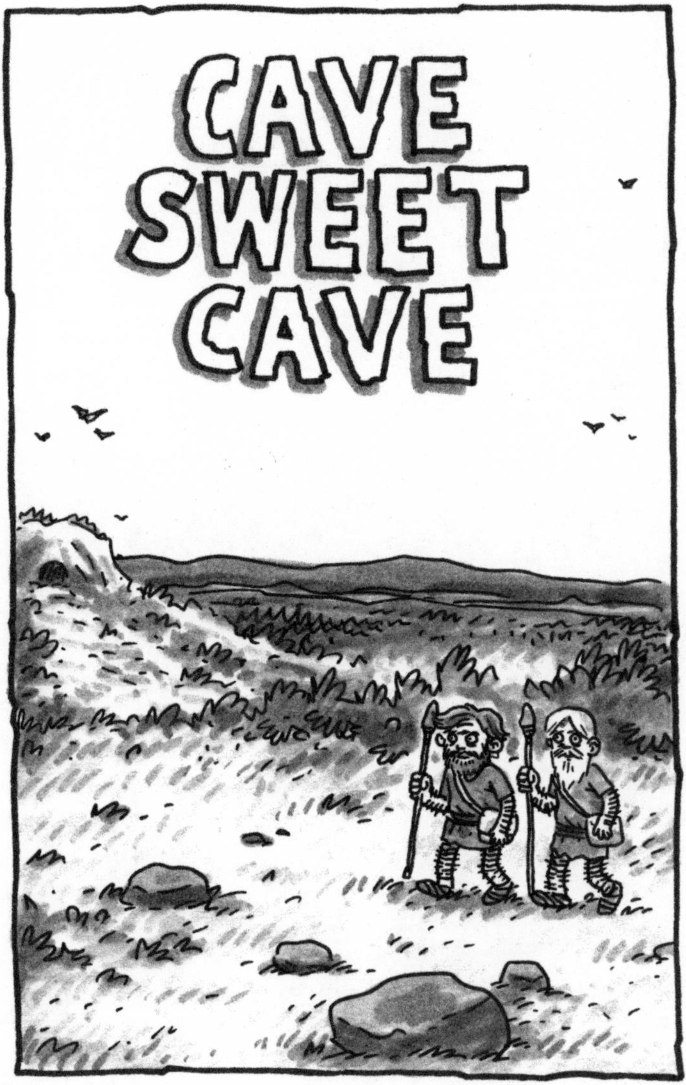
CAVE
SWEET
CAVE

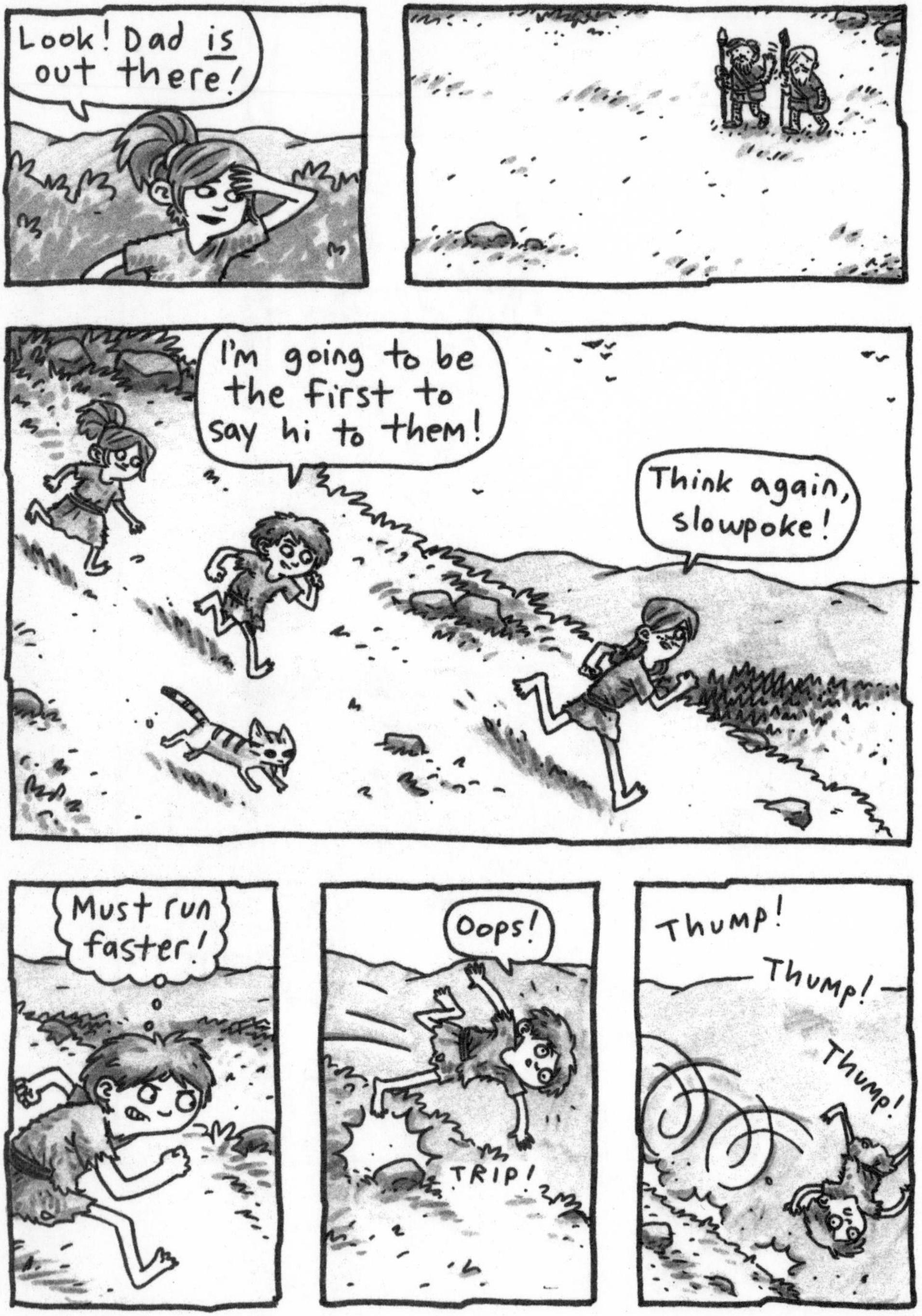
Look! Dad is out there!
I'm going to be the first to say hi to them!
Think again, slowpoke!
Must run faster!
Oops!
TRIP!
Thump!
Thump!
Thump!

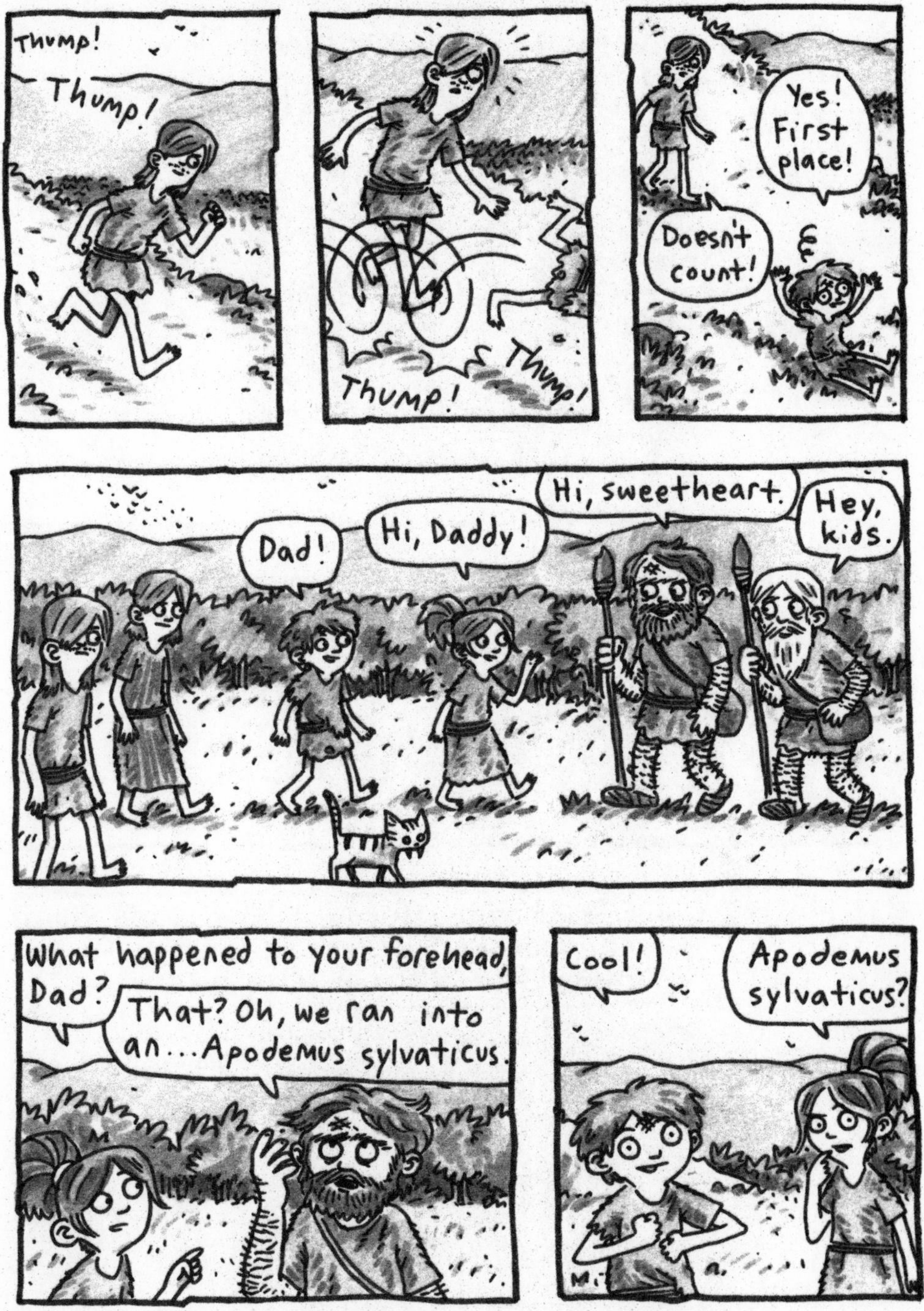
Thump!
Thump!
Thump!
Thump!
Yes! First place!
Doesn't count!
Dad!
Hi, Daddy!
Hi, sweetheart.
Hey, kids.
What happened to your forehead, Dad?
That? Oh, we ran into an...Apodemus sylvaticus.
Cool!
Apodemus sylvaticus?

Apodemus sylvaticus (common name: wood mouse)

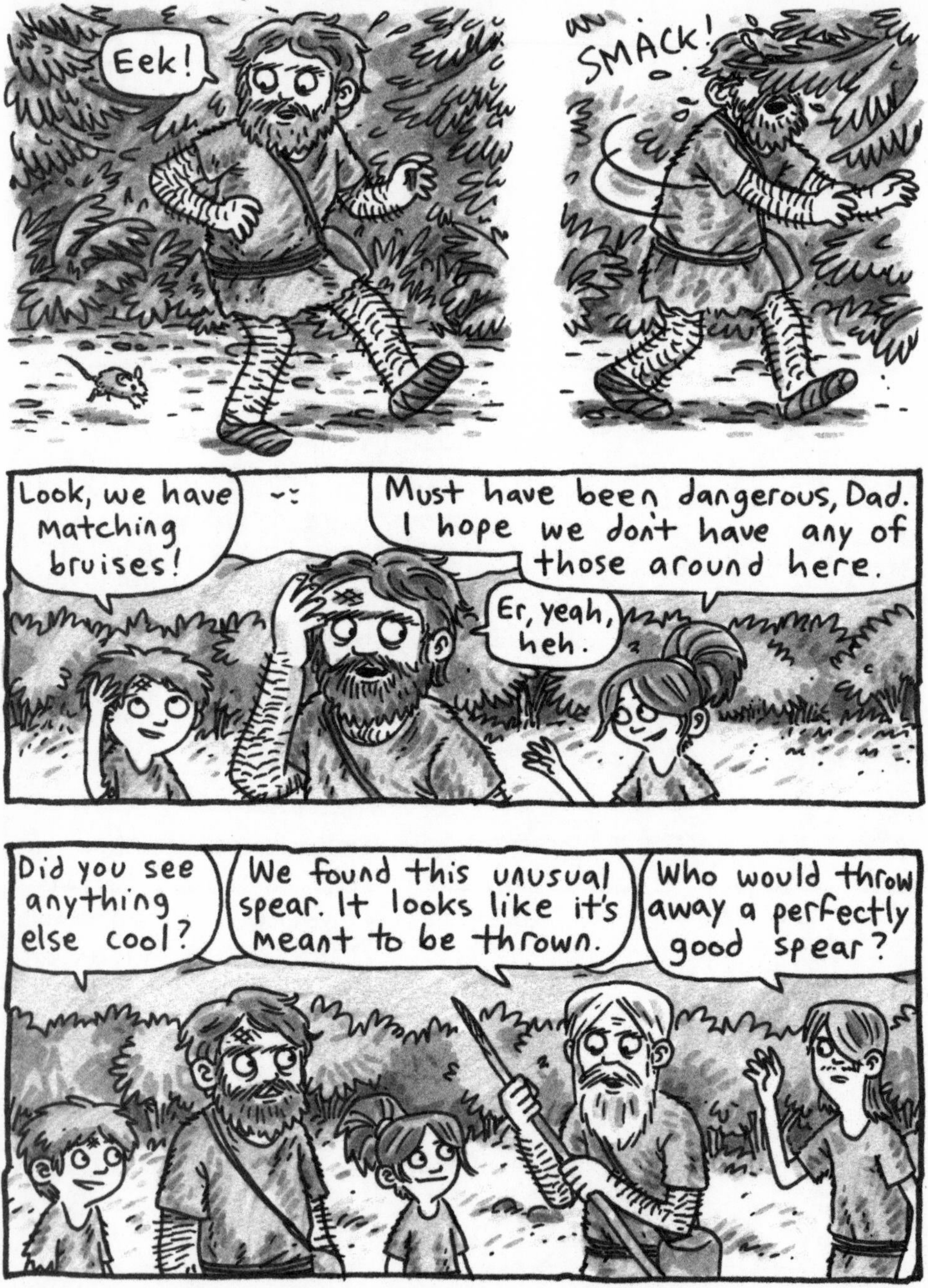
Eek!
SMACK!
Look, we have matching bruises!
Must have been dangerous, Dad. I hope we don't have any of those around here.
Er, yeah, heh.
Did you see anything else cool?
We found this unusual spear. It looks like it's meant to be thrown.
Who would throw away a perfectly good spear?

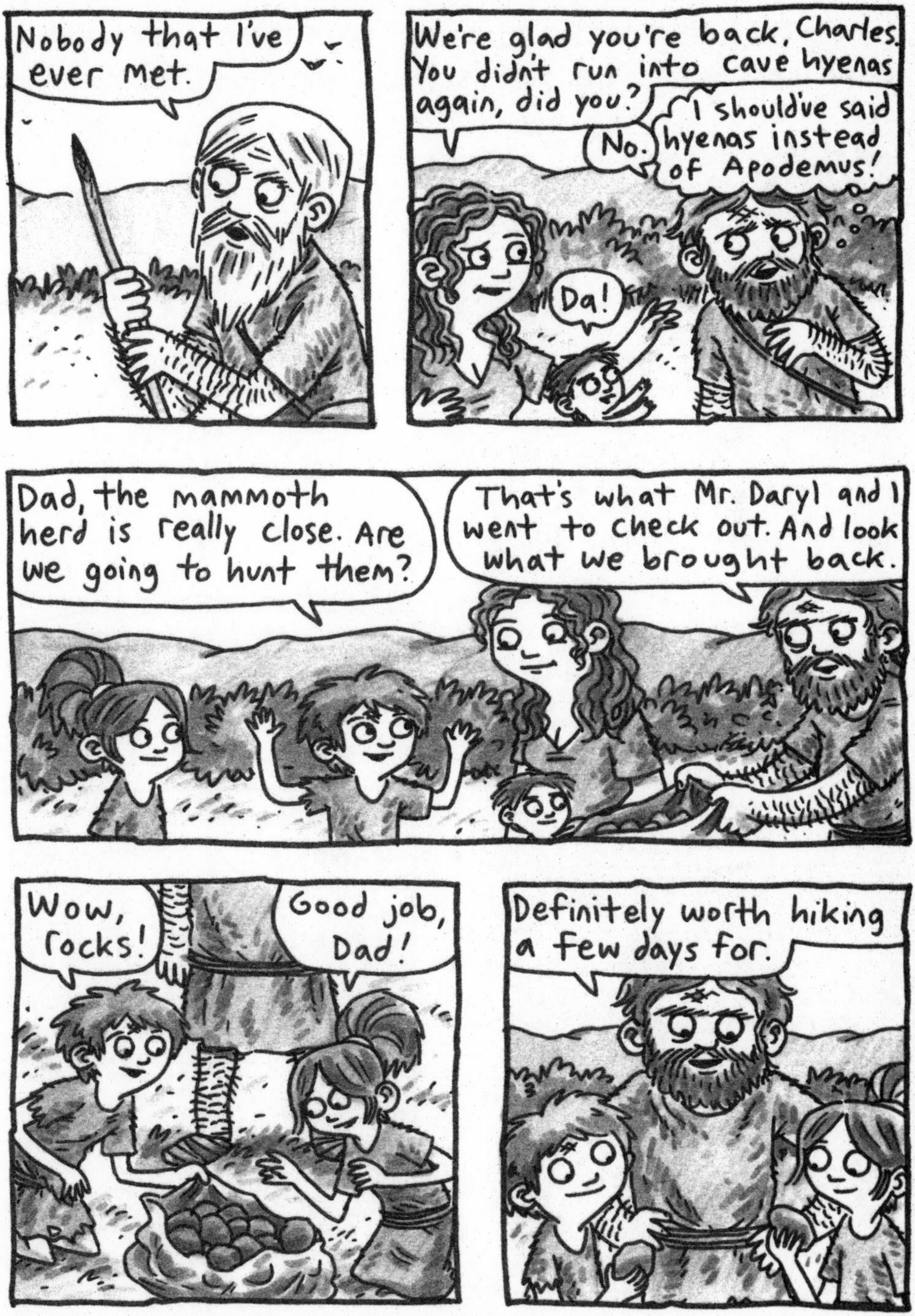
Nobody that I've ever met.
We're glad you're back, Charles. You didn't run into cave hyenas again, did you?
No.
I should've said hyenas instead of Apodemus!
Da!
Dad, the mammoth herd is really close. Are we going to hunt them?
That's what Mr. Daryl and I went to check out. And look what we brought back.
Wow, rocks!
Good job, Dad!
Definitely worth hiking a few days for.

The Stone Age gets its name from the material used at that time for toolmaking: Stone, of course!

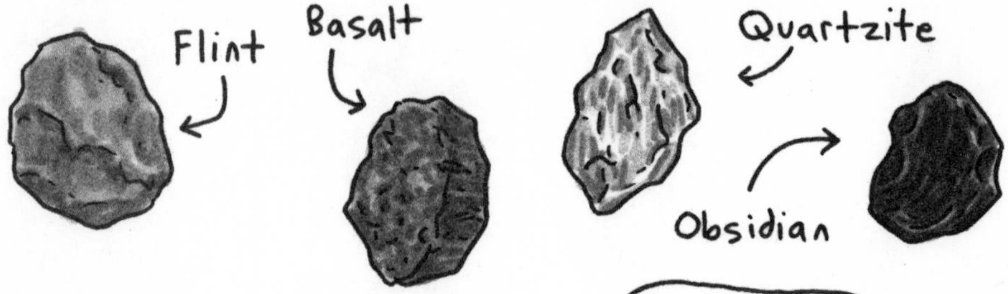
Flint
Basalt
Quartzite
Obsidian

Neanderthals created their tools using stones found nearby, but would also walk more than ten miles away to get better rocks that could be made into higher-quality tools.

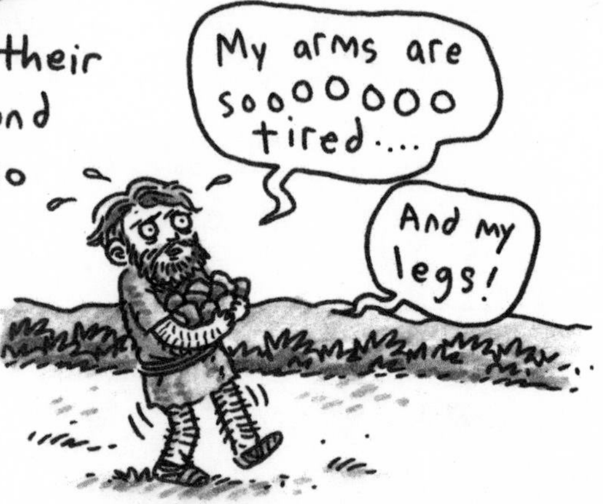
My arms are soooOOOOO tired....
And my legs!

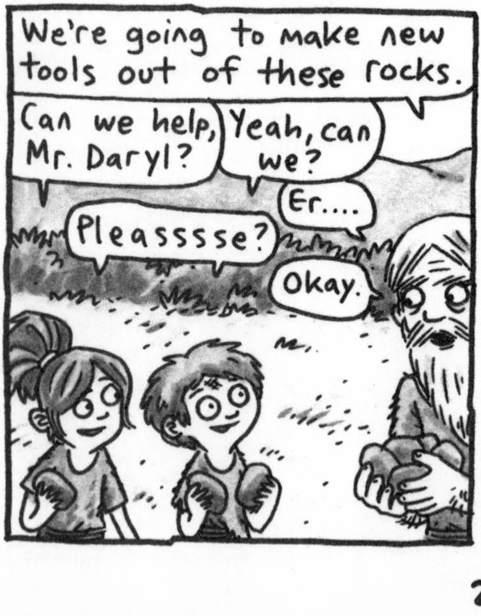
We're going to make new tools out of these rocks.
Can we help, Mr. Daryl?
Yeah, can we?
Er....
Pleasssse?
Okay.

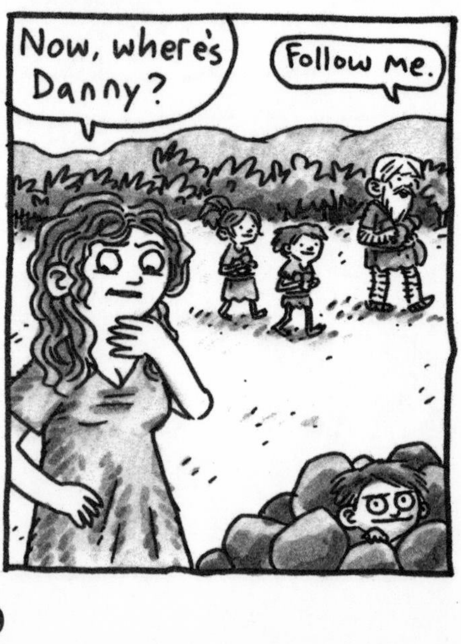
Now, where's Danny?
Follow me.

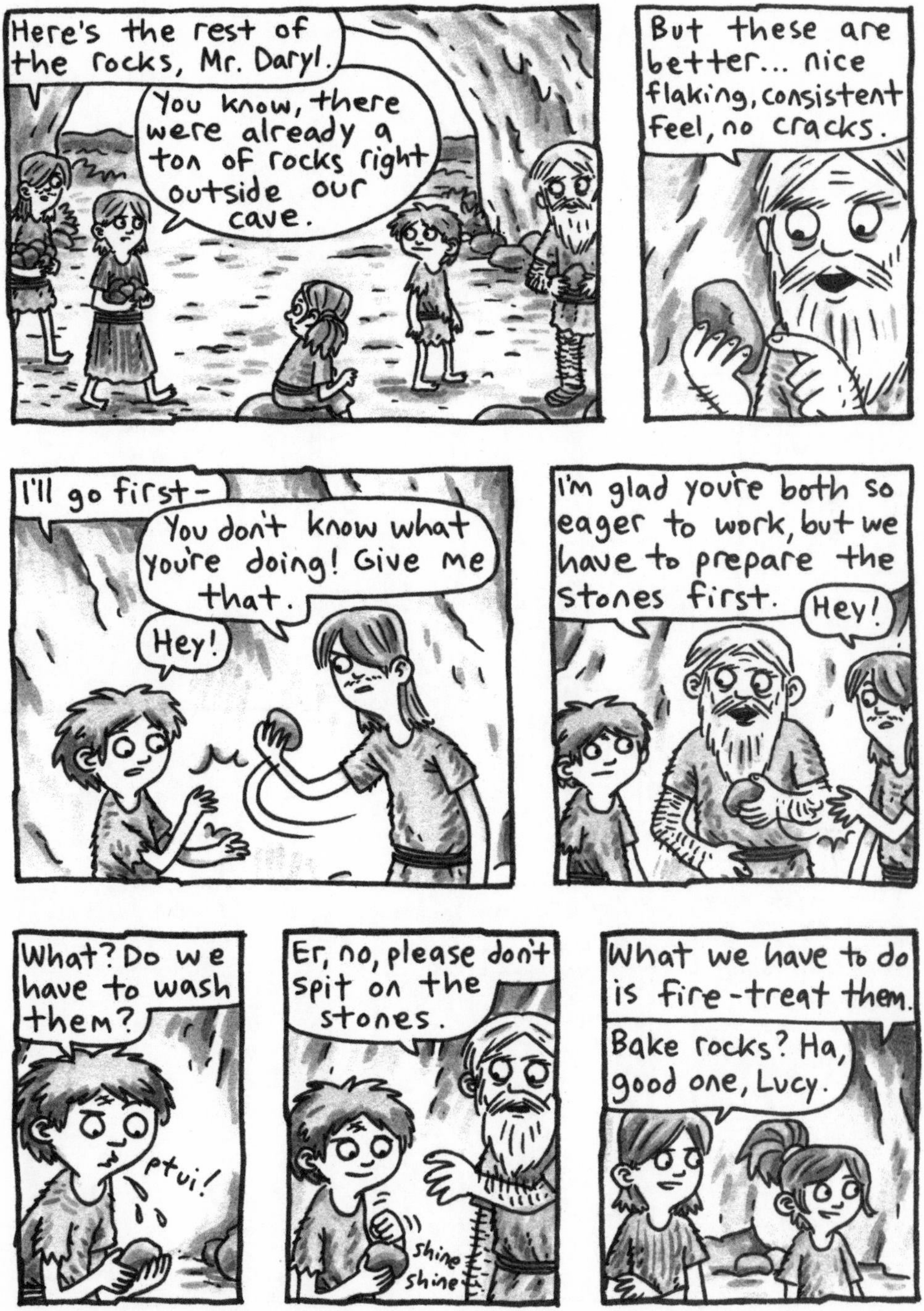
Here's the rest of the rocks, Mr. Daryl.
You know, there were already a ton of rocks right outside our cave.
But these are better... nice flaking, consistent feel, no cracks.
I'll go first-
You don't know what you're doing! Give me that.
Hey!
I'm glad you're both so eager to work, but we have to prepare the stones first.
Hey!
What? Do we have to wash them?
ptui!
Er, no, please don't spit on the stones.
shine
shine
What we have to do is fire-treat them.
Bake rocks? Ha, good one, Lucy.

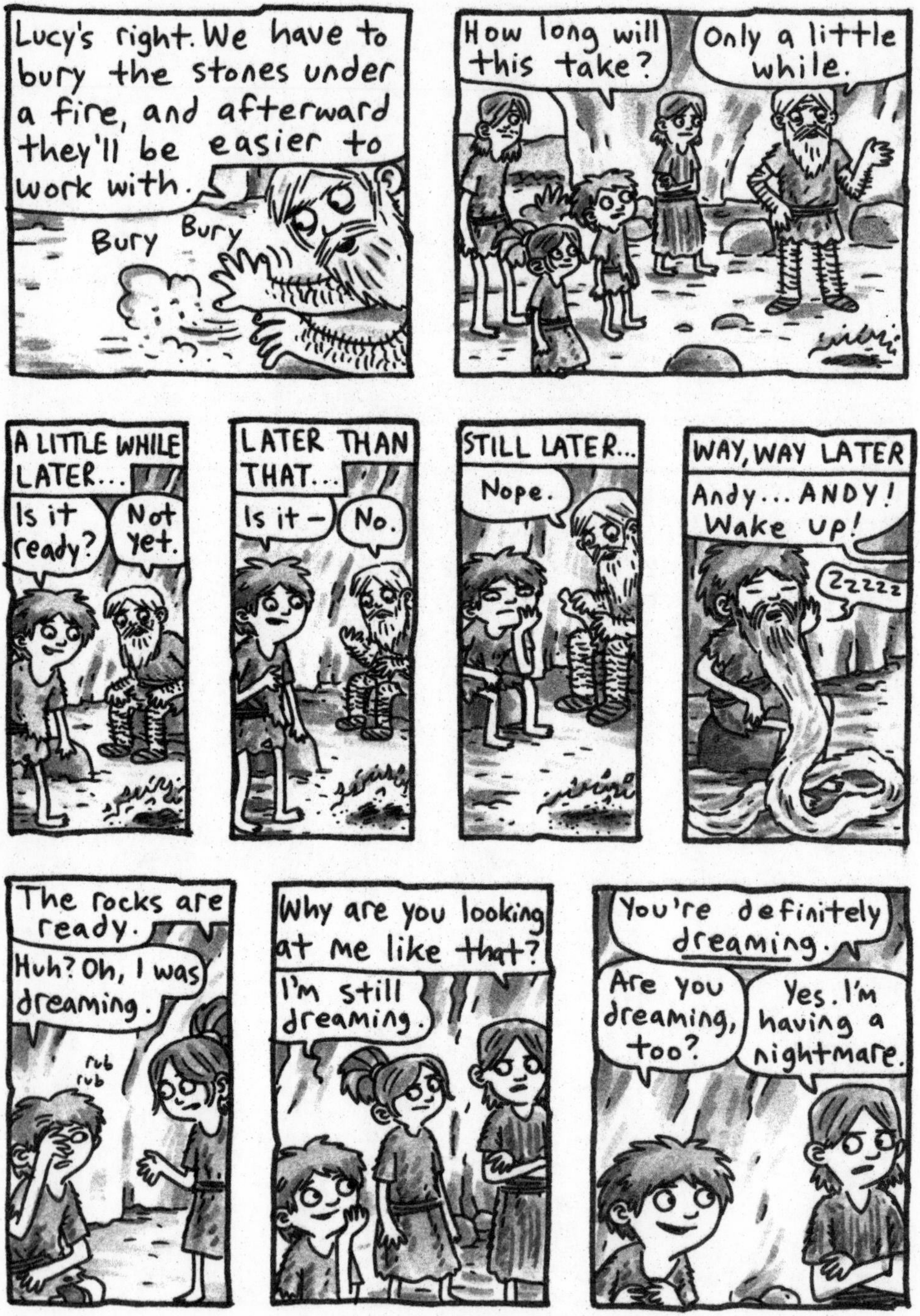

Lucy's right. We have to bury the stones under a fire, and afterward they'll be easier to work with.
Bury
Bury
How long will this take?
Only a little while.
A LITTLE WHILE LATER...
Is it ready?
Not yet.
LATER THAN THAT...
Is it –
No.
STILL LATER...
Nope.
WAY, WAY LATER
Andy... ANDY! Wake up!
Zzzzz
The rocks are ready.
Huh? Oh, I was dreaming.
rub rub
Why are you looking at me like that?
I'm still dreaming.
You're definitely dreaming.
Are you dreaming, too?
Yes. I'm having a nightmare.

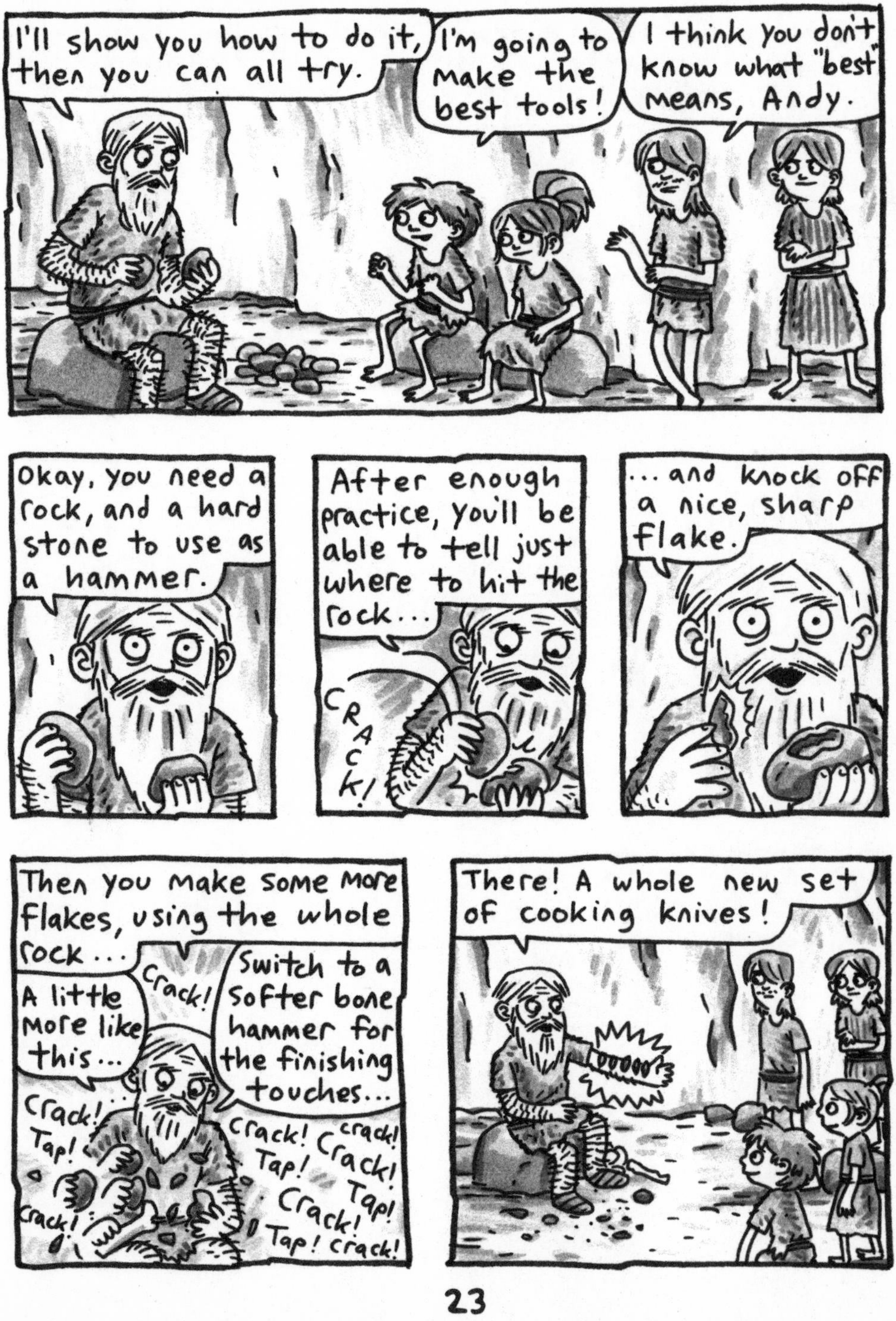
I'll show you how to do it, then you can all try.
I'm going to make the best tools!
I think you don't know what "best" means, Andy.
Okay, you need a rock, and a hard stone to use as a hammer.
After enough practice, you'll be able to tell just where to hit the rock...
CRACK!
...and knock off a nice, sharp flake.
Then you make some more flakes, using the whole rock...
A little more like this...
Crack!
Switch to a softer bone hammer for the finishing touches...
Crack! Tap!
Crack!
Crack! crack! Crack! Tap! Tap! Crack! Tap! crack!
There! A whole new set of cooking knives!

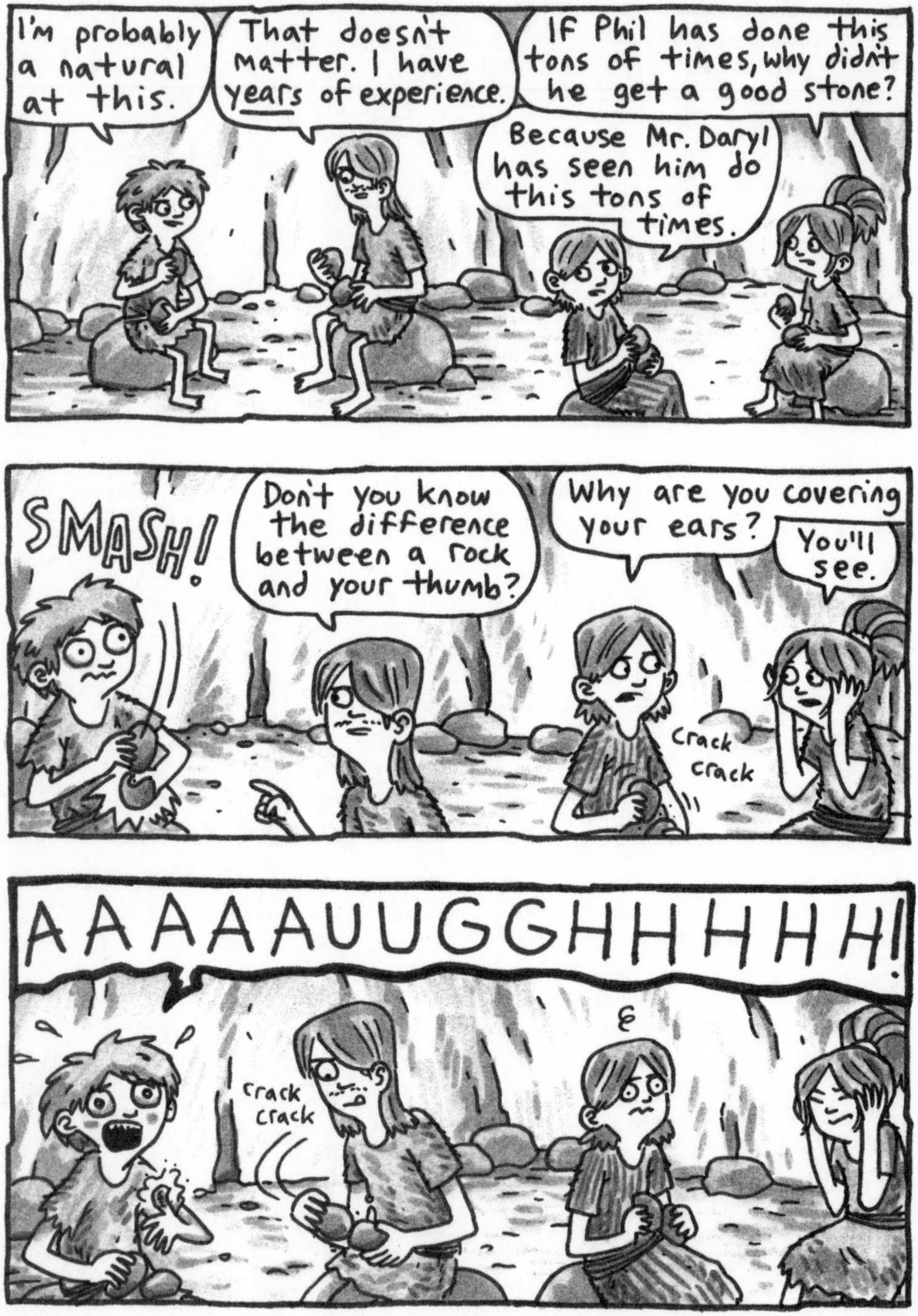
I'm probably a natural at this.
That doesn't matter. I have years of experience.
If Phil has done this tons of times, why didn't he get a good stone?
Because Mr. Daryl has seen him do this tons of times.
SMASH!
Don't you know the difference between a rock and your thumb?
Why are you covering your ears?
You'll see.
crack crack
AAAAAUUGGHHHHH!
crack crack

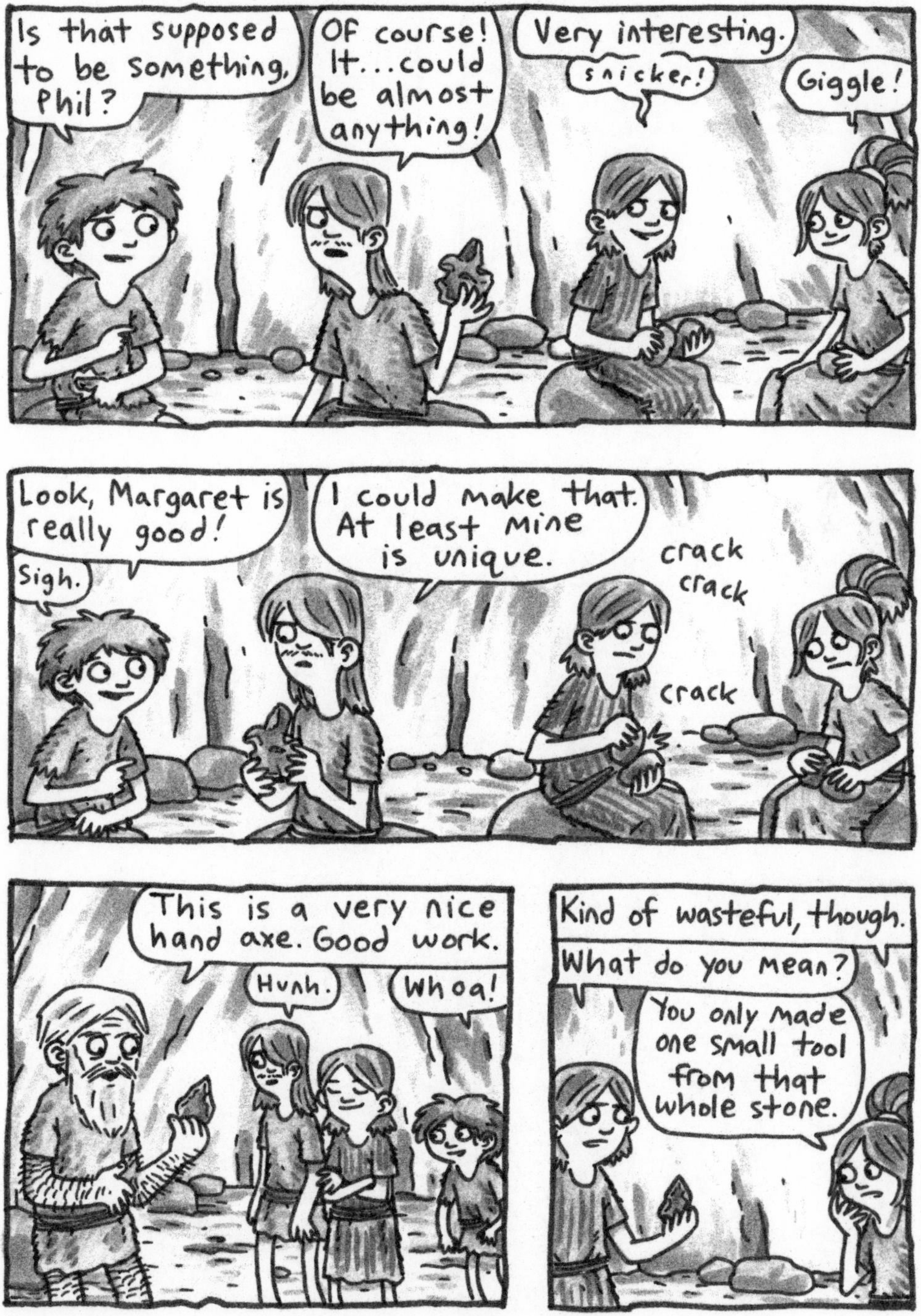
Is that supposed to be something, Phil?
Of course! It...could be almost anything!
Very interesting.
snicker!
Giggle!
Look, Margaret is really good!
Sigh.
I could make that. At least mine is unique.
crack
crack
crack
This is a very nice hand axe. Good work.
Hunh.
Whoa!
Kind of wasteful, though.
What do you mean?
You only made one small tool from that whole stone.

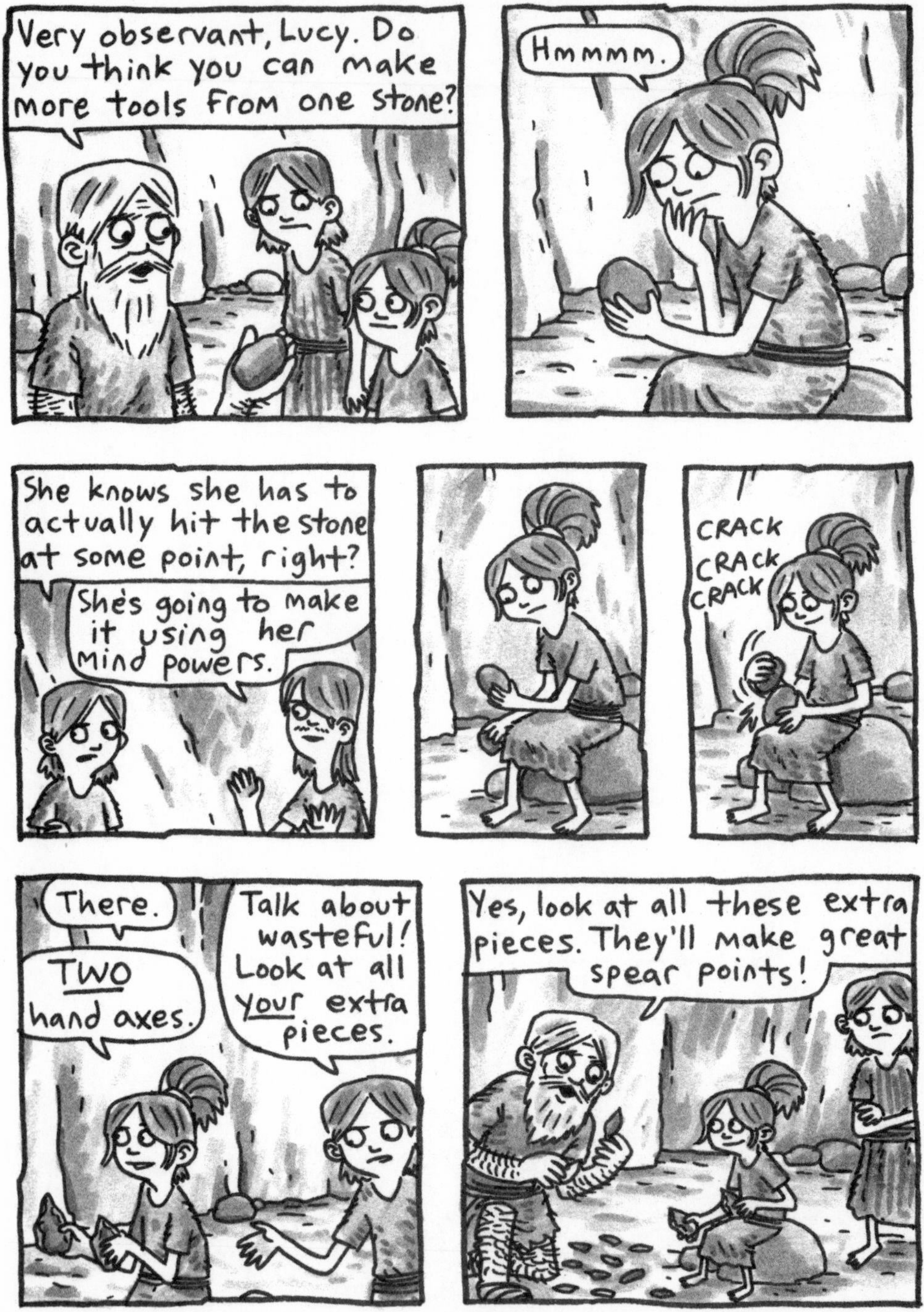
Very observant, Lucy. Do you think you can make more tools from one stone?
Hmmmm.
She knows she has to actually hit the stone at some point, right?
She's going to make it using her mind powers.
CRACK
CRACK
CRACK
There.
TWO hand axes.
Talk about wasteful! Look at all YOUR extra pieces.
Yes, look at all these extra pieces. They'll make great spear points!

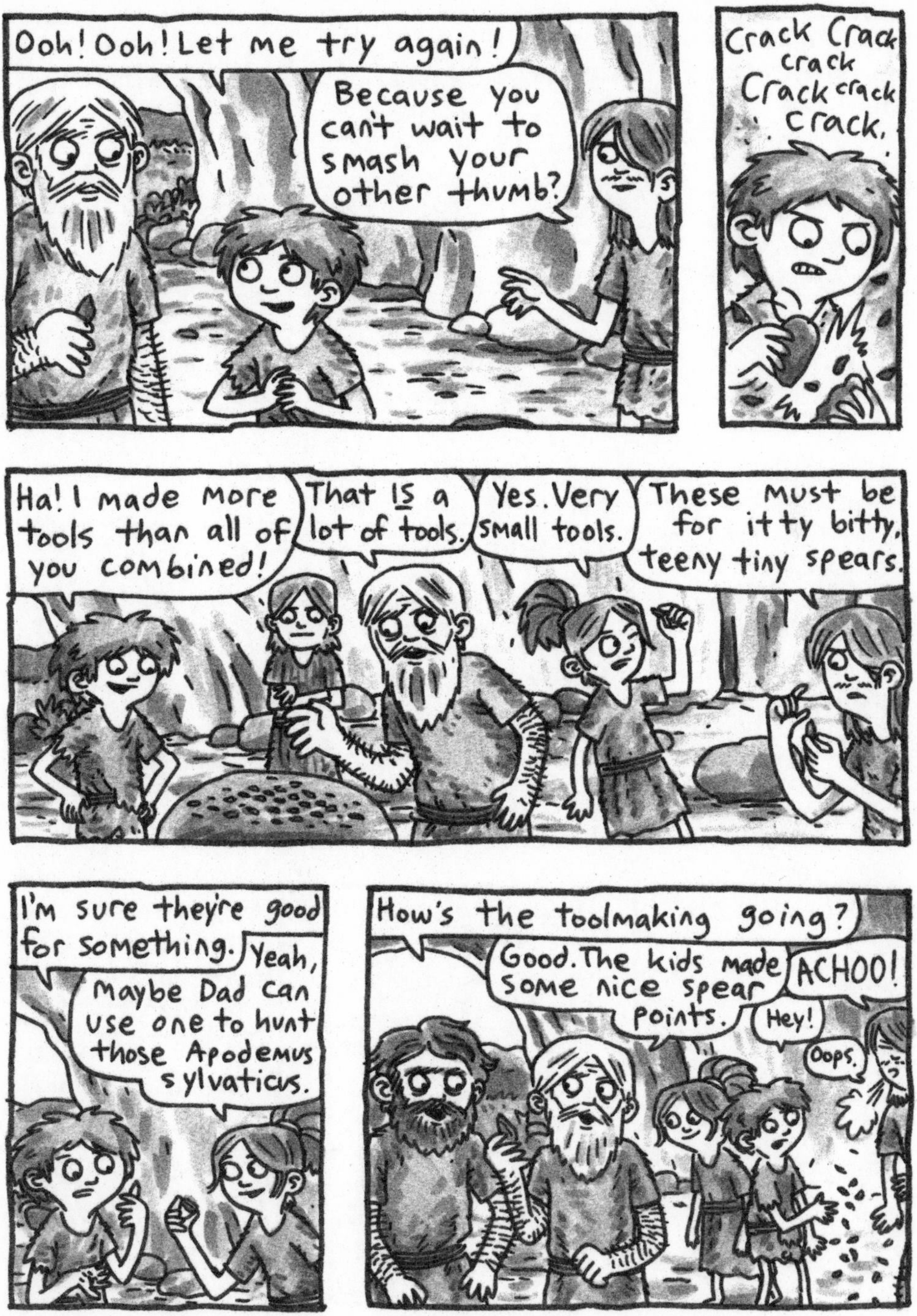
Ooh! Ooh! Let me try again!
Because you can't wait to smash your other thumb?
Crack Crack crack Crack crack Crack.
Ha! I made more tools than all of you combined!
That IS a lot of tools.
Yes. Very small tools.
These must be for itty bitty, teeny tiny spears.
I'm sure they're good for something.
Yeah, maybe Dad can use one to hunt those Apodemus sylvaticus.
How's the toolmaking going?
Good. The kids made some nice spear points.
ACHOO!
Hey!
Oops.

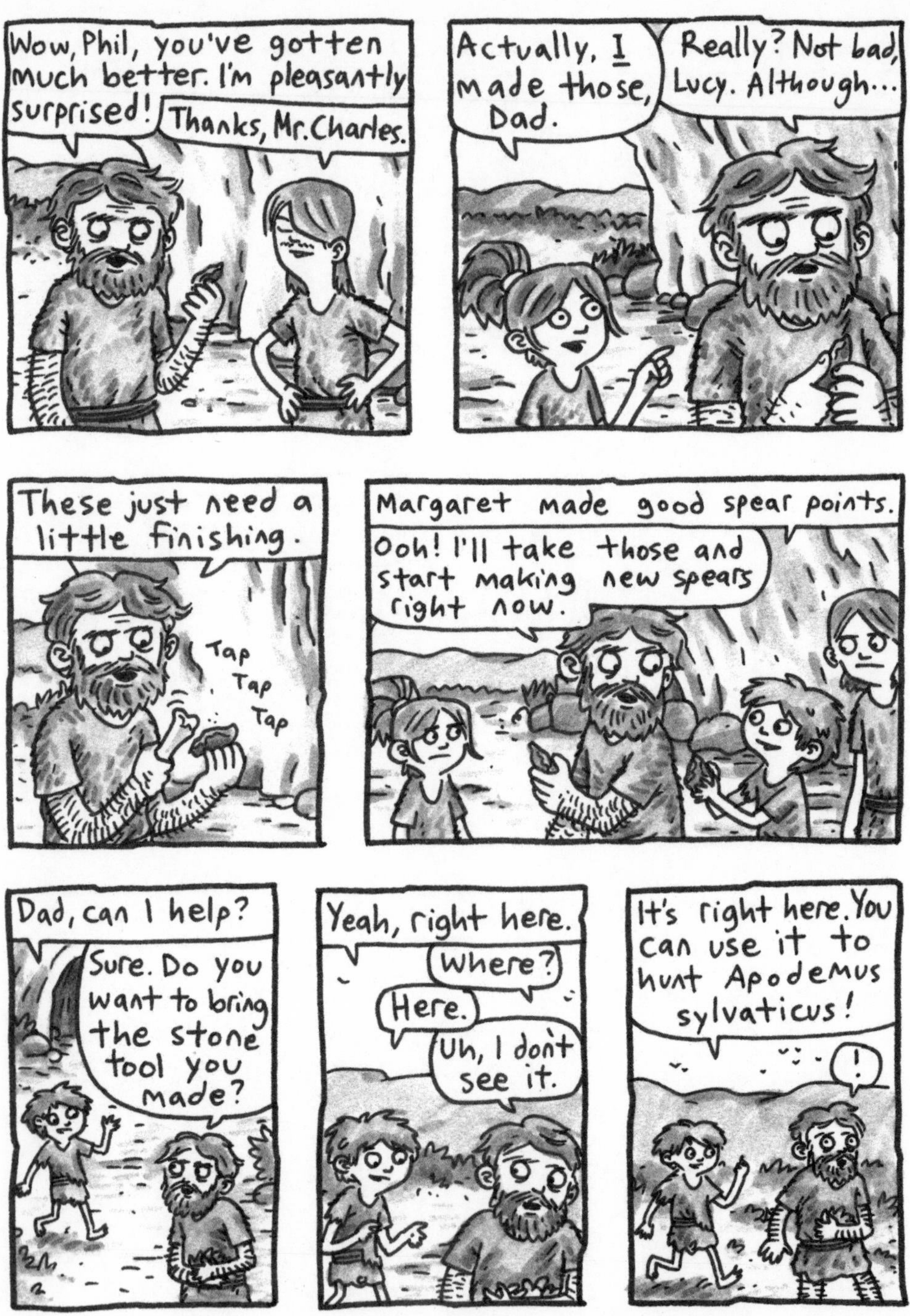
Wow, Phil, you've gotten much better. I'm pleasantly surprised!
Thanks, Mr. Charles.
Actually, I made those, Dad.
Really? Not bad, Lucy. Although...
These just need a little finishing.
Tap
Tap
Tap
Margaret made good spear points.
Ooh! I'll take those and start making new spears right now.
Dad, can I help?
Sure. Do you want to bring the stone tool you made?
Yeah, right here.
Where?
Here.
Uh, I don't see it.
It's right here. You can use it to hunt Apodemus sylvaticus!
!

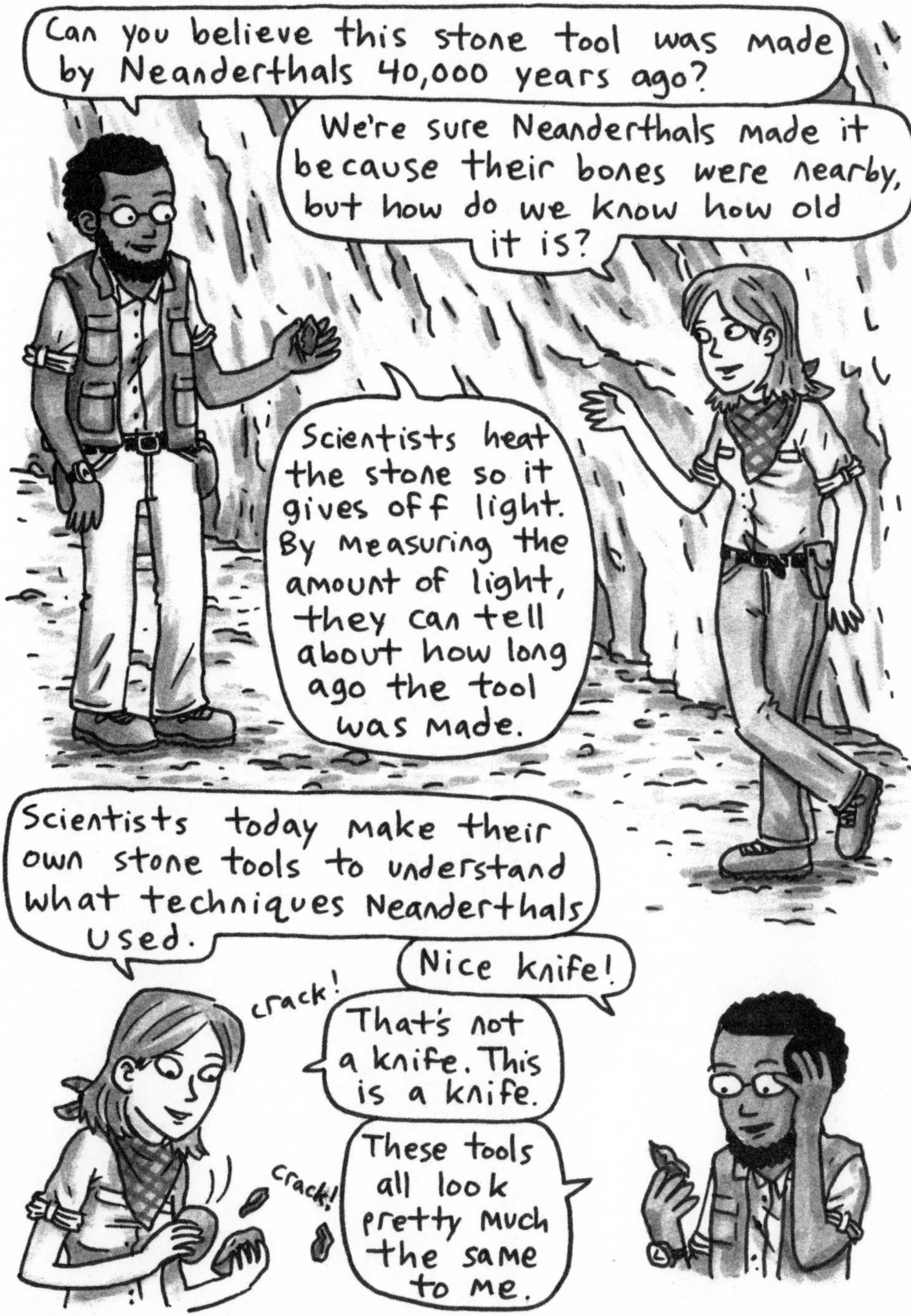

Can you believe this stone tool was made by Neanderthals 40,000 years ago?
We're sure Neanderthals made it because their bones were nearby, but how do we know how old it is?
Scientists heat the stone so it gives off light. By measuring the amount of light, they can tell about how long ago the tool was made.
Scientists today make their own stone tools to understand what techniques Neanderthals used.
Nice knife!
crack!
That's not a knife. This is a knife.
crack!
These tools all look pretty much the same to me.

By looking closely at Stone Age tools, scientists realized there were a few different types:

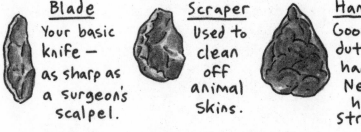

Blade
Your basic knife — as sharp as a surgeon's scalpel.

Scraper
Used to clean off animal skins.

Hand Axe
Good for heavy-duty cutting. No handle, but Neanderthals had very strong grips.

Point Attached to a spear using pitch, a sticky tar.

Sometimes we find stone flakes that came from the same original rock. We can put them together to see how different tools were made step by step.

I think I'm missing a piece.

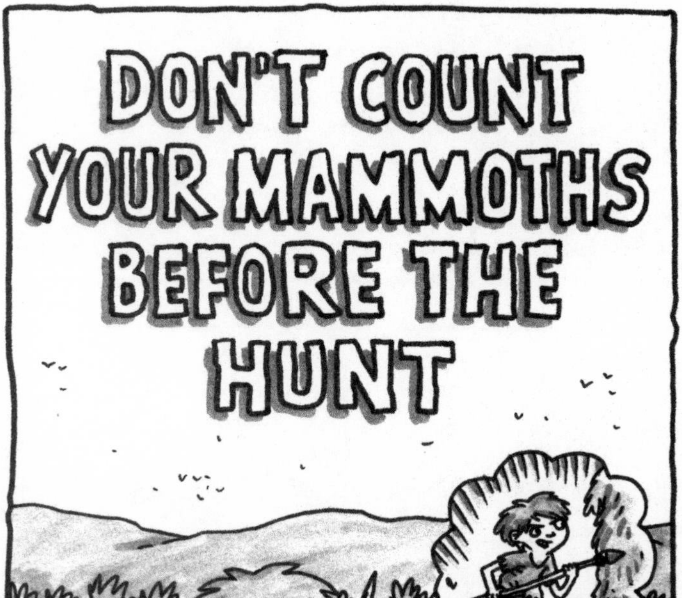
DON'T COUNT YOUR MAMMOTHS BEFORE THE HUNT

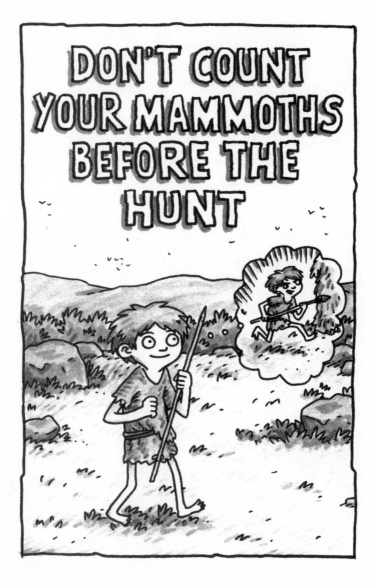

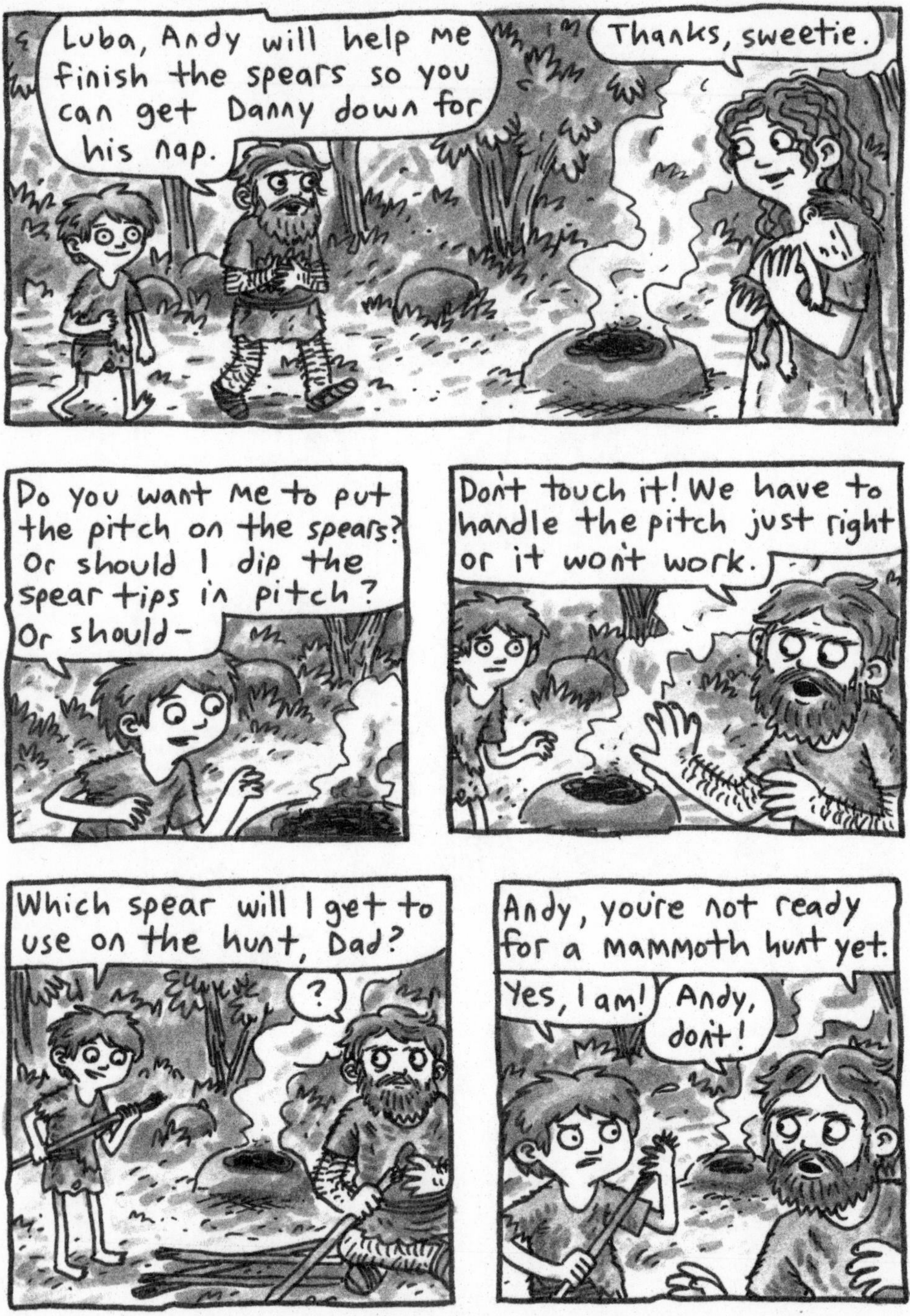
Luba, Andy will help me finish the spears so you can get Danny down for his nap.
Thanks, sweetie.
Do you want me to put the pitch on the spears? Or should I dip the spear tips in pitch? Or should–
Don't touch it! We have to handle the pitch just right or it won't work.
Which spear will I get to use on the hunt, Dad?
?
Andy, you're not ready for a mammoth hunt yet.
Yes, I am!
Andy, don't!

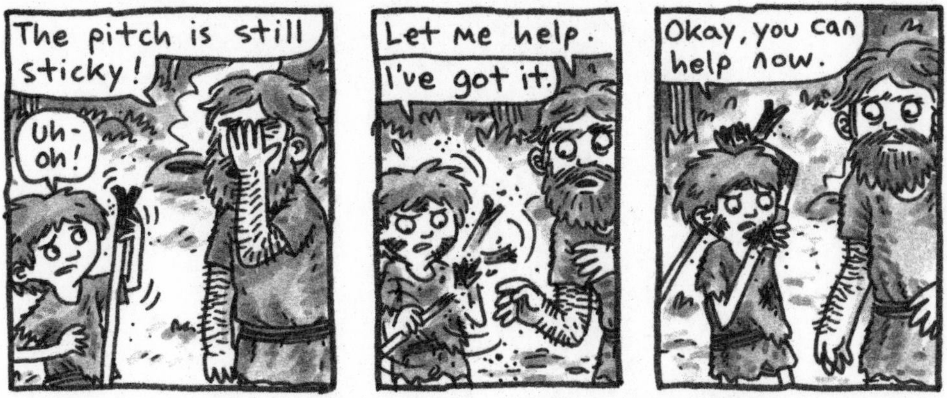
The pitch is still sticky!
Uh-oh!
Let me help.
I've got it.
Okay, you can help now.

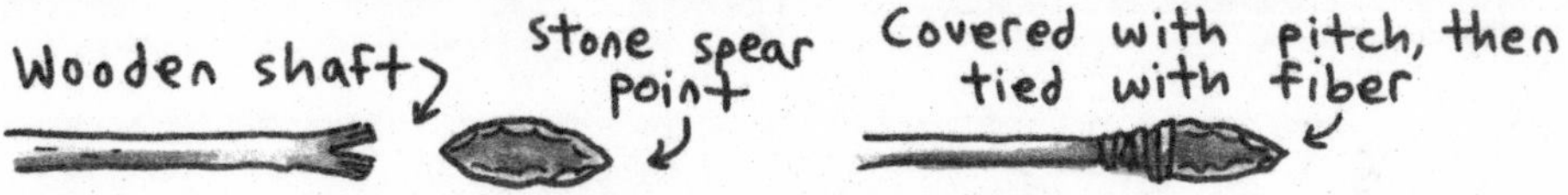
Wooden shaft
Stone spear point
Covered with pitch, then tied with fiber

Pitch is hard to make, so Neanderthals must have been smart and skilled to be able to make it!

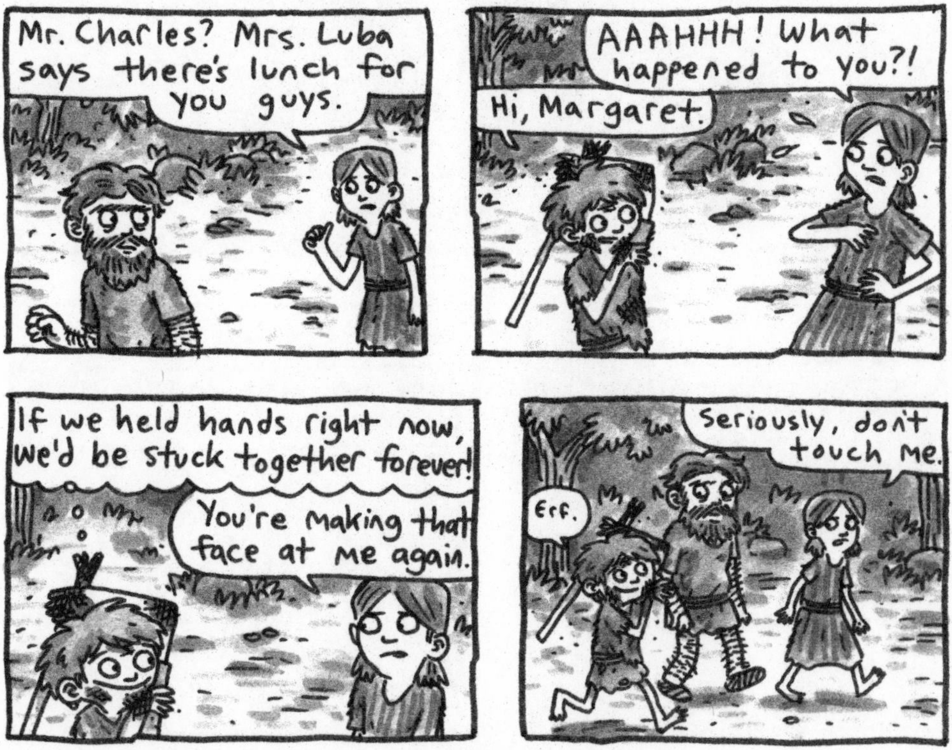
Mr. Charles? Mrs. Luba says there's lunch for you guys.
AAAHHH! What happened to you?!
Hi, Margaret.
If we held hands right now, we'd be stuck together forever!
You're making that face at me again.
Seriously, don't touch me.
Erf.

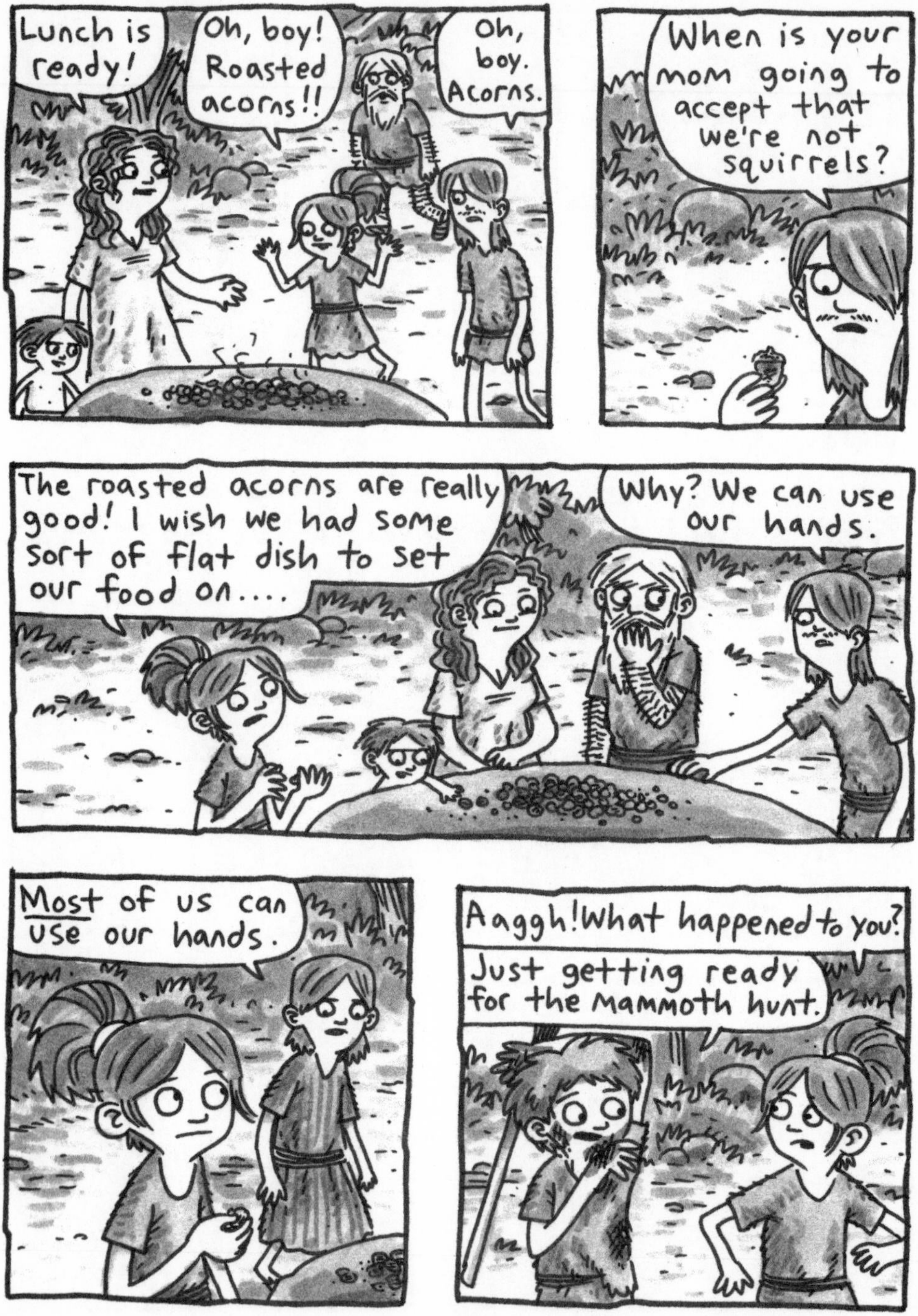
Lunch is ready!
Oh, boy! Roasted acorns!!
Oh, boy. Acorns.
When is your mom going to accept that we're not squirrels?
The roasted acorns are really good! I wish we had some sort of flat dish to set our food on....
Why? We can use our hands.
Most of us can use our hands.
Aaggh! What happened to you?
Just getting ready for the mammoth hunt.

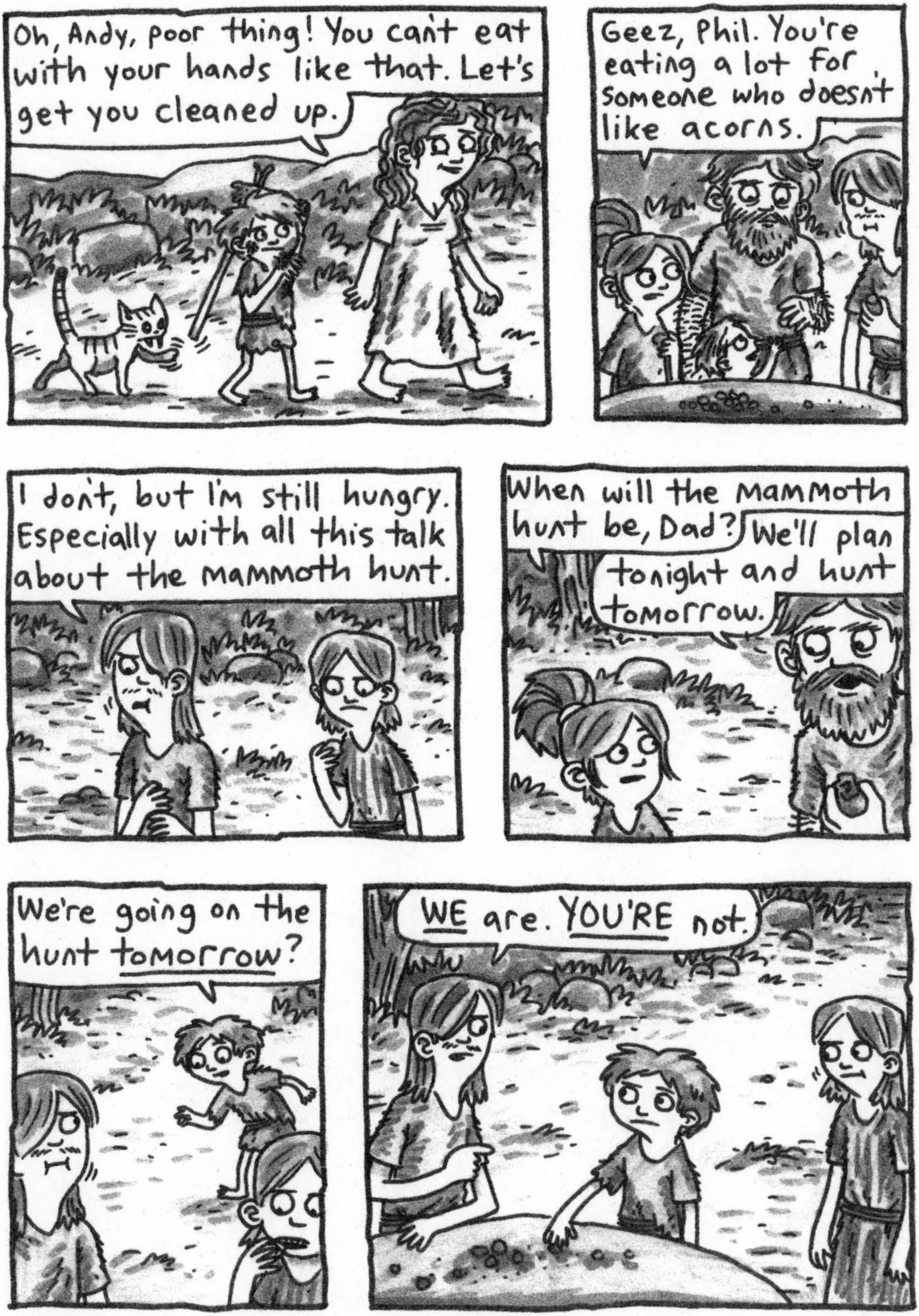
Oh, Andy, poor thing! You can't eat with your hands like that. Let's get you cleaned up.
Geez, Phil. You're eating a lot for someone who doesn't like acorns.
I don't, but I'm still hungry. Especially with all this talk about the mammoth hunt.
When will the mammoth hunt be, Dad?
We'll plan tonight and hunt tomorrow.
We're going on the hunt tomorrow?
WE are. YOU'RE not.

You're still a kid.
I'm not too young! My dad was younger when he went on his first hunt, right, Mom?
Well, yes, he was...
So, can I go?
I guess maybe you're old enough....
YES!
Just ask Dad if it's okay.
Nooooo.
If he says no, you'll have to stay at the cave with Margaret.
YES!
I don't care how clean your hands are, you still can't touch me.
Nooooo.
I don't see why I can't go.
It's not safe.
Kick!

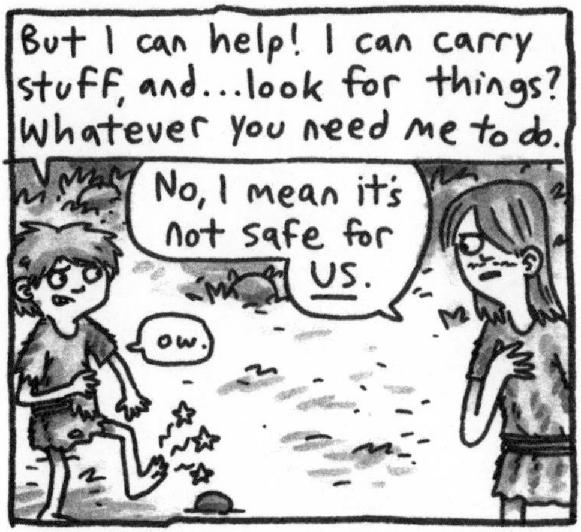
But I can help! I can carry stuff, and...look for things? Whatever you need me to do.
No, I mean it's not safe for US.
ow.

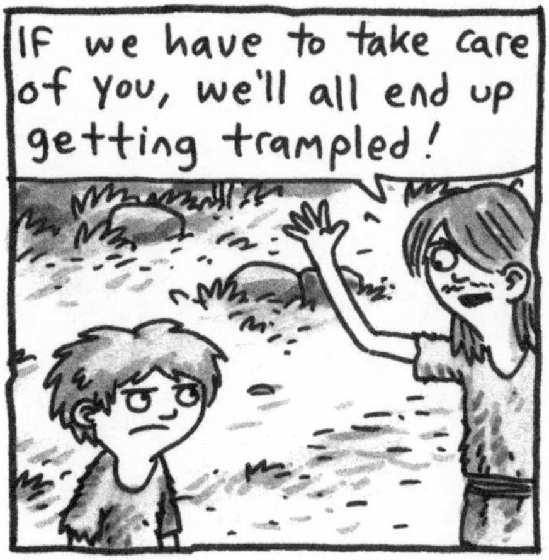
If we have to take care of you, we'll all end up getting trampled!

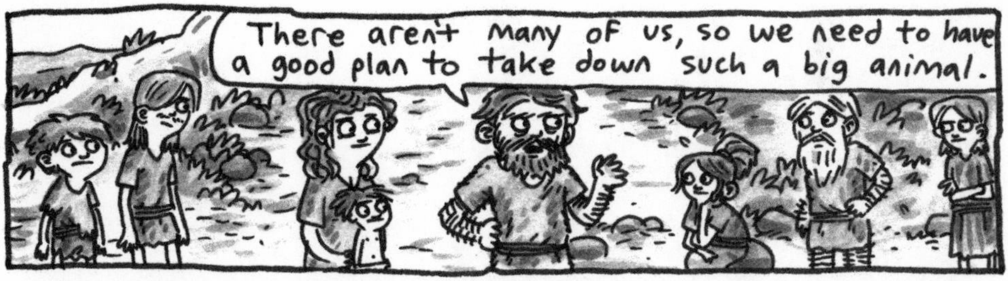
There aren't many of us, so we need to have a good plan to take down such a big animal.

The woolly mammoth lived in Europe and Asia until about 10,000 years ago.

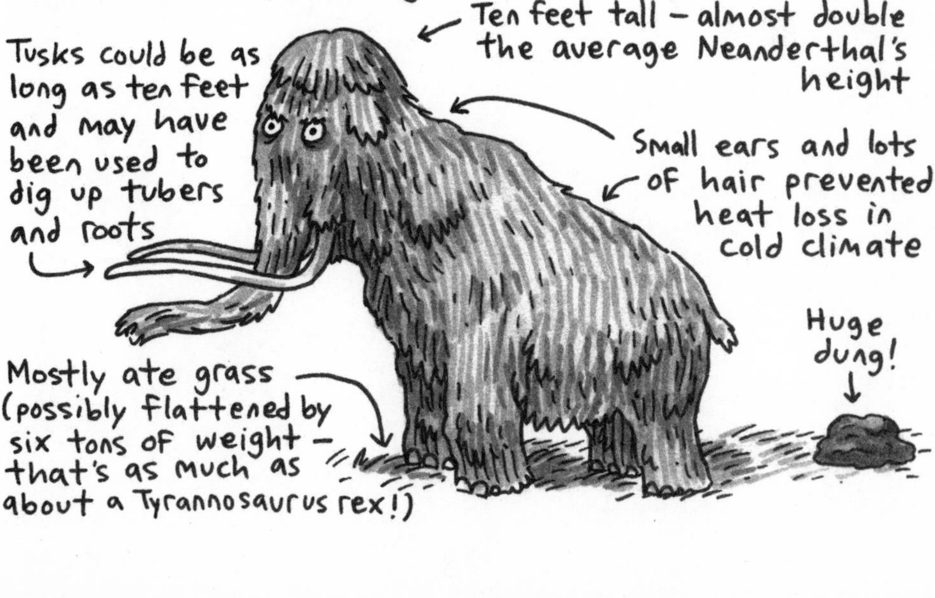
Ten feet tall – almost double the average Neanderthal's height
Tusks could be as long as ten feet and may have been used to dig up tubers and roots
Small ears and lots of hair prevented heat loss in cold climate
Huge dung!
Mostly ate grass (possibly flattened by six tons of weight – that's as much as about a Tyrannosaurus rex!)

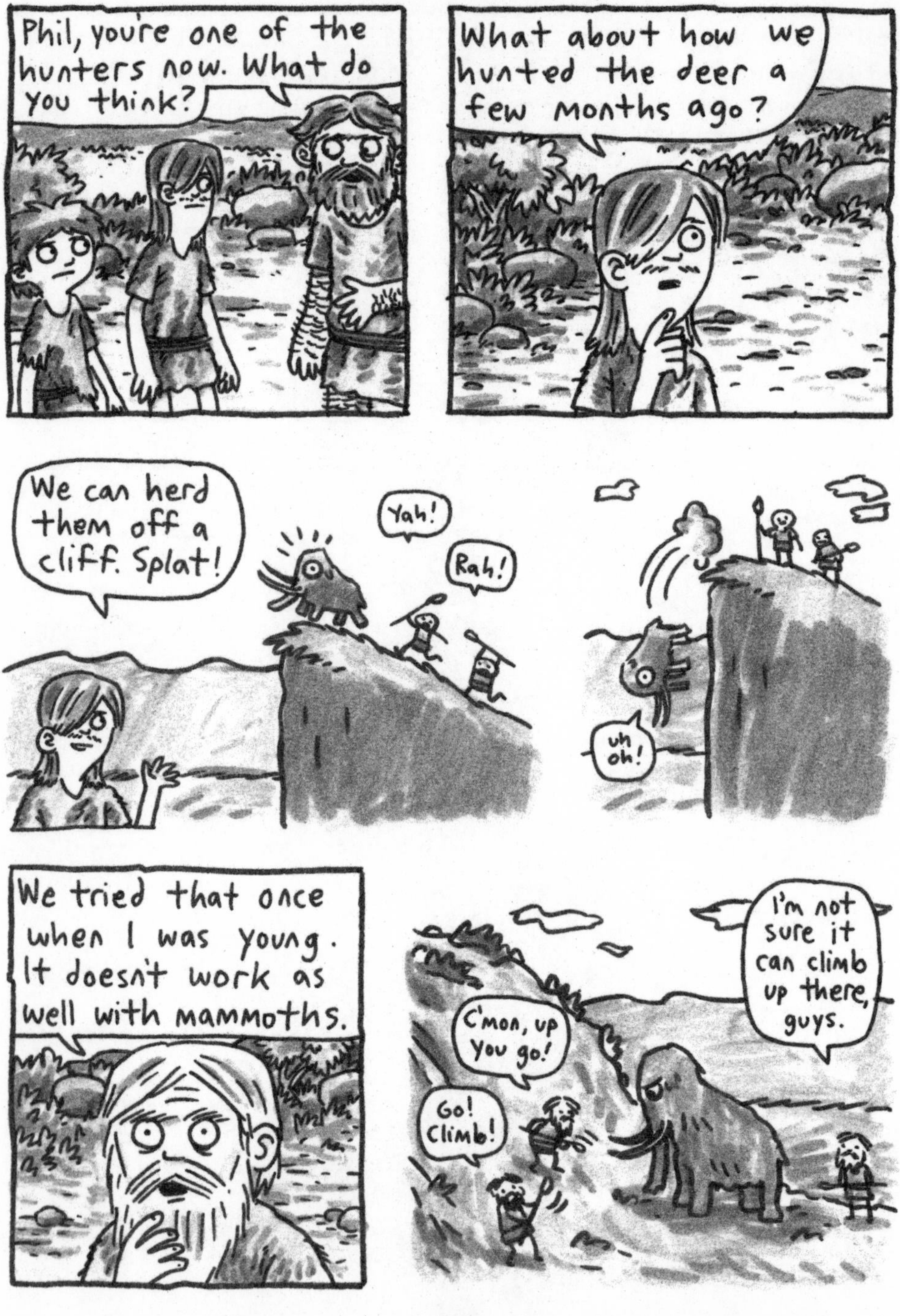

Phil, you're one of the hunters now. What do you think?
What about how we hunted the deer a few months ago?
We can herd them off a cliff. Splat!
Yah!
Rah!
uh oh!
We tried that once when I was young. It doesn't work as well with mammoths.
I'm not sure it can climb up there, guys.
C'mon, up you go!
Go! Climb!

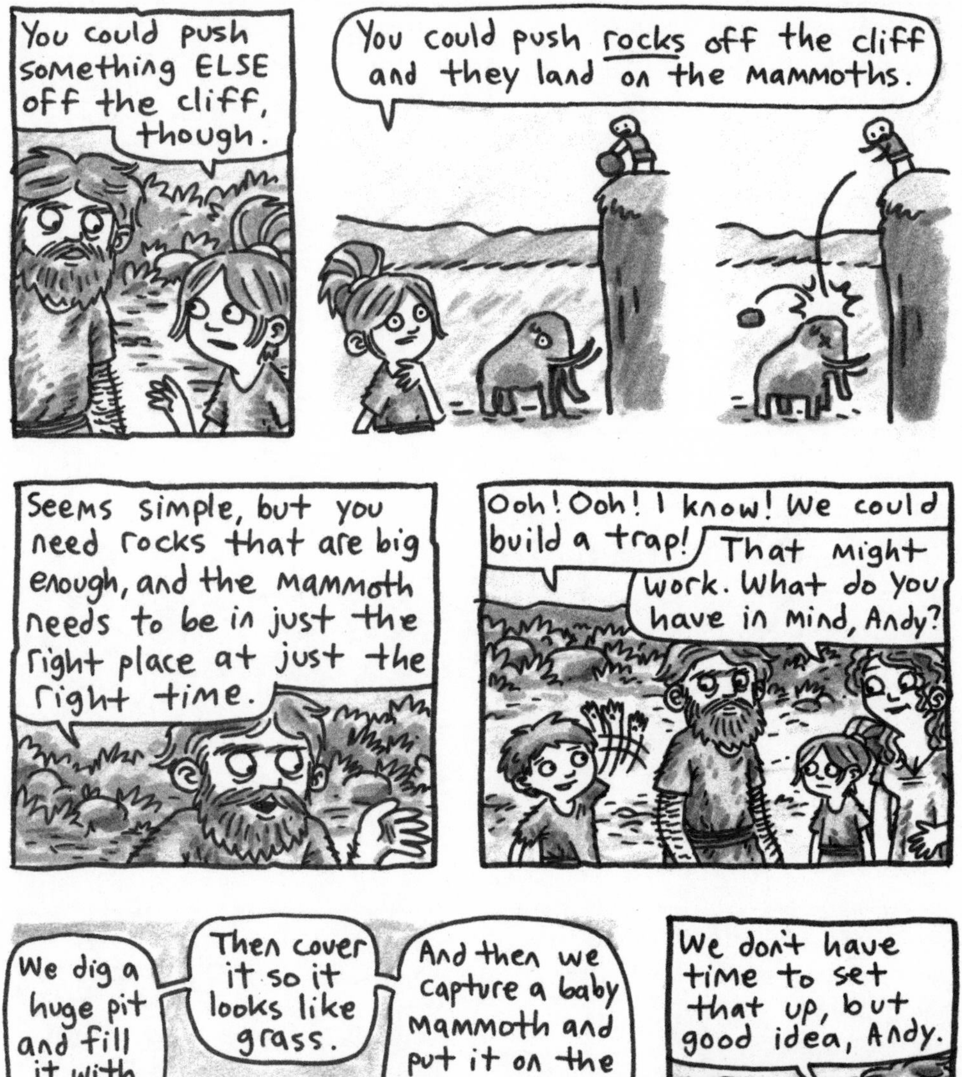
You could push something ELSE off the cliff, though.
You could push rocks off the cliff and they land on the mammoths.
Seems simple, but you need rocks that are big enough, and the mammoth needs to be in just the right place at just the right time.
Ooh! Ooh! I know! We could build a trap!
That might work. What do you have in mind, Andy?
We dig a huge pit and fill it with spears.
Then cover it so it looks like grass.
And then we capture a baby mammoth and put it on the other side so the mammoths come to rescue it but fall into the pit instead!
We don't have time to set that up, but good idea, Andy.
Pat pat

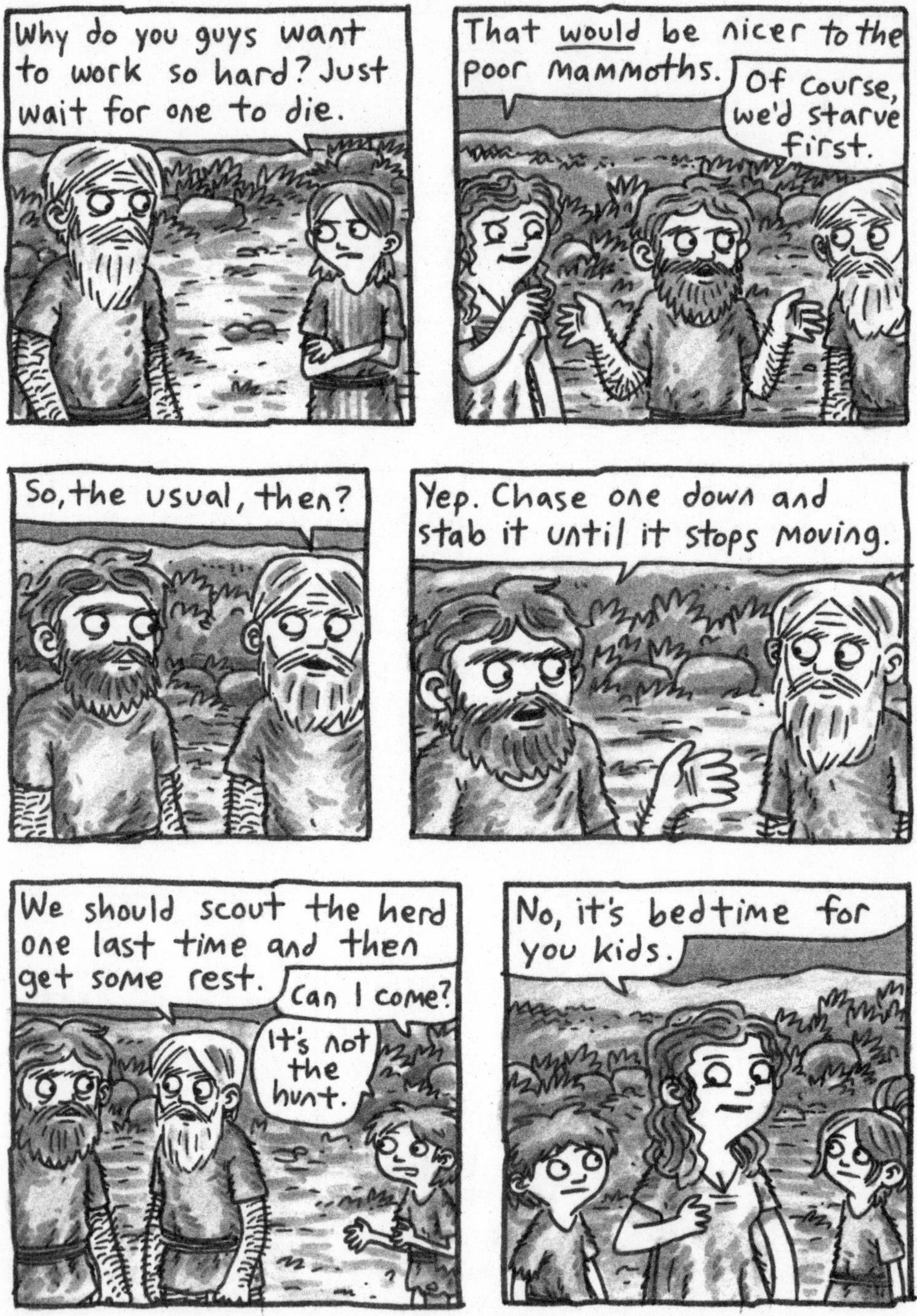
Why do you guys want to work so hard? Just wait for one to die.
That would be nicer to the poor mammoths.
Of course, we'd starve first.
So, the usual, then?
Yep. Chase one down and stab it until it stops moving.
We should scout the herd one last time and then get some rest.
Can I come?
It's not the hunt.
No, it's bedtime for you kids.

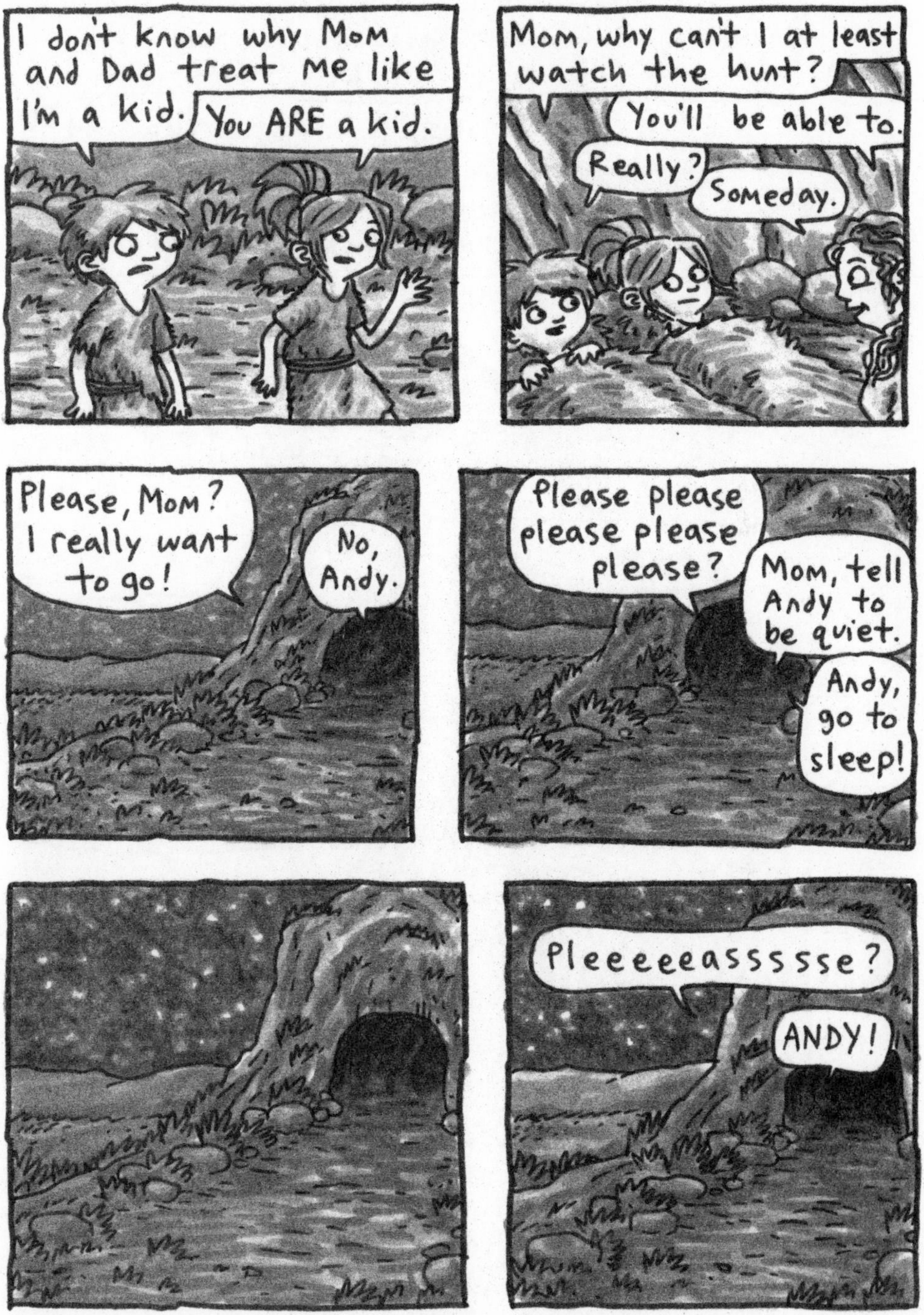
I don't know why Mom and Dad treat me like I'm a kid.
You ARE a kid.
Mom, why can't I at least watch the hunt?
You'll be able to.
Really?
Someday.
Please, Mom? I really want to go!
No, Andy.
Please please please please please?
Mom, tell Andy to be quiet.
Andy, go to sleep!
Pleeeeeeasssse?
ANDY!

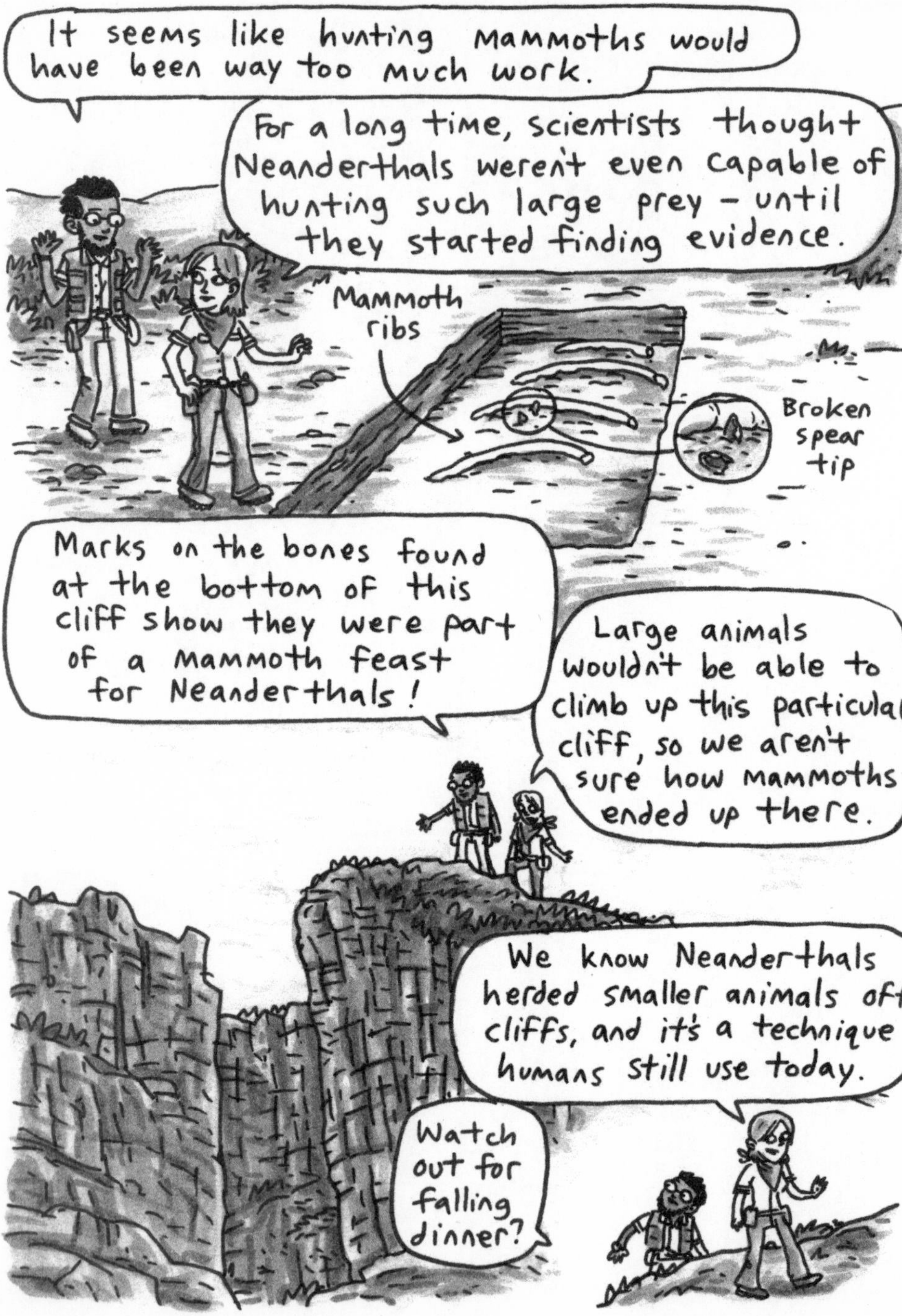
It seems like hunting mammoths would have been way too much work.
For a long time, scientists thought Neanderthals weren't even capable of hunting such large prey - until they started finding evidence.
Mammoth ribs
Broken spear tip
Marks on the bones found at the bottom of this cliff show they were part of a mammoth feast for Neanderthals!
Large animals wouldn't be able to climb up this particular cliff, so we aren't sure how mammoths ended up there.
We know Neanderthals herded smaller animals off cliffs, and it's a technique humans still use today.
Watch out for falling dinner?

REALLY, REALLY BIG GAME HUNTING

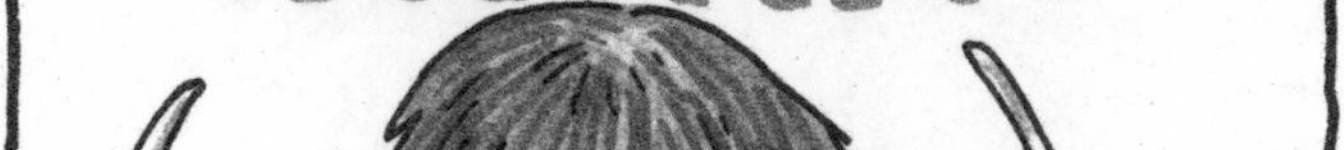

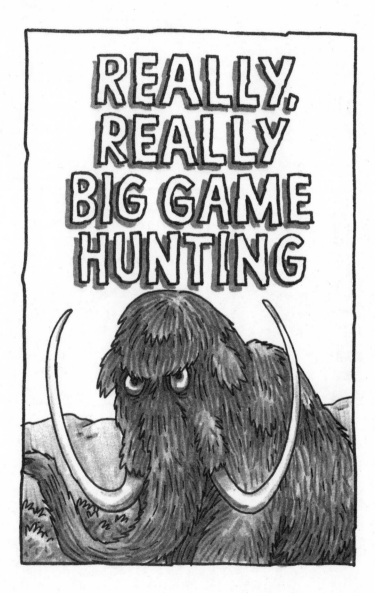

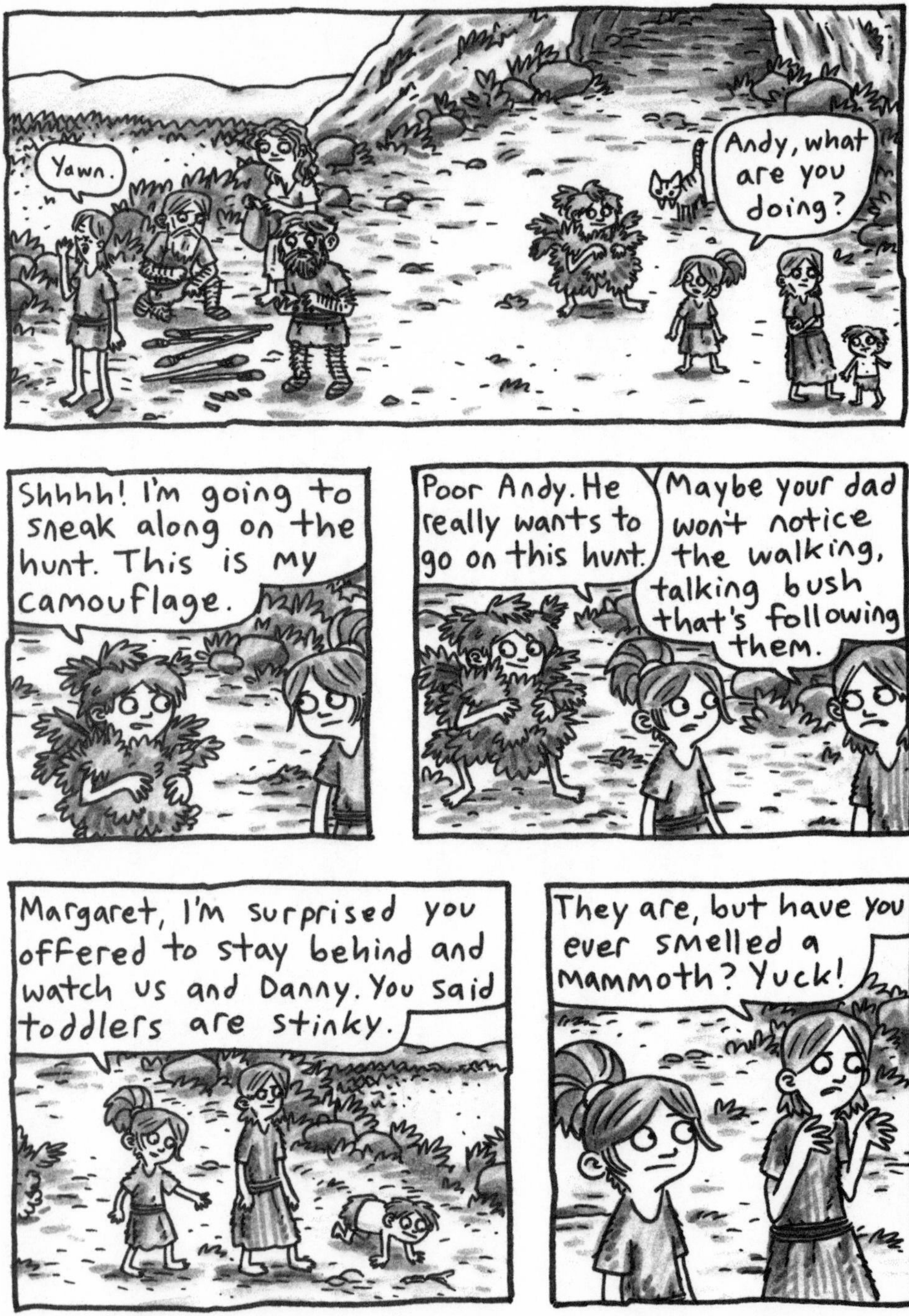

Yawn.
Andy, what are you doing?
Shhhh! I'm going to sneak along on the hunt. This is my camouflage.
Poor Andy. He really wants to go on this hunt.
Maybe your dad won't notice the walking, talking bush that's following them.
Margaret, I'm surprised you offered to stay behind and watch us and Danny. You said toddlers are stinky.
They are, but have you ever smelled a mammoth? Yuck!

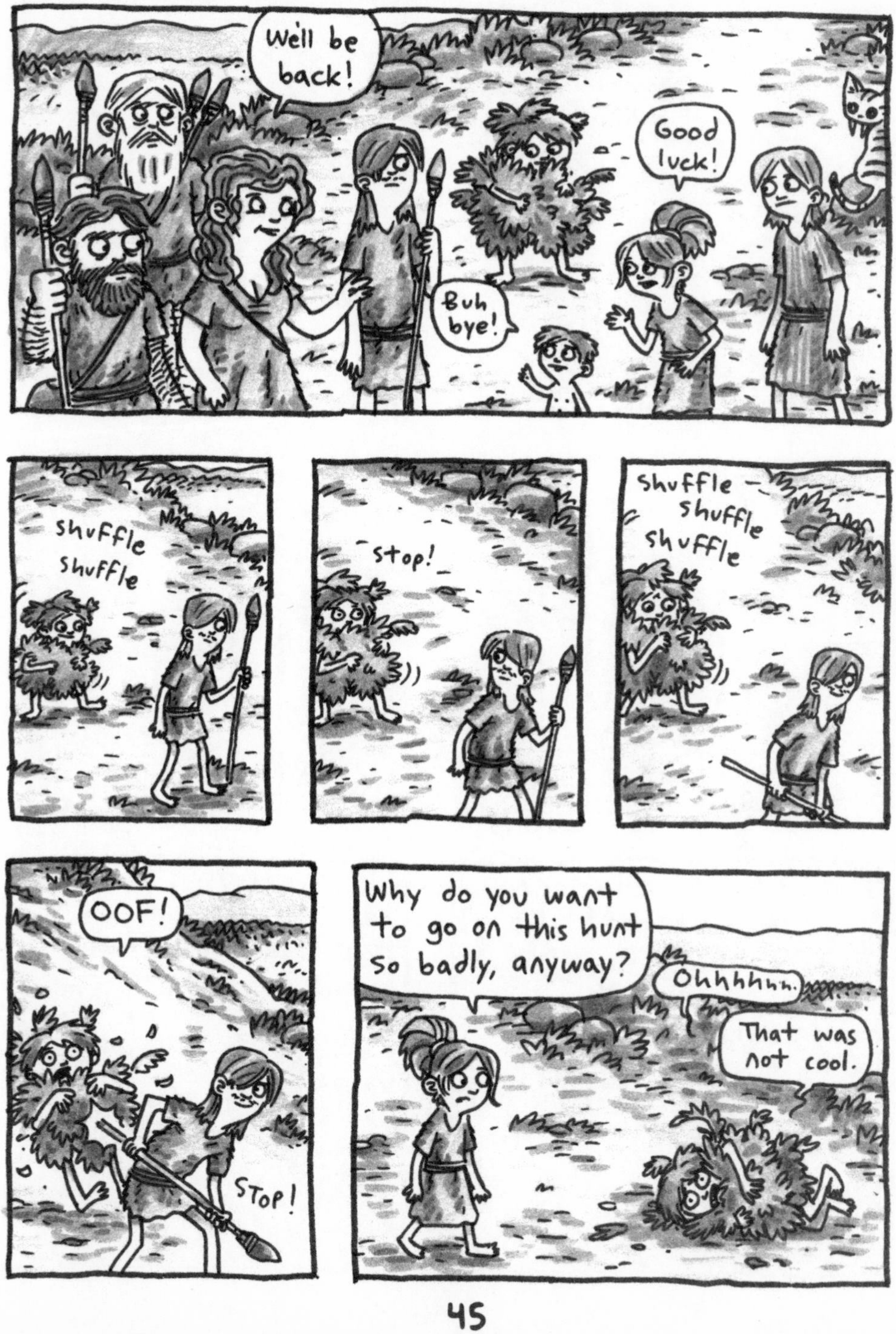
We'll be back!
Good luck!
Buh bye!
shuffle shuffle
stop!
shuffle shuffle shuffle
OOF!
STOP!
Why do you want to go on this hunt so badly, anyway?
Ohhhhhn.
That was not cool.

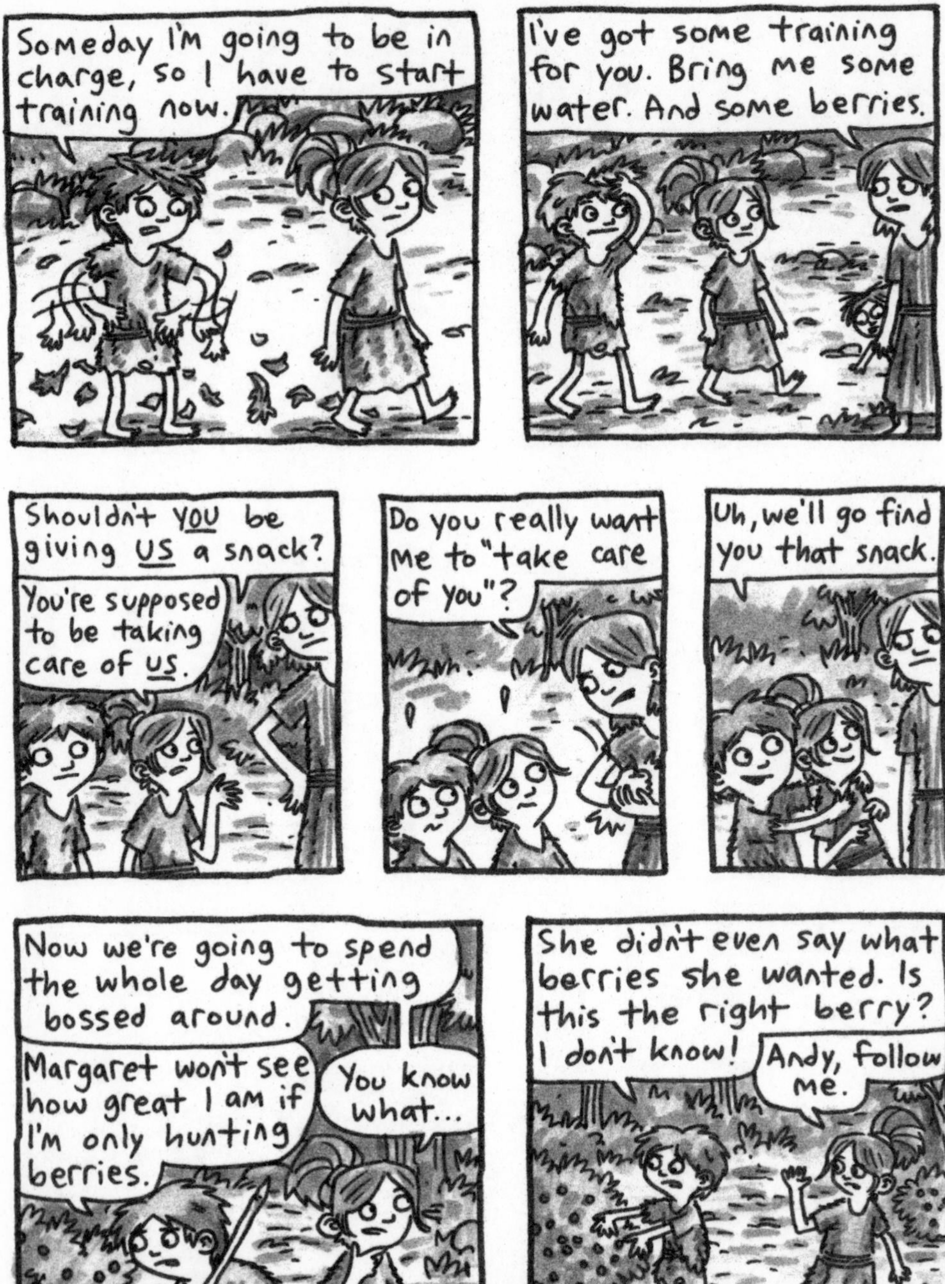
Someday I'm going to be in charge, so I have to start training now.
I've got some training for you. Bring me some water. And some berries.
Shouldn't YOU be giving US a snack?
You're supposed to be taking care of US.
Do you really want me to "take care of you"?
Uh, we'll go find you that snack.
Now we're going to spend the whole day getting bossed around.
Margaret won't see how great I am if I'm only hunting berries.
You know what...
She didn't even say what berries she wanted. Is this the right berry? I don't know!
Andy, follow me.

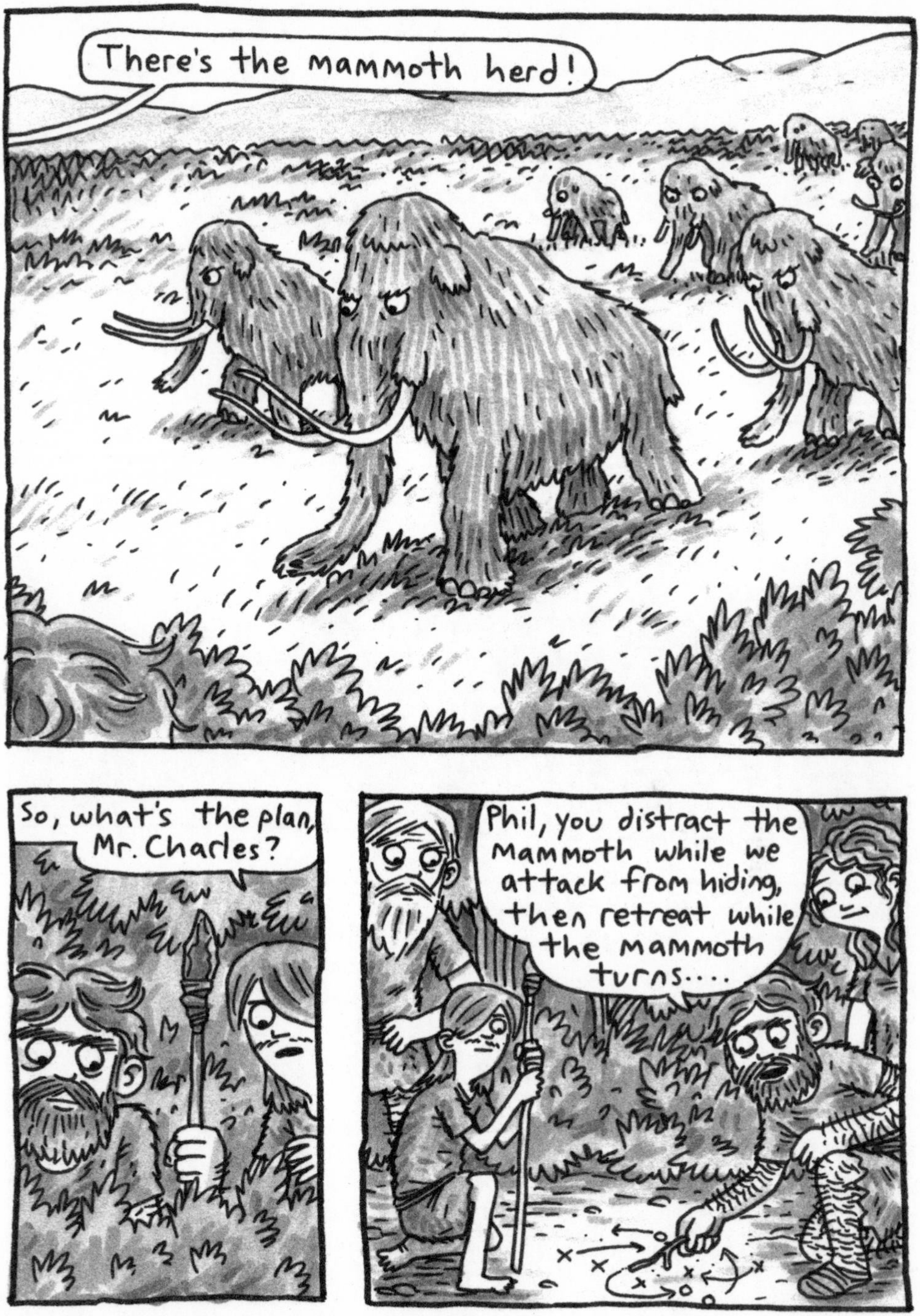
There's the mammoth herd!
So, what's the plan, Mr. Charles?
Phil, you distract the mammoth while we attack from hiding, then retreat while the mammoth turns....

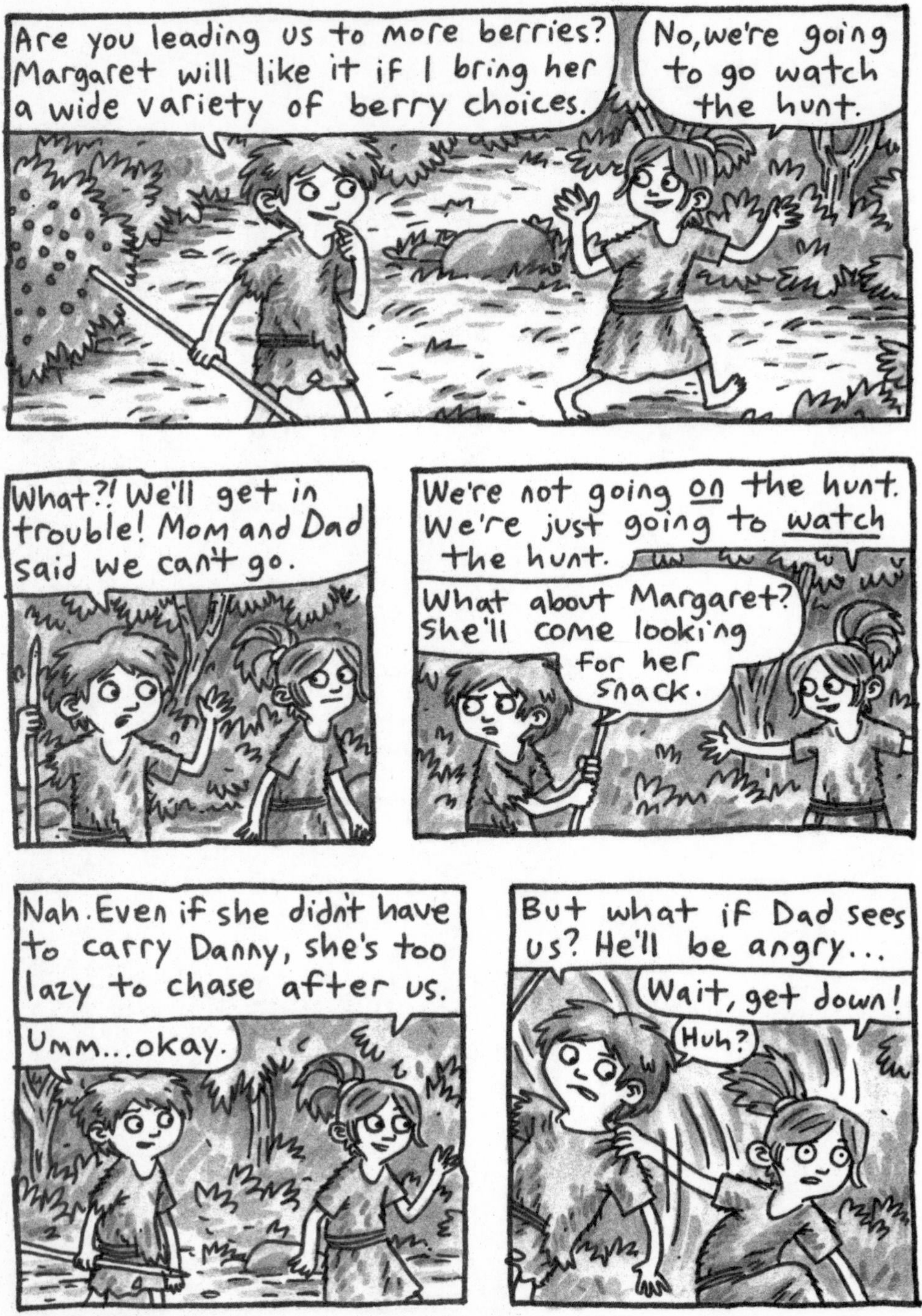
Are you leading us to more berries? Margaret will like it if I bring her a wide variety of berry choices.
No, we're going to go watch the hunt.
What?! We'll get in trouble! Mom and Dad said we can't go.
We're not going on the hunt. We're just going to watch the hunt.
What about Margaret? She'll come looking for her snack.
Nah. Even if she didn't have to carry Danny, she's too lazy to chase after us.
Umm...okay.
But what if Dad sees us? He'll be angry...
Wait, get down!
Huh?

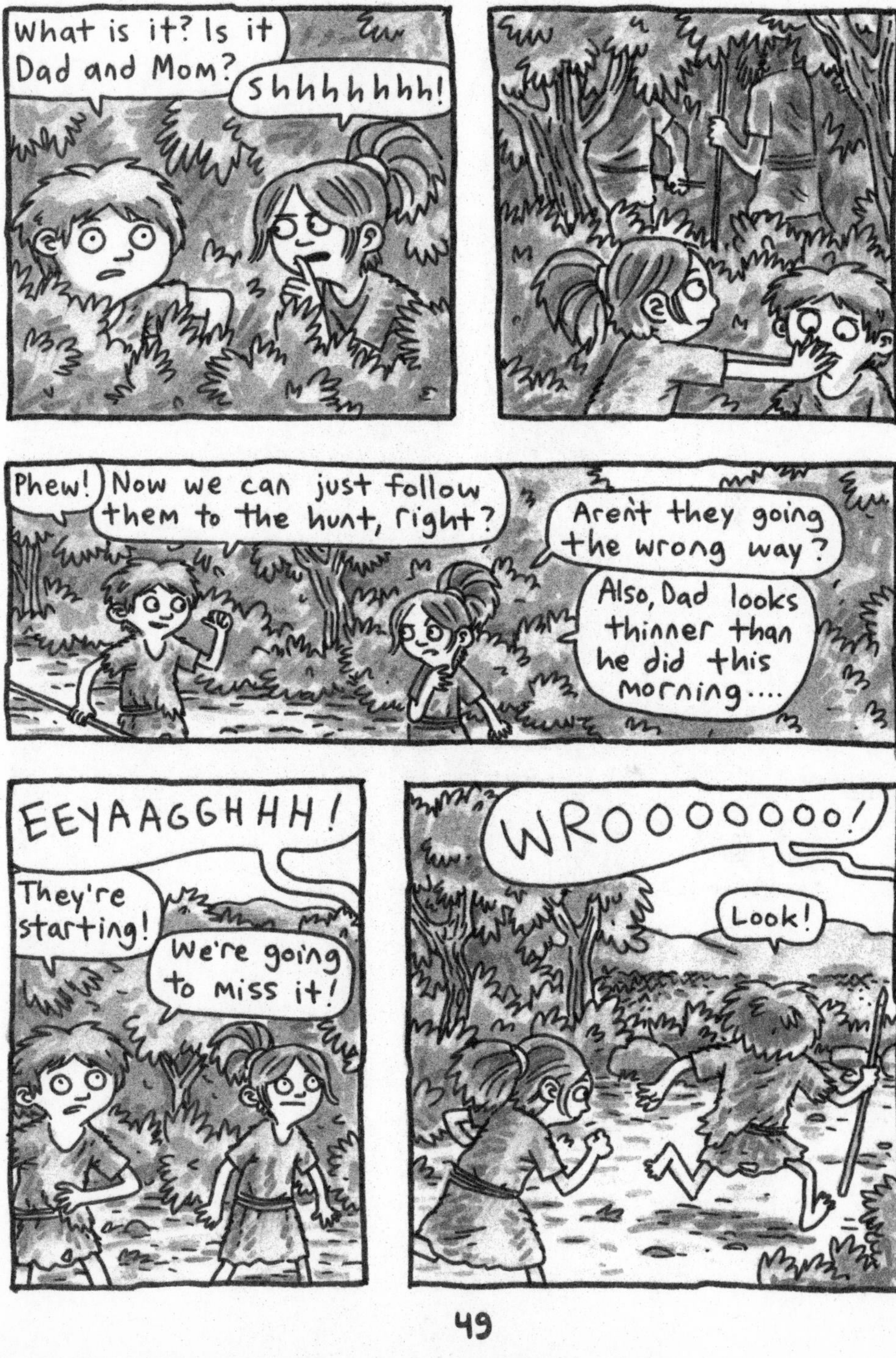
What is it? Is it Dad and Mom?
Shhhhhhhh!
Phew!
Now we can just follow them to the hunt, right?
Aren't they going the wrong way?
Also, Dad looks thinner than he did this morning....
EEYAAGGHHH!
They're starting!
We're going to miss it!
WROOOOOOOO!
Look!

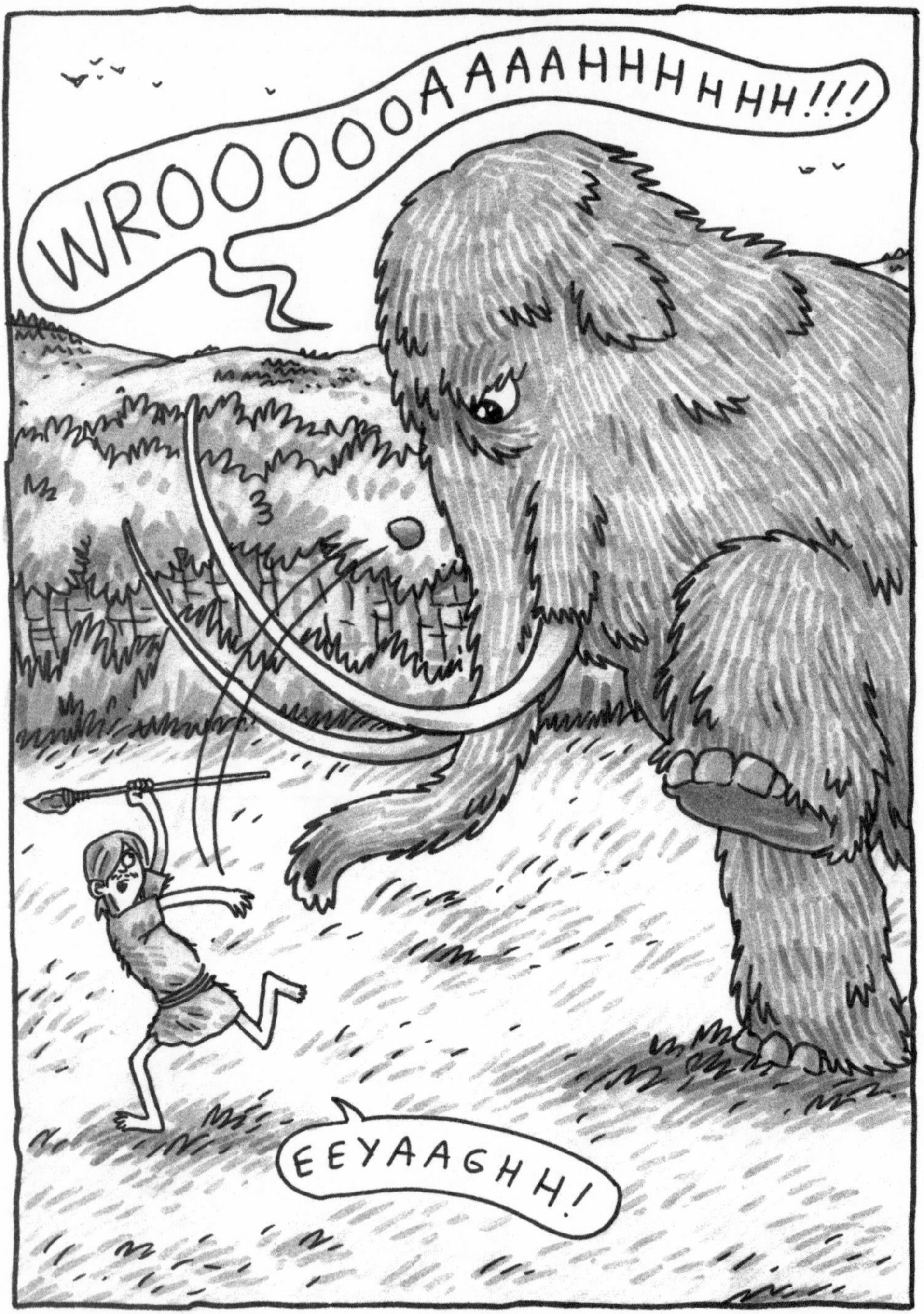
WROOOOOAAAAHHHHHHH!!!
EEYAAGHH!

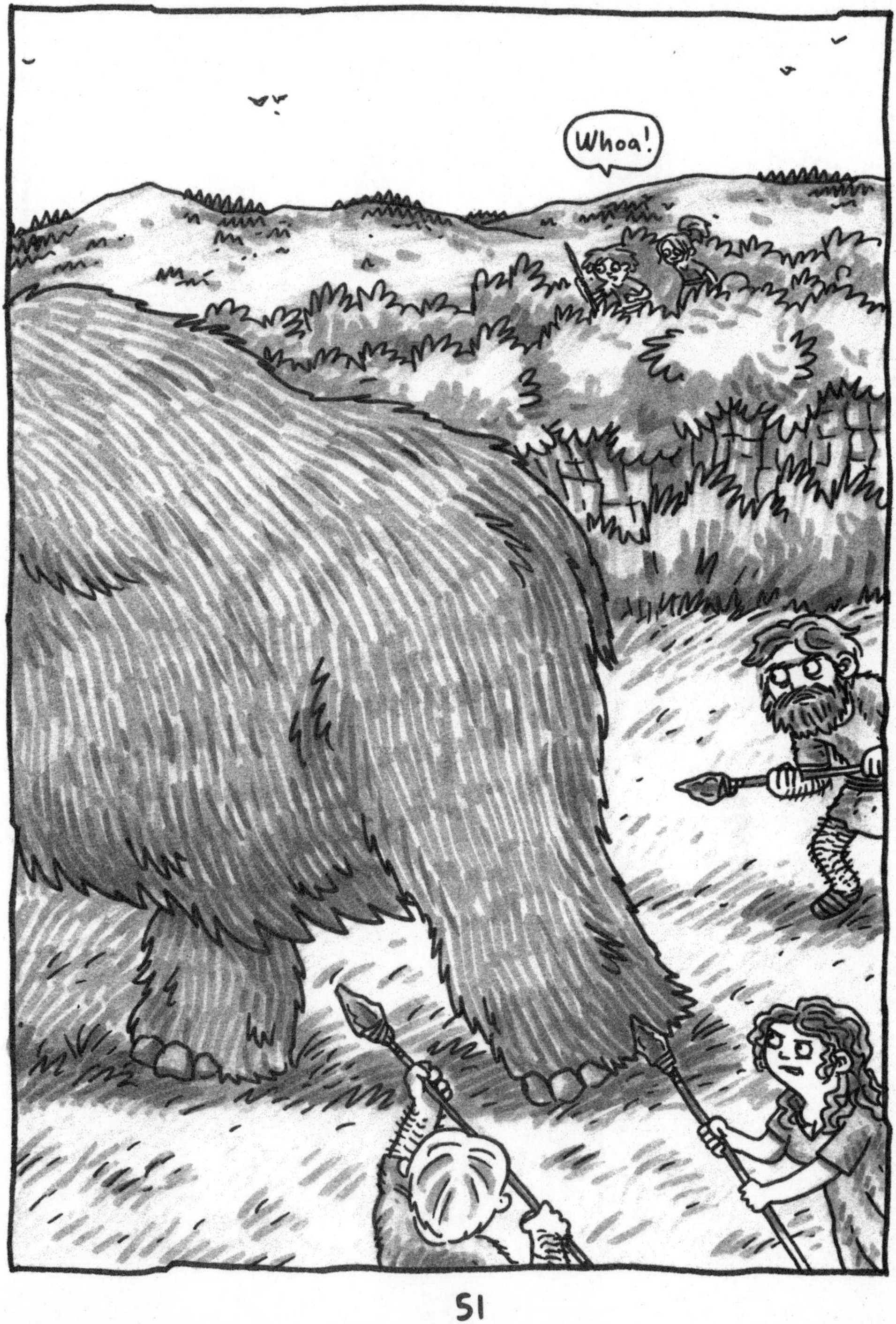
Whoa!

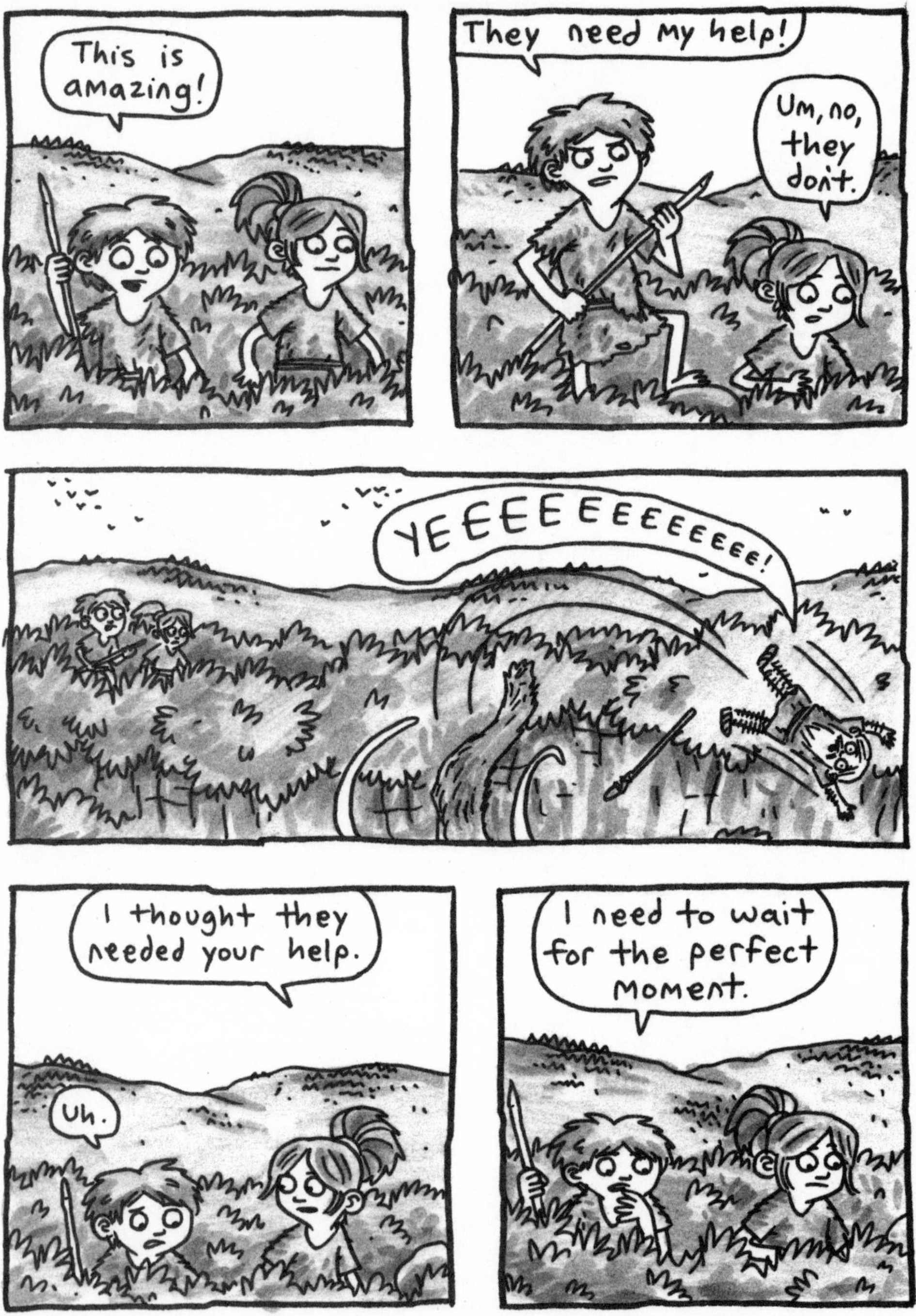
This is amazing!
They need my help!
Um, no, they don't.
YEEEEEEEEEEEEE!
I thought they needed your help.
Uh.
I need to wait for the perfect moment.

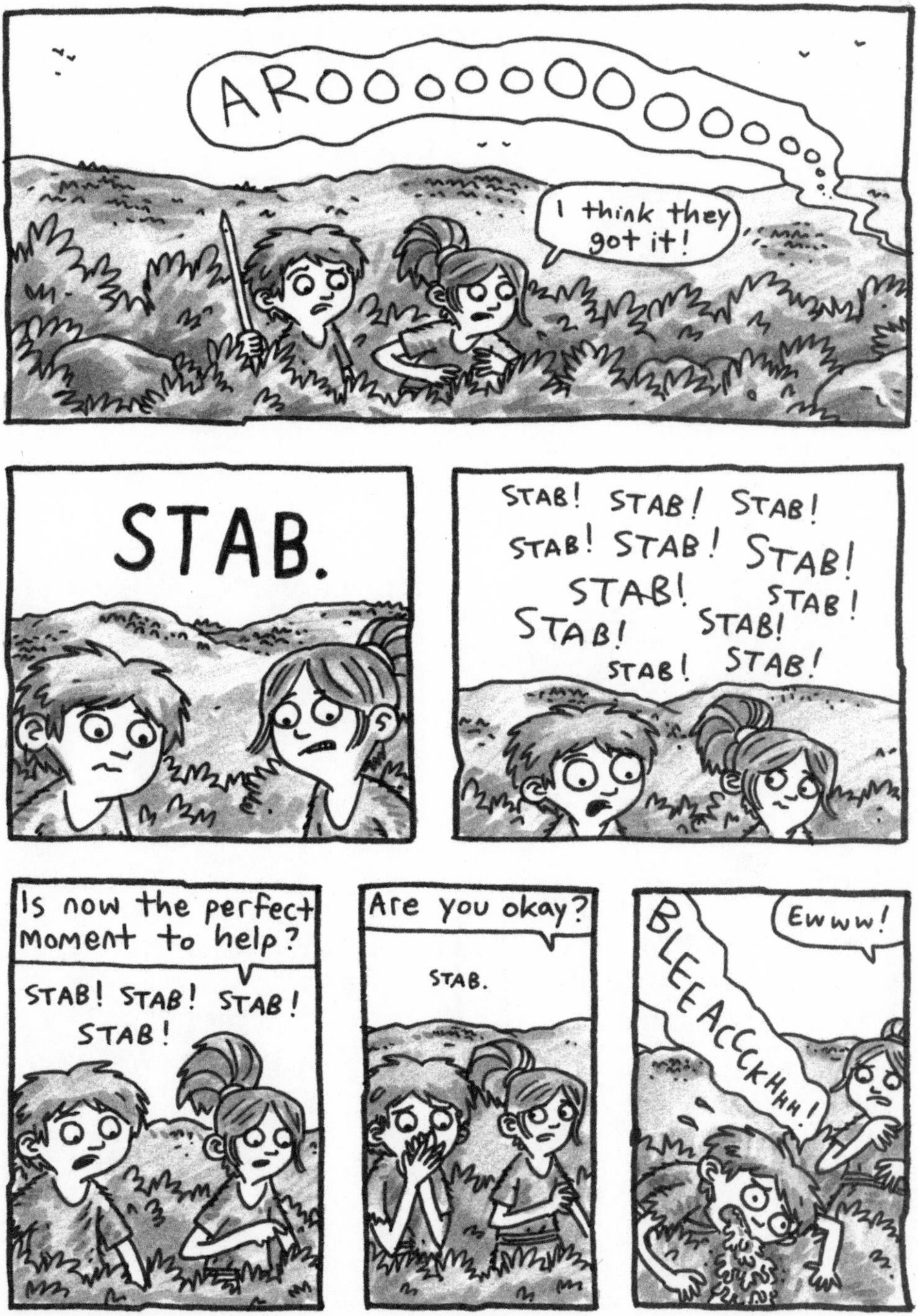

AROOOOOOOOOOOOOOooo
I think they got it!
STAB.
STAB! STAB! STAB!
STAB! STAB! STAB!
STAB! STAB!
STAB! STAB!
STAB! STAB!
Is now the perfect moment to help?
STAB! STAB! STAB!
STAB!
Are you okay?
STAB.
BLEEACCCKHHH!
Ewww!

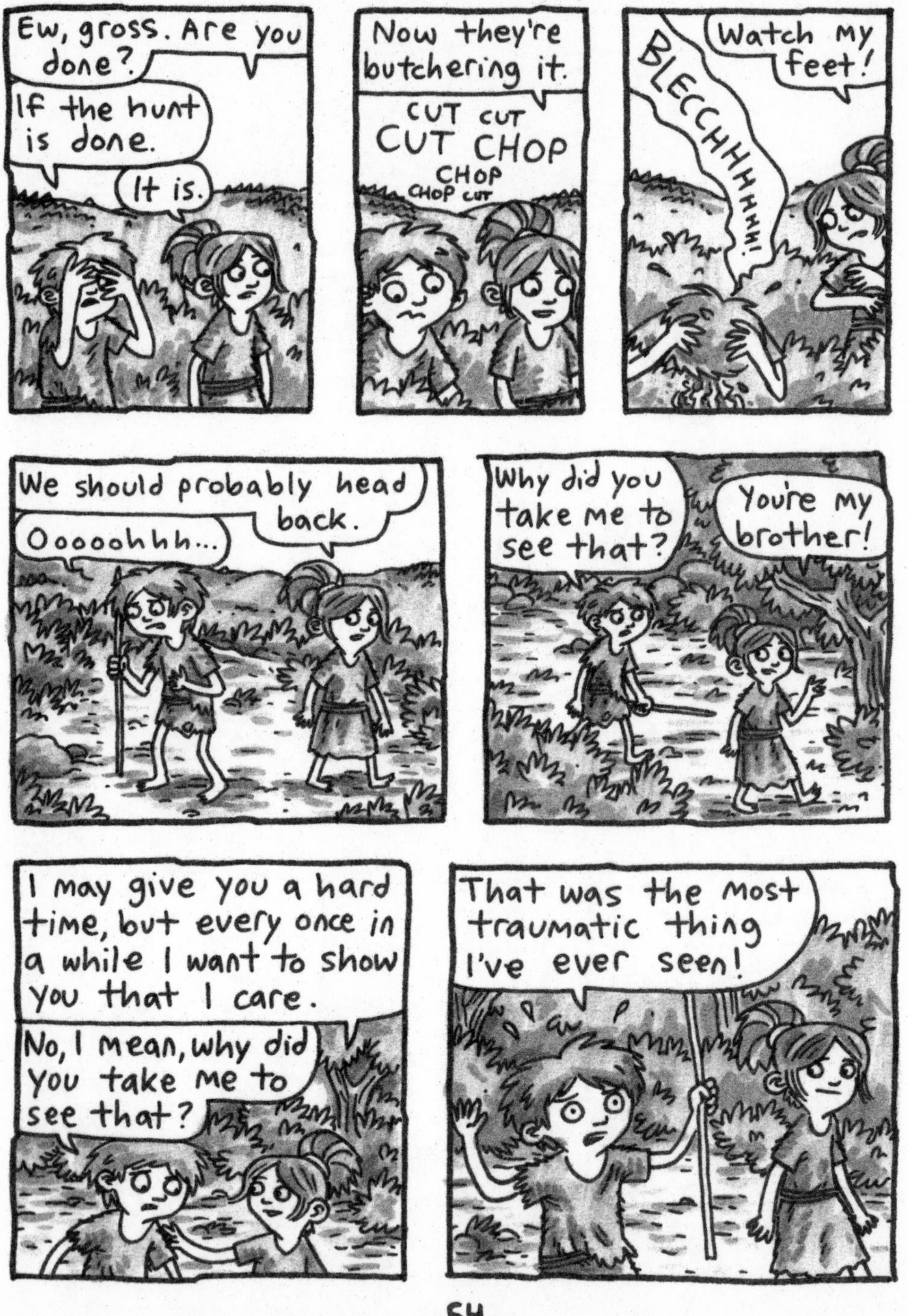

Ew, gross. Are you done?
If the hunt is done.
It is.
Now they're butchering it.
CUT CUT CUT CHOP CHOP CHOP CUT
BLECCHHHHHH!
Watch my feet!
We should probably head back.
Oooochhh...
Why did you take me to see that?
You're my brother!
I may give you a hard time, but every once in a while I want to show you that I care.
No, I mean, why did you take me to see that?
That was the most traumatic thing I've ever seen!

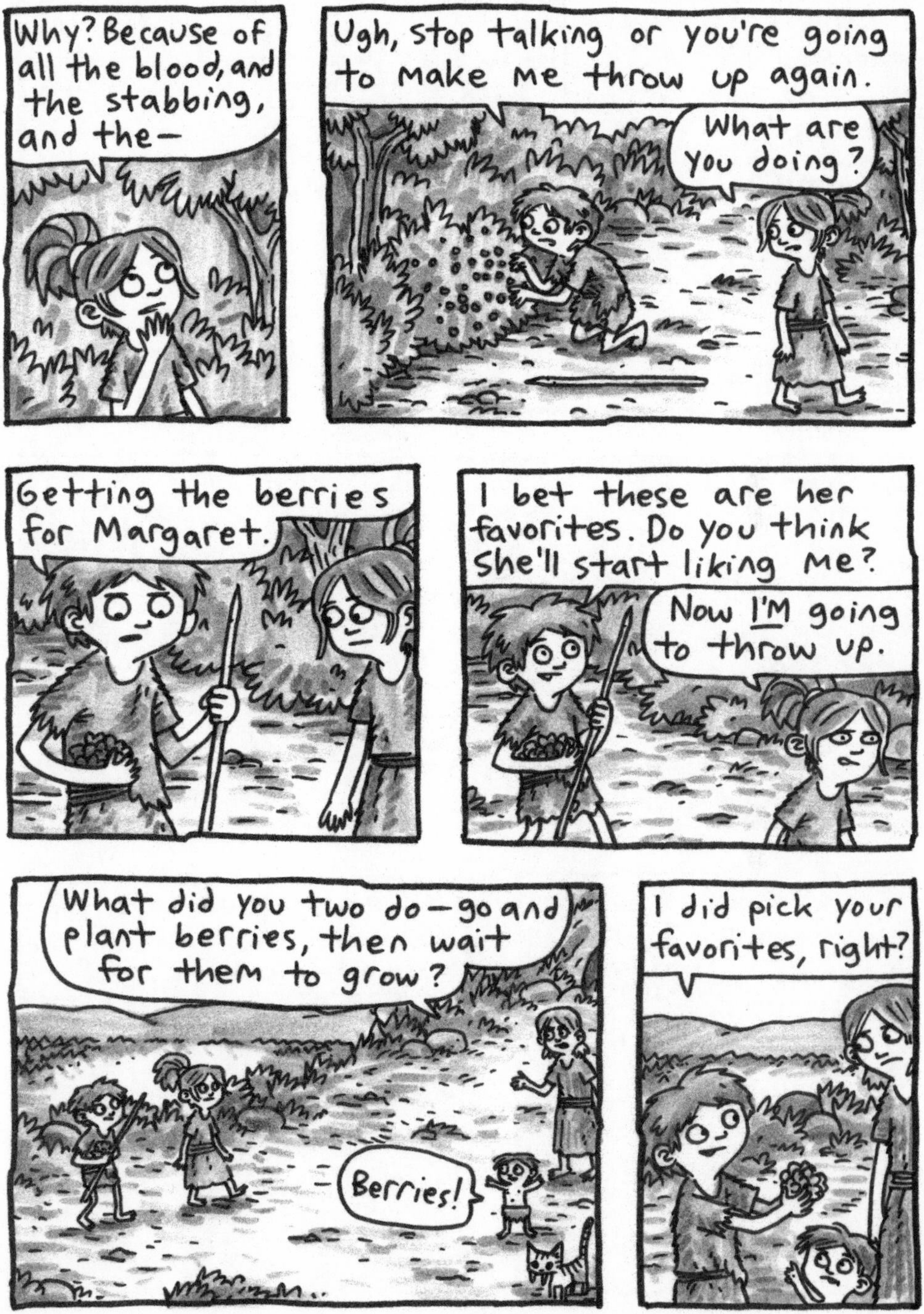
Why? Because of all the blood, and the stabbing, and the—
Ugh, stop talking or you're going to make me throw up again.
What are you doing?
Getting the berries for Margaret.
I bet these are her favorites. Do you think she'll start liking me?
Now I'M going to throw up.
What did you two do—go and plant berries, then wait for them to grow?
Berries!
I did pick your favorites, right?

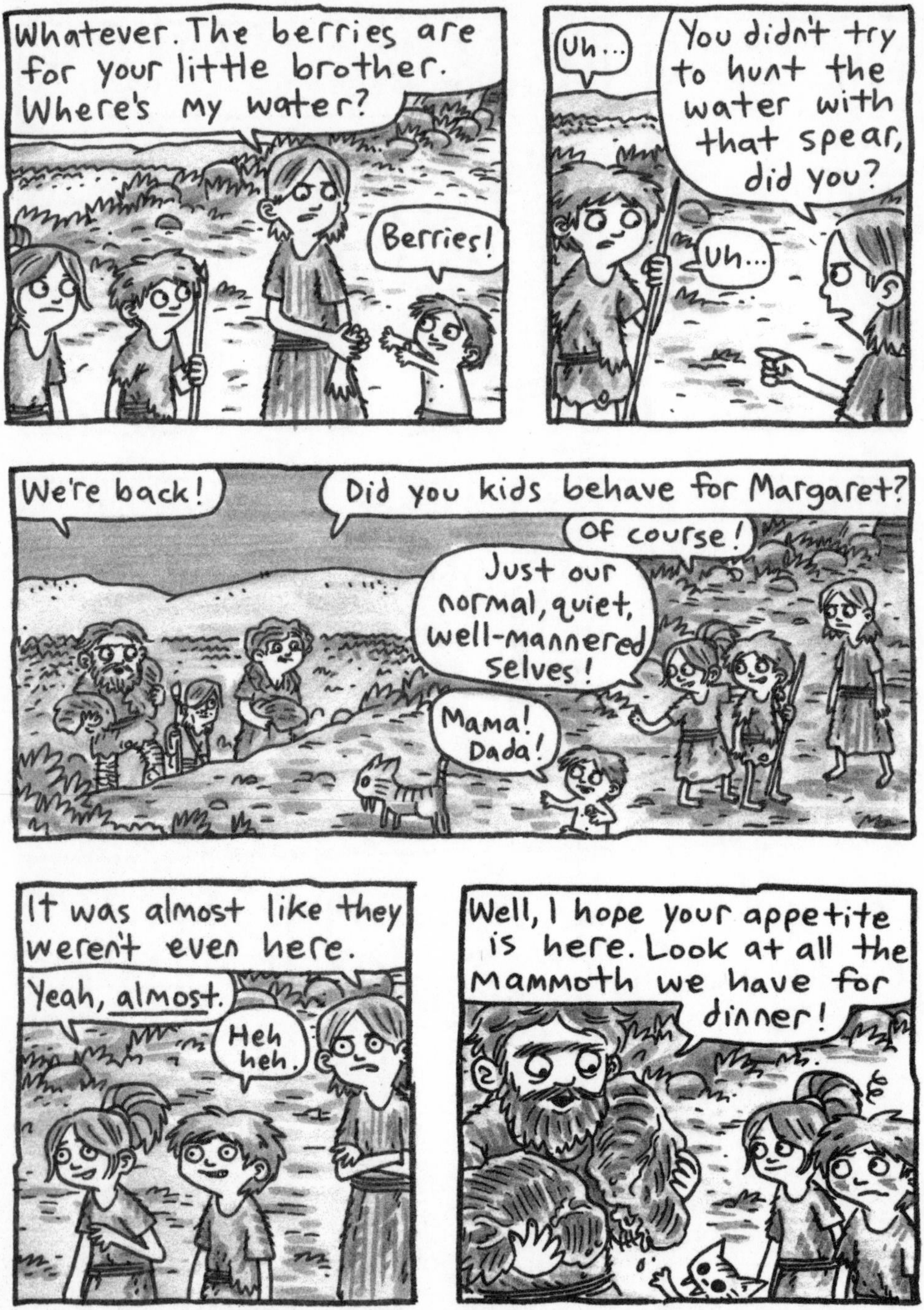

Whatever. The berries are for your little brother. Where's my water?
Berries!
Uh...
You didn't try to hunt the water with that spear, did you?
Uh...
We're back!
Did you kids behave for Margaret?
Of course!
Just our normal, quiet, well-mannered selves!
Mama! Dada!
It was almost like they weren't even here.
Yeah, almost.
Heh heh.
Well, I hope your appetite is here. Look at all the Mammoth we have for dinner!

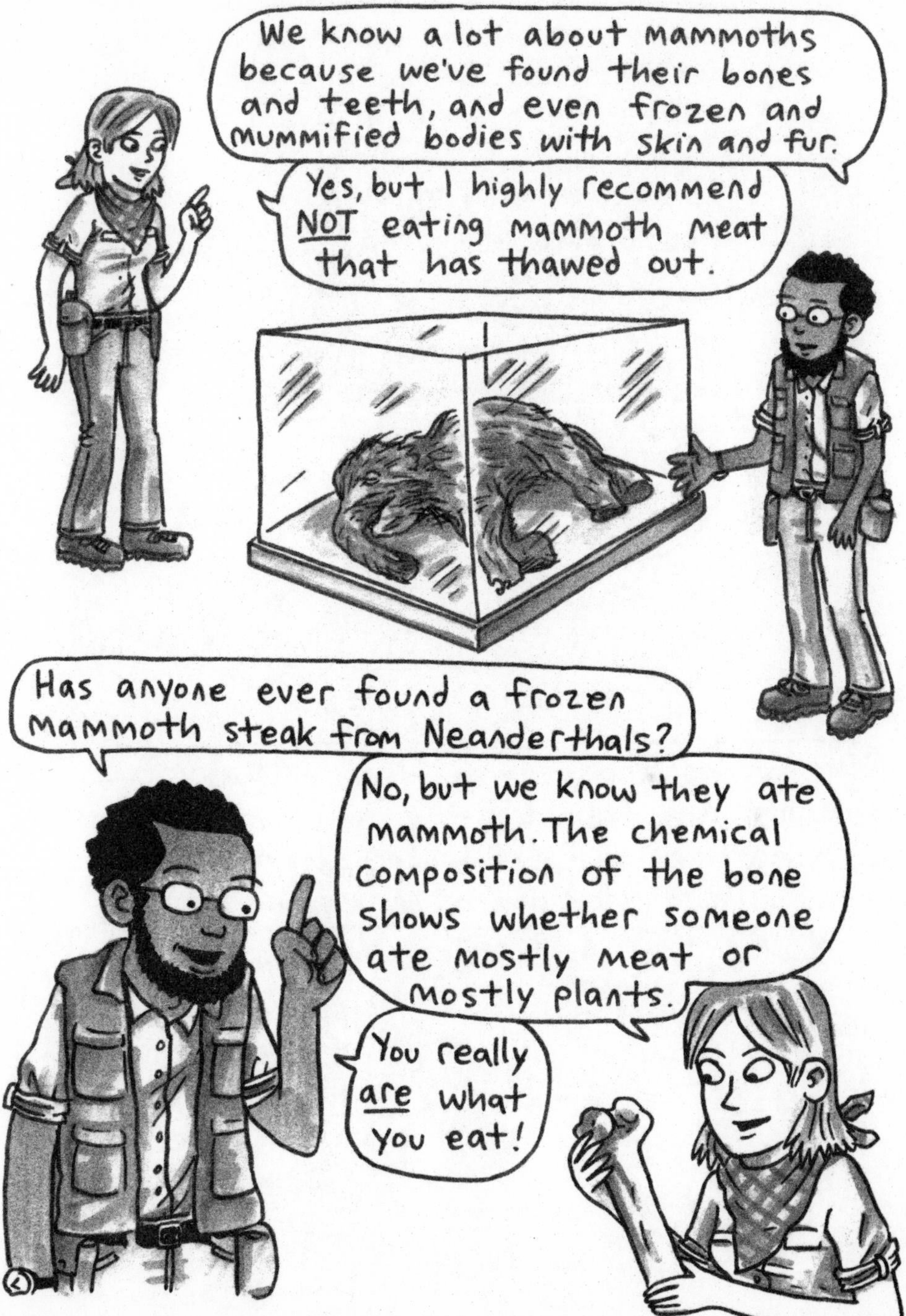
We know a lot about mammoths because we've found their bones and teeth, and even frozen and mummified bodies with skin and fur.
Yes, but I highly recommend NOT eating mammoth meat that has thawed out.
Has anyone ever found a frozen mammoth steak from Neanderthals?
No, but we know they ate mammoth. The chemical composition of the bone shows whether someone ate mostly meat or mostly plants.
You really are what you eat!

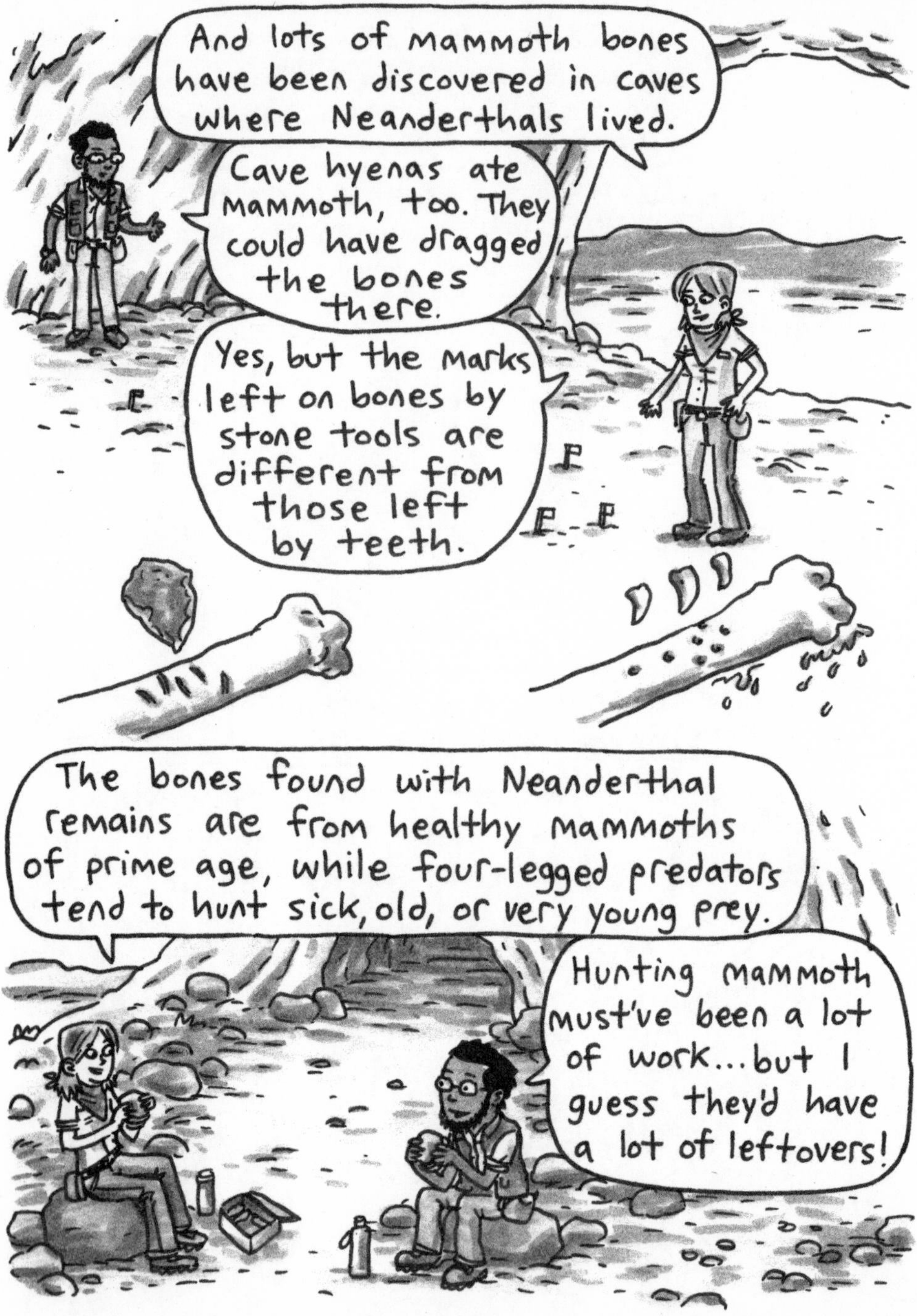
And lots of mammoth bones have been discovered in caves where Neanderthals lived.
Cave hyenas ate mammoth, too. They could have dragged the bones there.
Yes, but the marks left on bones by stone tools are different from those left by teeth.
The bones found with Neanderthal remains are from healthy mammoths of prime age, while four-legged predators tend to hunt sick, old, or very young prey.
Hunting mammoth must've been a lot of work...but I guess they'd have a lot of leftovers!

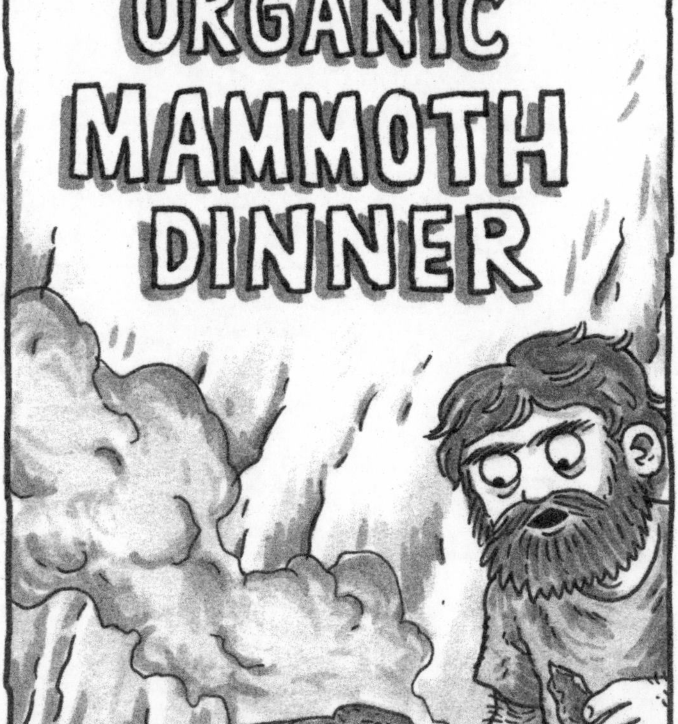
GLUTEN-FREE ORGANIC MAMMOTH DINNER

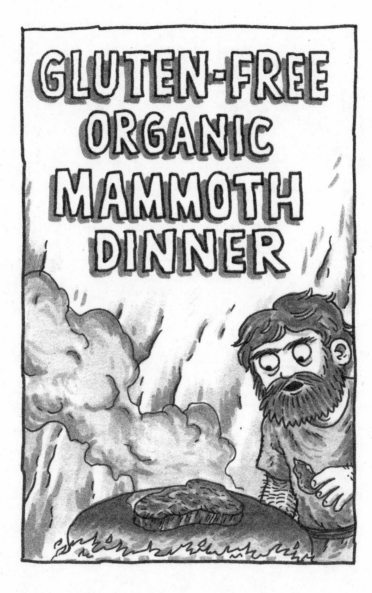

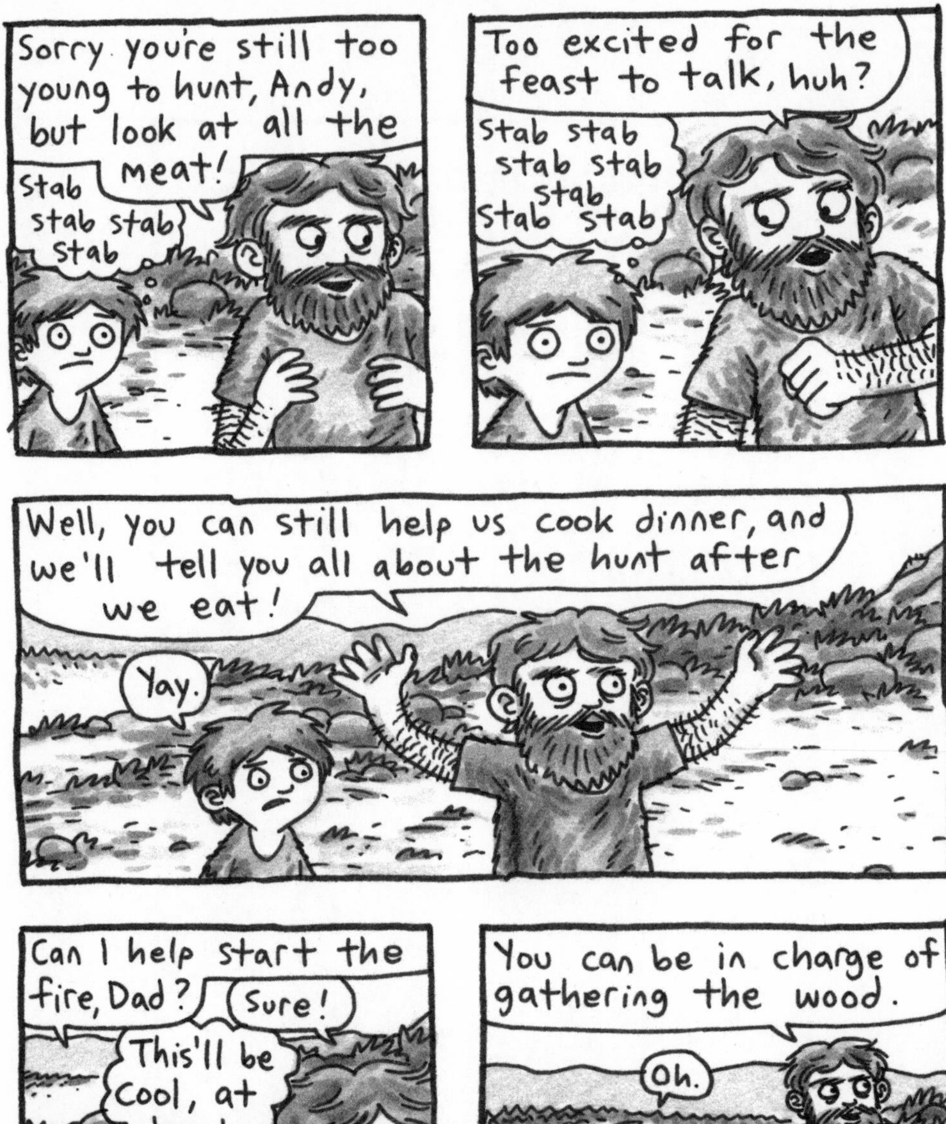

Sorry you're still too young to hunt, Andy, but look at all the meat!
Stab stab stab Stab
Too excited for the feast to talk, huh?
Stab stab stab stab Stab Stab stab
Well, you can still help us cook dinner, and we'll tell you all about the hunt after we eat!
Yay.
Can I help start the fire, Dad?
Sure!
This'll be cool, at least.
You can be in charge of gathering the wood.
Oh.

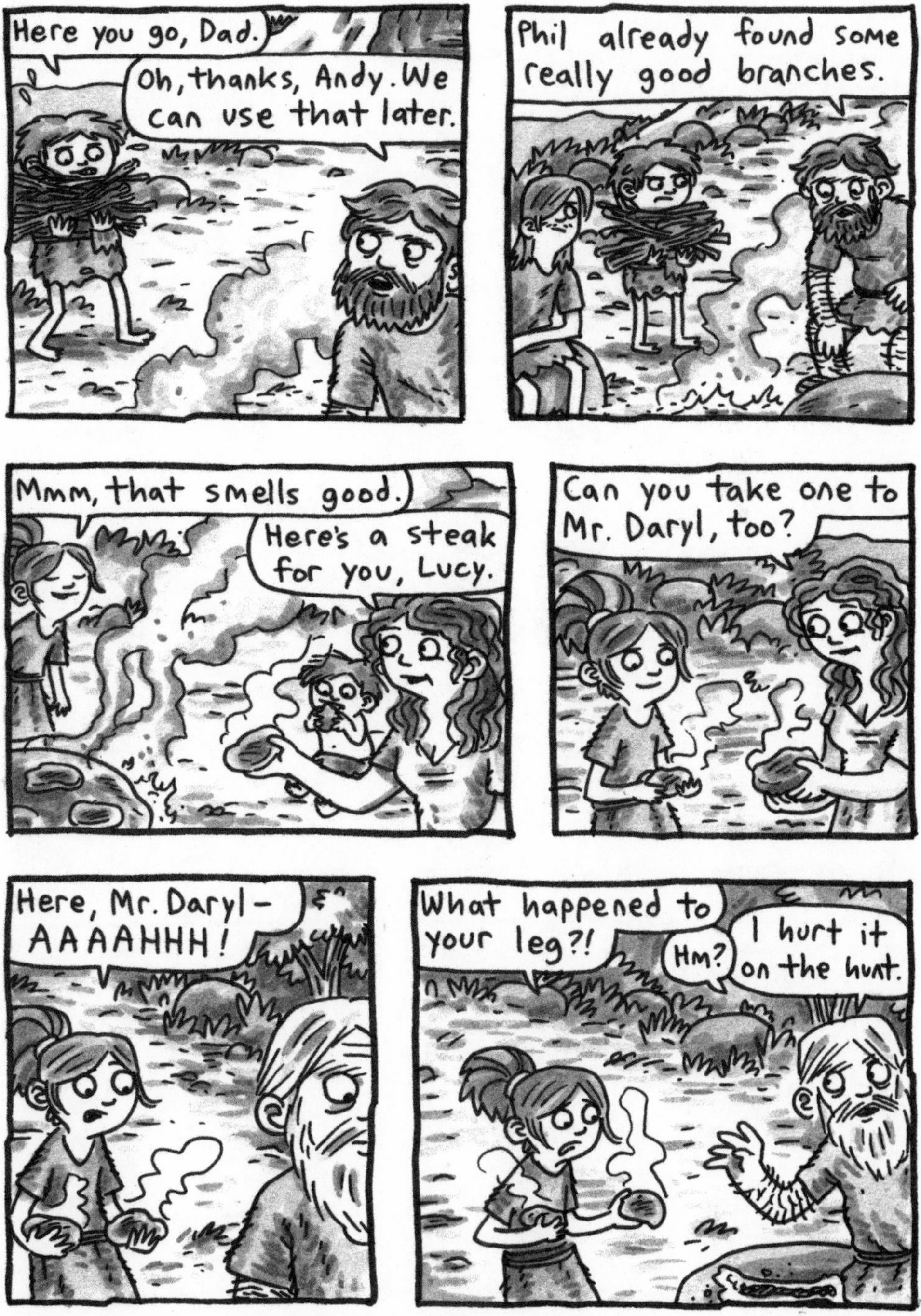
Here you go, Dad.
Oh, thanks, Andy. We can use that later.
Phil already found some really good branches.
Mmm, that smells good.
Here's a steak for you, Lucy.
Can you take one to Mr. Daryl, too?
Here, Mr. Daryl- AAAAHHH!
What happened to your leg?!
Hm?
I hurt it on the hunt.

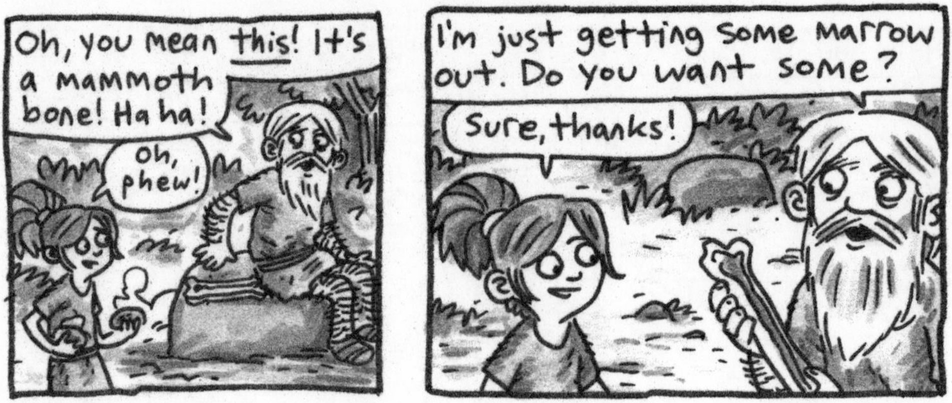
Oh, you mean this! It's a mammoth bone! Ha ha!
Oh, phew!
I'm just getting some marrow out. Do you want some?
Sure, thanks!

FATTY BONE MARROW!

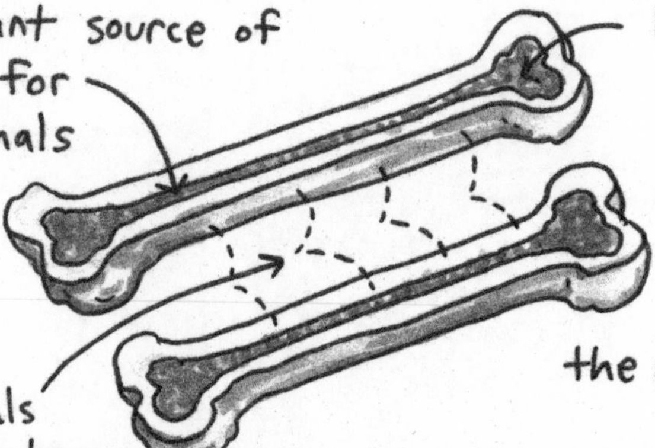
An important source of nutrition for Neanderthals
Hyenas shattered bones, and other carnivores chewed off the ends to get at the plentiful deposit.
Neanderthals would split bone to extract as much tissue as possible.

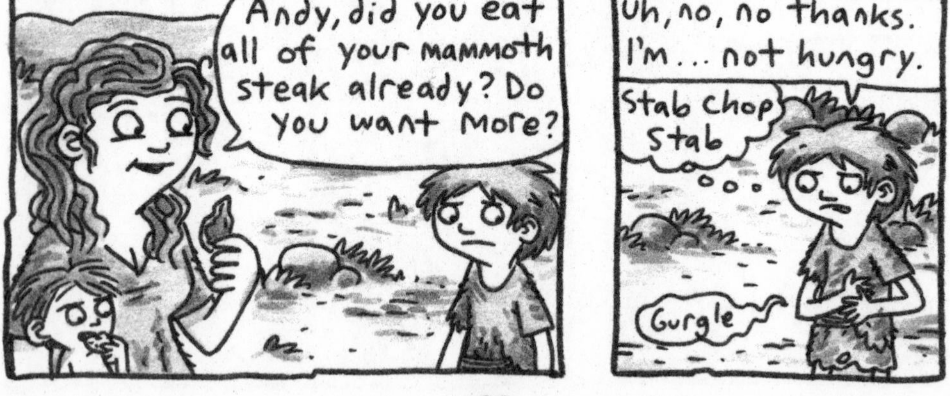
Andy, did you eat all of your mammoth steak already? Do you want more?
Uh, no, no thanks. I'm... not hungry.
Stab Chop Stab
Gurgle

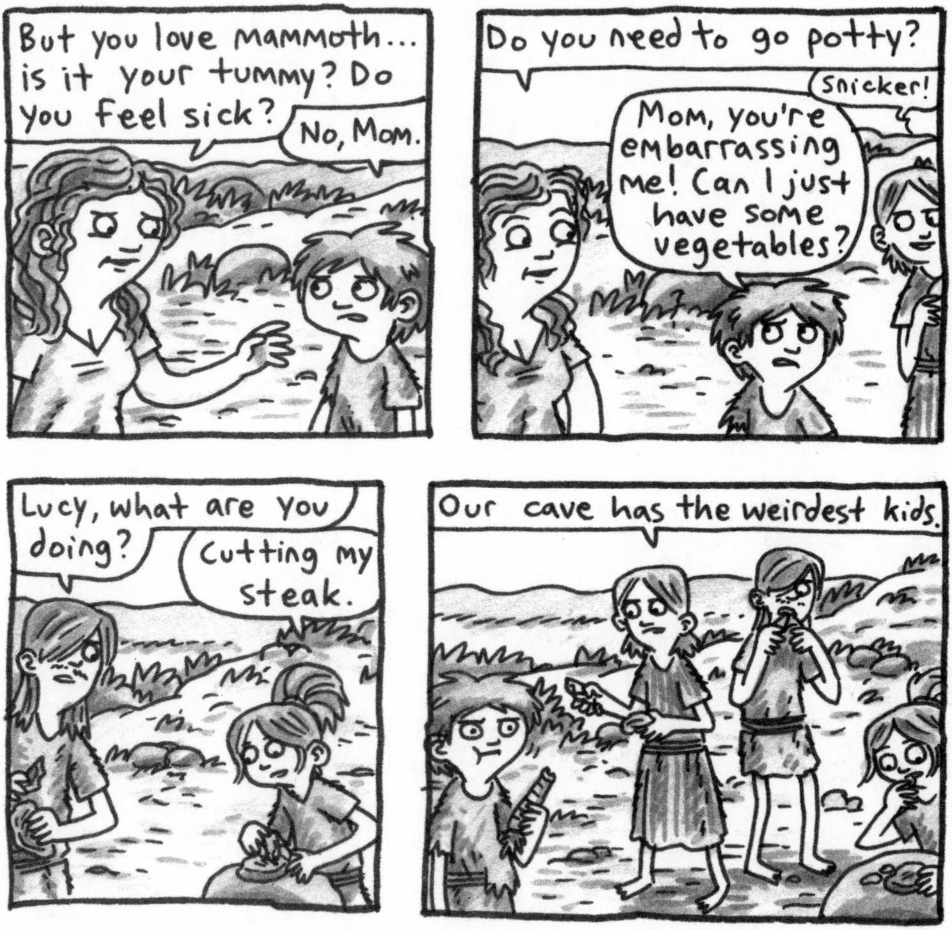
But you love mammoth... is it your tummy? Do you feel sick?
No, Mom.
Do you need to go potty?
Snicker!
Mom, you're embarrassing me! Can I just have some vegetables?
Lucy, what are you doing?
Cutting my steak.
Our cave has the weirdest kids.

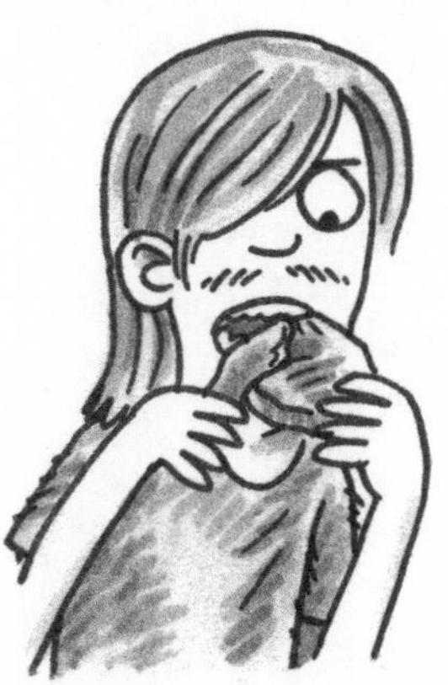

Like some modern-day human hunters, Neanderthals often held food with their teeth while cutting it. Scientists know this from tiny marks on Neanderthal teeth.

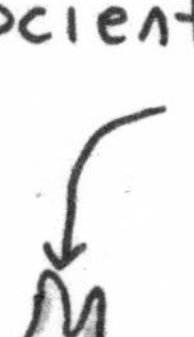

The location and angle of the marks also show that most Neanderthals were right-handed!

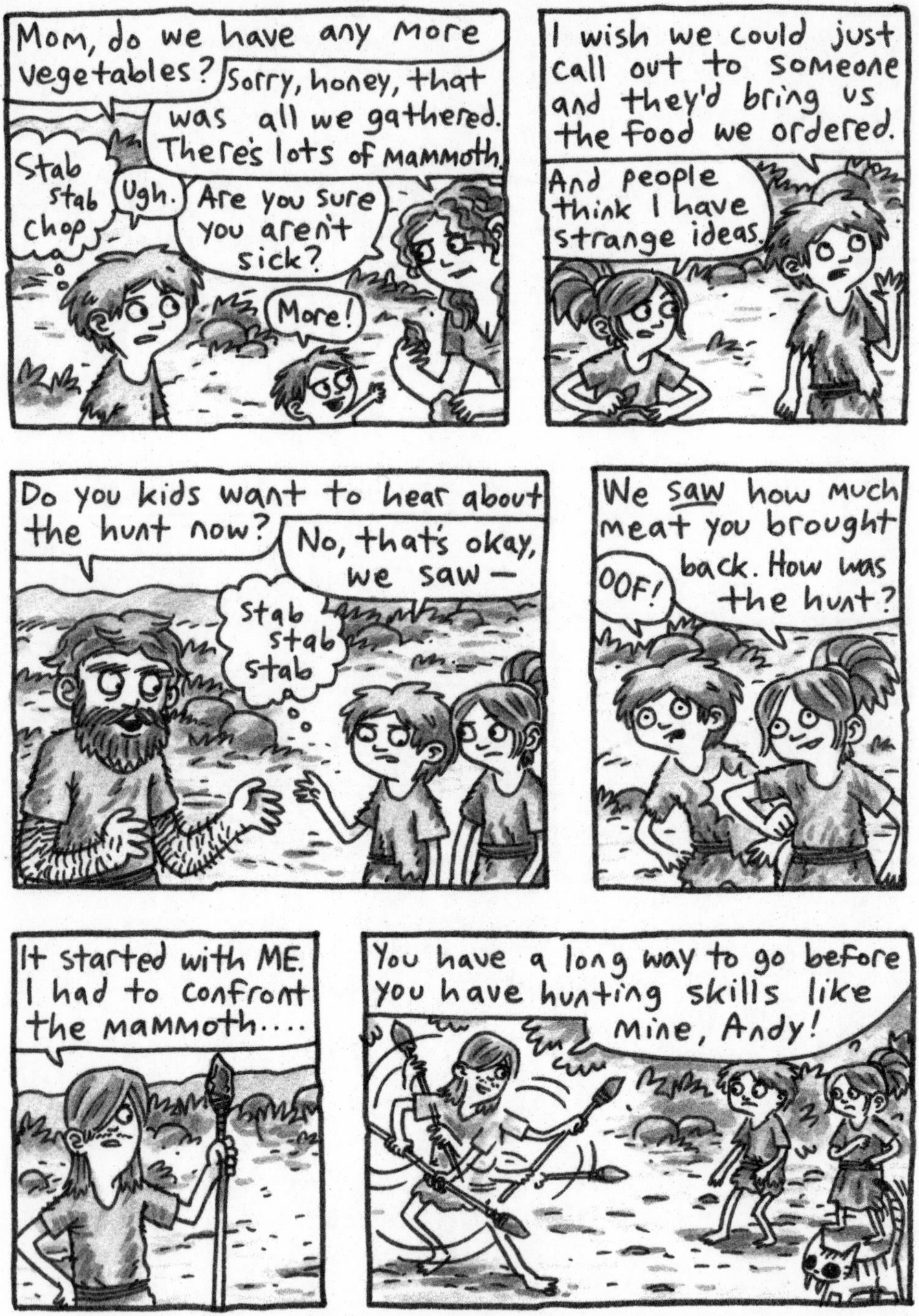
Mom, do we have any more vegetables?
Sorry, honey, that was all we gathered. There's lots of mammoth.
Stab stab chop
Ugh.
Are you sure you aren't sick?
More!
I wish we could just call out to someone and they'd bring us the food we ordered.
And people think I have strange ideas.
Do you kids want to hear about the hunt now?
No, that's okay, we saw—
Stab stab stab
We saw how much meat you brought back. How was the hunt?
OOF!
It started with ME. I had to confront the mammoth....
You have a long way to go before you have hunting skills like mine, Andy!

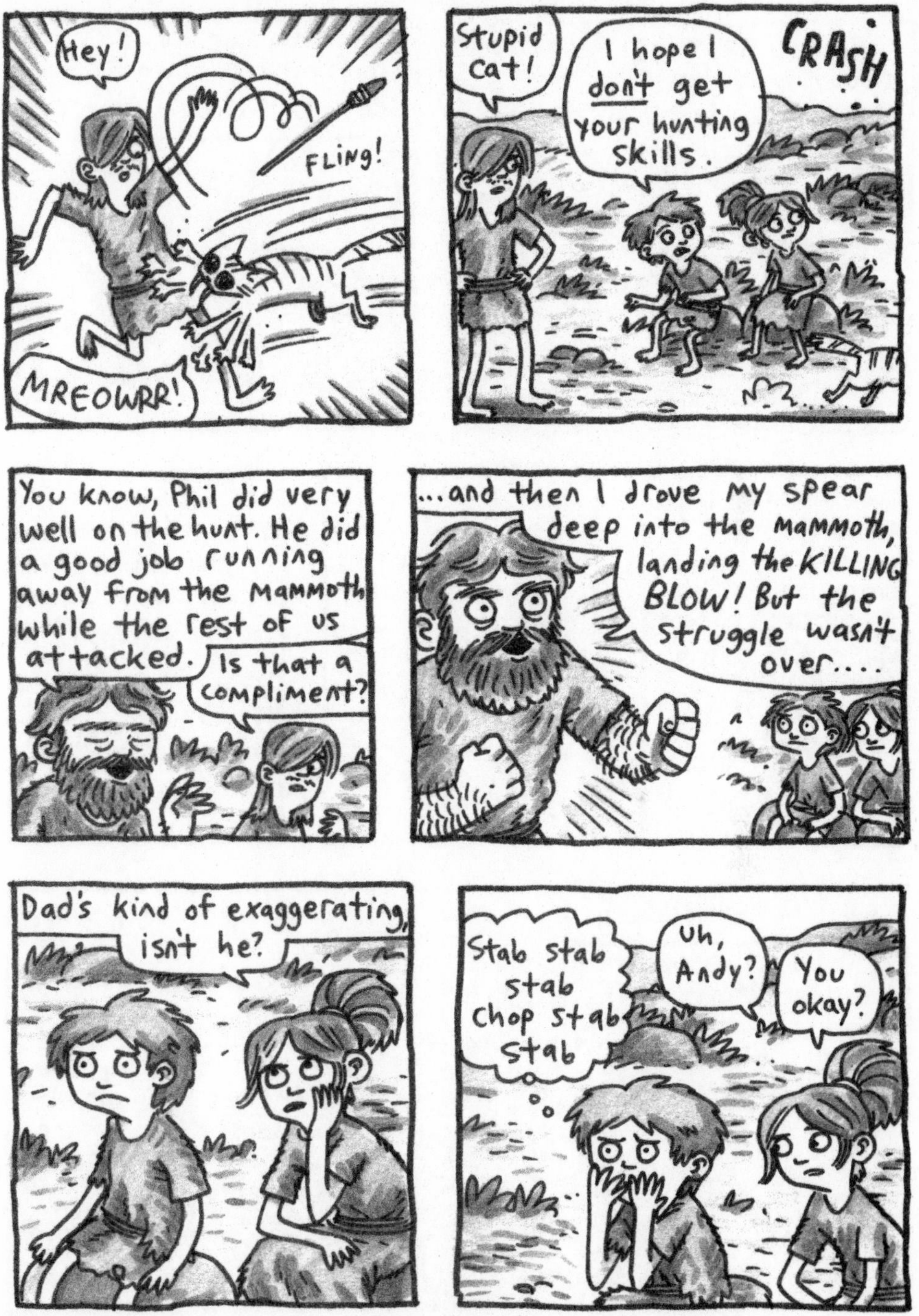
Hey!
FLING!
MREOWRR!
Stupid cat!
I hope I don't get your hunting skills.
CRASH
You know, Phil did very well on the hunt. He did a good job running away from the mammoth while the rest of us attacked.
Is that a compliment?
...and then I drove my spear deep into the mammoth, landing the KILLING BLOW! But the struggle wasn't over....
Dad's kind of exaggerating, isn't he?
Stab stab stab Chop stab stab
Uh, Andy?
You okay?

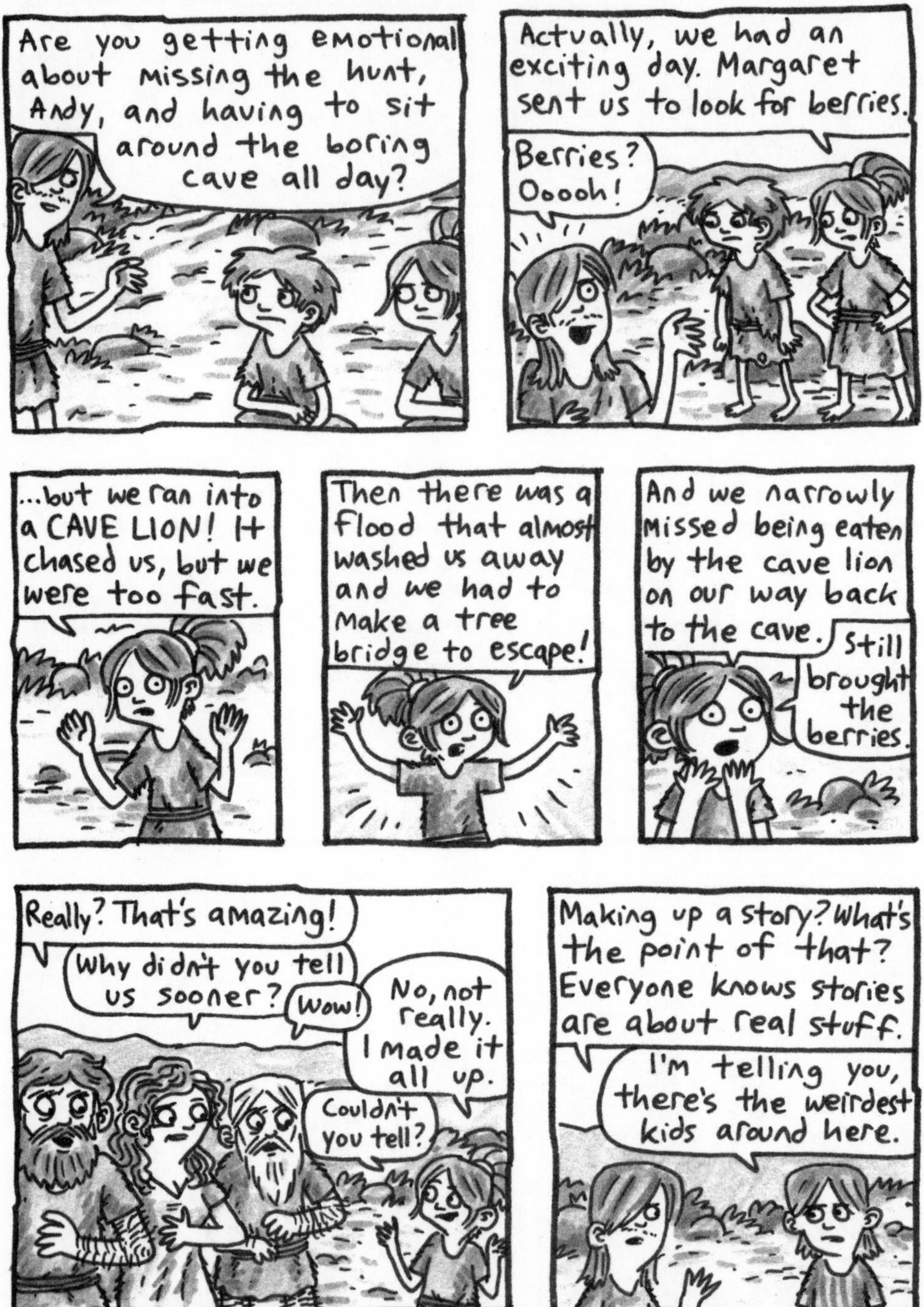

Are you getting emotional about missing the hunt, Andy, and having to sit around the boring cave all day?
Actually, we had an exciting day. Margaret sent us to look for berries.
Berries? Ooooh!
...but we ran into a CAVE LION! It chased us, but we were too fast.
Then there was a flood that almost washed us away and we had to make a tree bridge to escape!
And we narrowly missed being eaten by the cave lion on our way back to the cave.
Still brought the berries.
Really? That's amazing!
Why didn't you tell us sooner?
Wow!
No, not really. I made it all up.
Couldn't you tell?
Making up a story? What's the point of that? Everyone knows stories are about real stuff.
I'm telling you, there's the weirdest kids around here.

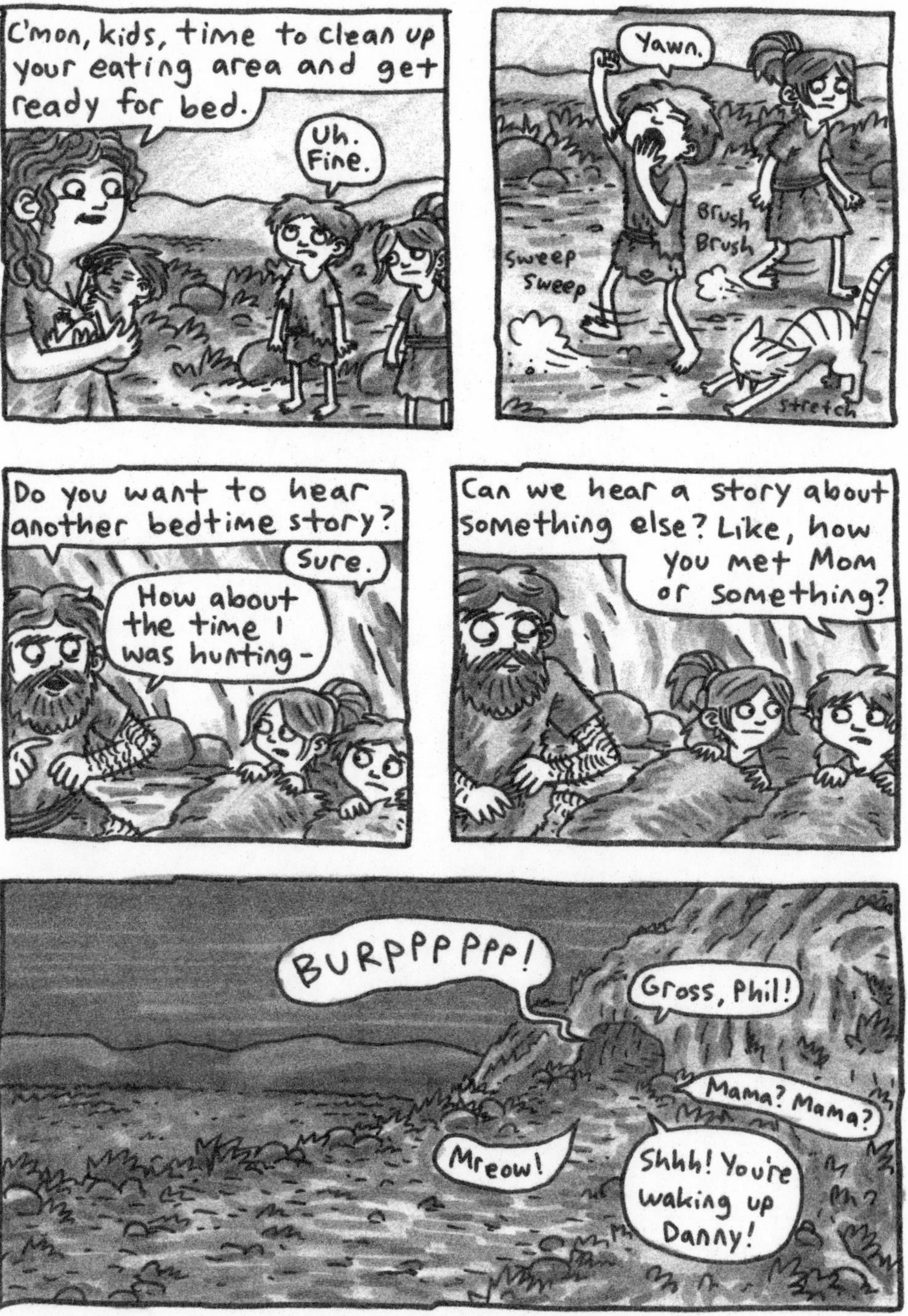
C'mon, kids, time to clean up your eating area and get ready for bed.
Uh. Fine.
Yawn.
Brush Brush
Sweep Sweep
stretch
Do you want to hear another bedtime story?
Sure.
How about the time I was hunting-
Can we hear a story about something else? Like, how you met Mom or something?
BURPPPPPP!
Gross, Phil!
Mama? Mama?
Mreow!
Shhh! You're waking up Danny!

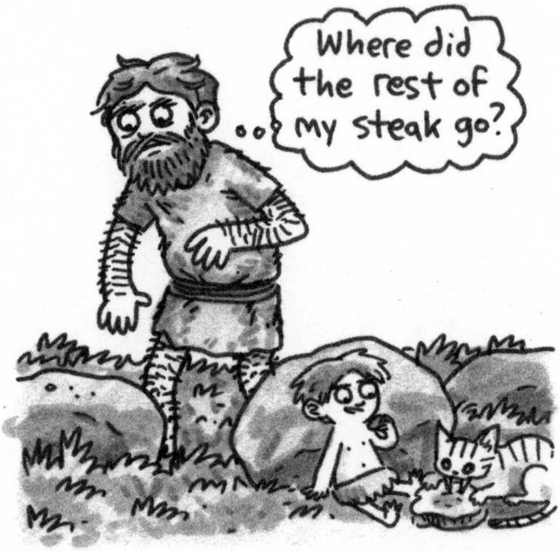
Where did the rest of my steak go?

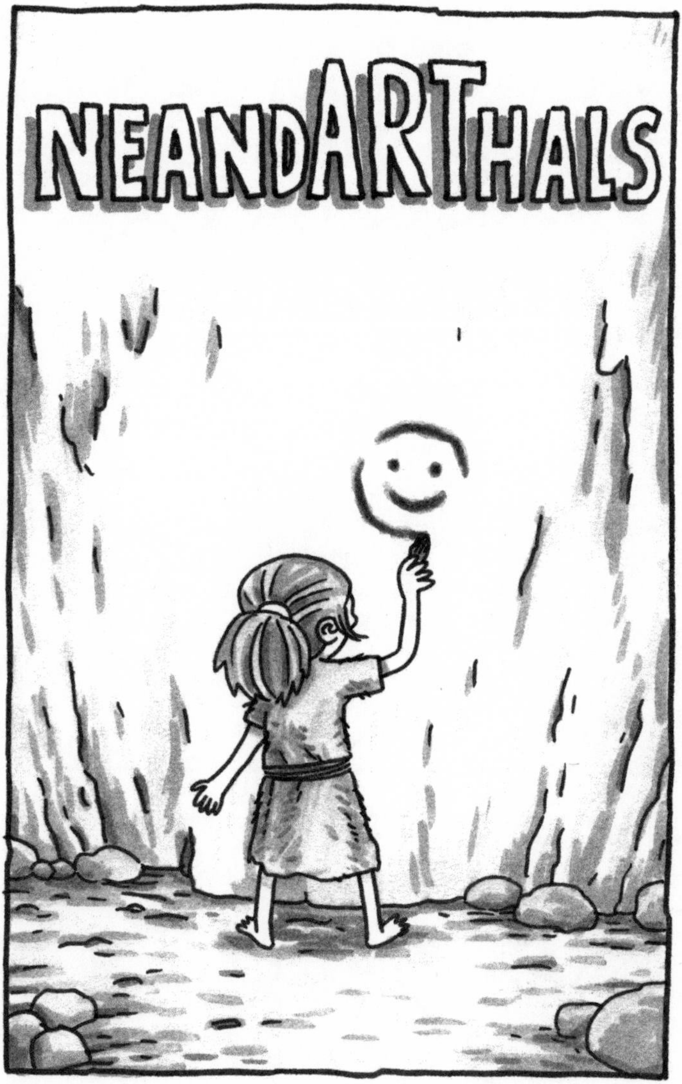
NEANDARTHALS

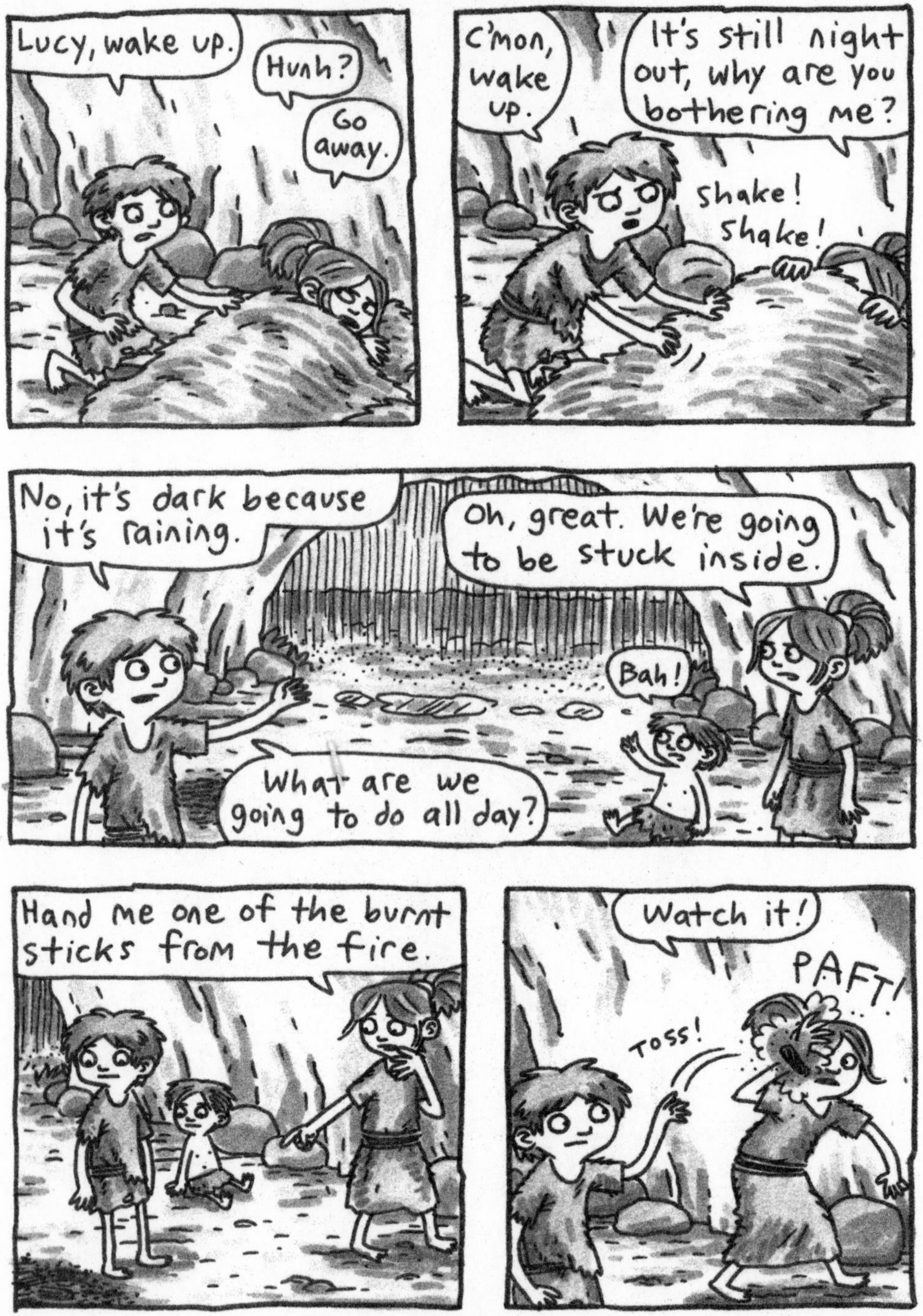
Lucy, wake up.
Hunh?
Go away.
C'mon, wake up.
It's still night out, why are you bothering me?
Shake! Shake!
No, it's dark because it's raining.
Oh, great. We're going to be stuck inside.
Bah!
What are we going to do all day?
Hand me one of the burnt sticks from the fire.
Watch it!
PAFT!
TOSS!

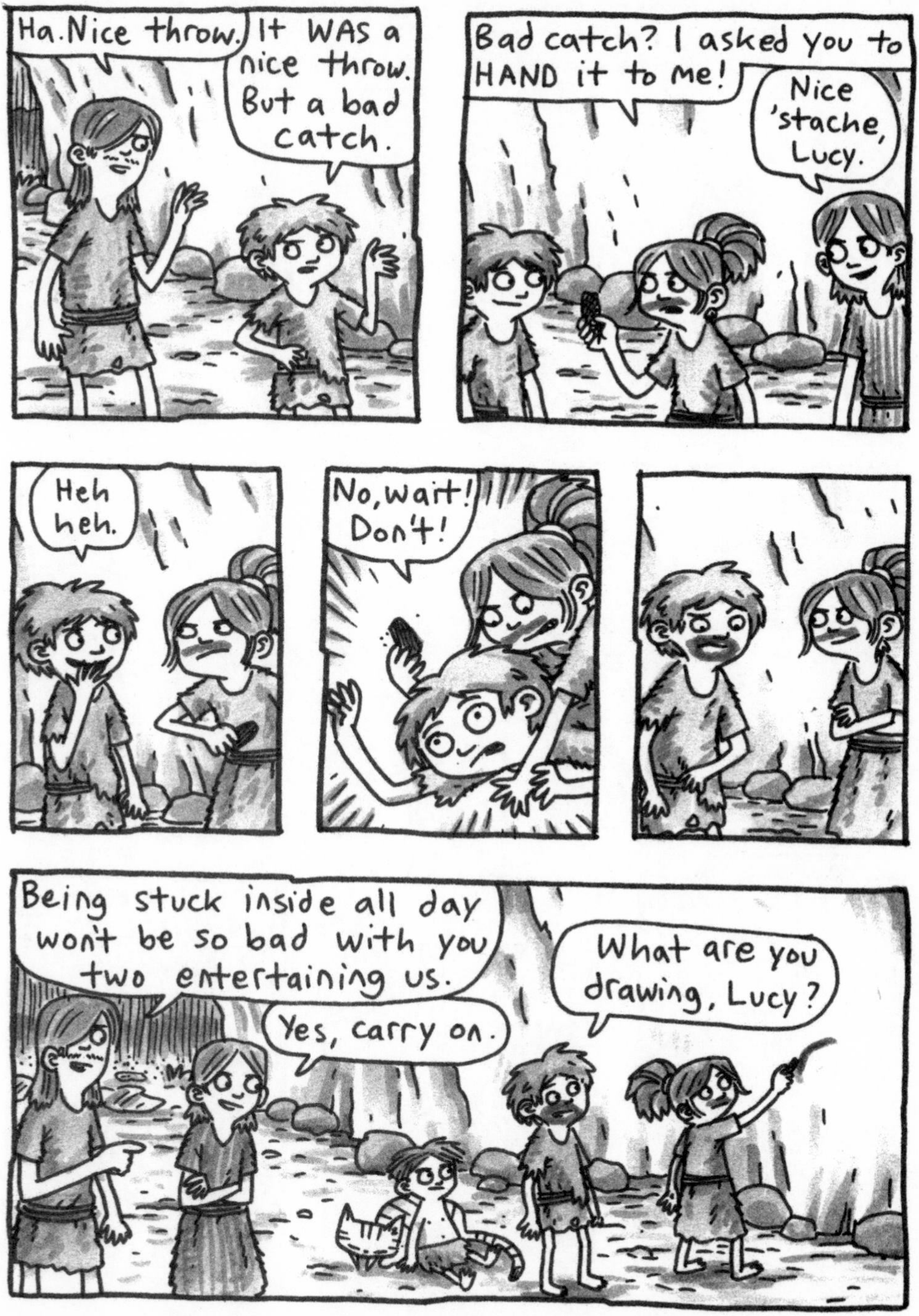
Ha. Nice throw.
It WAS a nice throw. But a bad catch.
Bad catch? I asked you to HAND it to me!
Nice 'stache, Lucy.
Heh heh.
No, wait! Don't!
Being stuck inside all day won't be so bad with you two entertaining us.
Yes, carry on.
What are you drawing, Lucy?

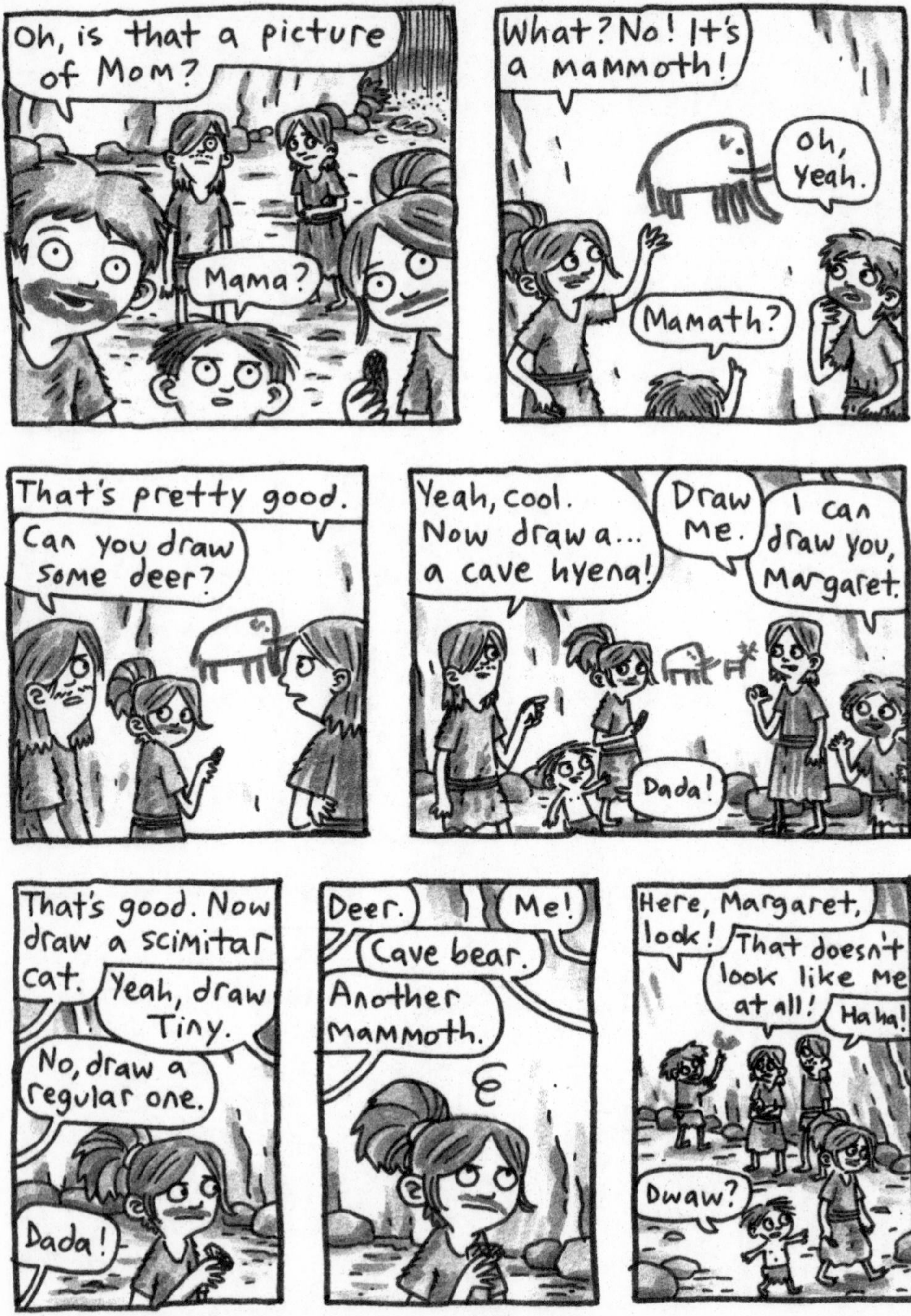
Oh, is that a picture of Mom?
Mama?
What? No! It's a mammoth!
Oh, yeah.
Mamath?
That's pretty good.
Can you draw some deer?
Yeah, cool. Now draw a... a cave hyena!
Draw Me.
I can draw you, Margaret.
Dada!
That's good. Now draw a scimitar cat.
Yeah, draw Tiny.
No, draw a regular one.
Dada!
Deer.
Me!
Cave bear.
Another mammoth.
Here, Margaret, look!
That doesn't look like me at all!
Ha ha!
Dwaw?

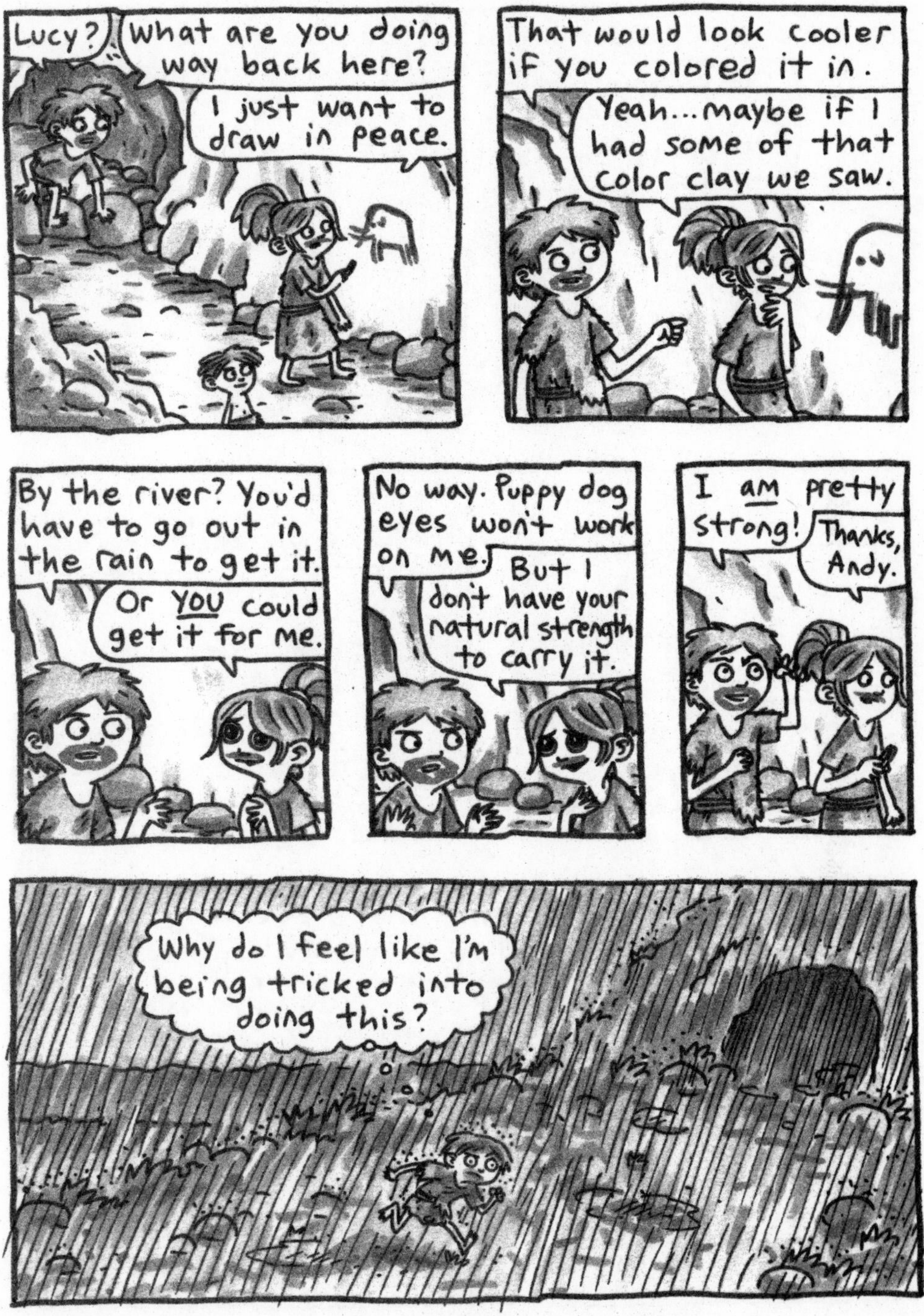
Lucy?
What are you doing way back here?
I just want to draw in peace.
That would look cooler if you colored it in.
Yeah... maybe if I had some of that color clay we saw.
By the river? You'd have to go out in the rain to get it.
Or YOU could get it for me.
No way. Puppy dog eyes won't work on me.
But I don't have your natural strength to carry it.
I AM pretty strong!
Thanks, Andy.
Why do I feel like I'm being tricked into doing this?

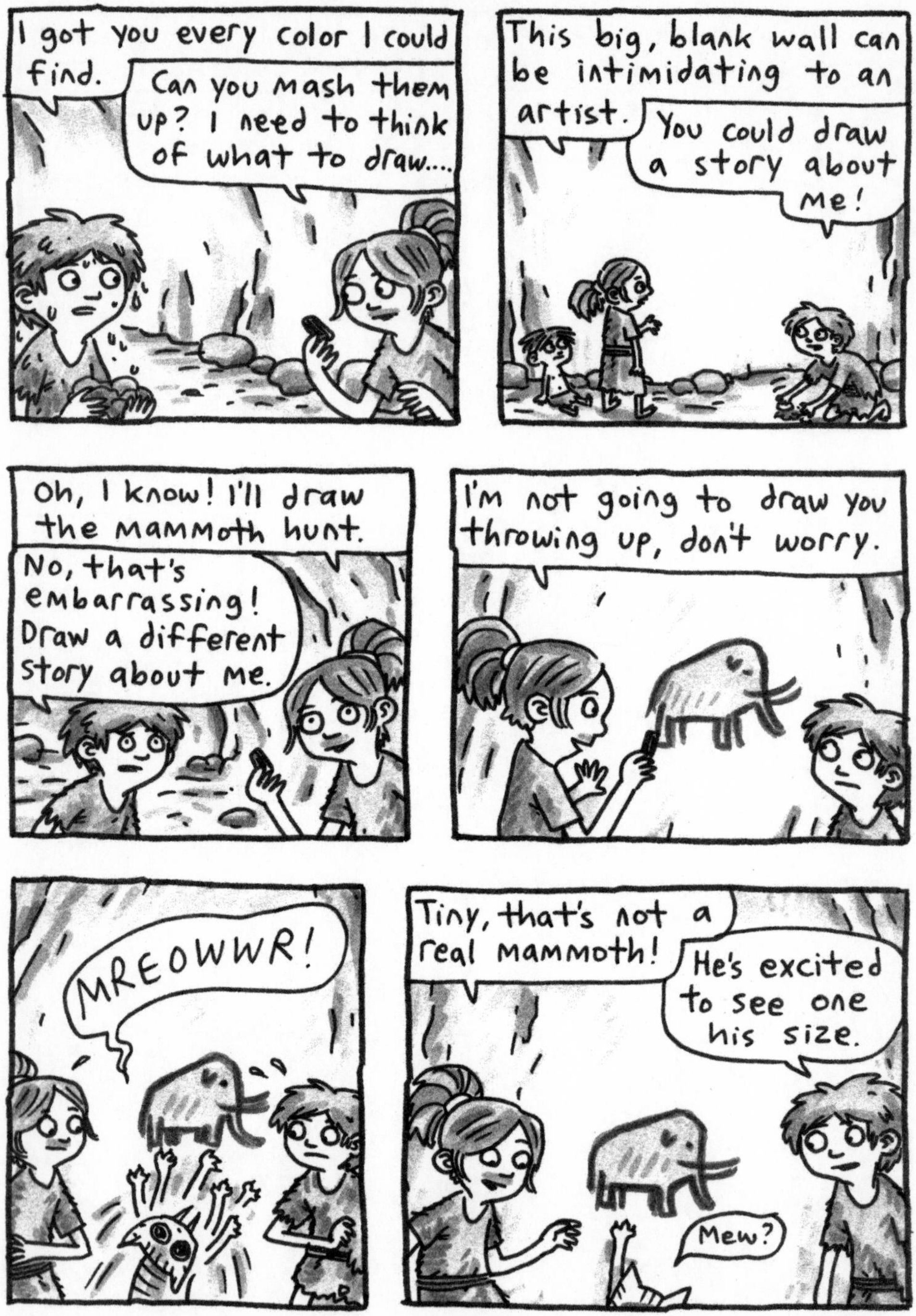

I got you every color I could find.
Can you mash them up? I need to think of what to draw....
This big, blank wall can be intimidating to an artist.
You could draw a story about me!
Oh, I know! I'll draw the mammoth hunt.
No, that's embarrassing! Draw a different story about me.
I'm not going to draw you throwing up, don't worry.
MREOWWR!
Tiny, that's not a real mammoth!
He's excited to see one his size.
Mew?

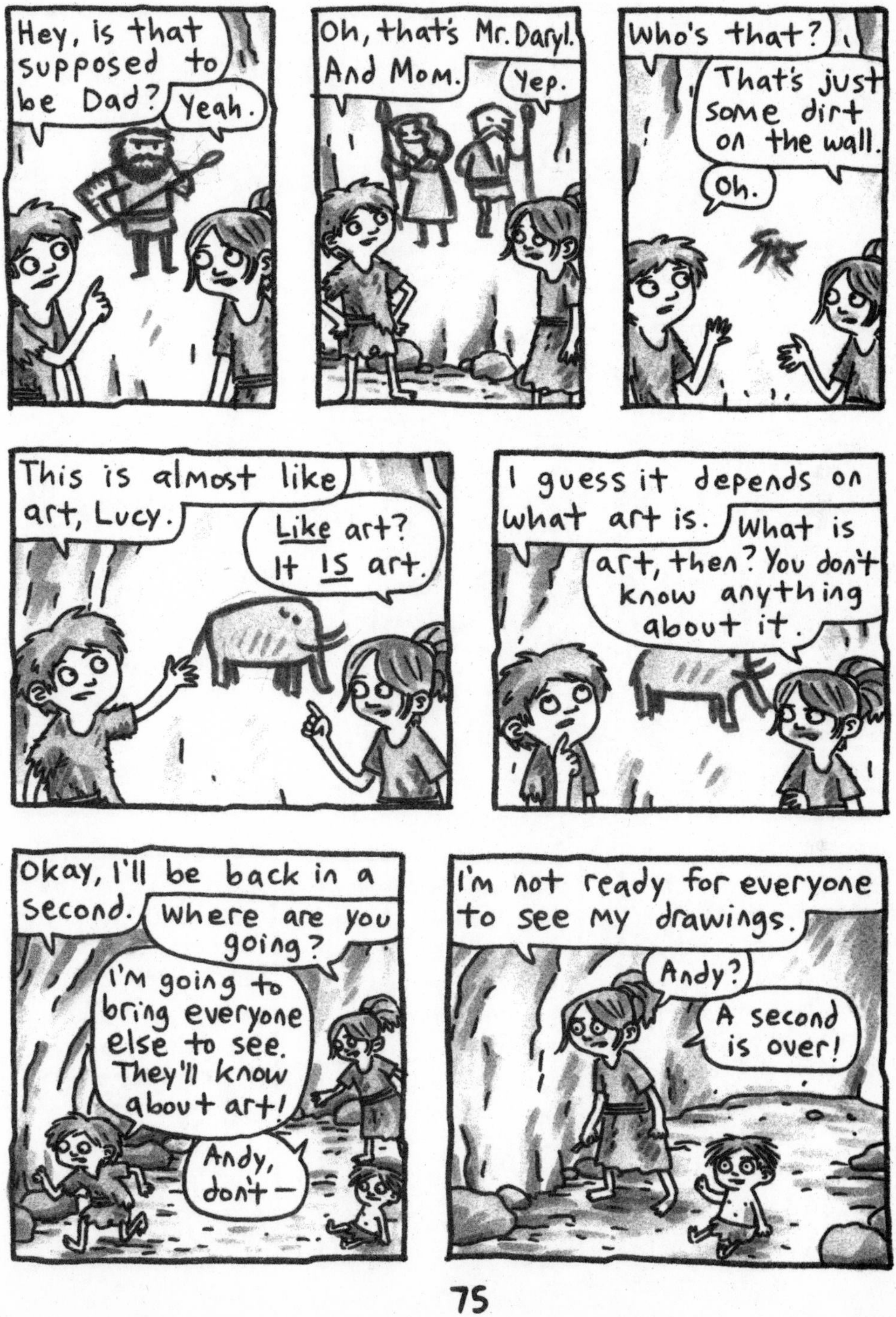
Hey, is that supposed to be Dad?
Yeah.
Oh, that's Mr. Daryl. And Mom.
Yep.
Who's that?
That's just some dirt on the wall.
Oh.
This is almost like art, Lucy.
Like art? It IS art.
I guess it depends on what art is.
What is art, then? You don't know anything about it.
Okay, I'll be back in a second.
Where are you going?
I'm going to bring everyone else to see. They'll know about art!
Andy, don't—
I'm not ready for everyone to see my drawings.
Andy?
A second is over!

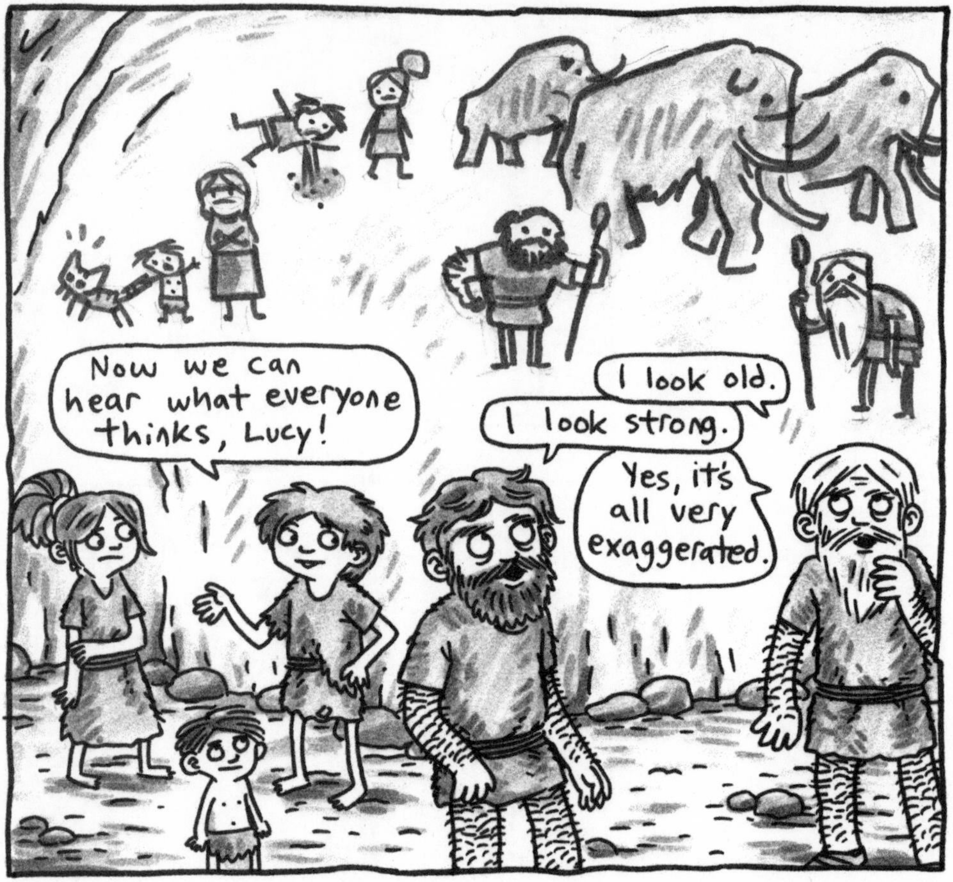
Now we can hear what everyone thinks, Lucy!
I look strong.
I look old.
Yes, it's all very exaggerated.

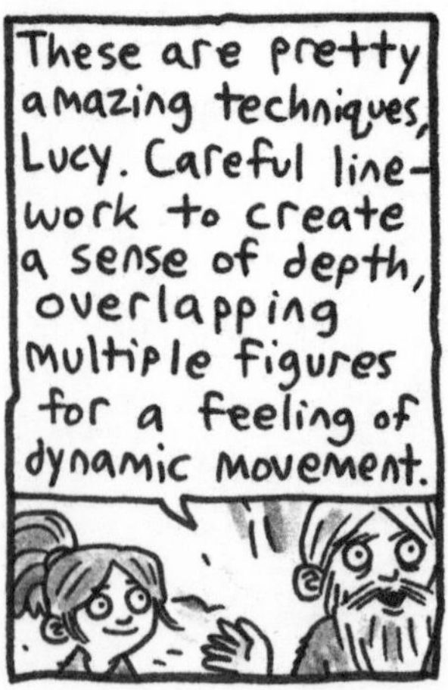
These are pretty amazing techniques, Lucy. Careful line-work to create a sense of depth, overlapping multiple figures for a feeling of dynamic movement.

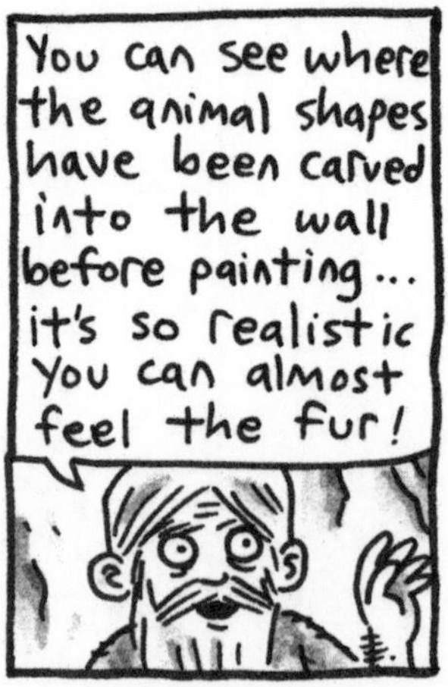
You can see where the animal shapes have been carved into the wall before painting... it's so realistic you can almost feel the fur!

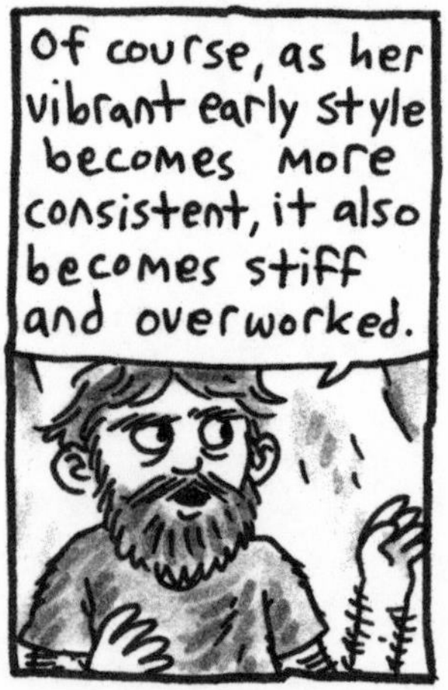
Of course, as her vibrant early style becomes more consistent, it also becomes stiff and overworked.

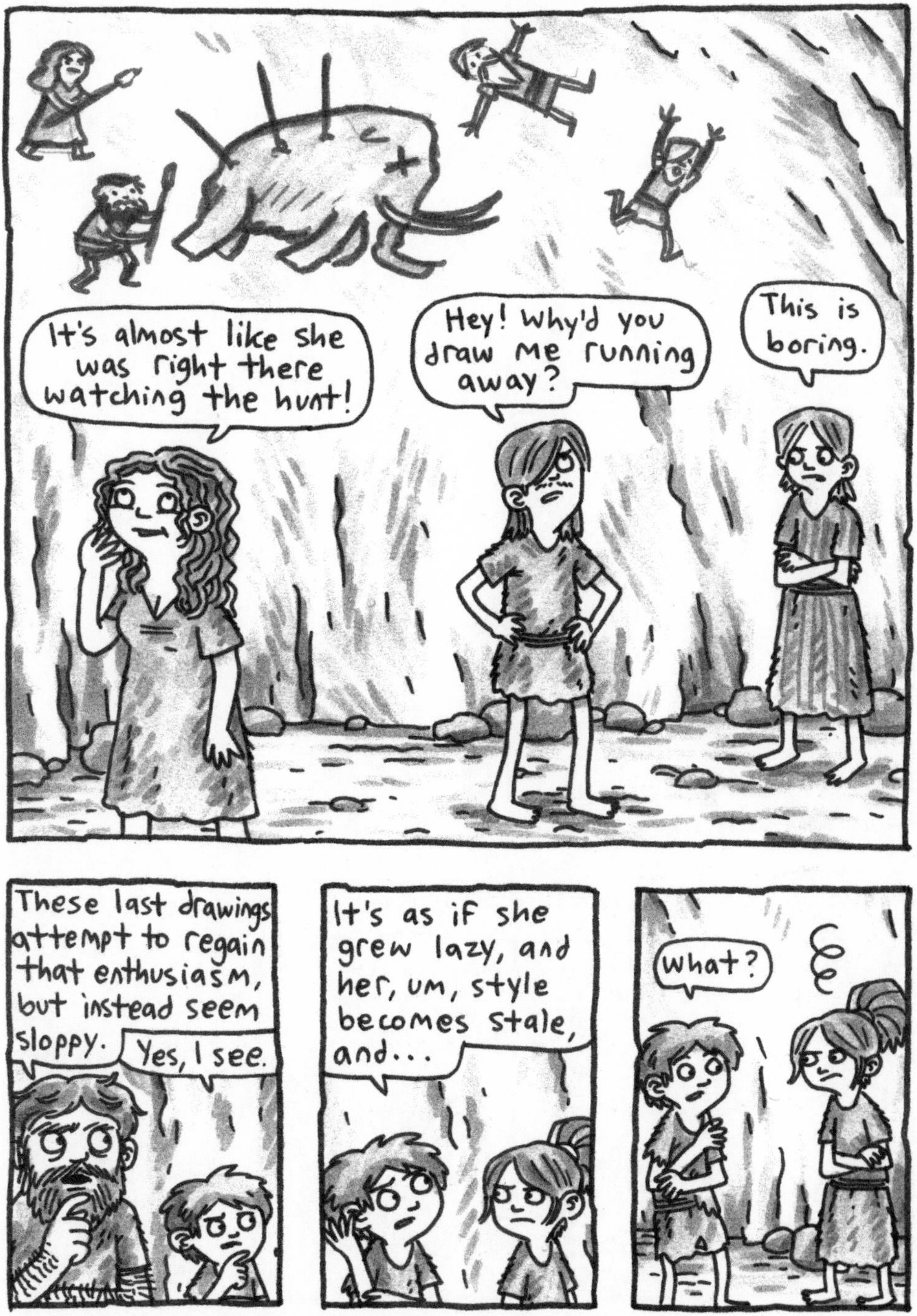
It's almost like she was right there watching the hunt!
Hey! Why'd you draw me running away?
This is boring.
These last drawings attempt to regain that enthusiasm, but instead seem sloppy.
Yes, I see.
It's as if she grew lazy, and her, um, style becomes stale, and...
What?

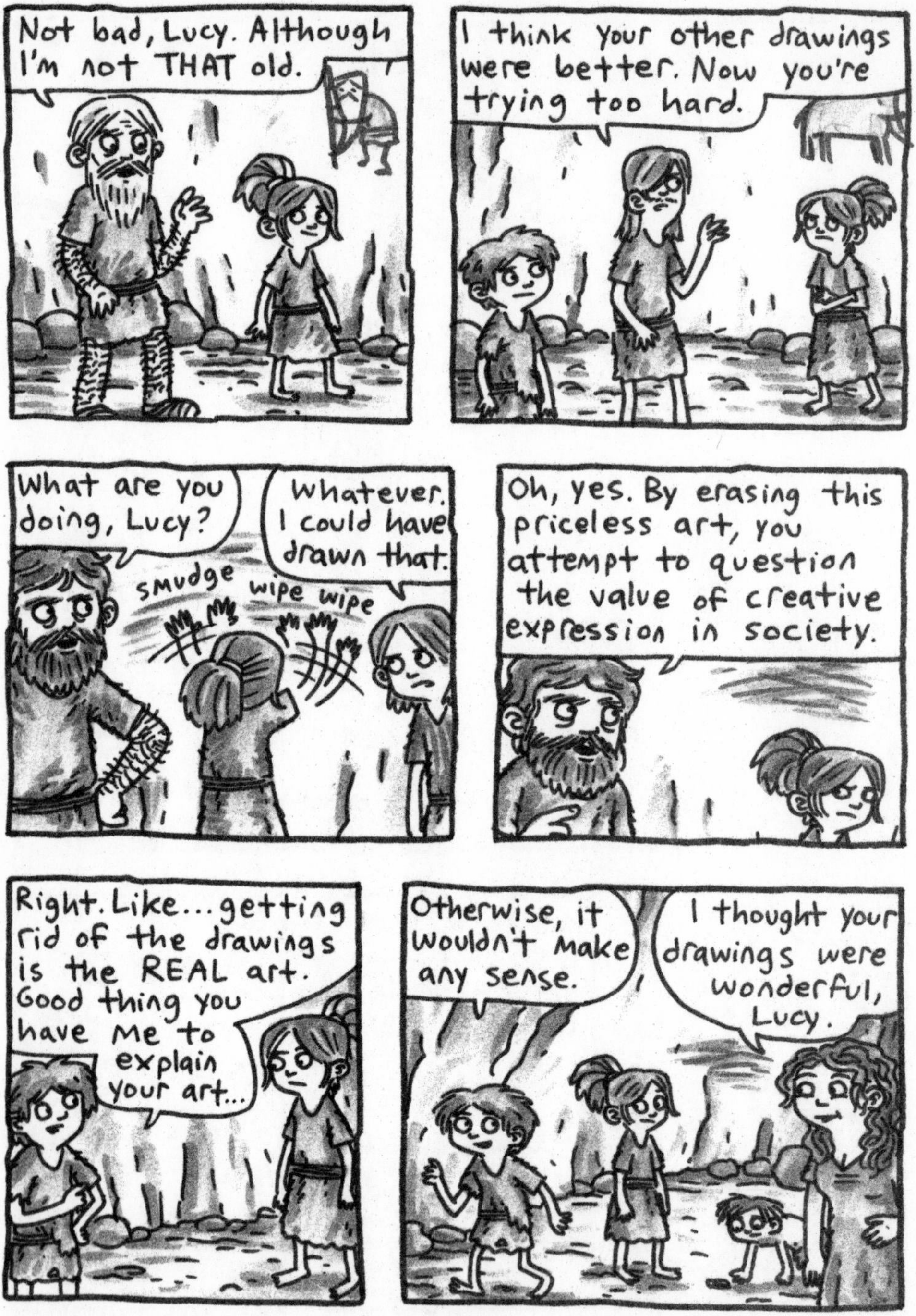
Not bad, Lucy. Although I'm not THAT old.
I think your other drawings were better. Now you're trying too hard.
What are you doing, Lucy?
Whatever. I could have drawn that.
SMUDGE
WIPE WIPE
Oh, yes. By erasing this priceless art, you attempt to question the value of creative expression in society.
Right. Like... getting rid of the drawings is the REAL art. Good thing you have me to explain your art...
Otherwise, it wouldn't make any sense.
I thought your drawings were wonderful, Lucy.

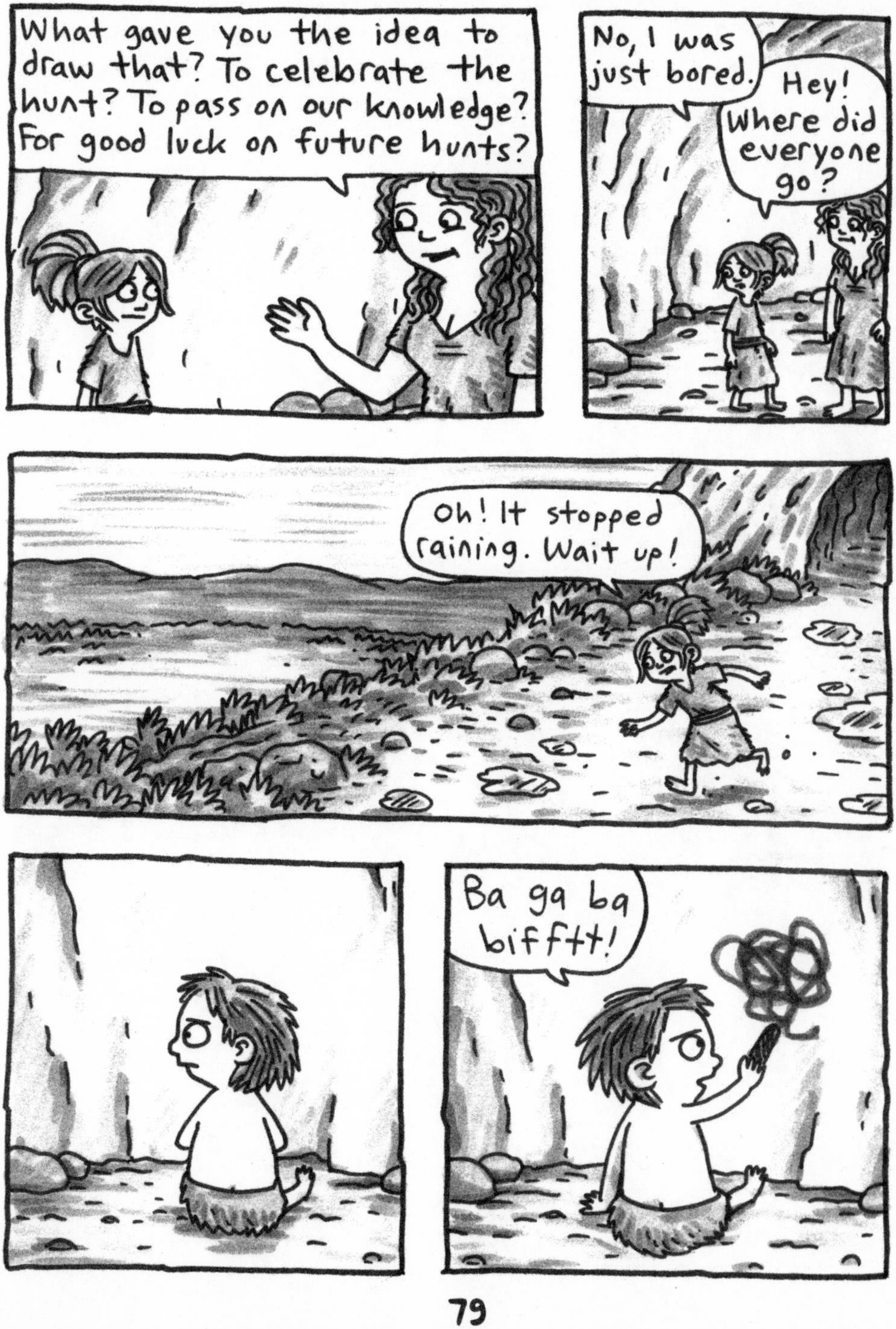
What gave you the idea to draw that? To celebrate the hunt? To pass on our knowledge? For good luck on future hunts?
No, I was just bored.
Hey! Where did everyone go?
Oh! It stopped raining. Wait up!
Ba ga ba bifftt!

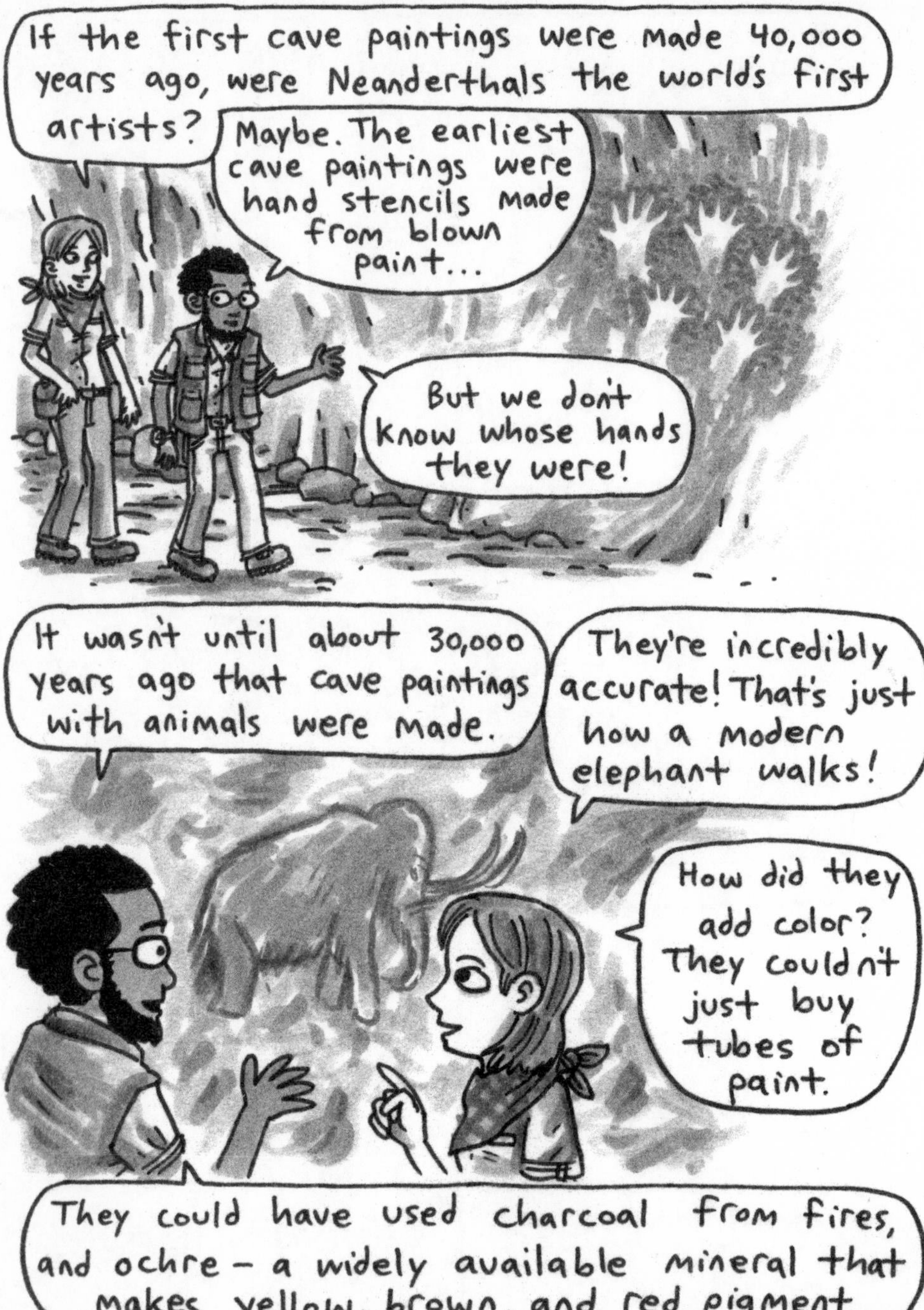

If the first cave paintings were made 40,000 years ago, were Neanderthals the world's first artists?
Maybe. The earliest cave paintings were hand stencils made from blown paint...
But we don't know whose hands they were!
It wasn't until about 30,000 years ago that cave paintings with animals were made.
They're incredibly accurate! That's just how a modern elephant walks!
How did they add color? They couldn't just buy tubes of paint.
They could have used charcoal from fires, and ochre - a widely available mineral that makes yellow, brown, and red pigment.

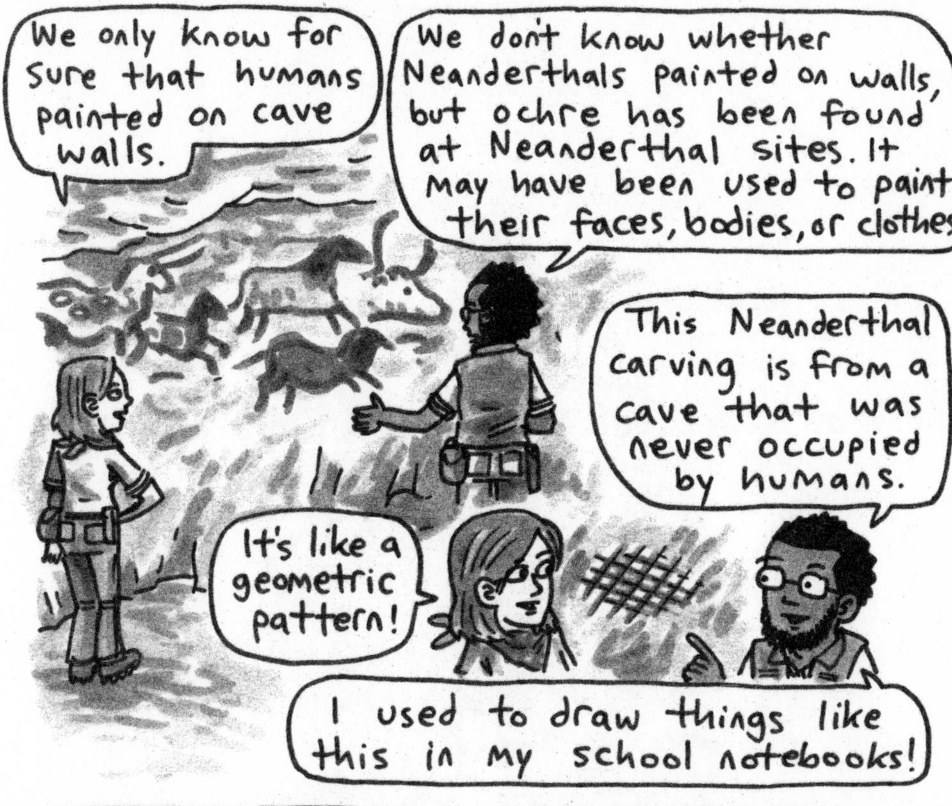
We only know for sure that humans painted on cave walls.
We don't know whether Neanderthals painted on walls, but ochre has been found at Neanderthal sites. It may have been used to paint their faces, bodies, or clothes.
This Neanderthal carving is from a cave that was never occupied by humans.
It's like a geometric pattern!
I used to draw things like this in my school notebooks!
These early sculptures were made by humans. Did Neanderthals make any?
Not that we've found. They collected these shells and drilled holes in them. They could be art.
We don't know who the first artists were - humans or Neanderthals - but it's cool that people have been making art as long as they have!

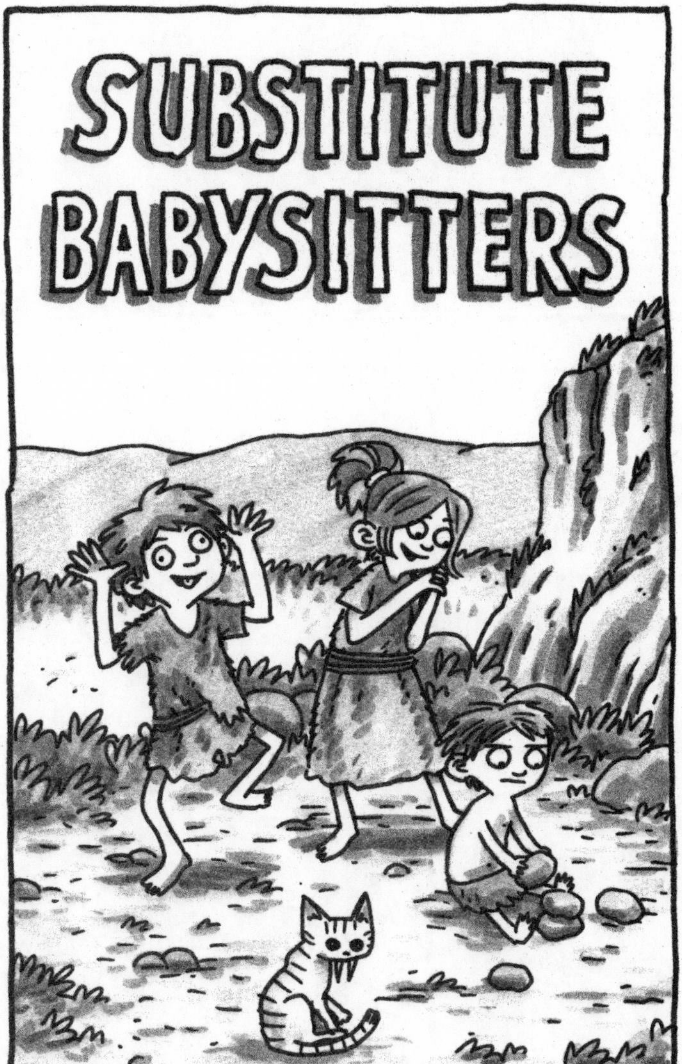
SUBSTITUTE
BABYSITTERS

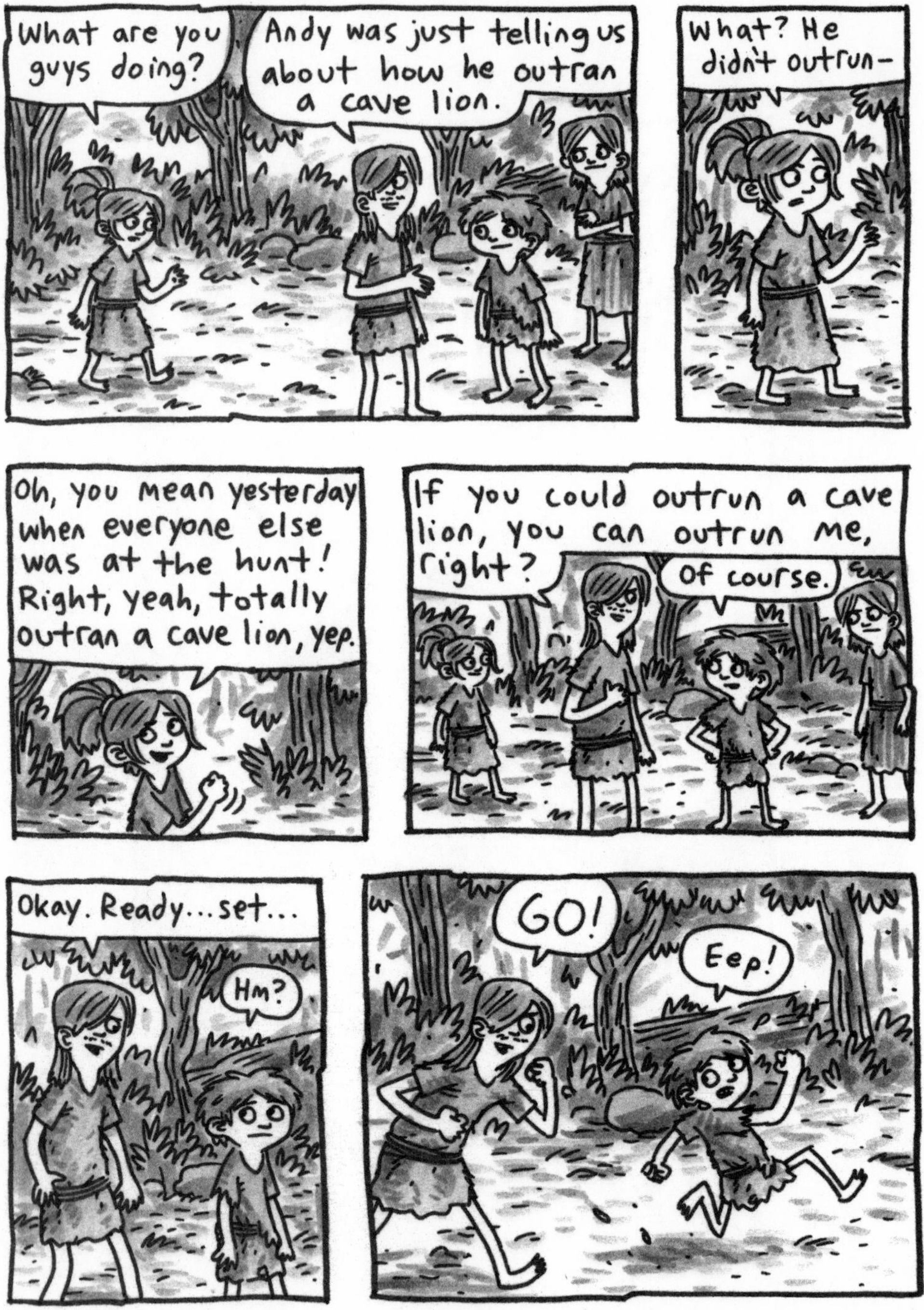
What are you guys doing?
Andy was just telling us about how he outran a cave lion.
What? He didn't outrun-
Oh, you mean yesterday when everyone else was at the hunt! Right, yeah, totally outran a cave lion, yep.
If you could outrun a cave lion, you can outrun me, right?
Of course.
Okay. Ready...set...
Hm?
GO!
Eep!

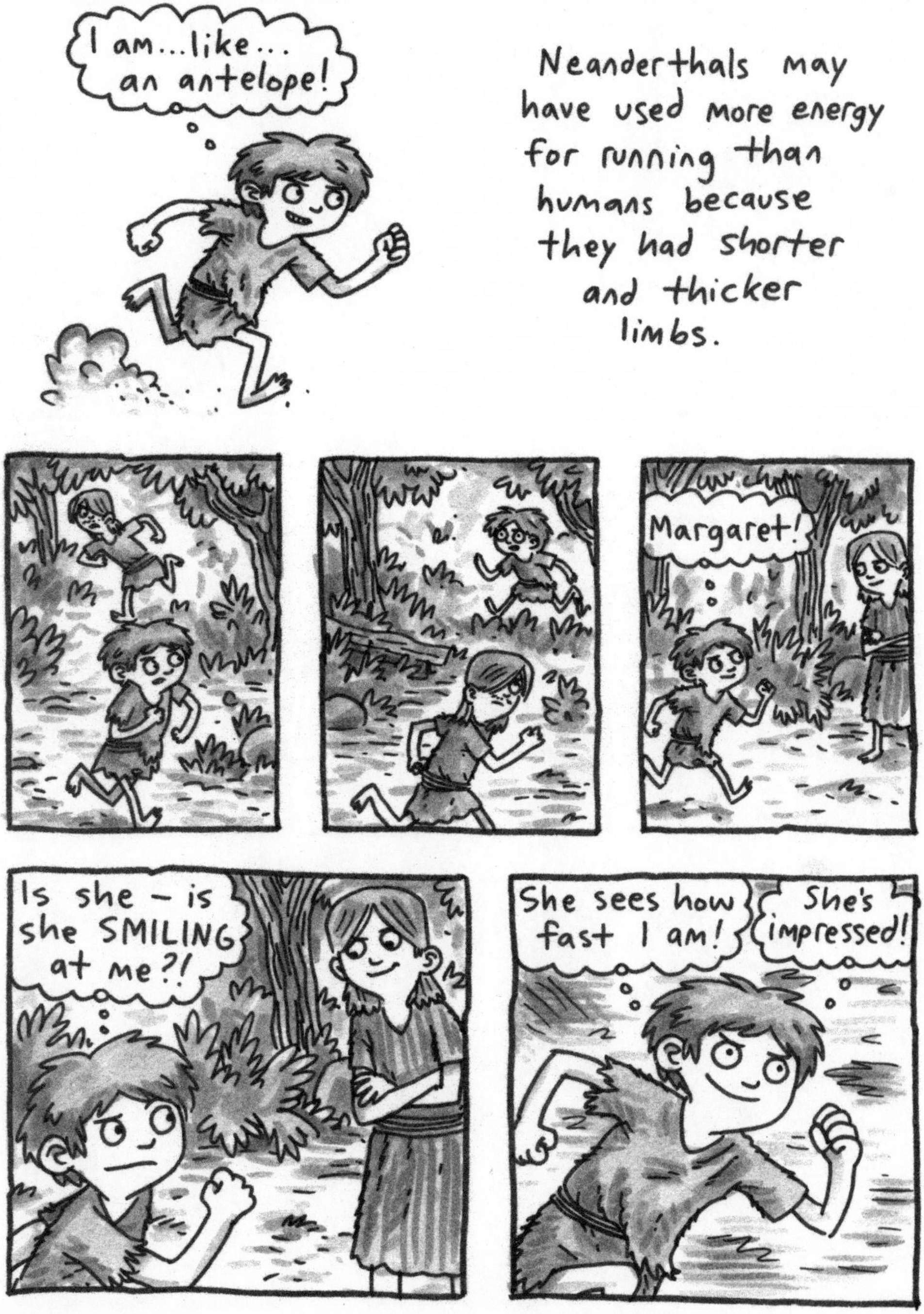
I am...like...
an antelope!
Neanderthals may have used more energy for running than humans because they had shorter and thicker limbs.
Margaret!
Is she - is she SMILING at me?!
She sees how fast I am!
She's impressed!

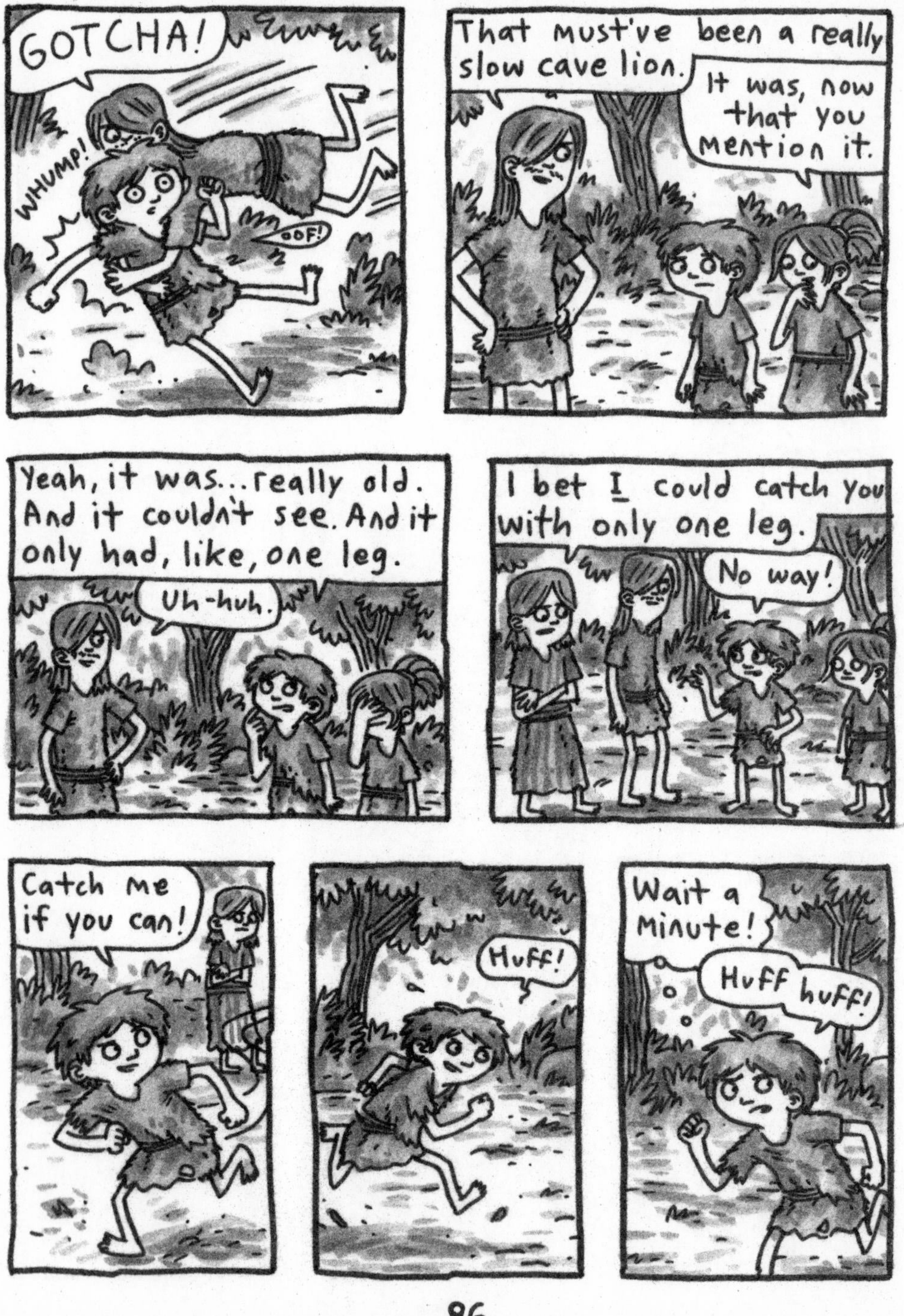
GOTCHA!
WHUMP!
OOF!
That must've been a really slow cave lion.
It was, now that you mention it.
Yeah, it was...really old. And it couldn't see. And it only had, like, one leg.
Uh-huh.
I bet I could catch you with only one leg.
No way!
Catch me if you can!
Huff!
Wait a minute!
Huff huff!

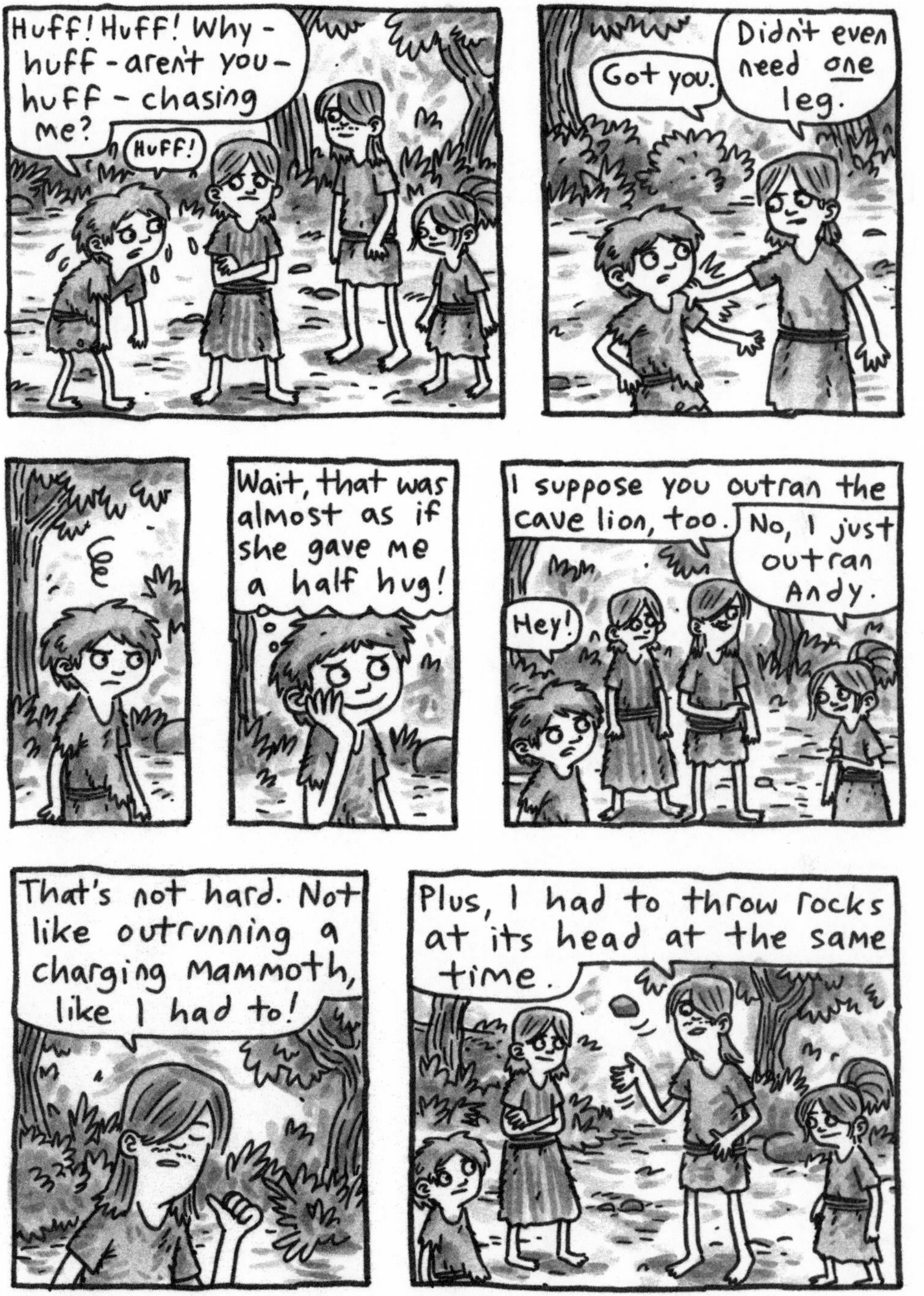

Huff! Huff! Why - huff - aren't you - huff - chasing me?
HUFF!
Got you.
Didn't even need one leg.
Wait, that was almost as if she gave me a half hug!
I suppose you outran the cave lion, too.
No, I just outran Andy.
Hey!
That's not hard. Not like outrunning a charging mammoth, like I had to!
Plus, I had to throw rocks at its head at the same time.

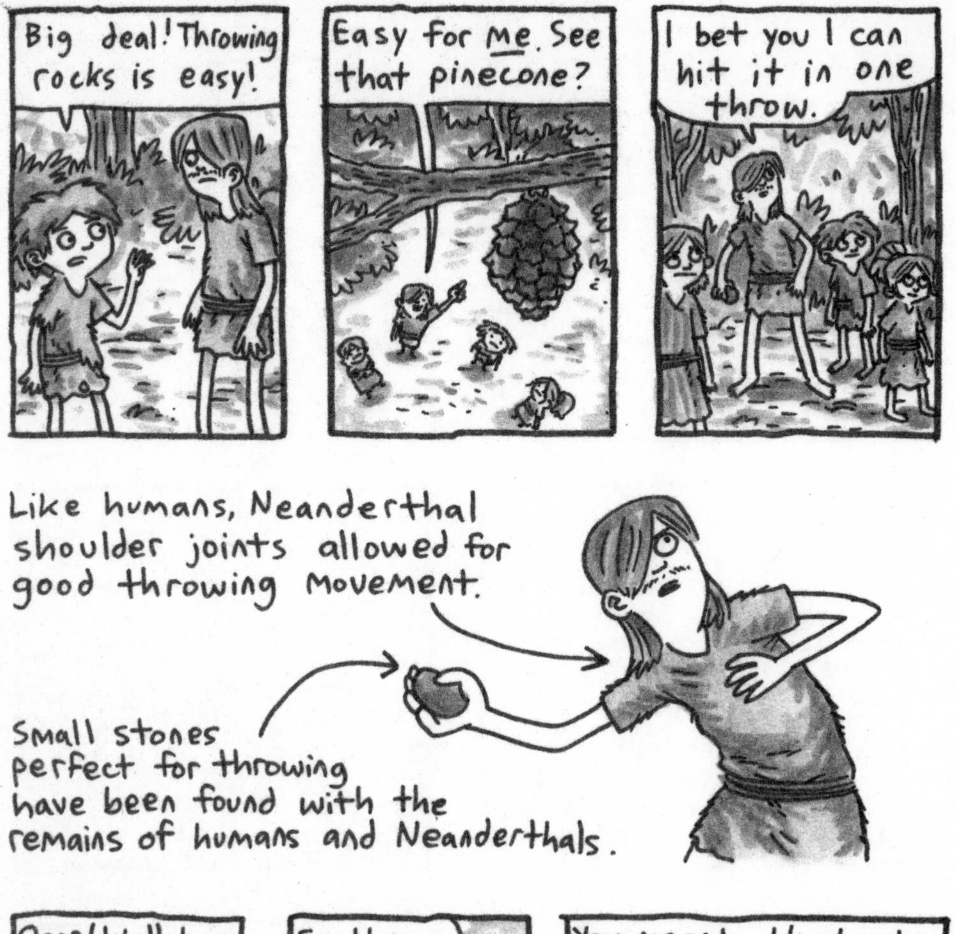
Big deal! Throwing rocks is easy!
Easy for me. See that pinecone?
I bet you I can hit it in one throw.
Like humans, Neanderthal shoulder joints allowed for good throwing movement.
Small stones perfect for throwing have been found with the remains of humans and Neanderthals.
Oops! Well, I can do it in two throws.
Er, three.
Four.
Five.
You meant that when you finally hit it, that's one throw?
Like you could do it.
I bet I can.

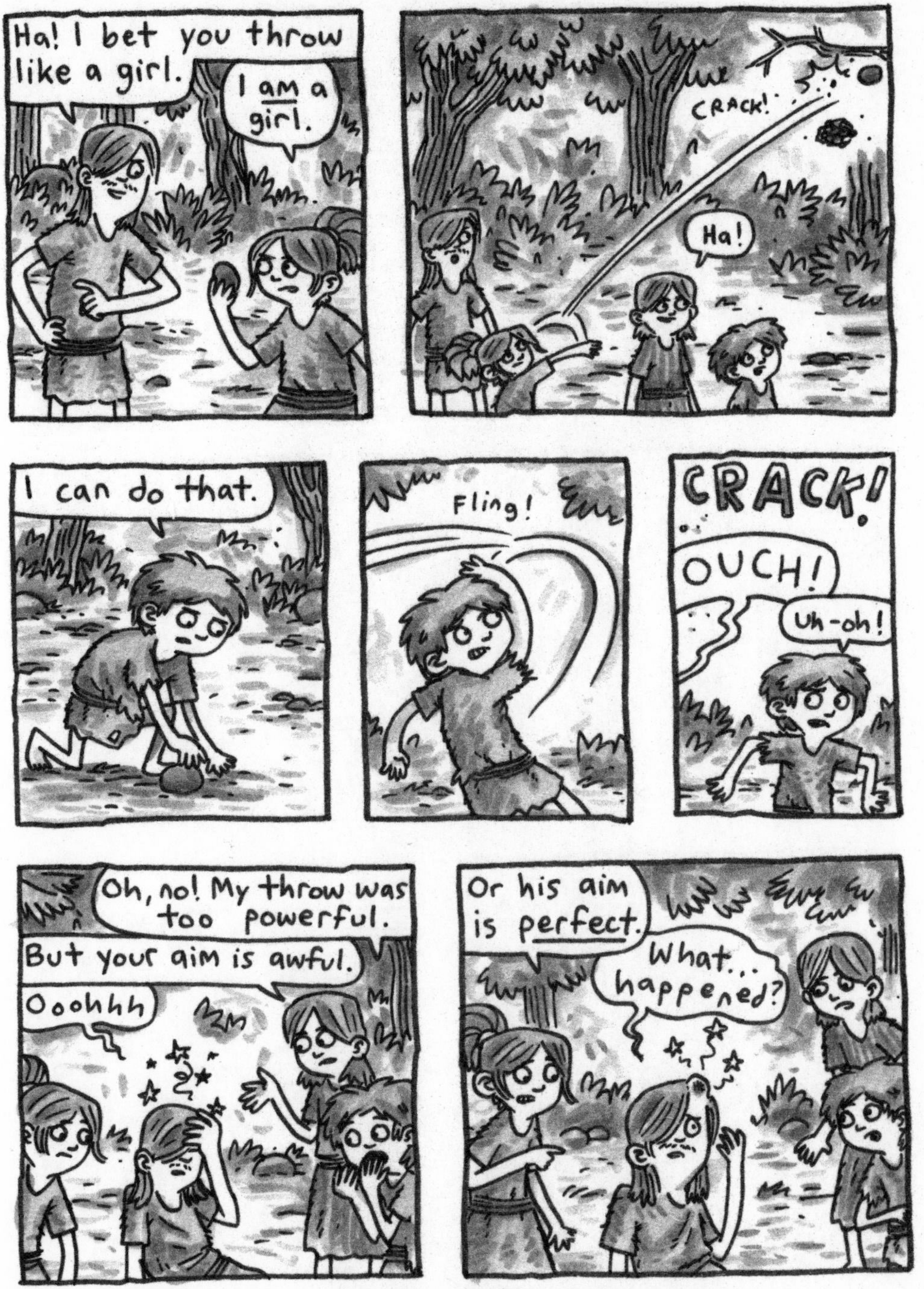
Ha! I bet you throw like a girl.
I am a girl.
CRACK!
Ha!
I can do that.
Fling!
CRACK!
OUCH!
Uh-oh!
Oh, no! My throw was too powerful.
But your aim is awful.
Ooohhh
Or his aim is perfect.
What... happened?

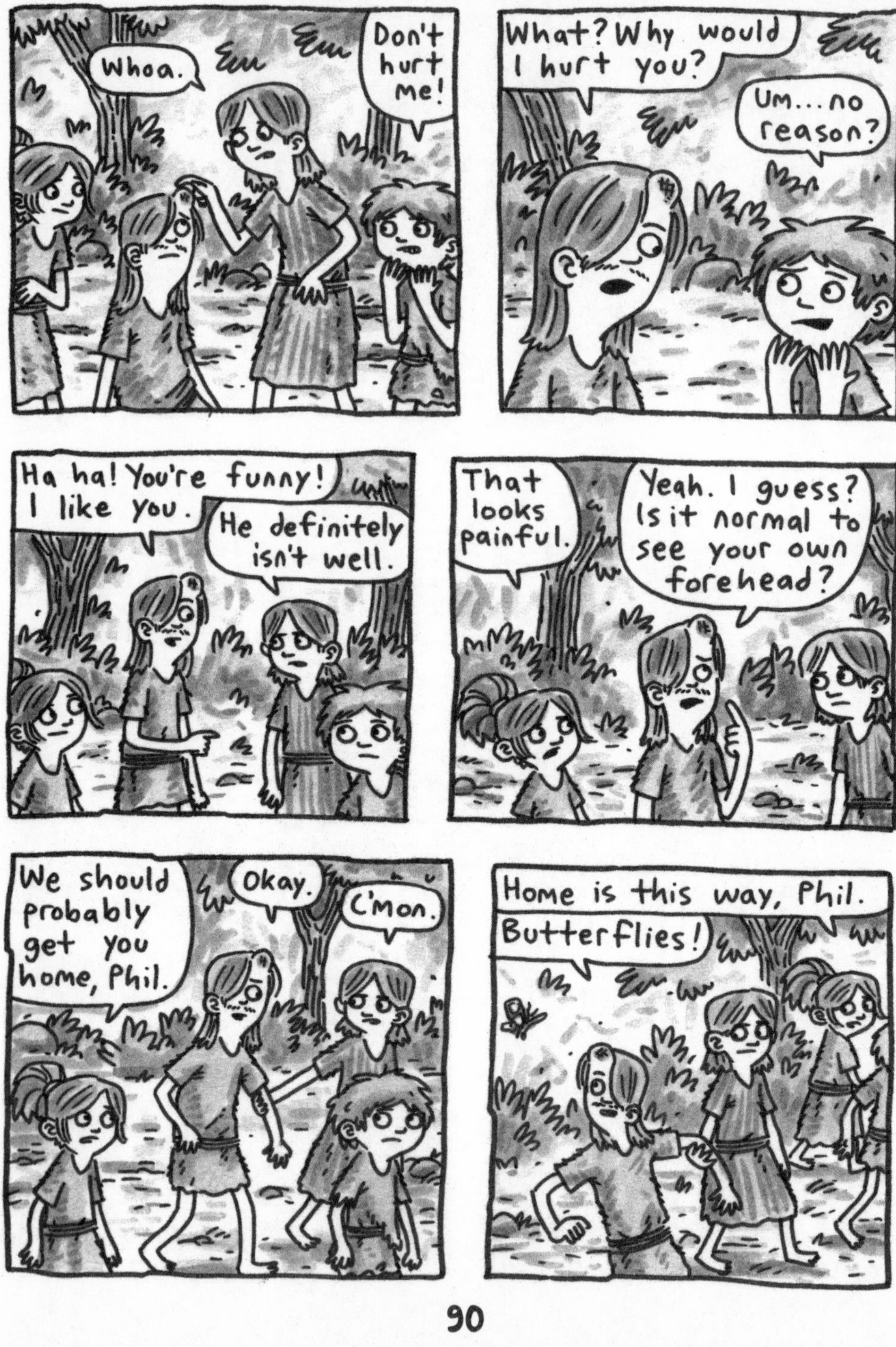
Whoa.
Don't hurt me!
What? Why would I hurt you?
Um... no reason?
Ha ha! You're funny! I like you.
He definitely isn't well.
That looks painful.
Yeah. I guess? Is it normal to see your own forehead?
We should probably get you home, Phil.
Okay.
C'mon.
Home is this way, Phil.
Butterflies!

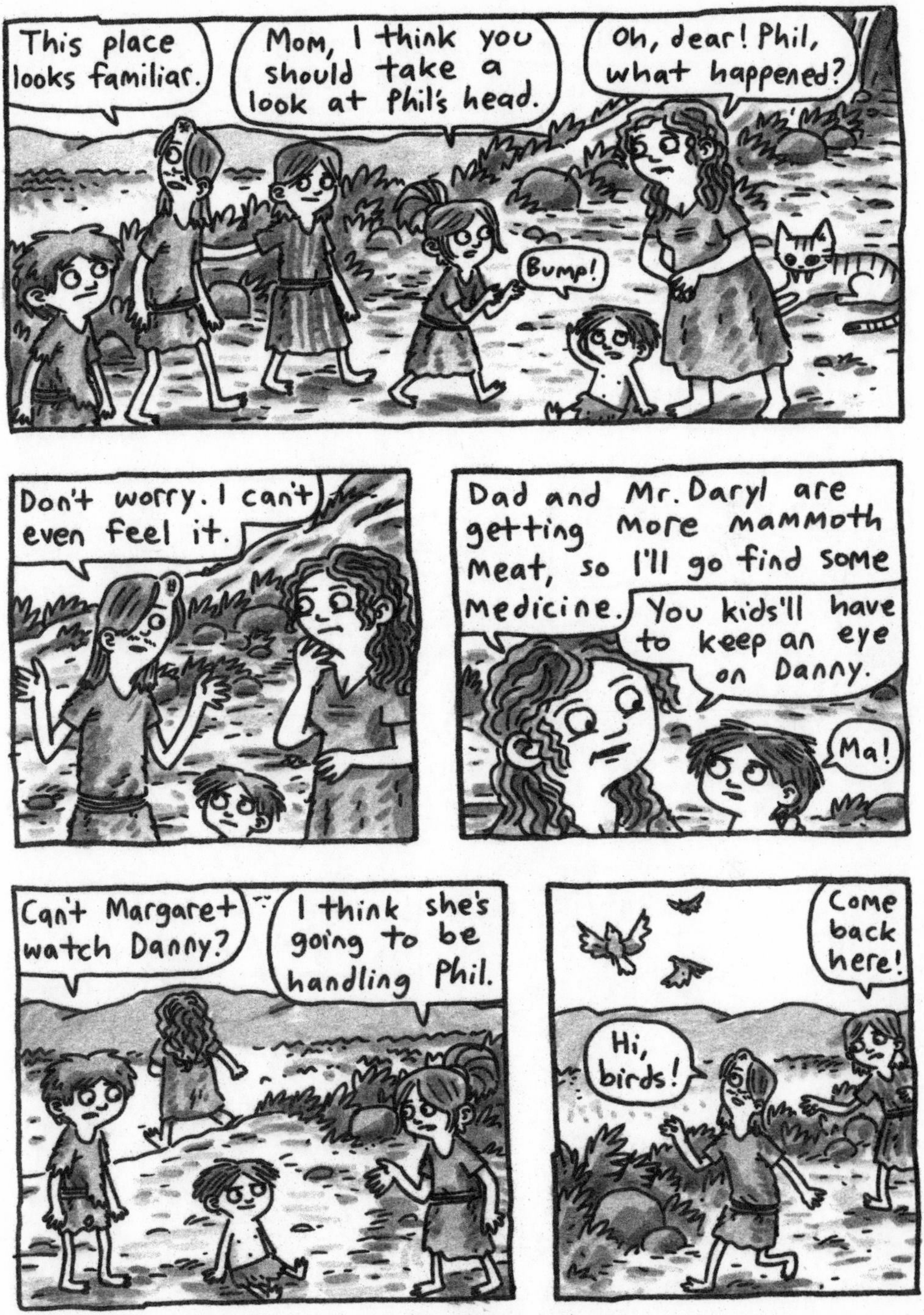
This place looks familiar.
Mom, I think you should take a look at Phil's head.
Oh, dear! Phil, what happened?
Bump!
Don't worry. I can't even feel it.
Dad and Mr. Daryl are getting more mammoth meat, so I'll go find some medicine.
You kids'll have to keep an eye on Danny.
Ma!
Can't Margaret watch Danny?
I think she's going to be handling Phil.
Come back here!
Hi, birds!

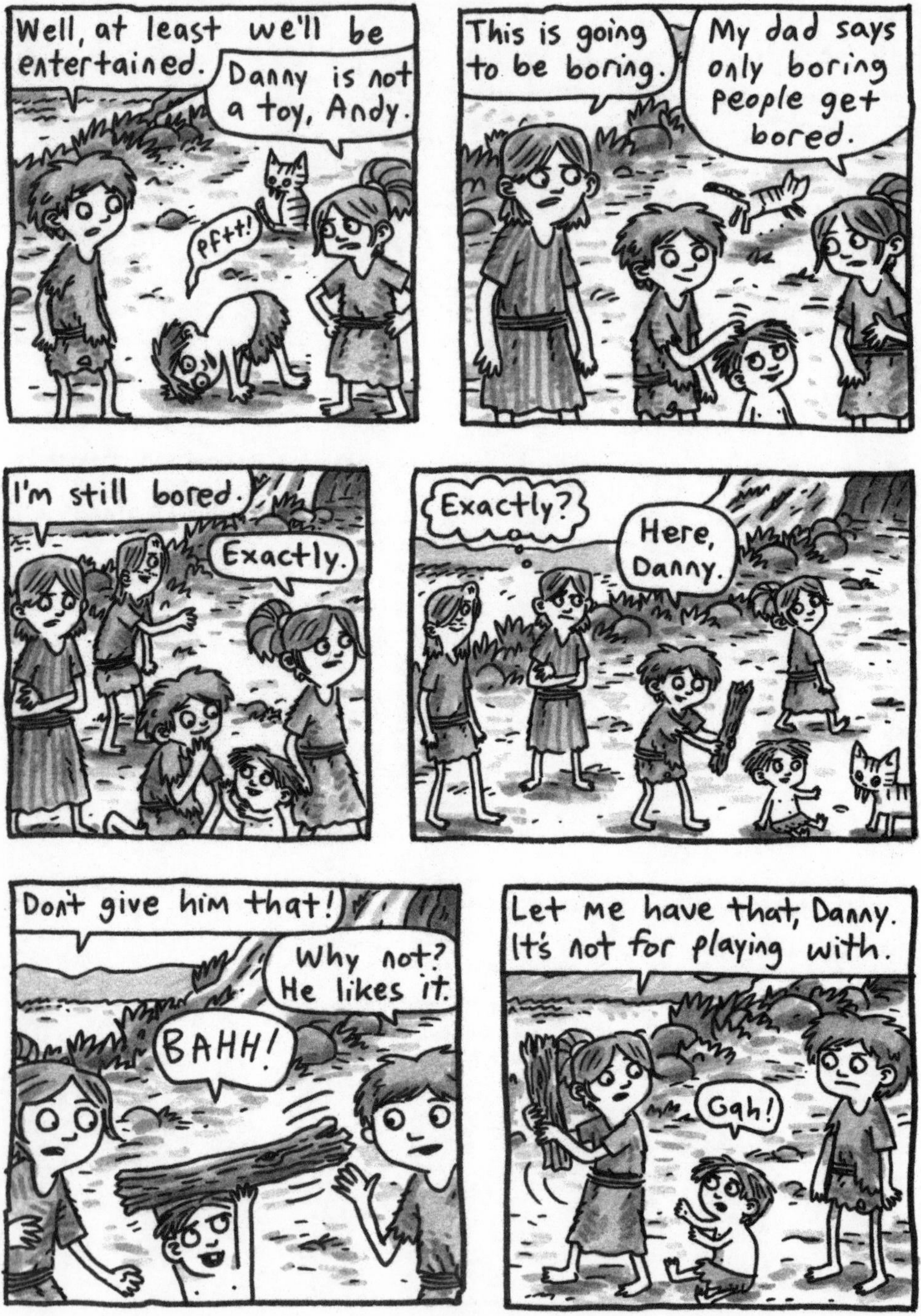
Well, at least we'll be entertained.
Danny is not a toy, Andy.
pftt!
This is going to be boring.
My dad says only boring people get bored.
I'm still bored.
Exactly.
Exactly?
Here, Danny.
Don't give him that!
Why not? He likes it.
BAHH!
Let me have that, Danny. It's not for playing with.
Gah!

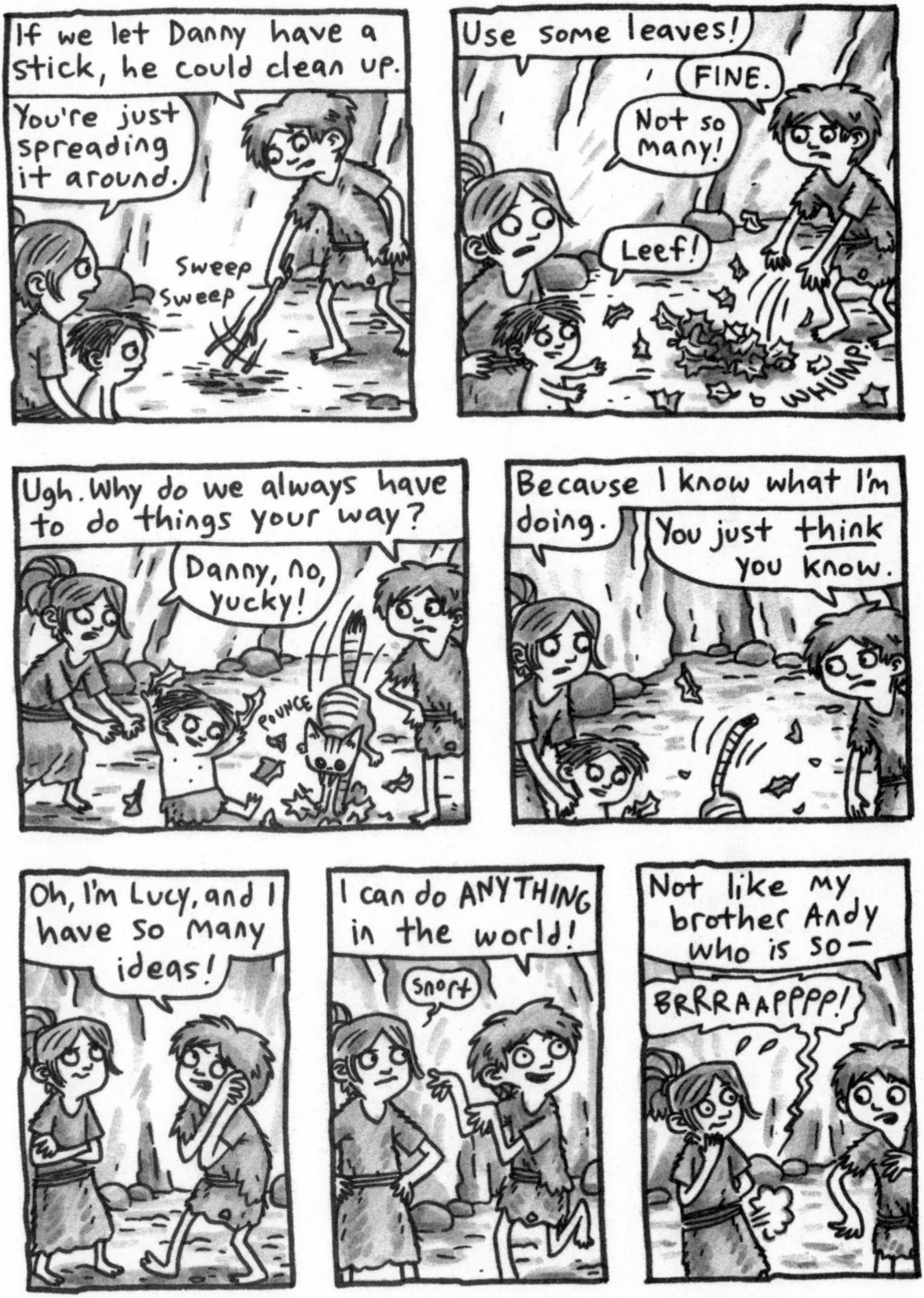
If we let Danny have a stick, he could clean up.
You're just spreading it around.
Sweep
Sweep
Use some leaves!
FINE.
Not so many!
Leef!
WHUMP!
Ugh. Why do we always have to do things your way?
Danny, no, yucky!
POUNCE
Because I know what I'm doing.
You just think you know.
Oh, I'm Lucy, and I have so many ideas!
I can do ANYTHING in the world!
Snort
Not like my brother Andy who is so—
BRRRAAPPPP!

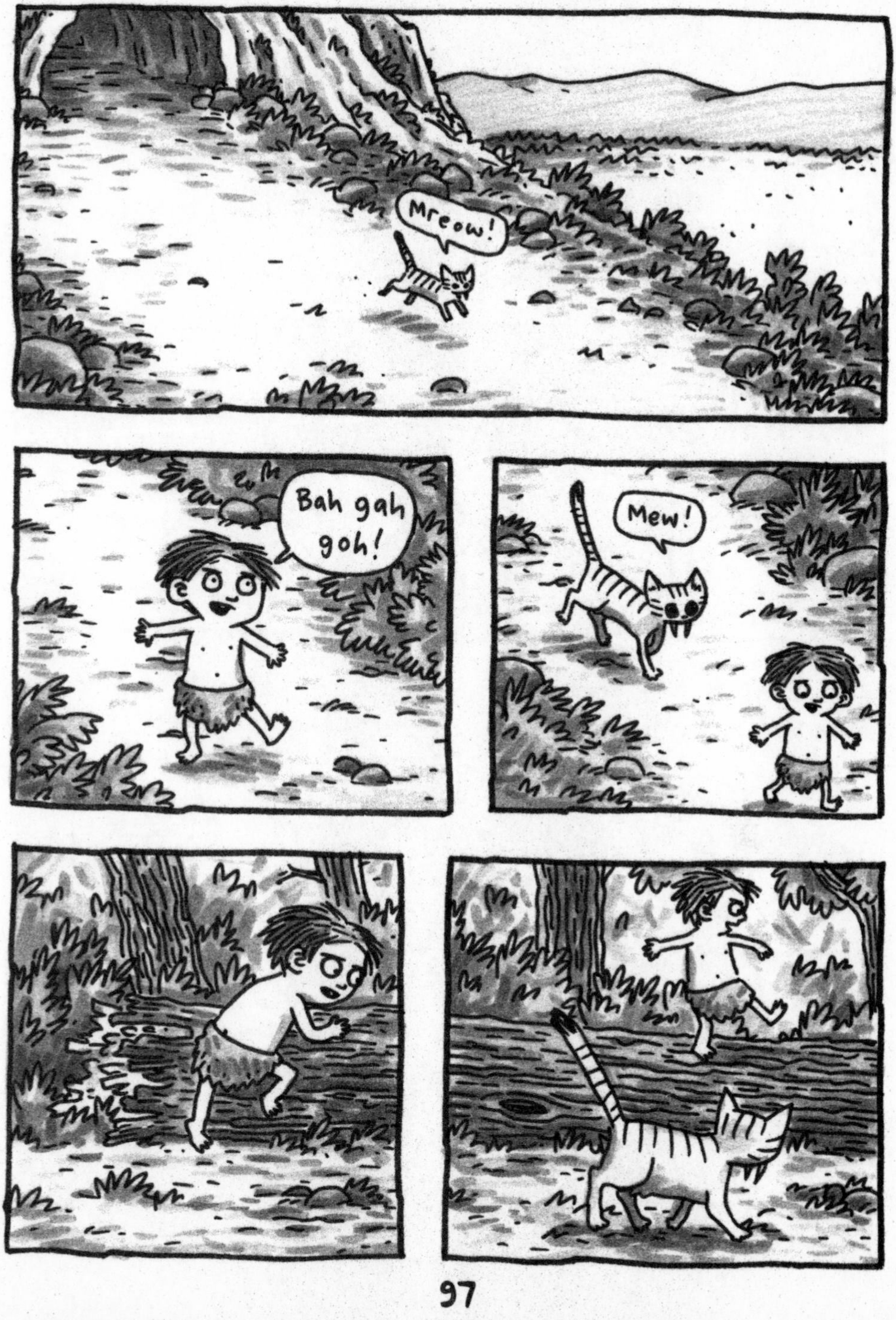
Mreow!
Bah gah goh!
Mew!

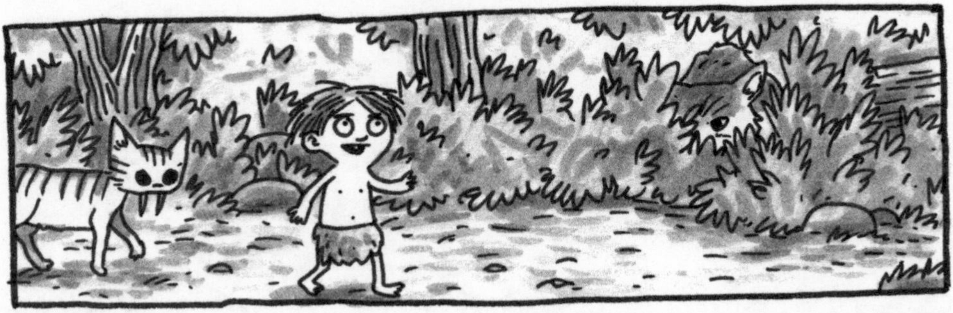

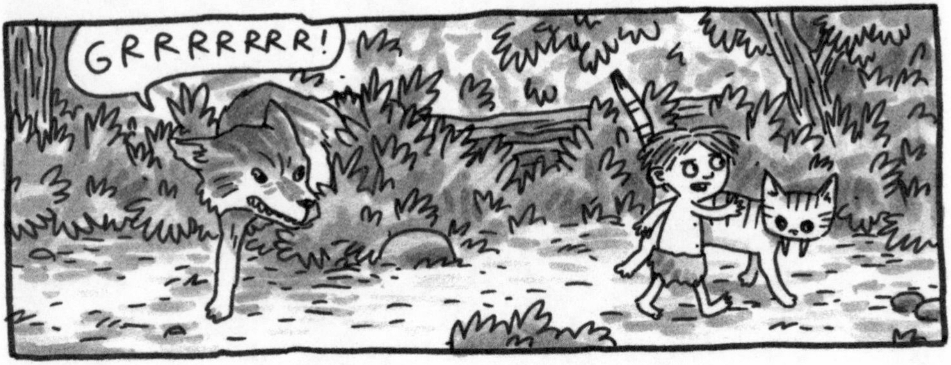
GRRRRRRR!

The largest and deadliest canine to ever live was the dire wolf. Fortunately for Neanderthals, dire wolves lived only in North and South America, while wolves in Europe were more like modern-day wolves.

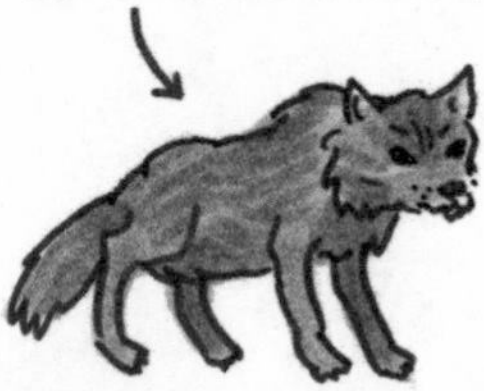

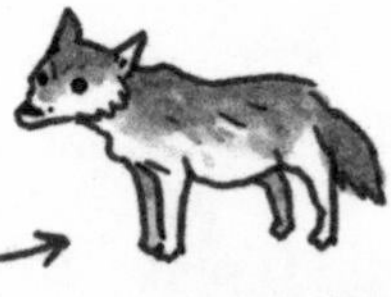

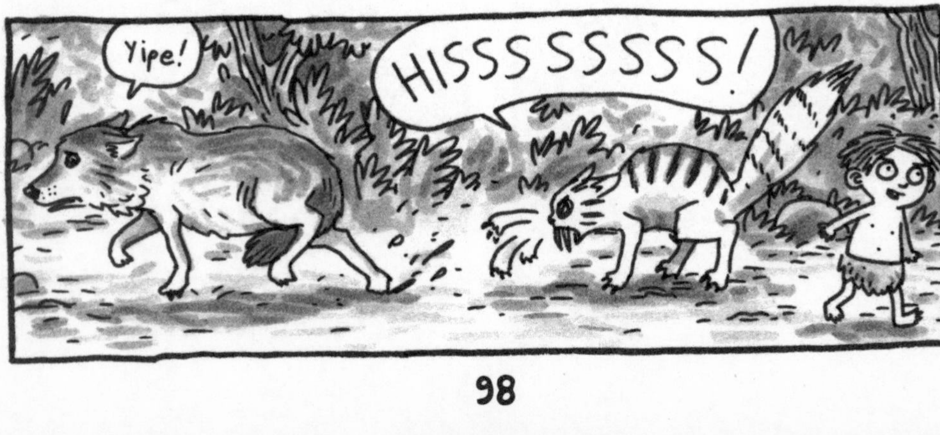
Yipe!
HISSSSSSSS!

Danny?

Danny!

We have to find him, or Mom and Dad will think I'm not ready for more responsibility.

Who's Danny?

You mean we have to find him before he gets HURT?!

That too.

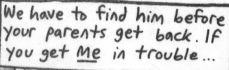

We have to find him before your parents get back. If you get ME in trouble...

Eeek!

Don't worry, look!

What is that?!

It's a fake Danny. We can leave it here and no one will be suspicious while we're looking for Danny.

Creepy.

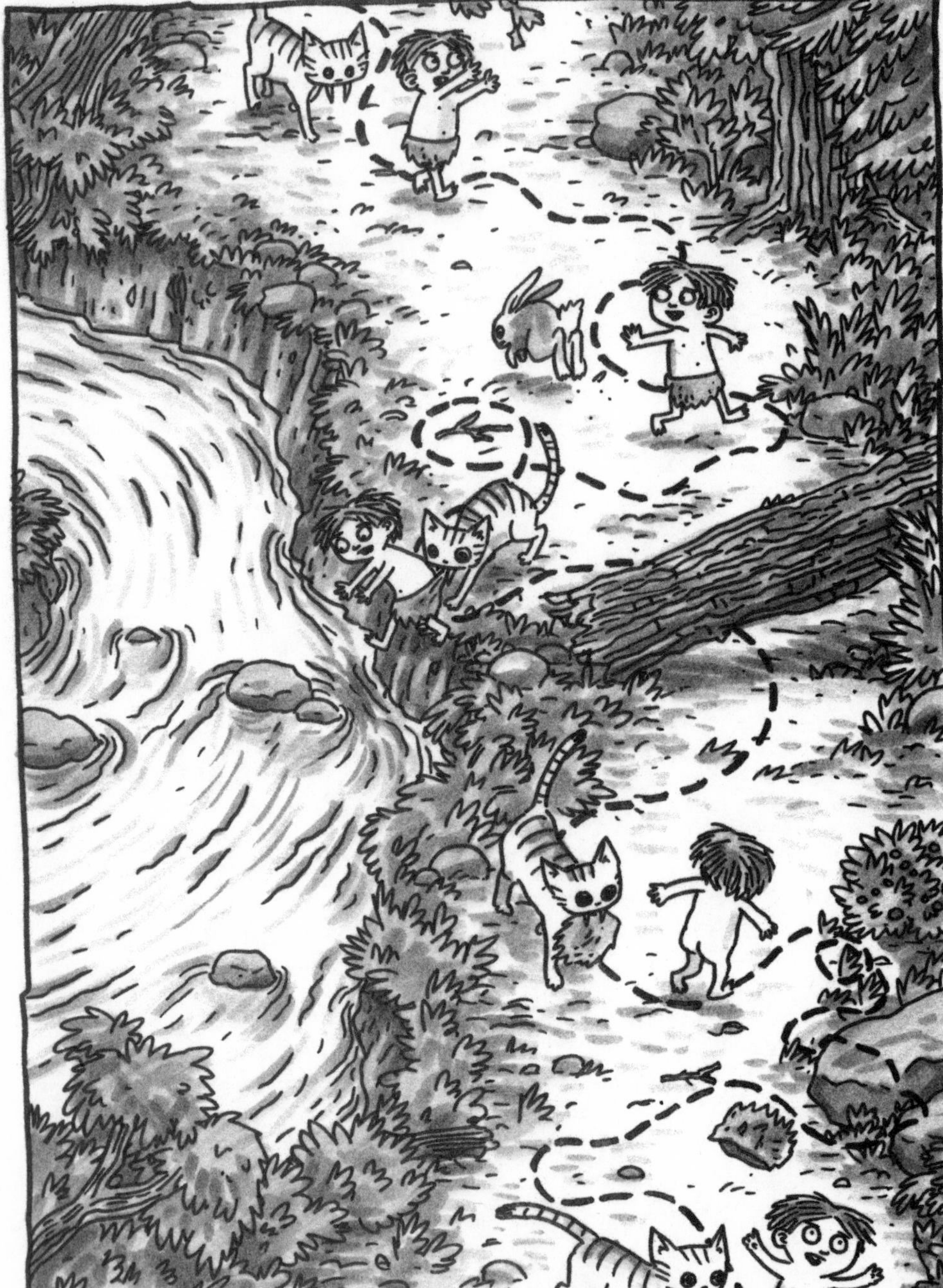

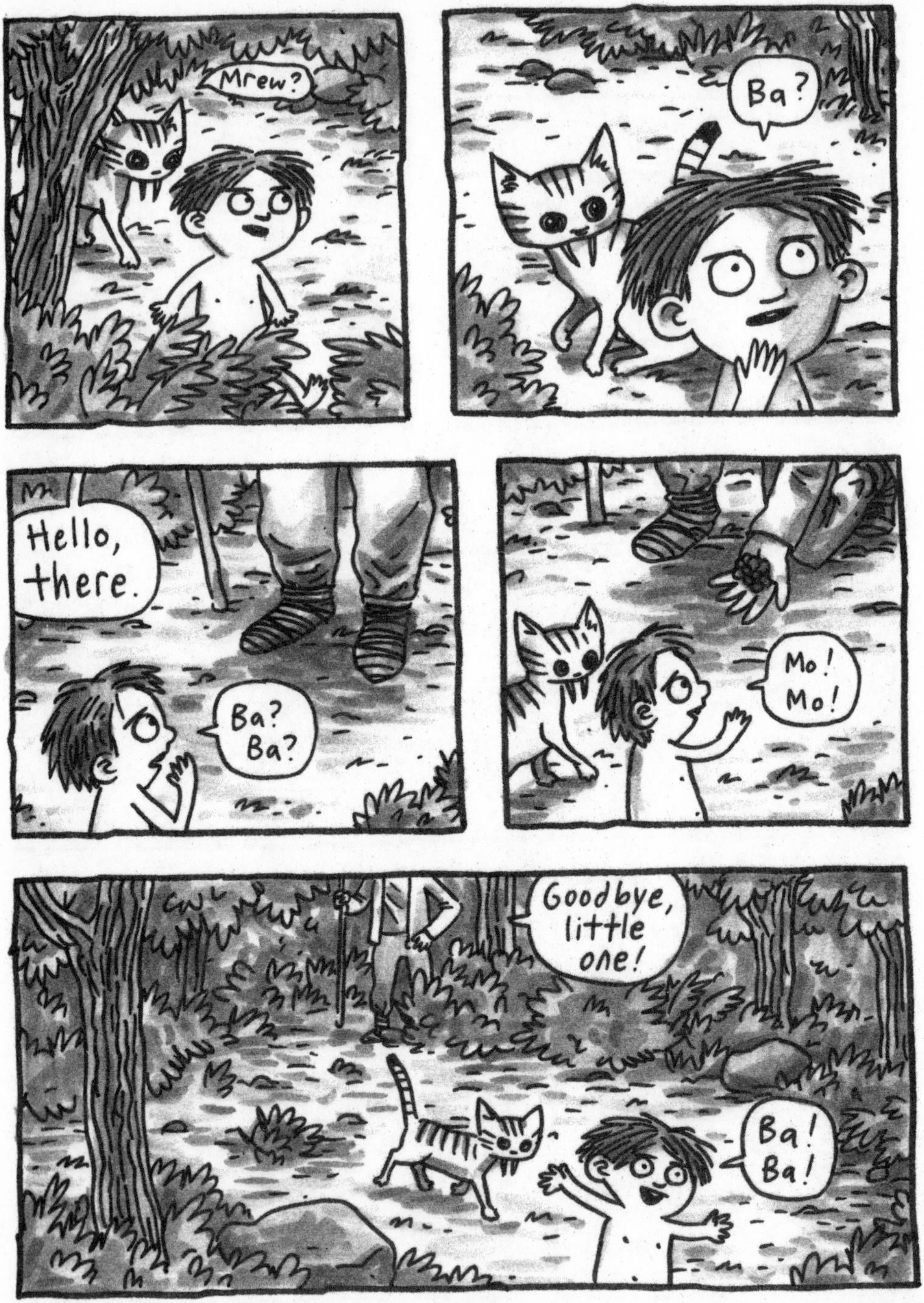
Mrew?
Ba?
Hello, there.
Ba? Ba?
Mo! Mo!
Goodbye, little one!
Ba! Ba!

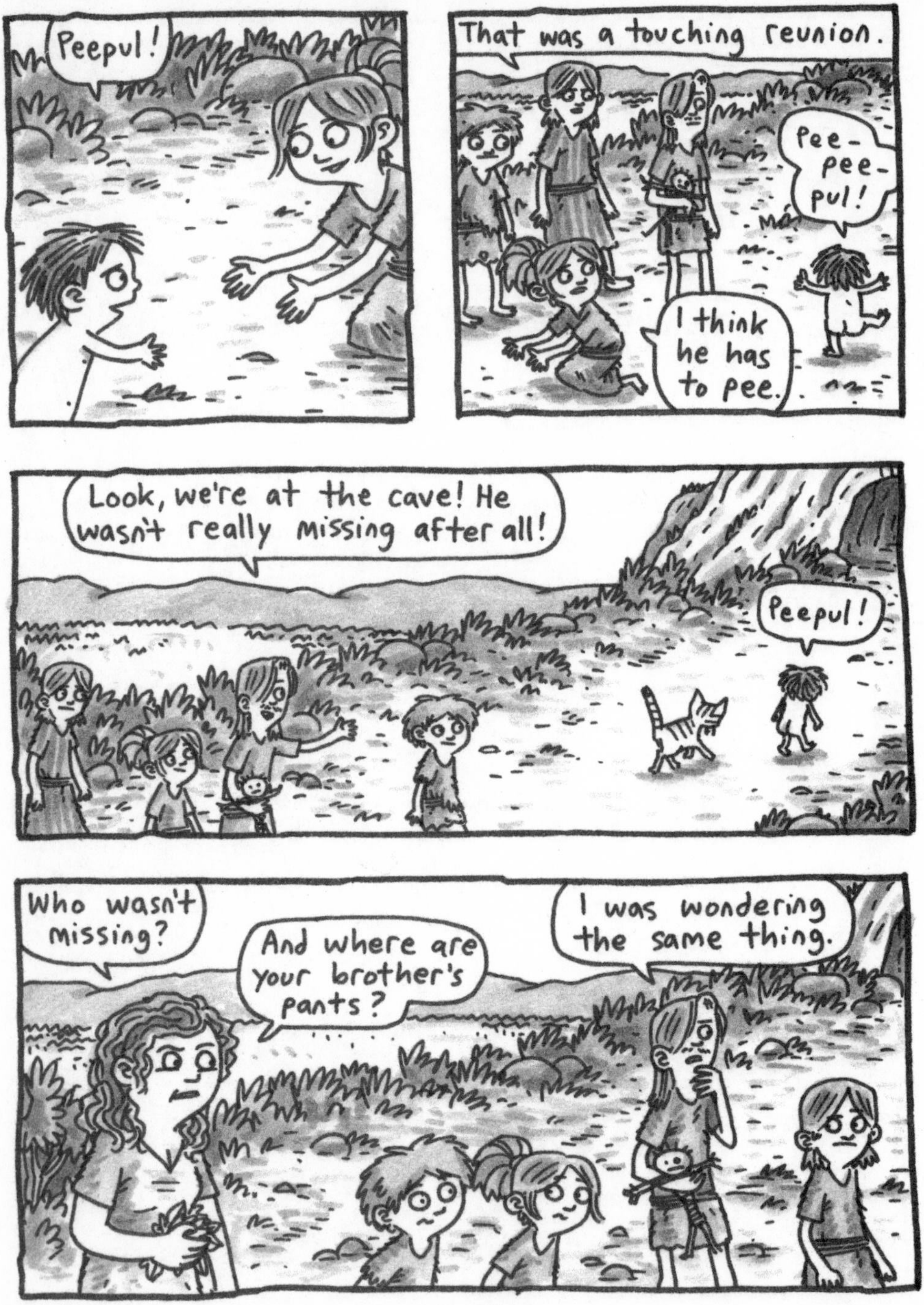
Peepul!
That was a touching reunion.
Pee-pee-pul!
I think he has to pee.
Look, we're at the cave! He wasn't really missing after all!
Peepul!
Who wasn't missing?
And where are your brother's pants?
I was wondering the same thing.

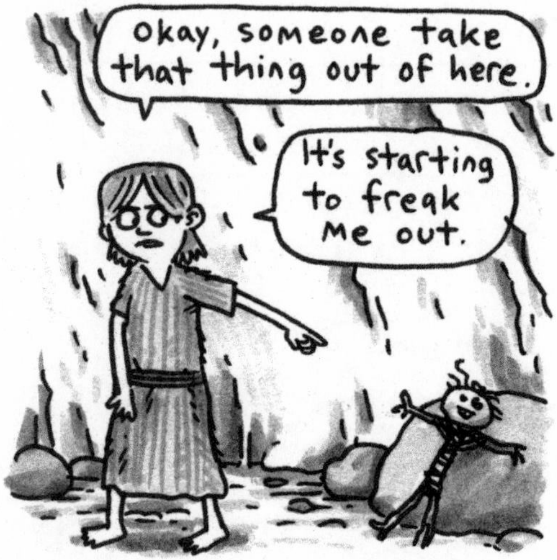
Okay, someone take that thing out of here.
It's starting to freak me out.

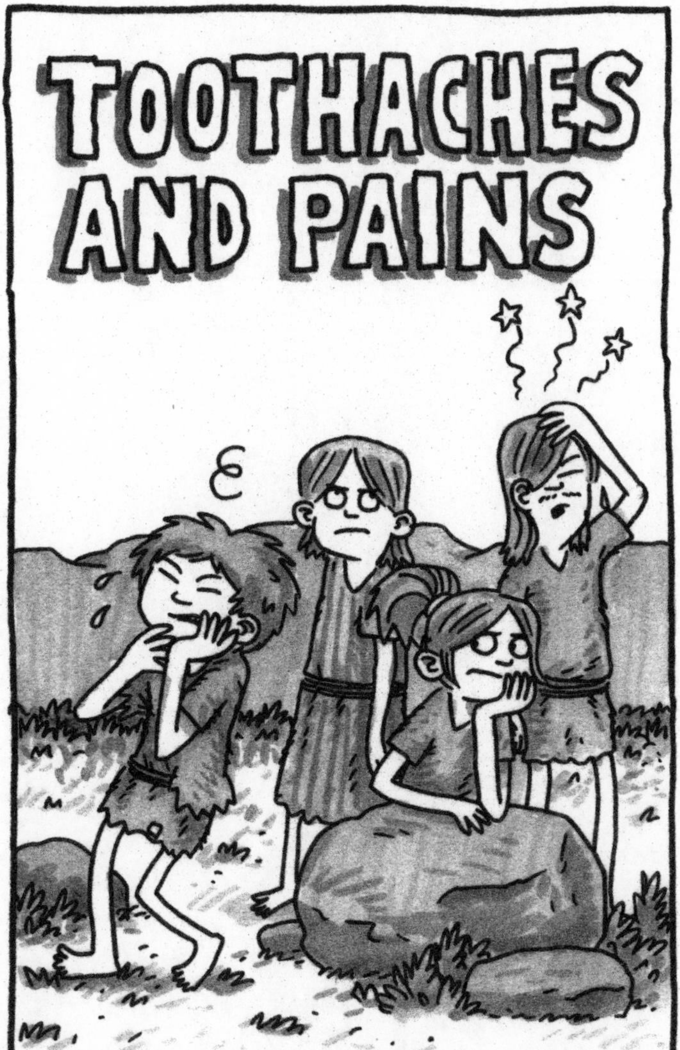
TOOTHACHES AND PAINS

108

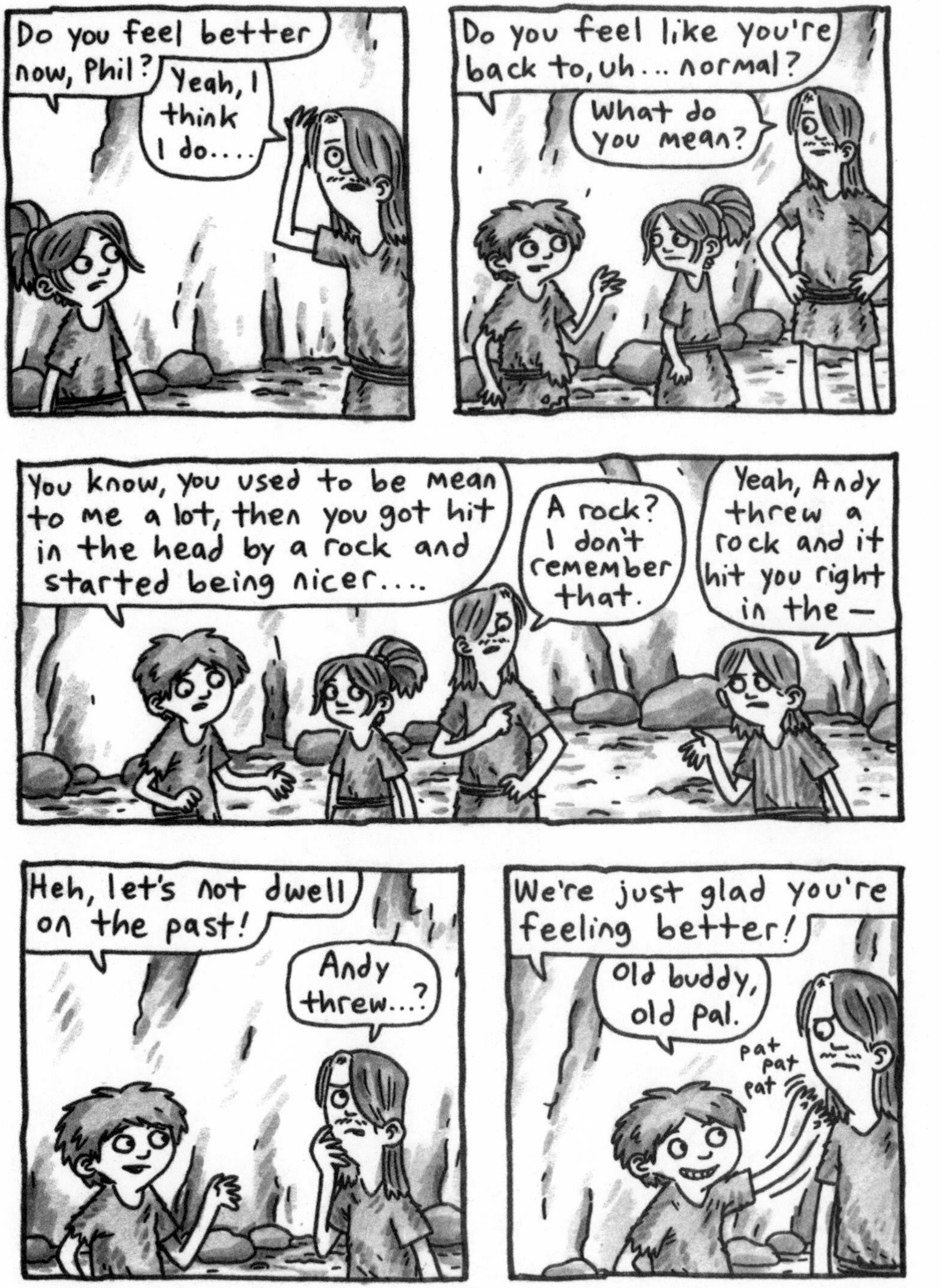
Do you feel better now, Phil?
Yeah, I think I do....
Do you feel like you're back to, uh... normal?
What do you mean?
You know, you used to be mean to me a lot, then you got hit in the head by a rock and started being nicer....
A rock? I don't remember that.
Yeah, Andy threw a rock and it hit you right in the—
Heh, let's not dwell on the past!
Andy threw...?
We're just glad you're feeling better!
Old buddy, old pal.
pat pat pat

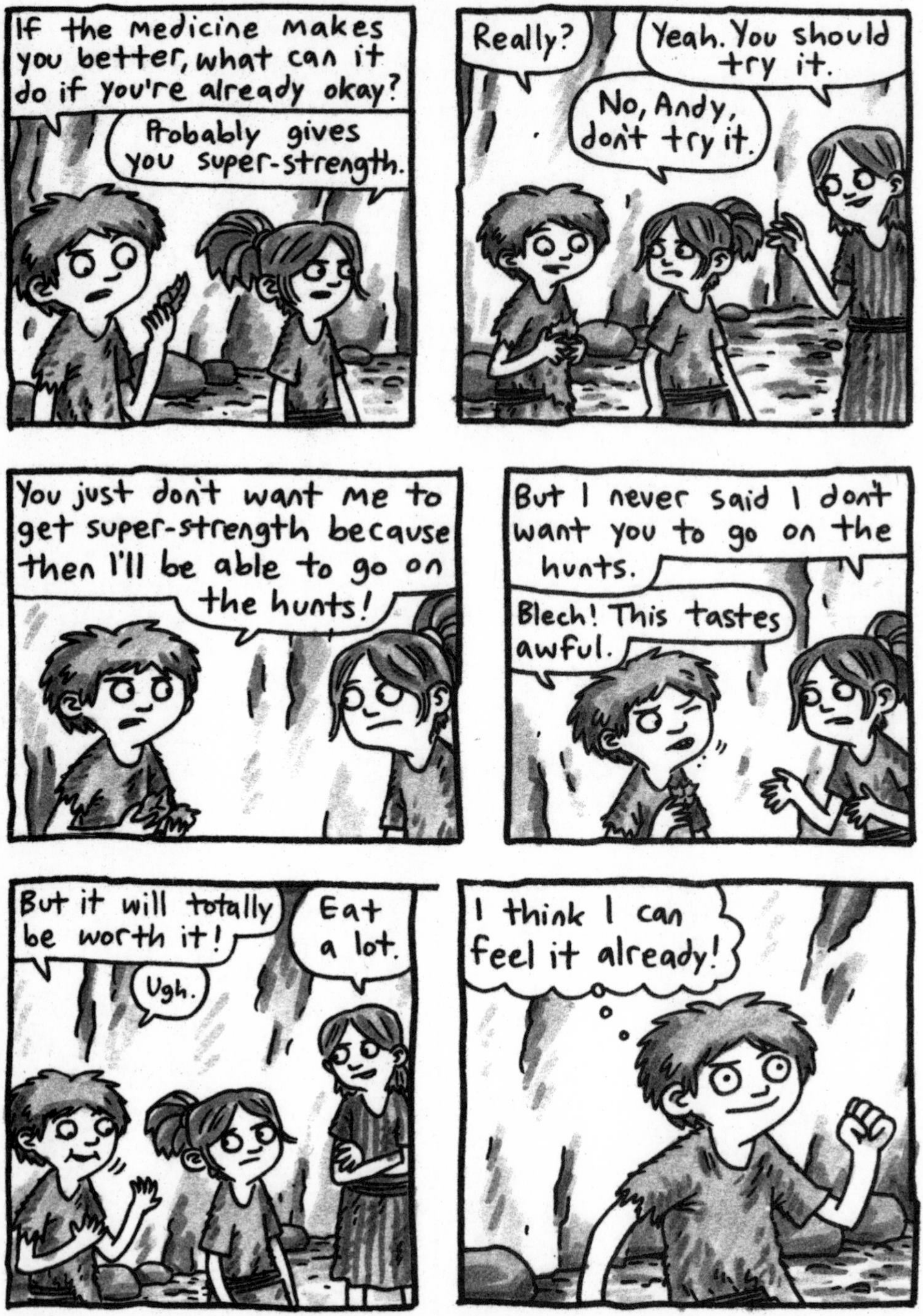
If the medicine makes you better, what can it do if you're already okay?
Probably gives you super-strength.
Really?
Yeah. You should try it.
No, Andy, don't try it.
You just don't want me to get super-strength because then I'll be able to go on the hunts!
But I never said I don't want you to go on the hunts.
Blech! This tastes awful.
But it will totally be worth it!
Eat a lot.
Ugh.
I think I can feel it already!

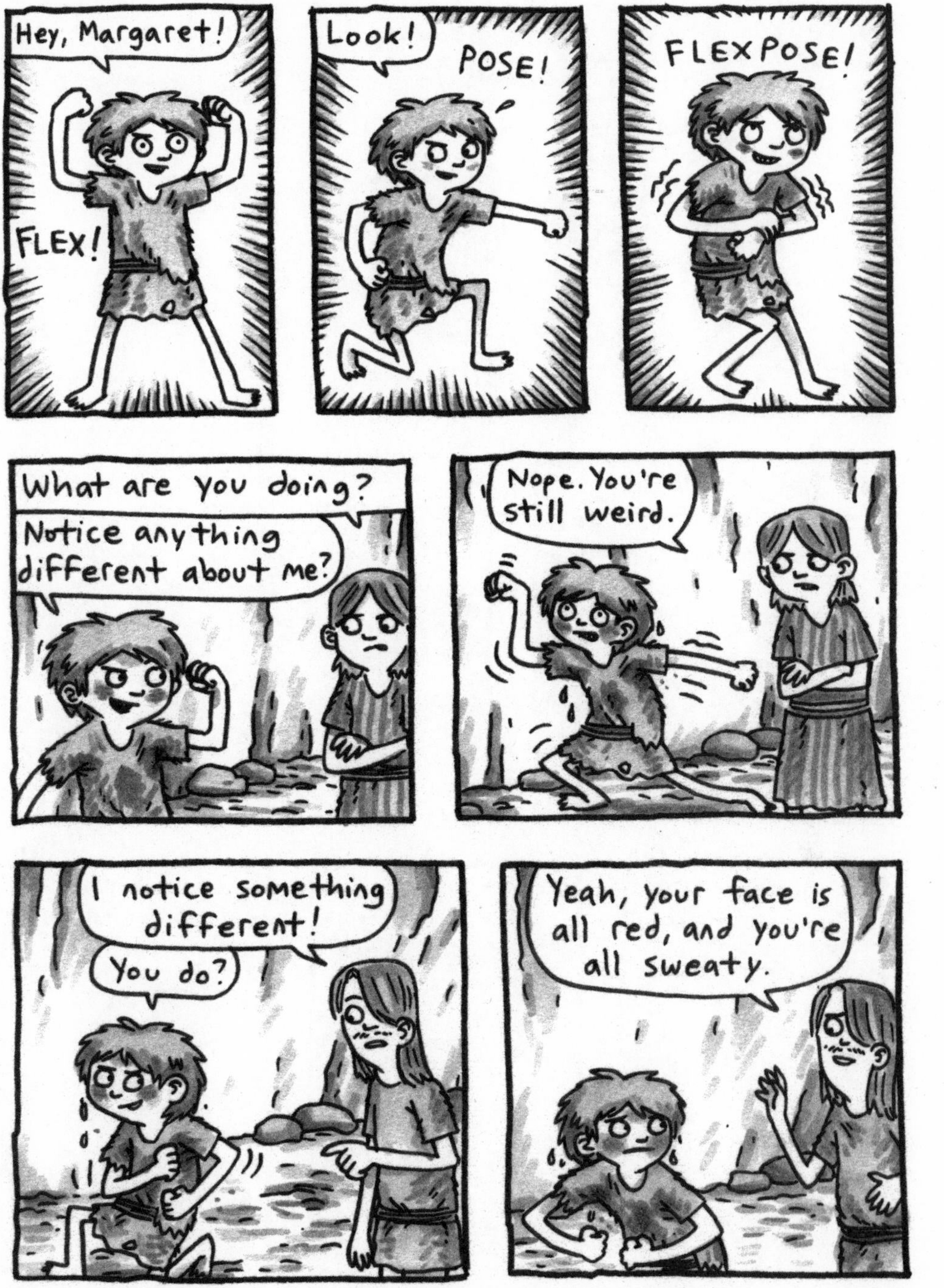
Hey, Margaret!
FLEX!
Look!
POSE!
FLEXPOSE!
What are you doing?
Notice anything different about me?
Nope. You're still weird.
I notice something different!
You do?
Yeah, your face is all red, and you're all sweaty.

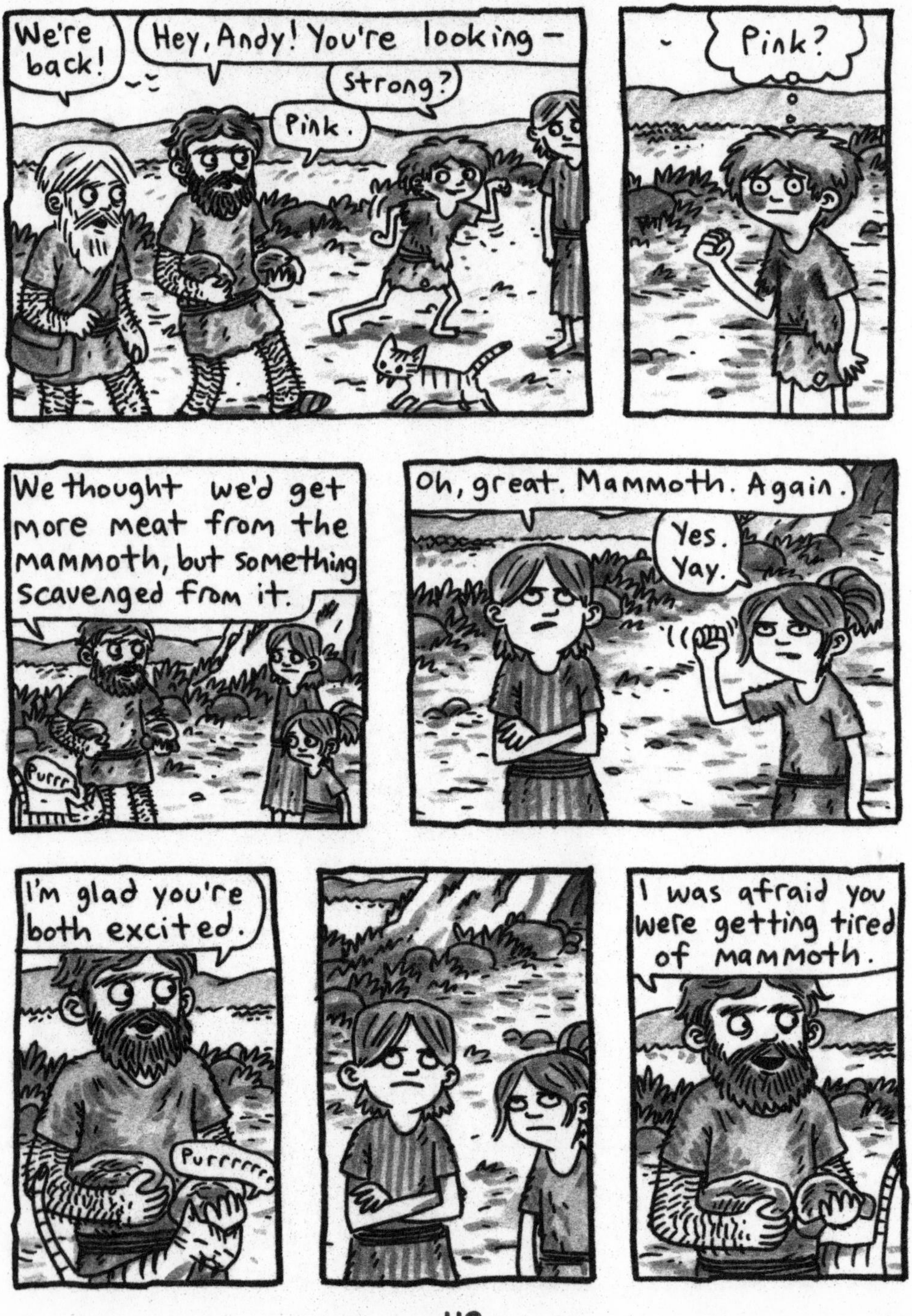

We're back!
Hey, Andy! You're looking—
Strong?
Pink.
Pink?
We thought we'd get more meat from the mammoth, but something scavenged from it.
Purrr
Oh, great. Mammoth. Again.
Yes. Yay.
I'm glad you're both excited.
Purrrrrr
I was afraid you were getting tired of mammoth.

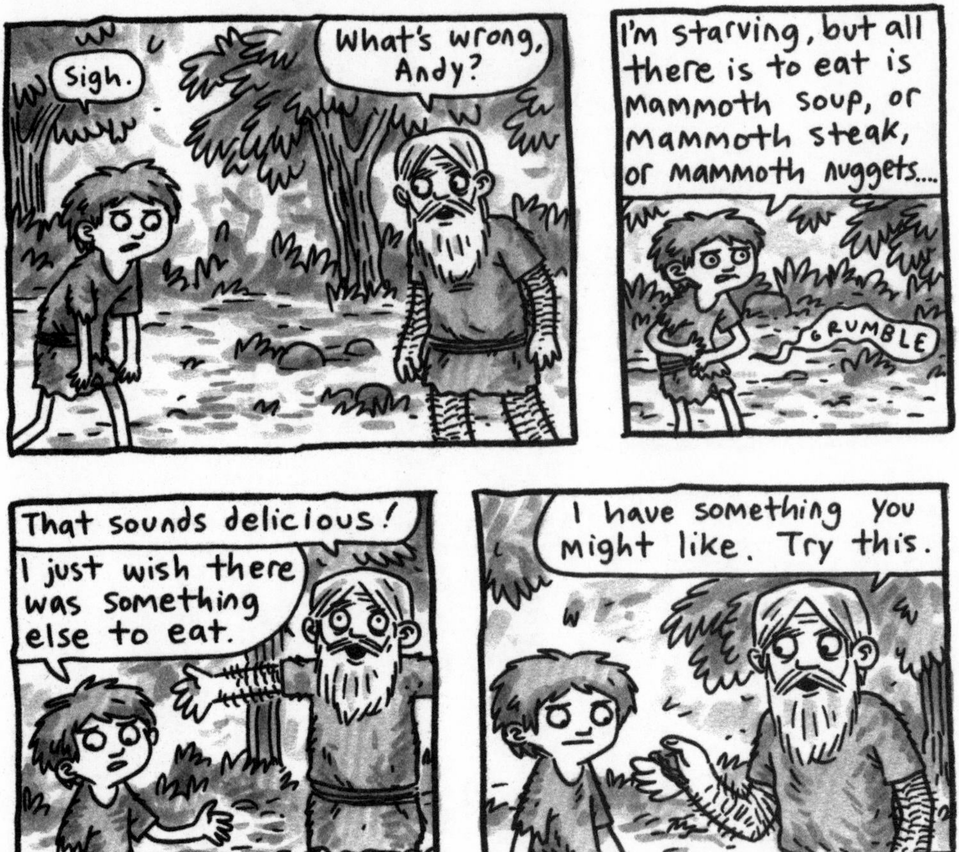
Sigh.
What's wrong, Andy?
I'm starving, but all there is to eat is mammoth soup, or mammoth steak, or mammoth nuggets....
GRUMBLE
That sounds delicious!
I just wish there was something else to eat.
I have something you might like. Try this.
Smells okay.
sniff
sniff
Nibble
chew chew
chew
Whoa! This is REALLY good!!
Andy, your face is scaring me.

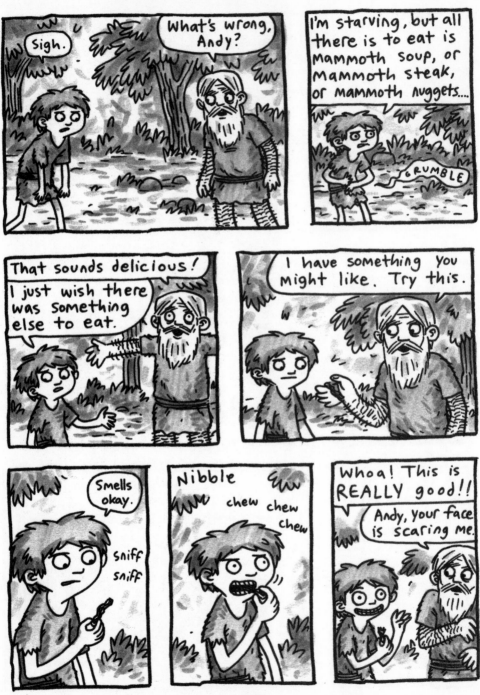

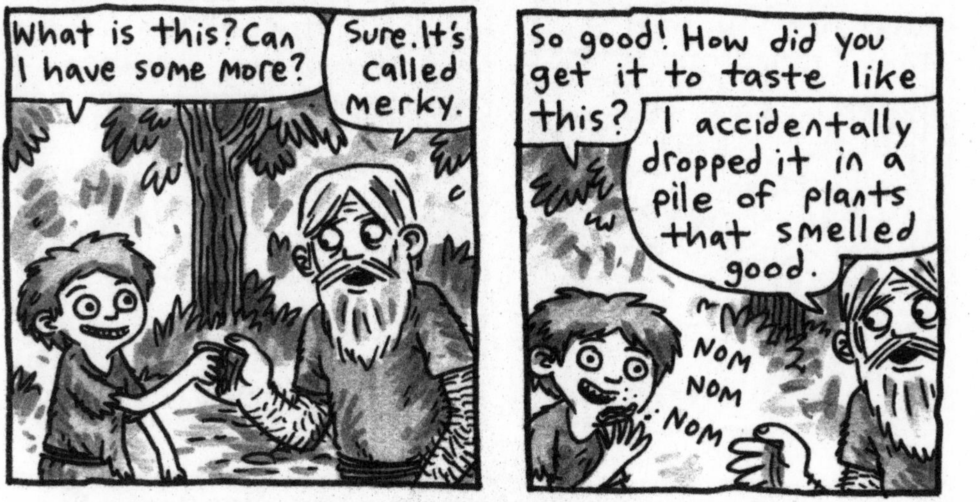
What is this? Can I have some more?
Sure. It's called merky.
So good! How did you get it to taste like this?
I accidentally dropped it in a pile of plants that smelled good.
NOM NOM NOM

Neanderthals didn't seem to use spices. They didn't even have salt or pepper!

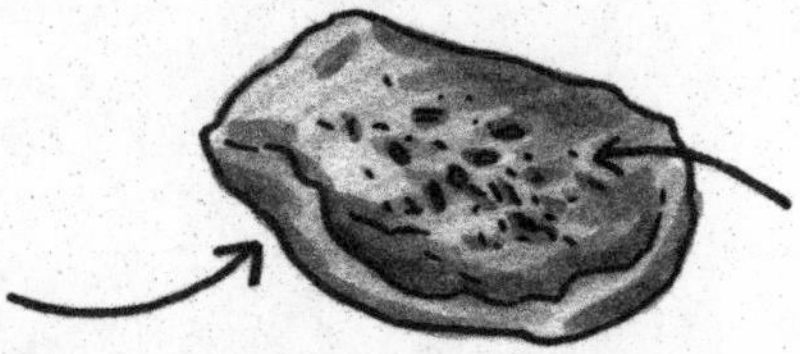
First clear evidence of cooking with spices: 6,000 years ago
Really, really old mustard

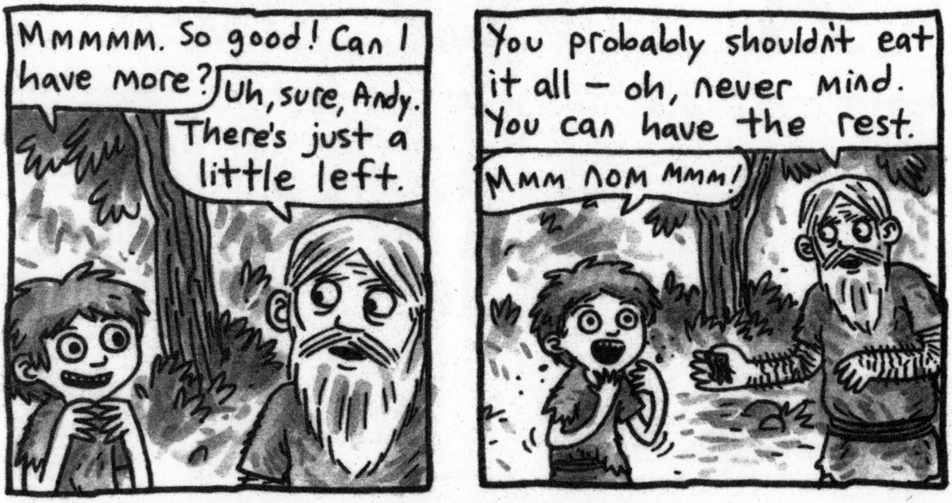
MMMMM. So good! Can I have more?
Uh, sure, Andy. There's just a little left.
You probably shouldn't eat it all – oh, never mind. You can have the rest.
MMM NOM MMM!

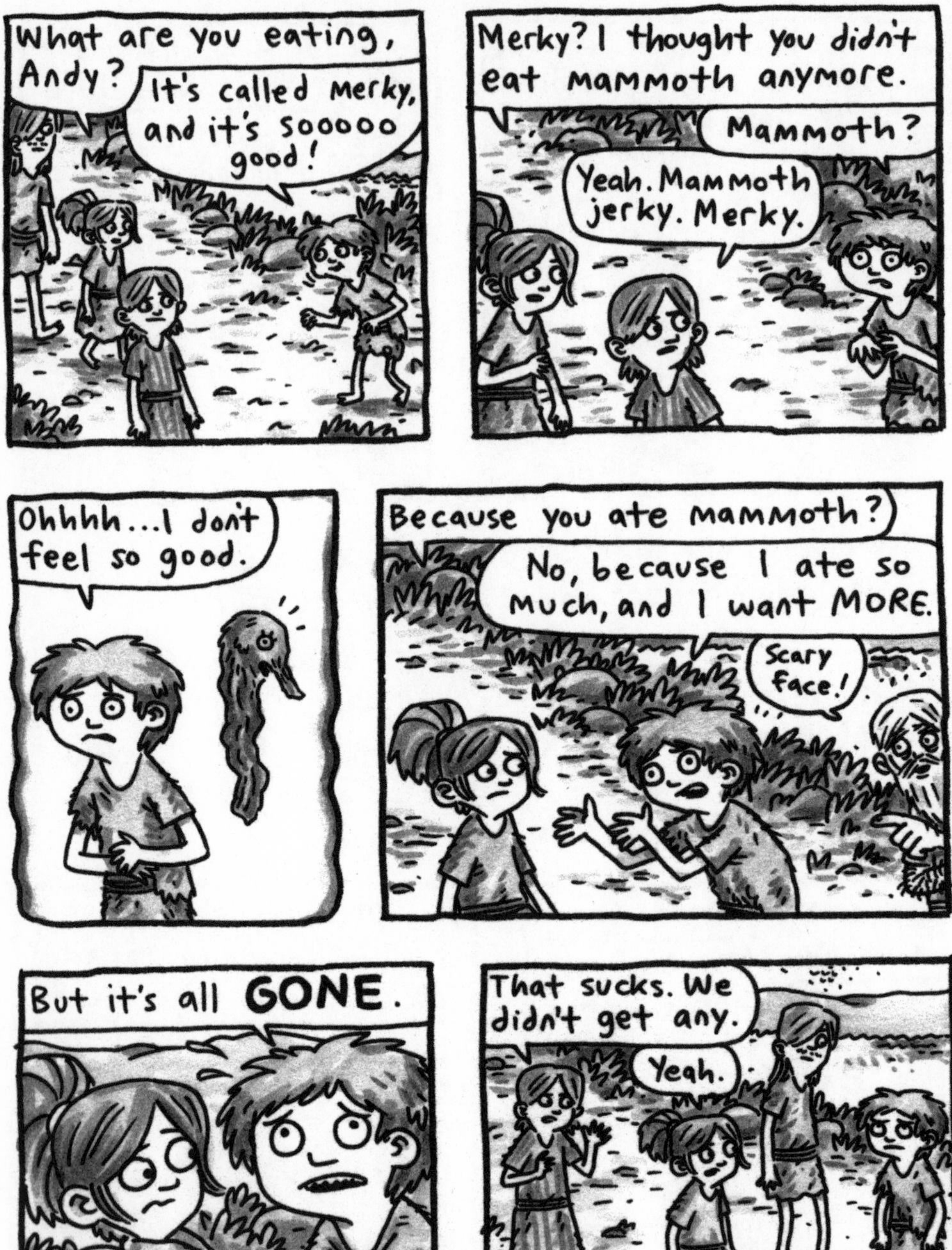
What are you eating, Andy?
It's called merky, and it's sooooo good!
Merky? I thought you didn't eat mammoth anymore.
Mammoth?
Yeah. Mammoth jerky. Merky.
Ohhhh... I don't feel so good.
Because you ate mammoth?
No, because I ate so much, and I want MORE.
Scary face!
But it's all **GONE**.
That sucks. We didn't get any.
Yeah.

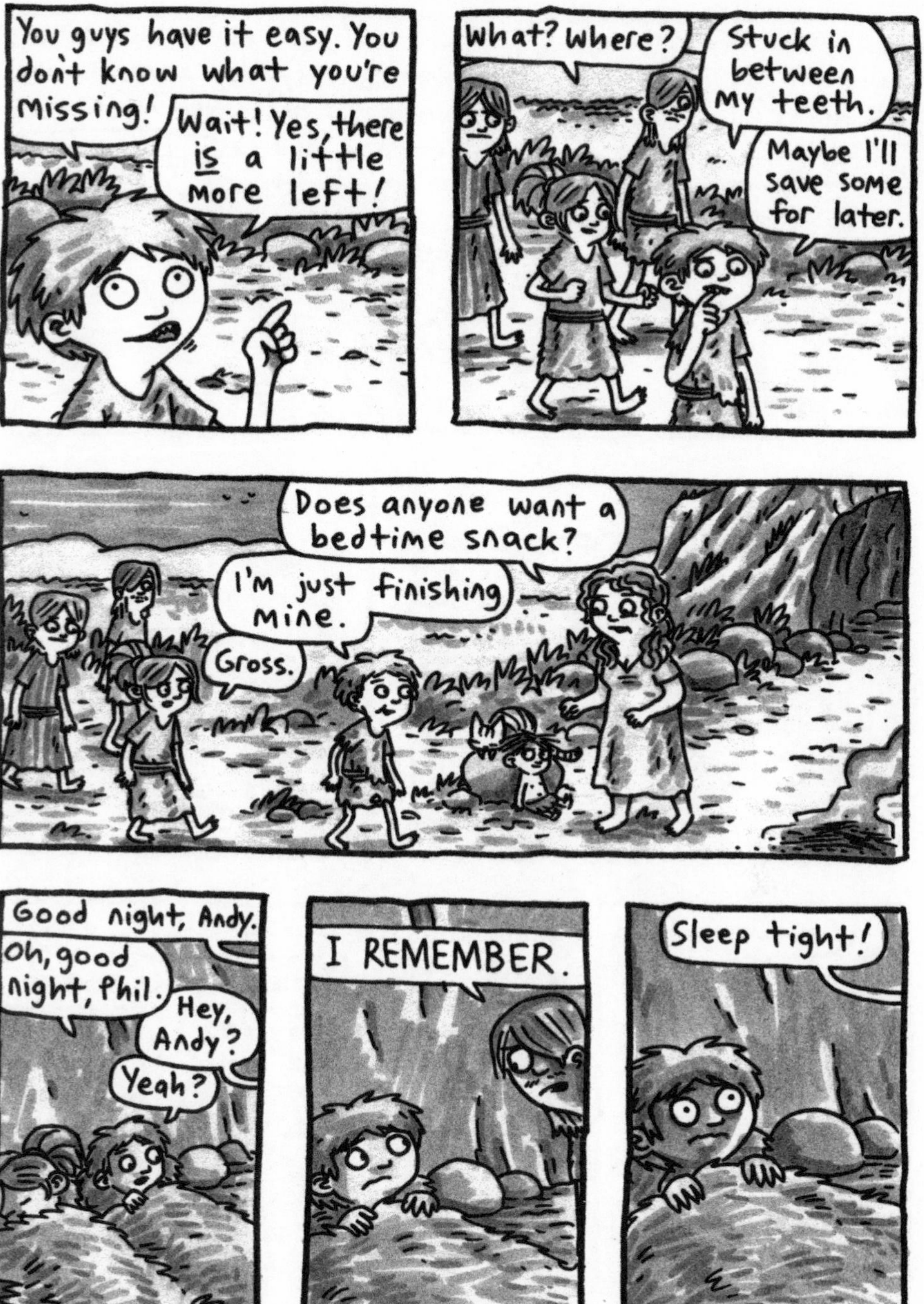
You guys have it easy. You don't know what you're missing!
Wait! Yes, there is a little more left!
What? Where?
Stuck in between my teeth.
Maybe I'll save some for later.
Does anyone want a bedtime snack?
I'm just finishing mine.
Gross.
Good night, Andy.
Oh, good night, Phil.
Hey, Andy?
Yeah?
I REMEMBER.
Sleep tight!

118

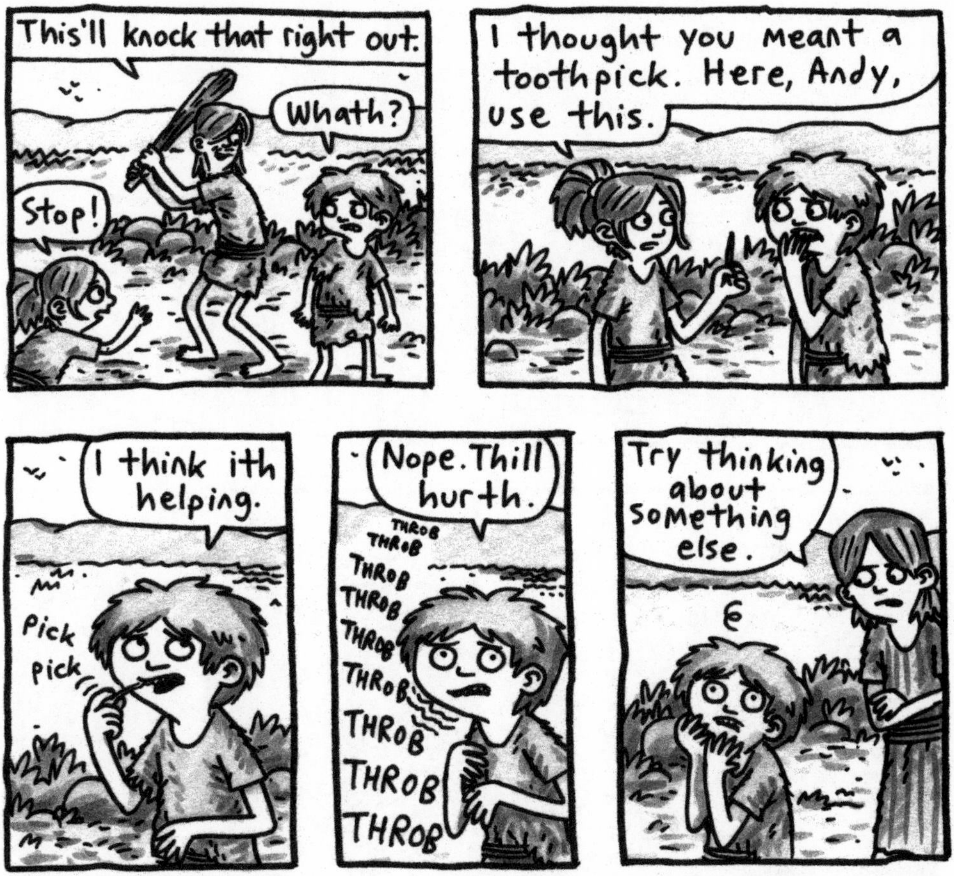
This'll knock that right out.
Whath?
Stop!
I thought you meant a toothpick. Here, Andy, use this.
I think ith helping.
Pick pick
Nope. Thill hurth.
THROB THROB THROB THROB THROB THROB THROB THROB THROB
Try thinking about something else.
I can't think about anything, ith driving me craythy!
Maybe it's the ghost of the mammoth haunting you.
AAAAAHHHHHH!

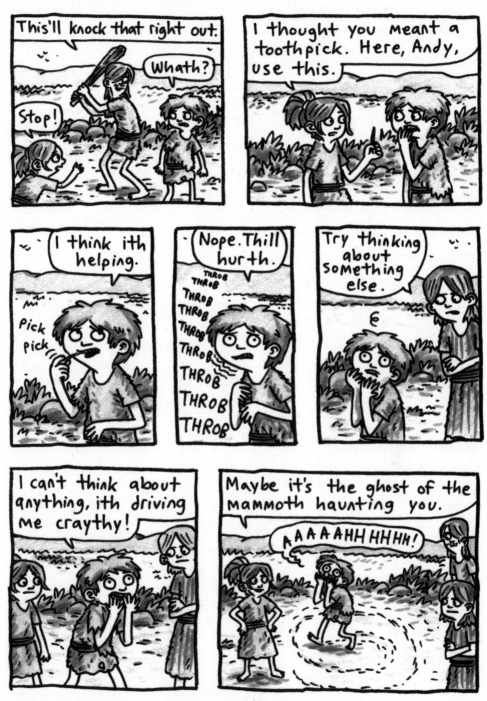

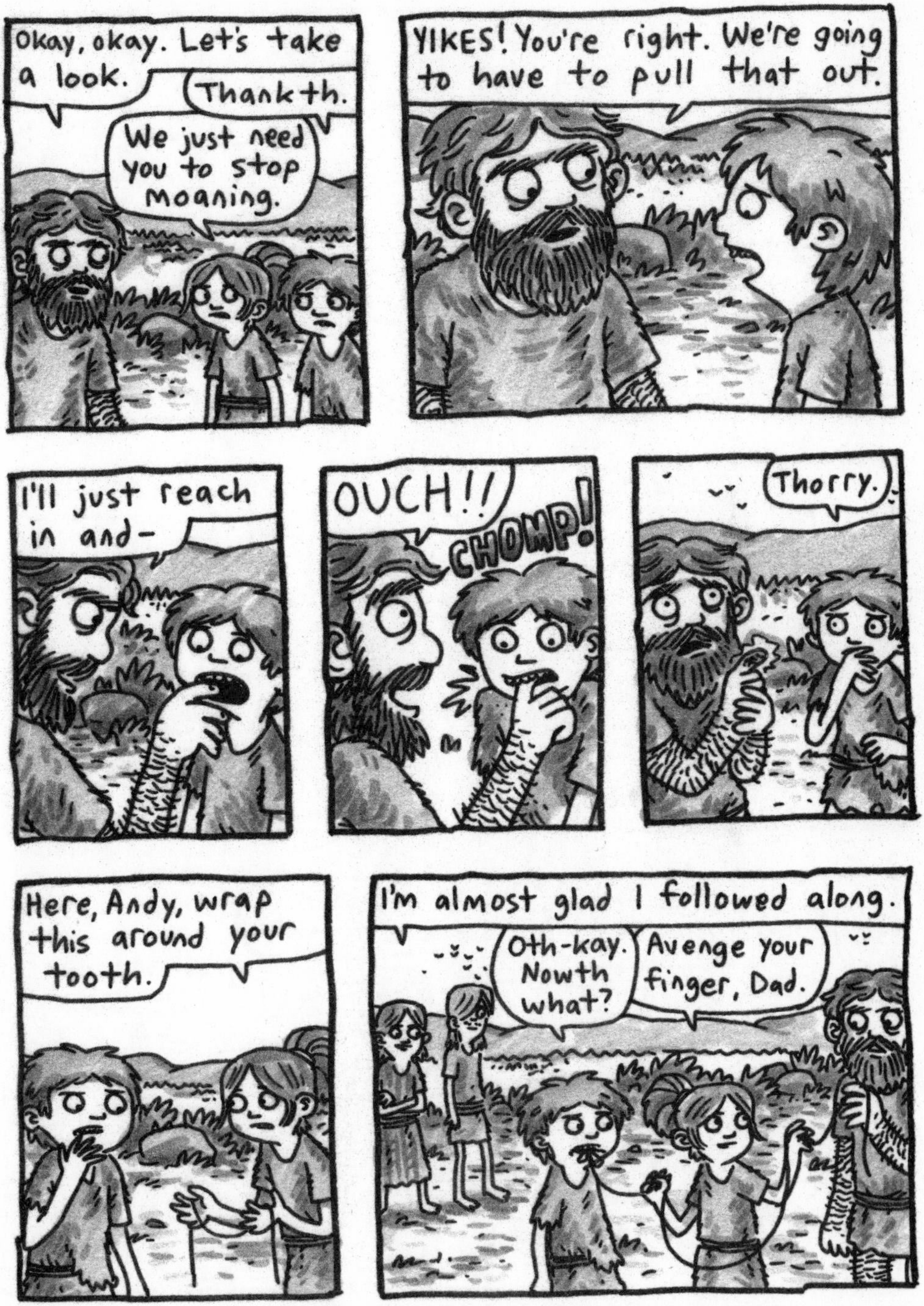
Okay, okay. Let's take a look.
Thank th.
We just need you to stop moaning.
YIKES! You're right. We're going to have to pull that out.
I'll just reach in and-
OUCH!!
CHOMP!
Thorry.
Here, Andy, wrap this around your tooth.
I'm almost glad I followed along.
Oth-kay. Nowth what?
Avenge your finger, Dad.

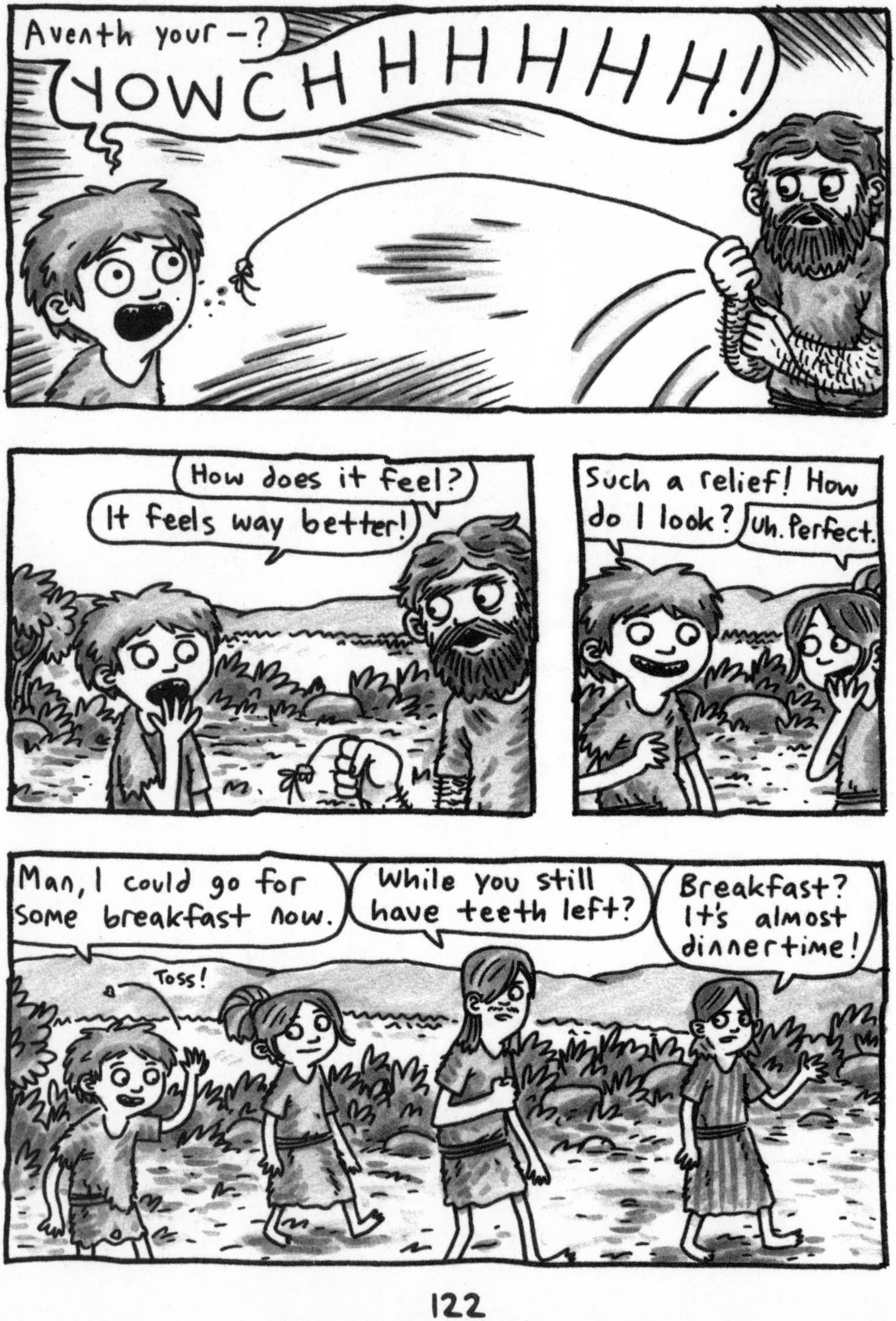
Aventh your—?
YOWCHHHHHHH!
How does it feel?
It feels way better!
Such a relief! How do I look?
Uh. Perfect.
Man, I could go for some breakfast now.
Toss!
While you still have teeth left?
Breakfast? It's almost dinnertime!

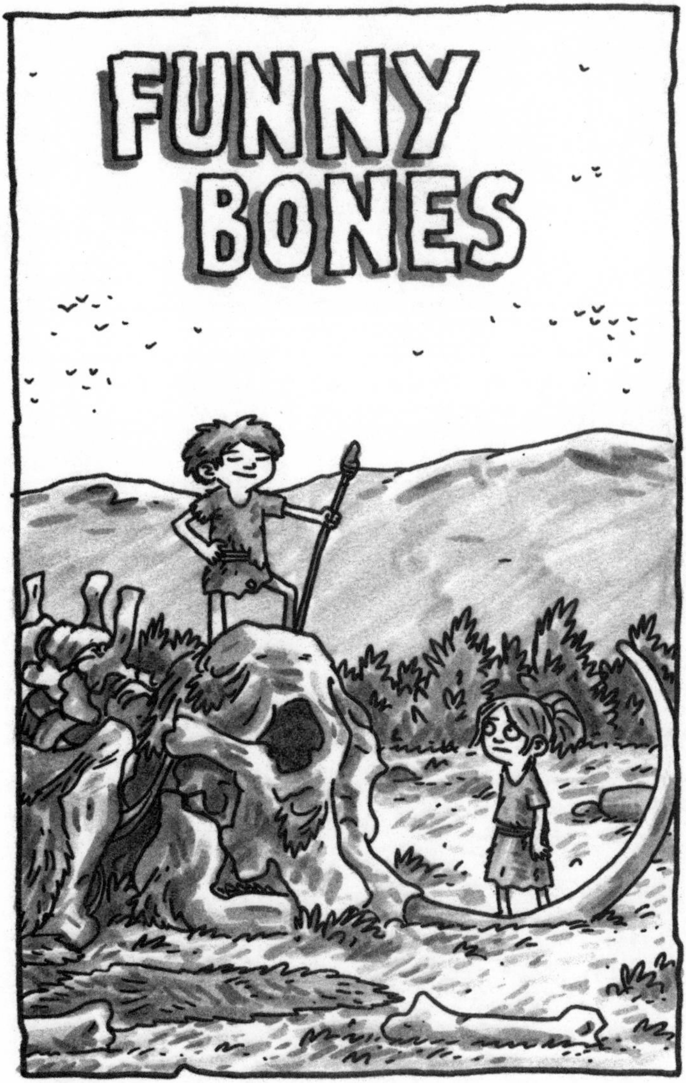
FUNNY BONES

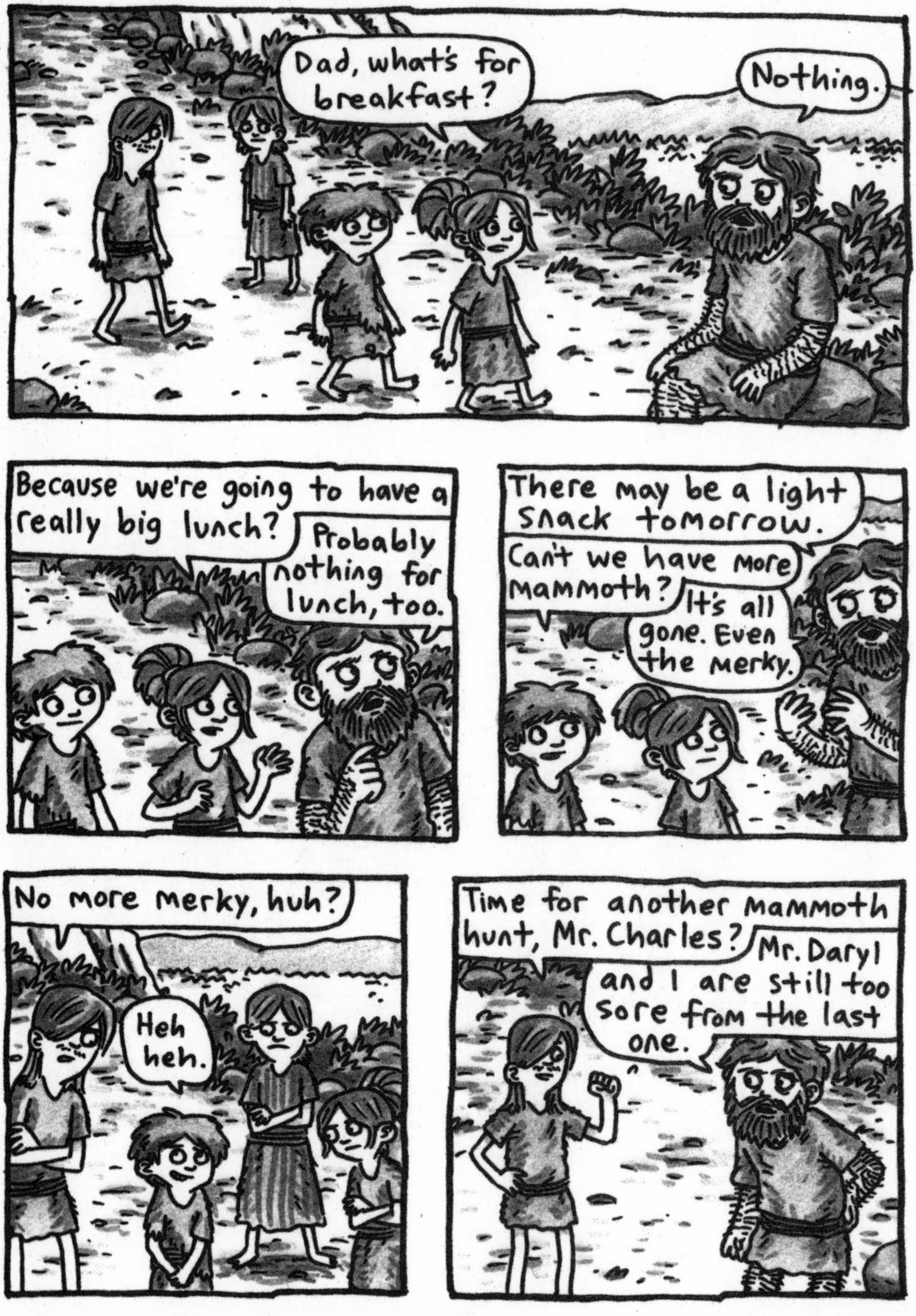
Dad, what's for breakfast?
Nothing.
Because we're going to have a really big lunch?
Probably nothing for lunch, too.
There may be a light snack tomorrow.
Can't we have more mammoth?
It's all gone. Even the merky.
No more merky, huh?
Heh heh.
Time for another mammoth hunt, Mr. Charles?
Mr. Daryl and I are still too sore from the last one.

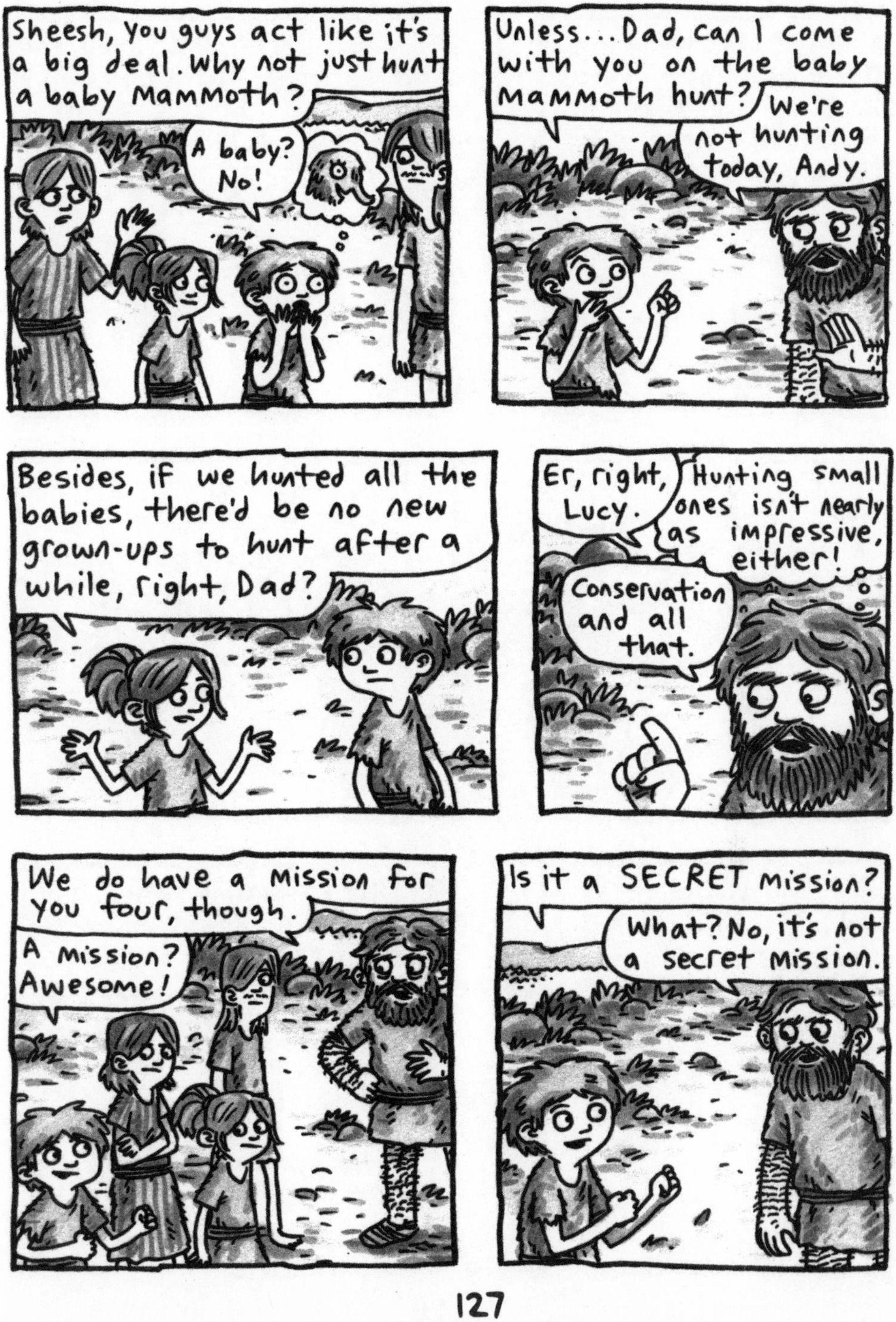
Sheesh, you guys act like it's a big deal. Why not just hunt a baby Mammoth?
A baby? No!
Unless... Dad, can I come with you on the baby Mammoth hunt?
We're not hunting today, Andy.
Besides, if we hunted all the babies, there'd be no new grown-ups to hunt after a while, right, Dad?
Er, right, Lucy.
Hunting small ones isn't nearly as impressive, either!
Conservation and all that.
We do have a mission for you four, though.
A mission? Awesome!
Is it a SECRET mission?
What? No, it's not a secret mission.

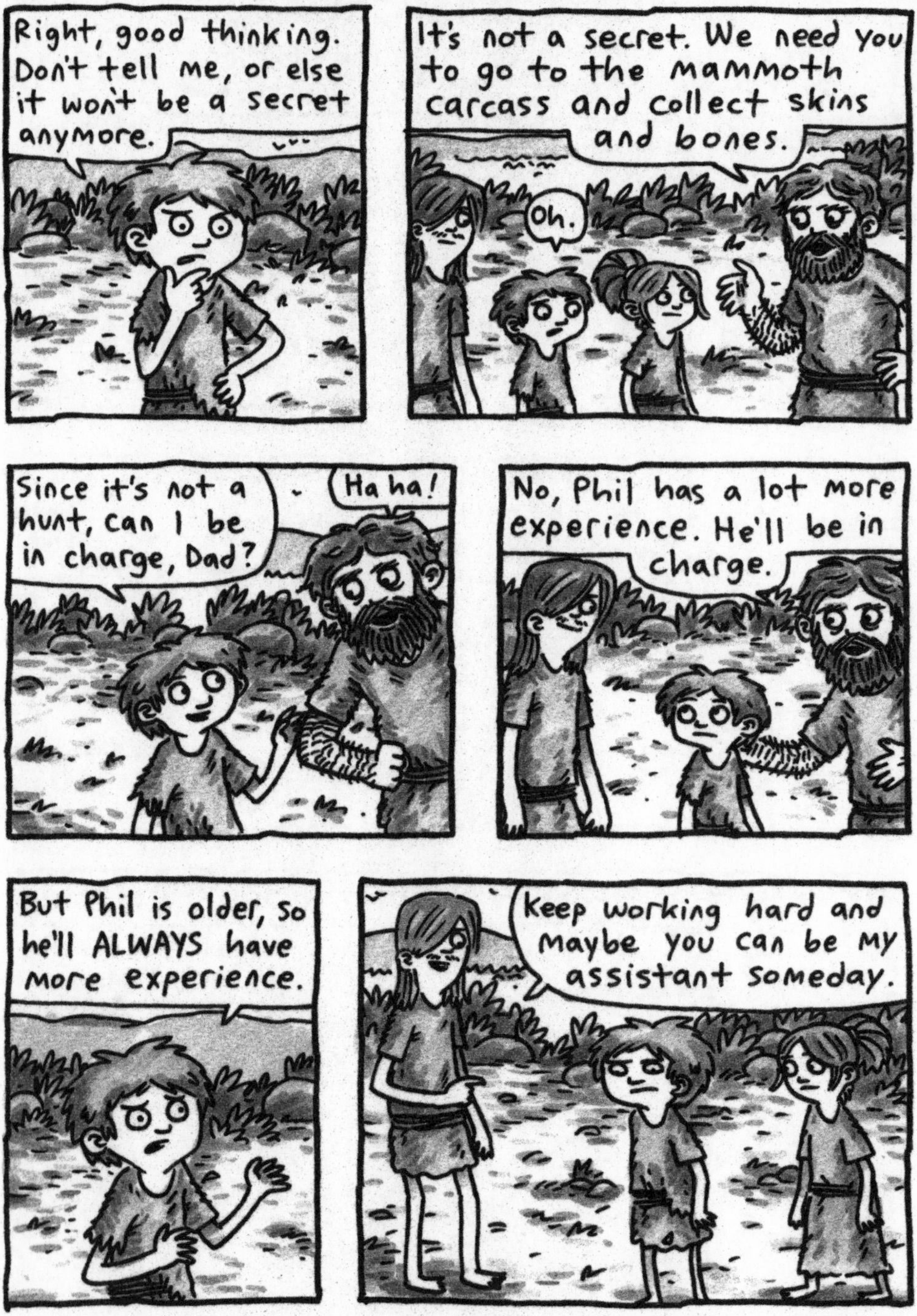
Right, good thinking. Don't tell me, or else it won't be a secret anymore.
It's not a secret. We need you to go to the mammoth carcass and collect skins and bones.
Oh.
Since it's not a hunt, can I be in charge, Dad?
Ha ha!
No, Phil has a lot more experience. He'll be in charge.
But Phil is older, so he'll ALWAYS have more experience.
Keep working hard and maybe you can be my assistant someday.

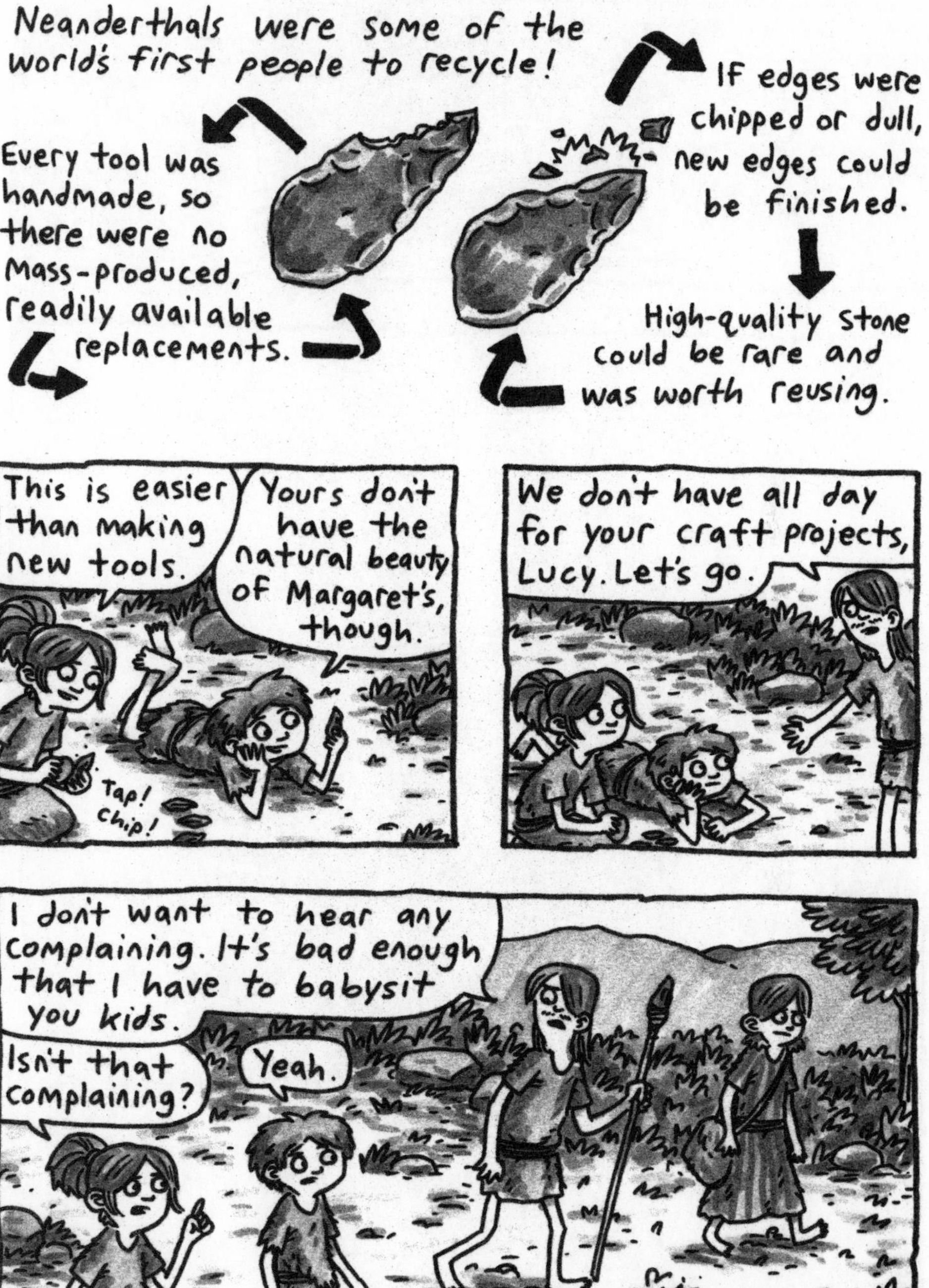
Neanderthals were some of the world's first people to recycle!
Every tool was handmade, so there were no mass-produced, readily available replacements.
If edges were chipped or dull, new edges could be finished.
High-quality stone could be rare and was worth reusing.
This is easier than making new tools.
Yours don't have the natural beauty of Margaret's, though.
Tap! Chip!
We don't have all day for your craft projects, Lucy. Let's go.
I don't want to hear any complaining. It's bad enough that I have to babysit you kids.
Isn't that complaining?
Yeah.

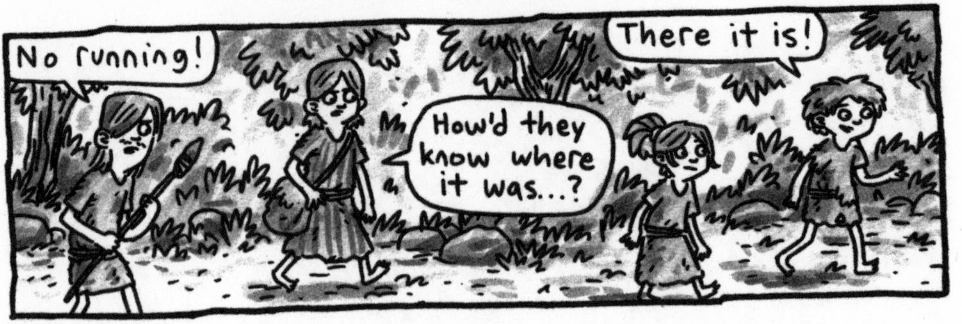
No running!
How'd they know where it was...?
There it is!

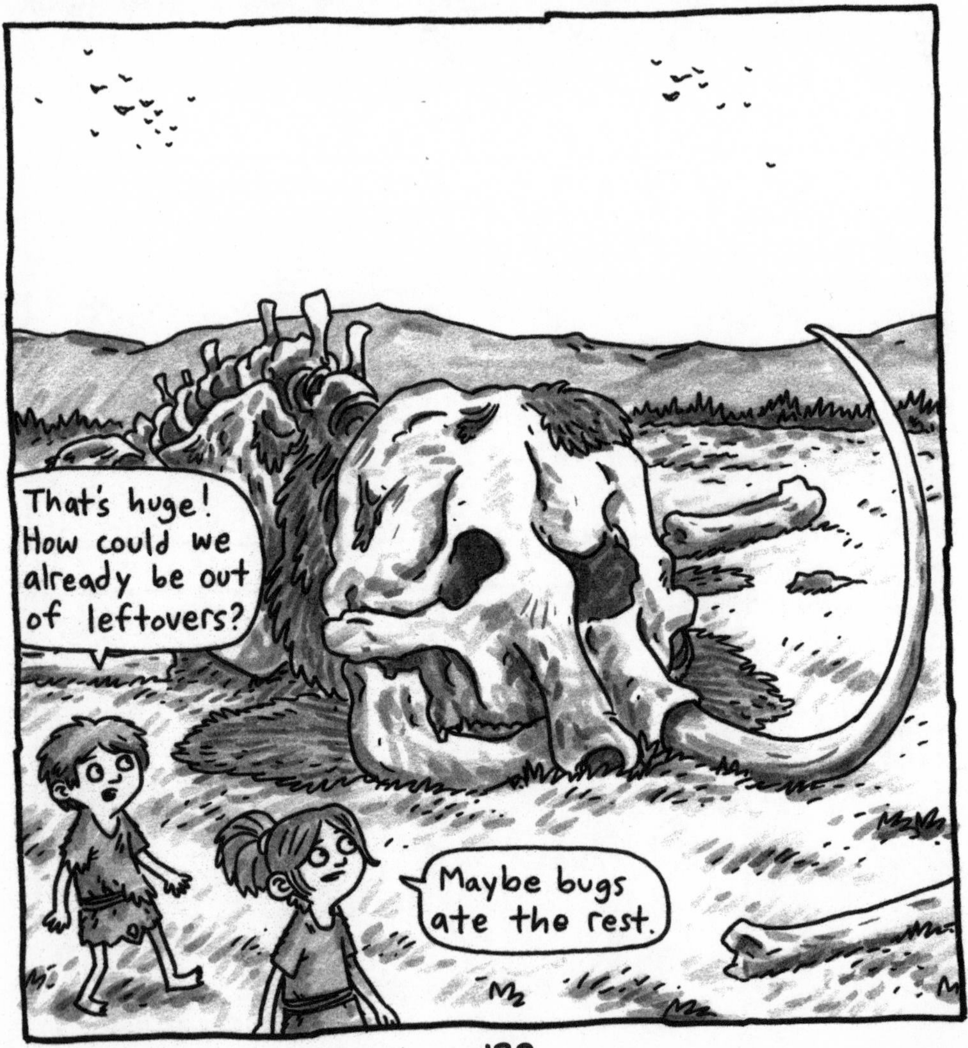
That's huge! How could we already be out of leftovers?
Maybe bugs ate the rest.

Museums use dermestid beetles to clean bones of flesh and organic matter, for easier study!

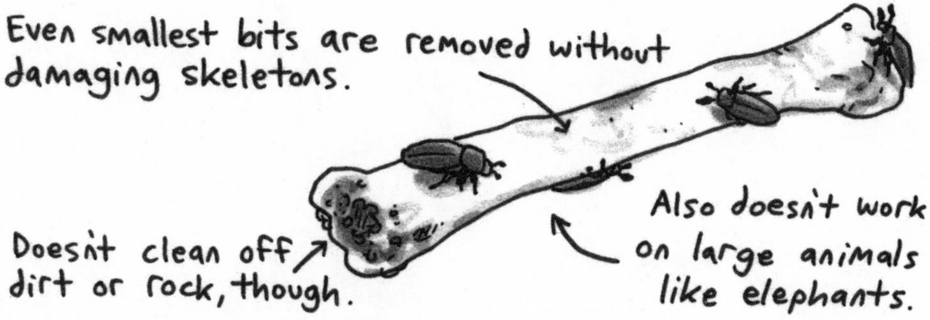

Even smallest bits are removed without damaging skeletons.
Doesn't clean off dirt or rock, though.
Also doesn't work on large animals like elephants.

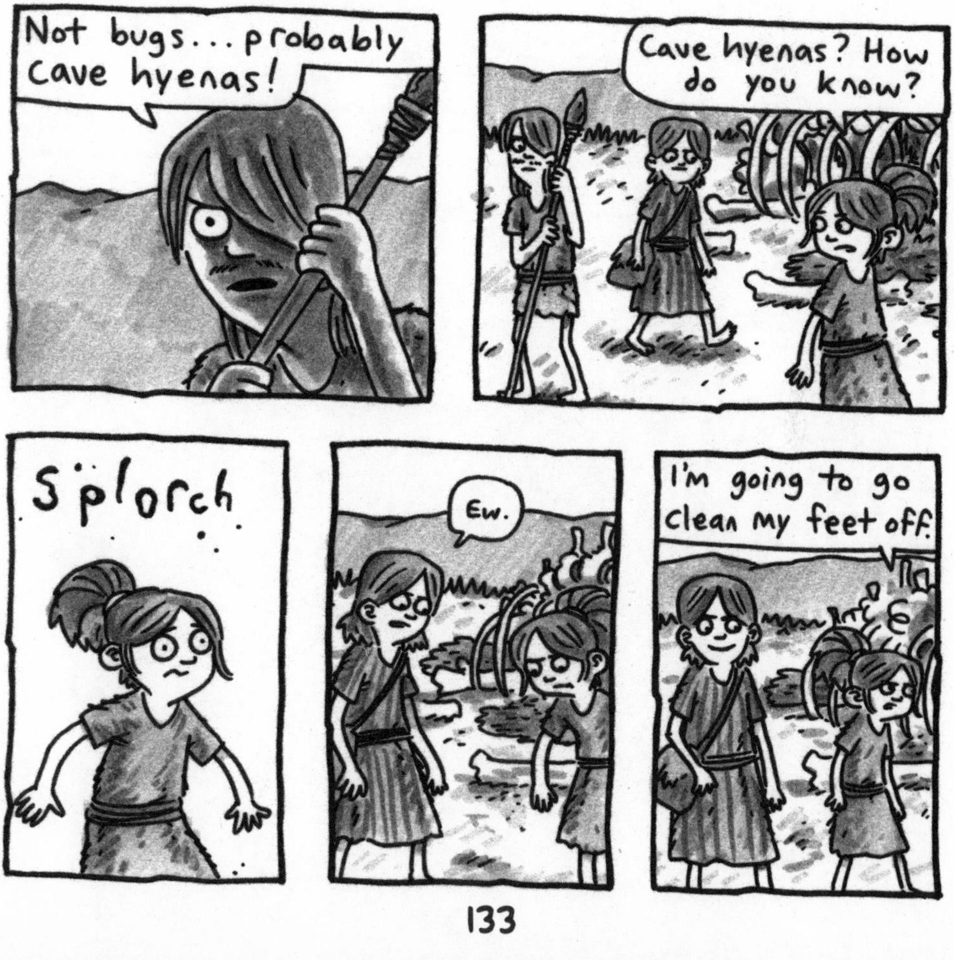

Not bugs... probably cave hyenas!
Cave hyenas? How do you know?
Splorch
Ew.
I'm going to go clean my feet off.

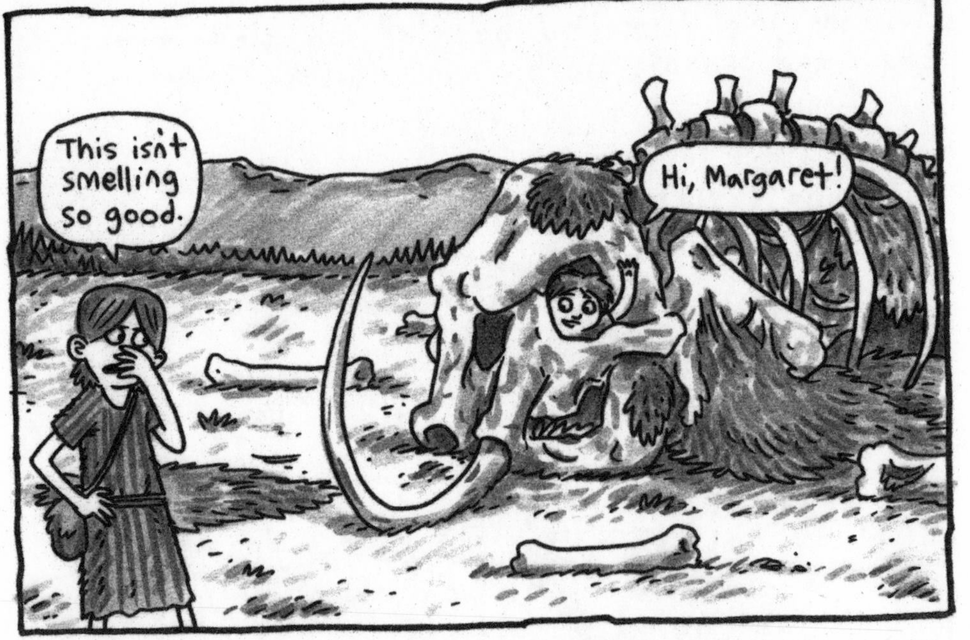
This isn't smelling so good.
Hi, Margaret!

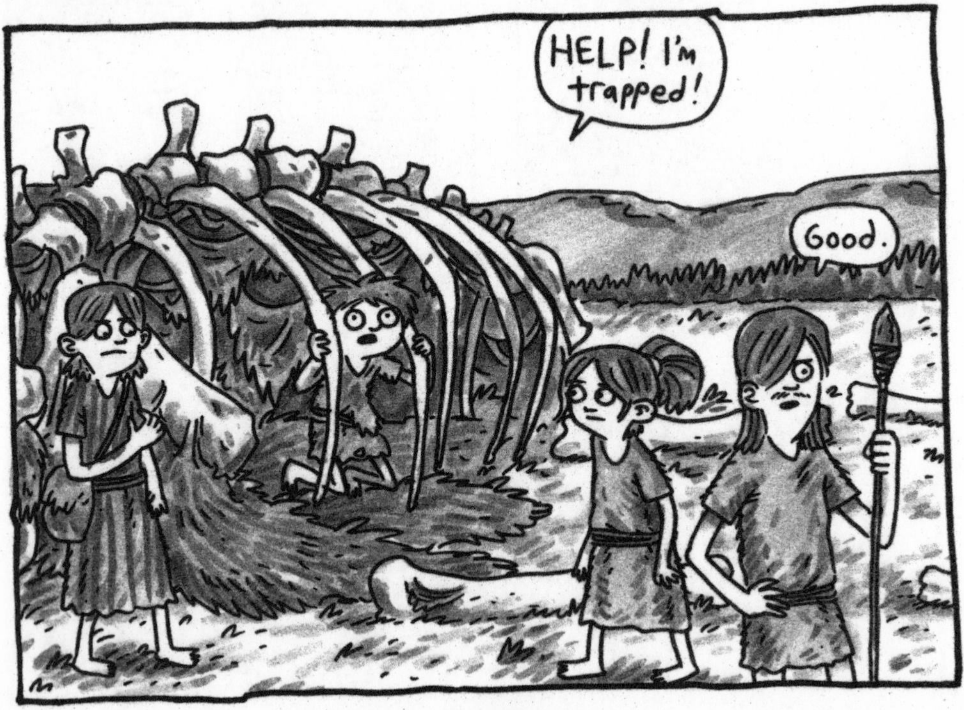
HELP! I'm trapped!
Good.

135

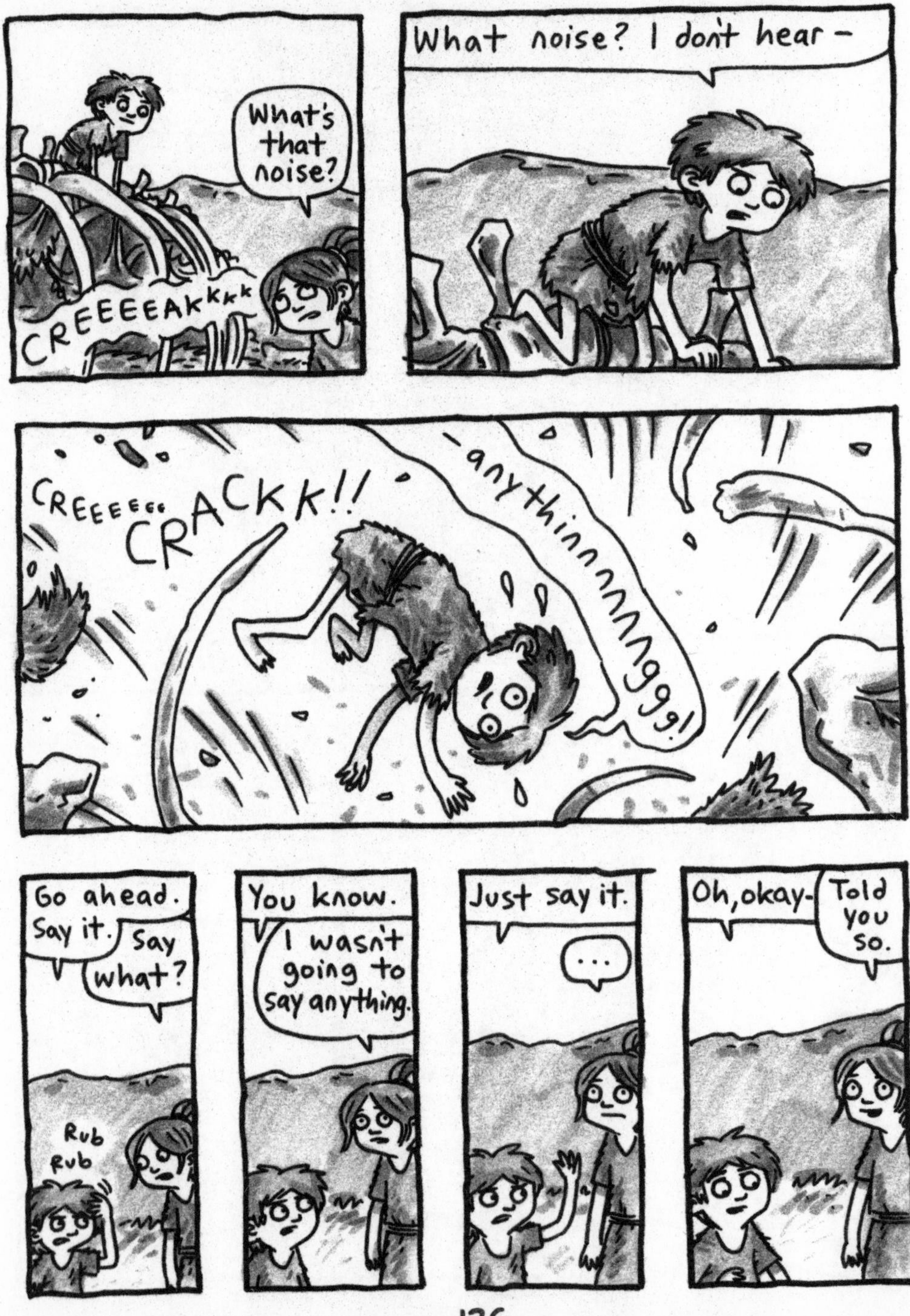
What's that noise?
CREEEEEAKkkk
What noise? I don't hear -
CREEEEEEE CRACKK!!
-anythinnnnnNNggg!
Go ahead. Say it.
Say what?
Rub Rub
You know.
I wasn't going to say anything.
Just say it.
...
Oh, okay-
Told you so.

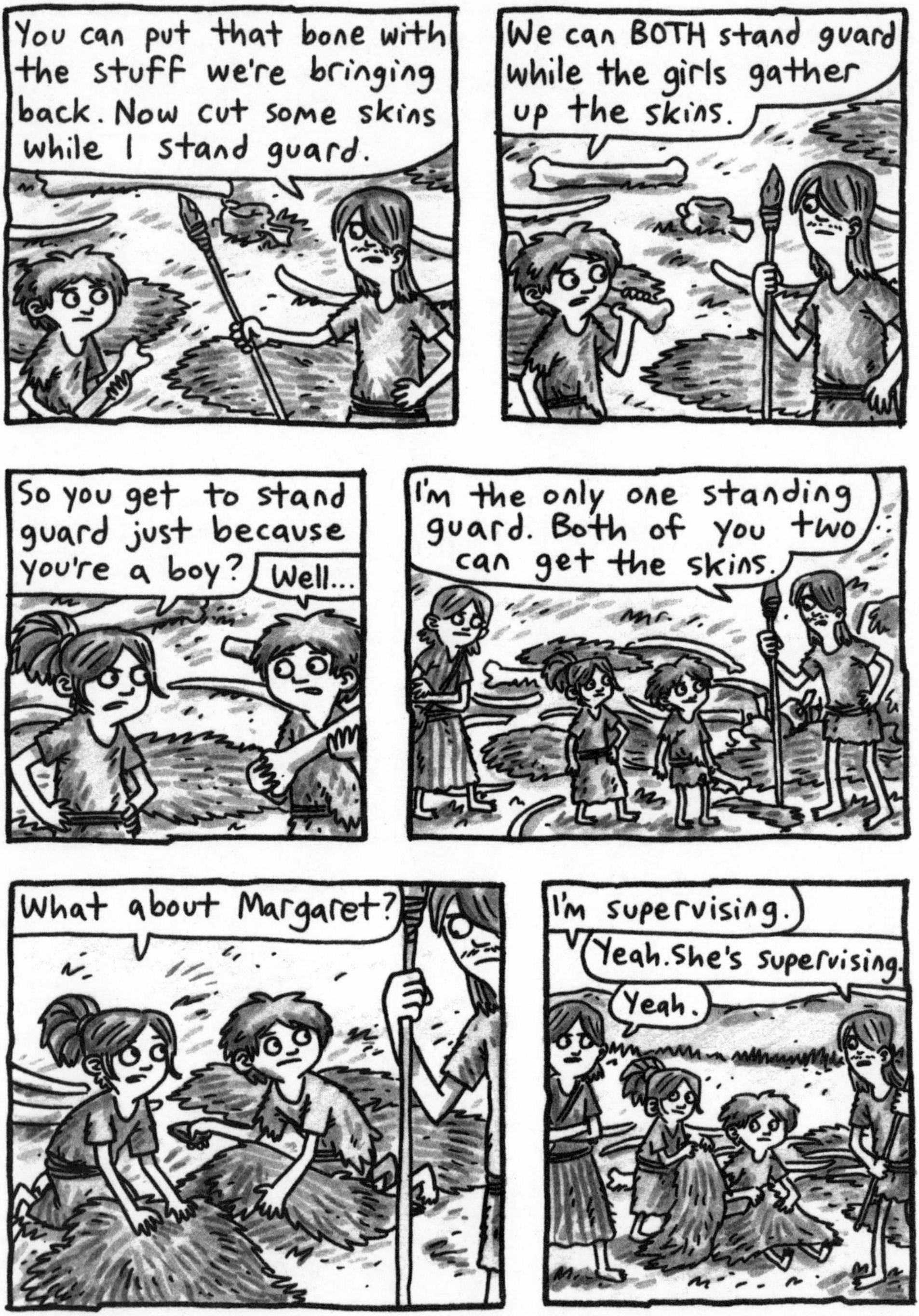
You can put that bone with the stuff we're bringing back. Now cut some skins while I stand guard.
We can BOTH stand guard while the girls gather up the skins.
So you get to stand guard just because you're a boy?
Well...
I'm the only one standing guard. Both of you two can get the skins.
What about Margaret?
I'm supervising.
Yeah. She's supervising.
Yeah.

140

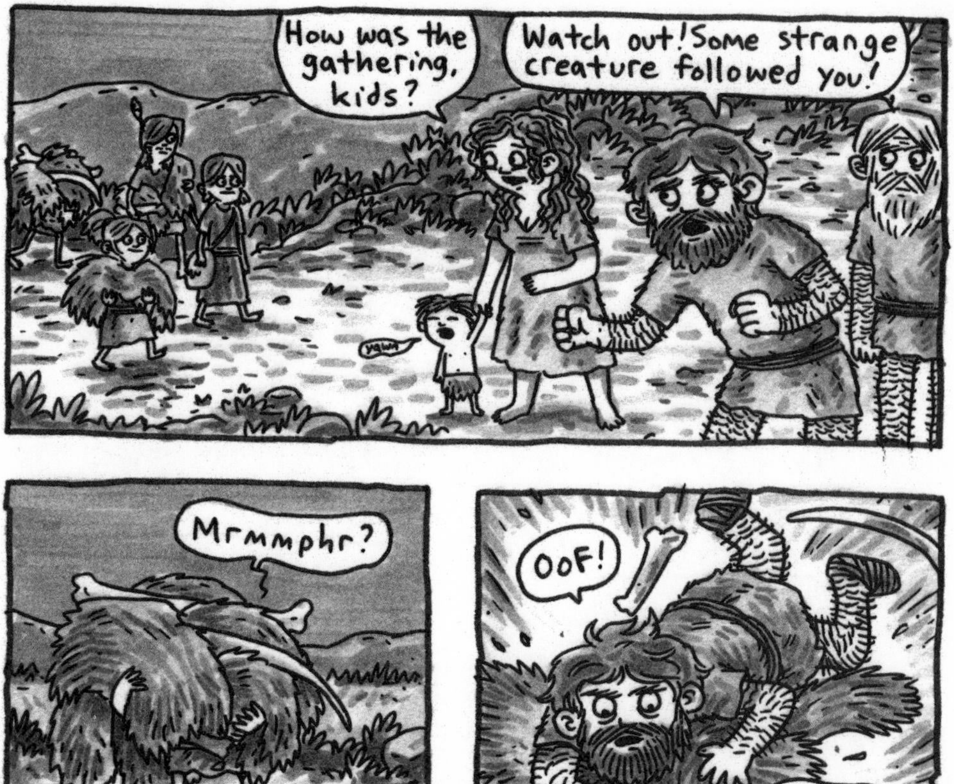
How was the gathering, kids?
Watch out! Some strange creature followed you!
Mrmmphr?
OOF!
AIEEE!
That's weird. It talks.
Can't... breathe...
Okay, time for bed!
ROARR!
OOF!
At least your camouflage is getting better, Andy.

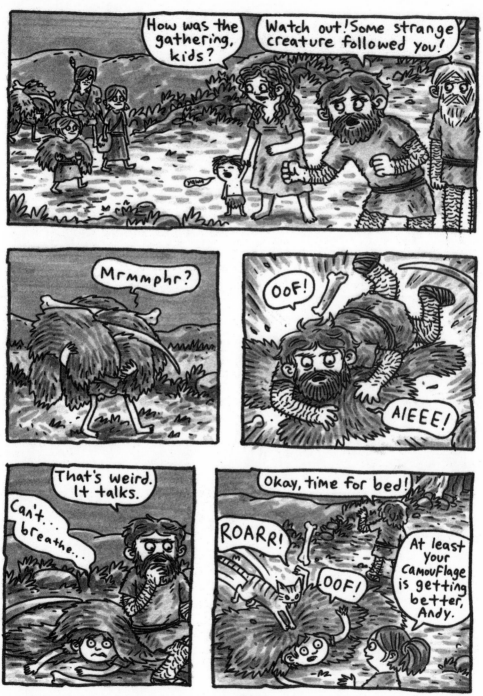

UP CLOTHES AND PERSONAL

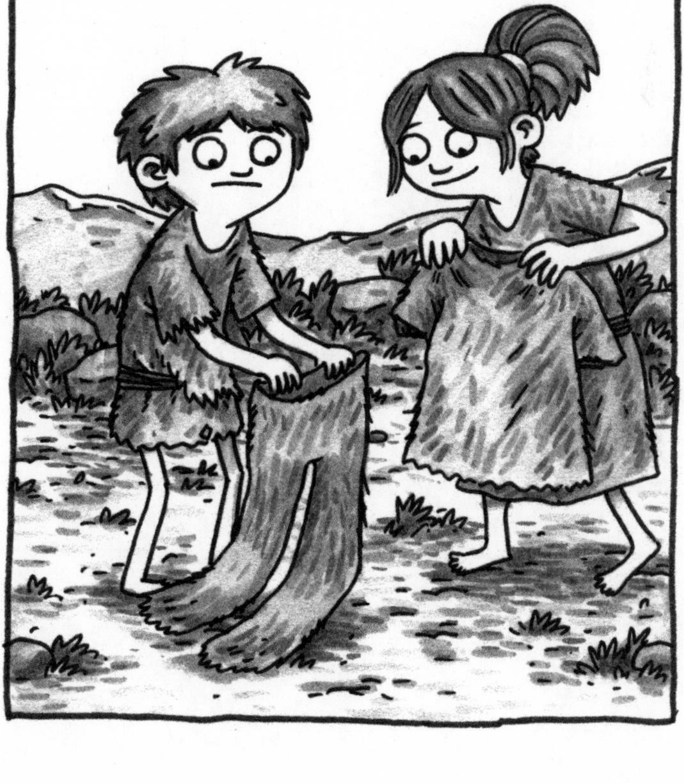

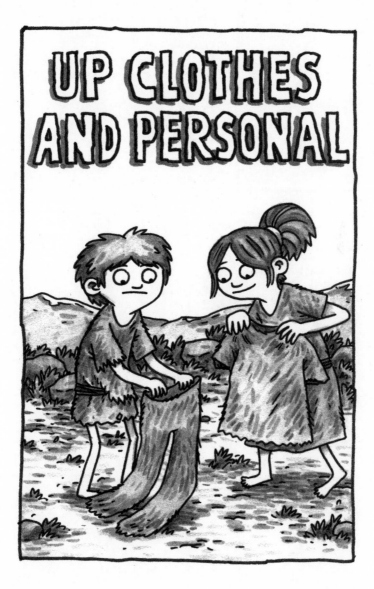

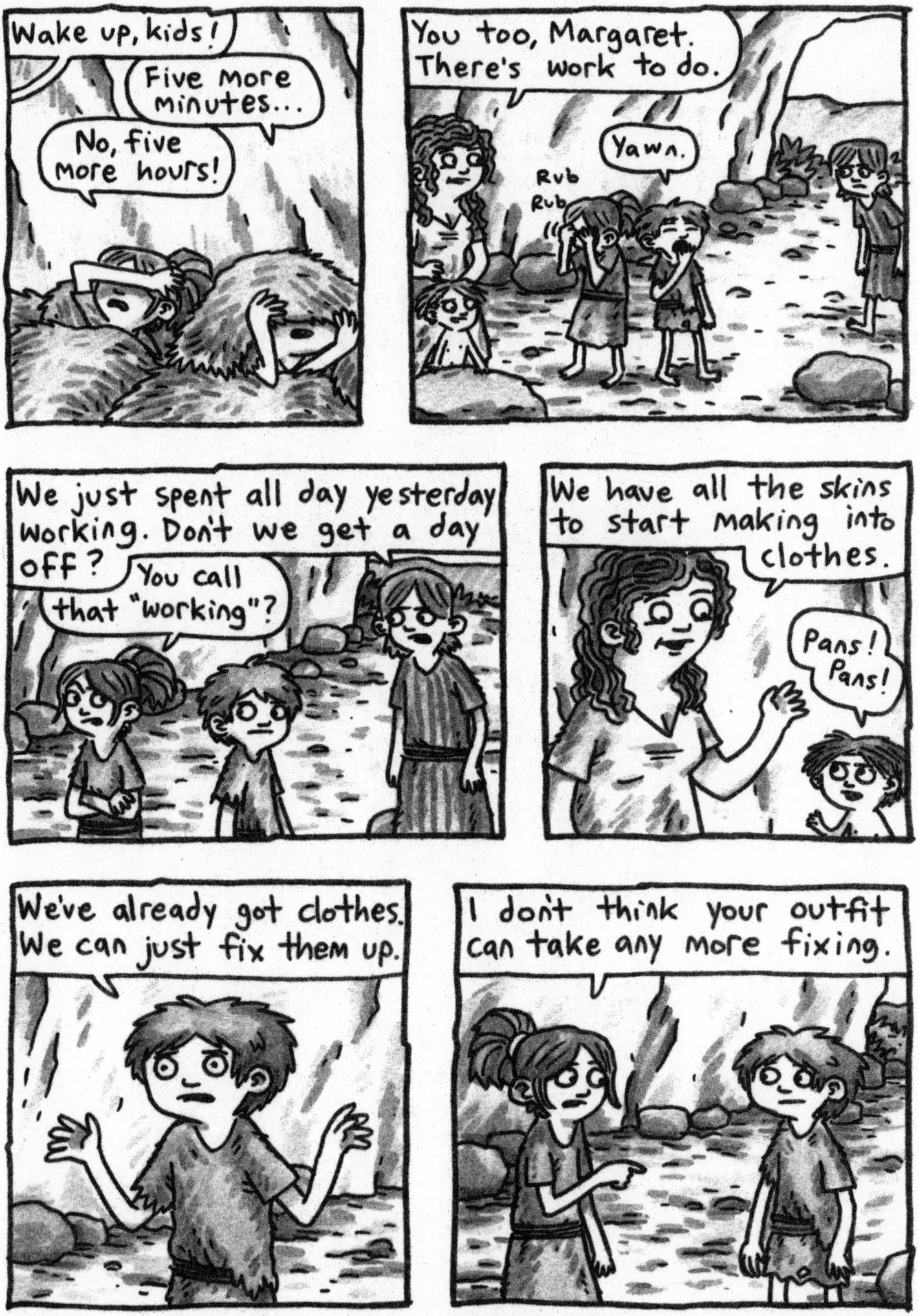
Wake up, kids!
Five more minutes...
No, five more hours!
You too, Margaret. There's work to do.
Yawn.
Rub Rub
We just spent all day yesterday working. Don't we get a day off?
You call that "working"?
We have all the skins to start making into clothes.
Pans! Pans!
We've already got clothes. We can just fix them up.
I don't think your outfit can take any more fixing.

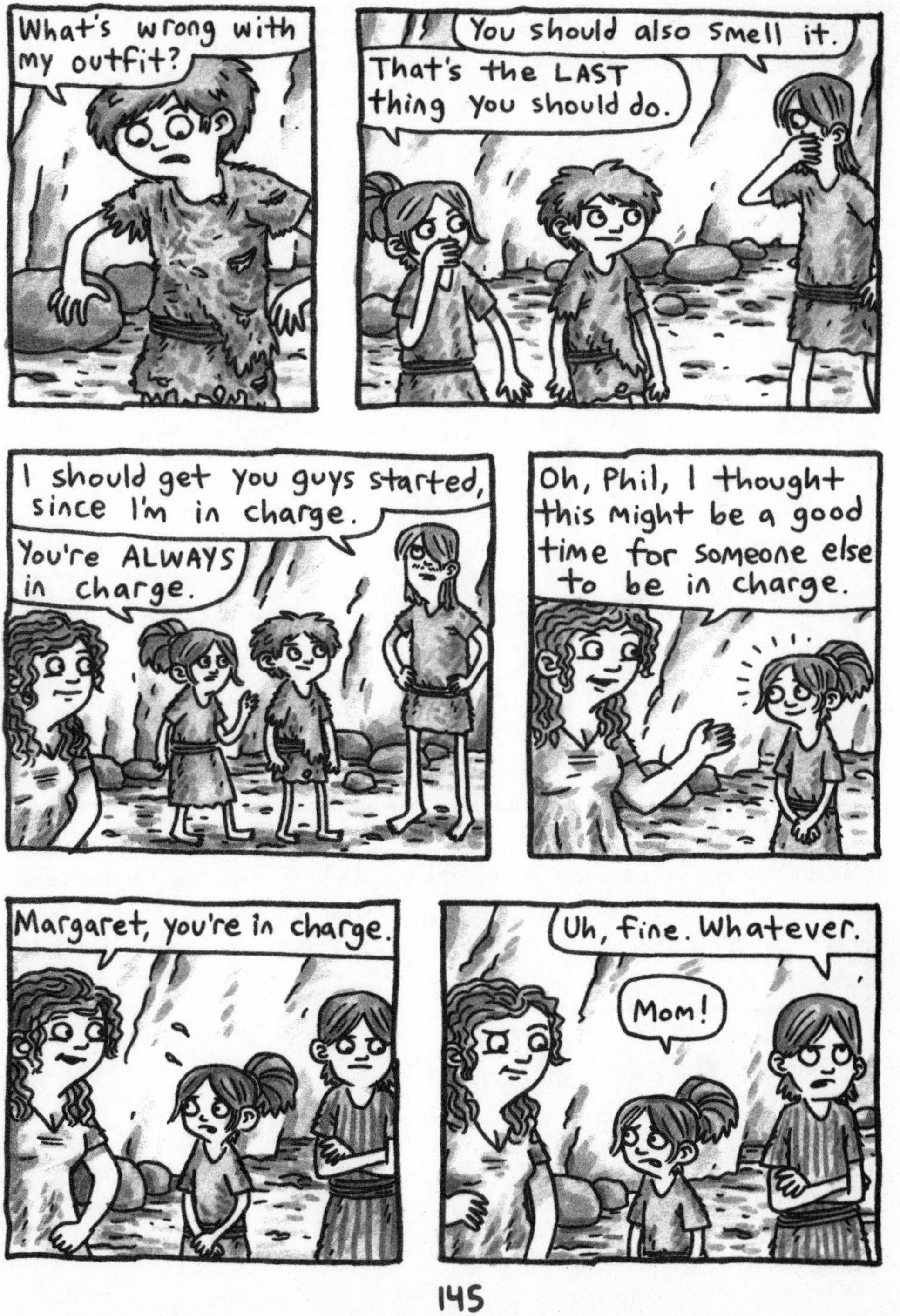
What's wrong with my outfit?
You should also smell it.
That's the LAST thing you should do.
I should get you guys started, since I'm in charge.
You're ALWAYS in charge.
Oh, Phil, I thought this might be a good time for someone else to be in charge.
Margaret, you're in charge.
Uh, fine. Whatever.
Mom!

147

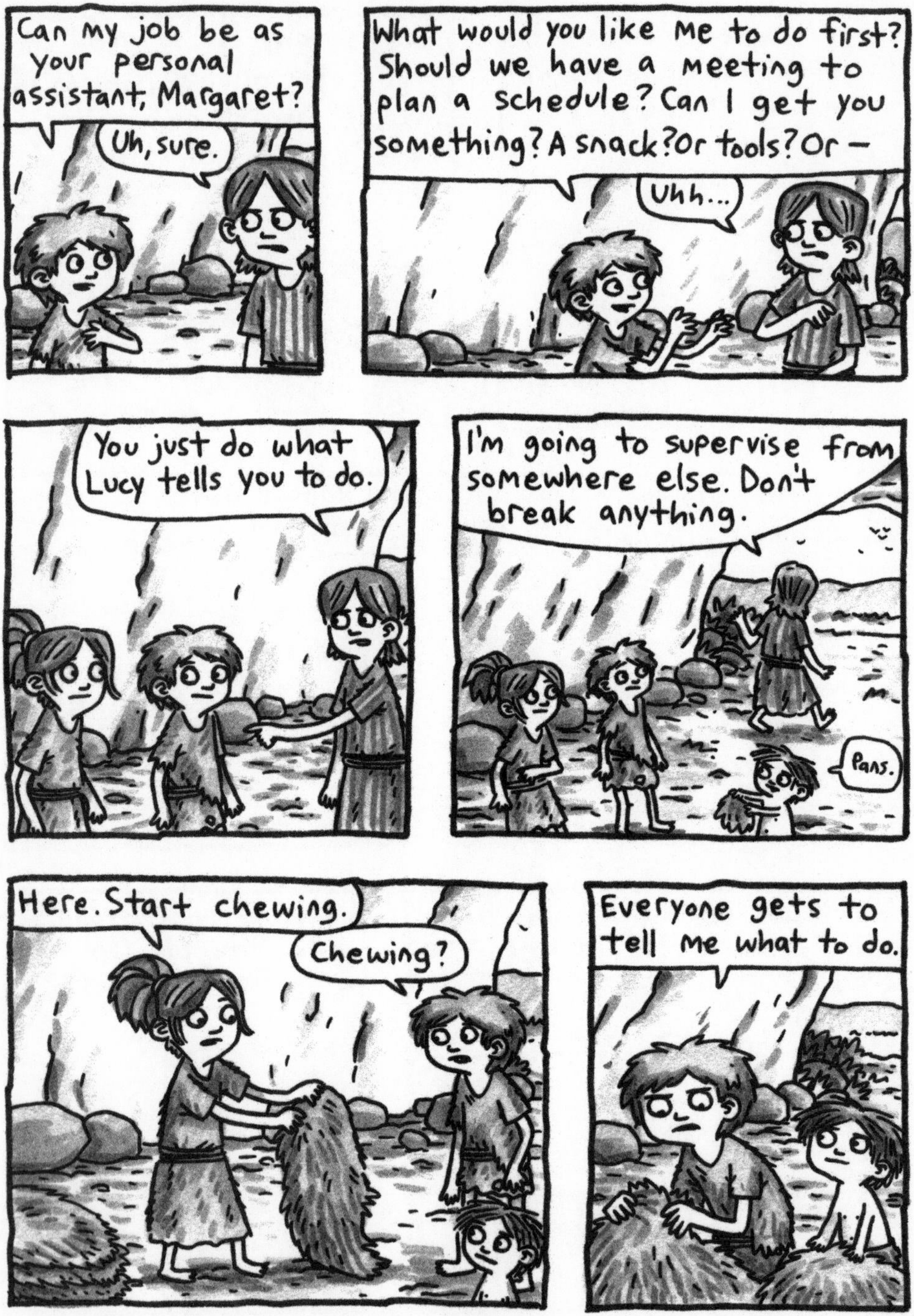
Can my job be as your personal assistant, Margaret?
Uh, sure.
What would you like me to do first? Should we have a meeting to plan a schedule? Can I get you something? A snack? Or tools? Or —
Uhh...
You just do what Lucy tells you to do.
I'm going to supervise from somewhere else. Don't break anything.
Pans.
Here. Start chewing.
Chewing?
Everyone gets to tell me what to do.

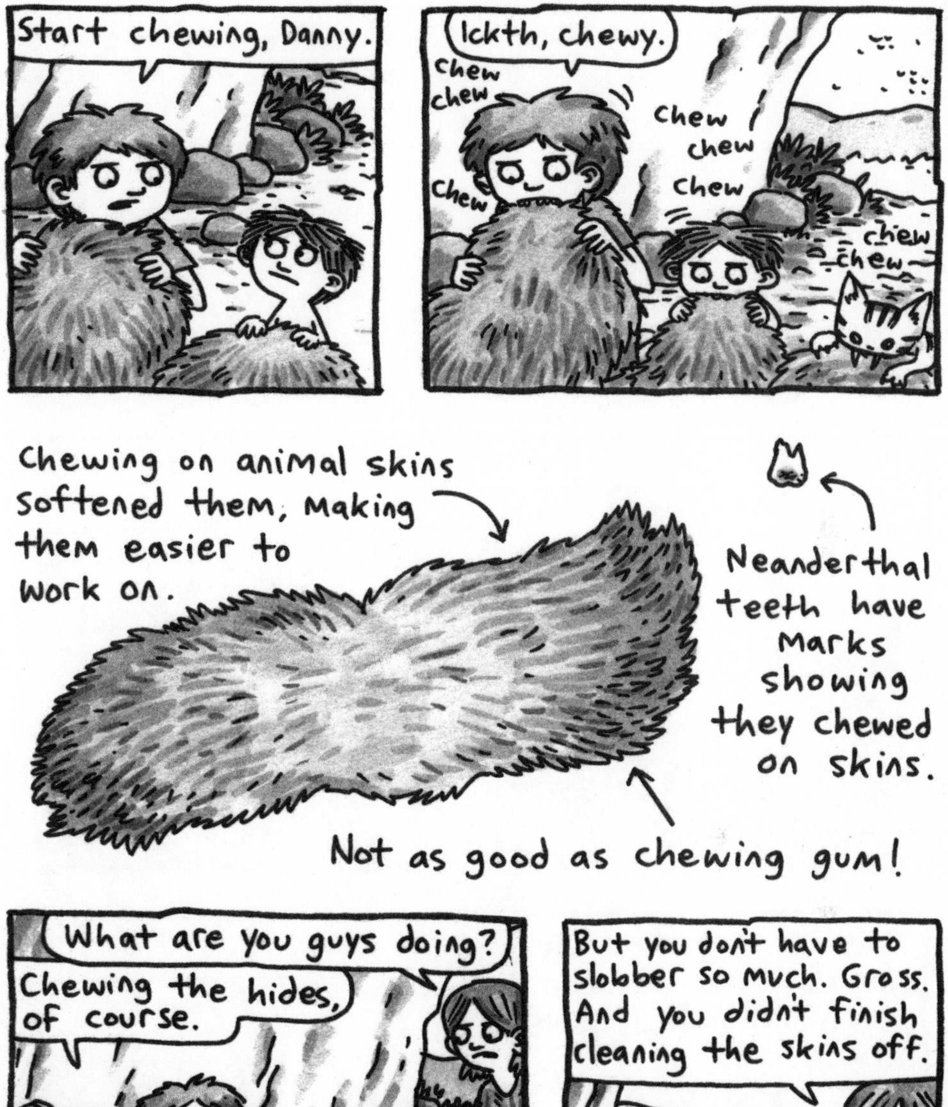
Start chewing, Danny.
Ickth, chewy.
chew chew
Chew
Chew chew chew
chew chew
Chewing on animal skins softened them, making them easier to work on.
Neanderthal teeth have marks showing they chewed on skins.
Not as good as chewing gum!
What are you guys doing?
Chewing the hides, of course.
But you don't have to slobber so much. Gross. And you didn't finish cleaning the skins off.

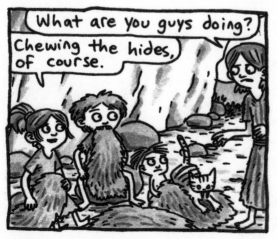

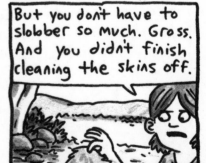

152

Twisted plant fibers were used as string!

Doesn't naturally grow that way!

The fibers have been found in Neanderthal territory from a time before humans. This shows that Neanderthals didn't always copy them.

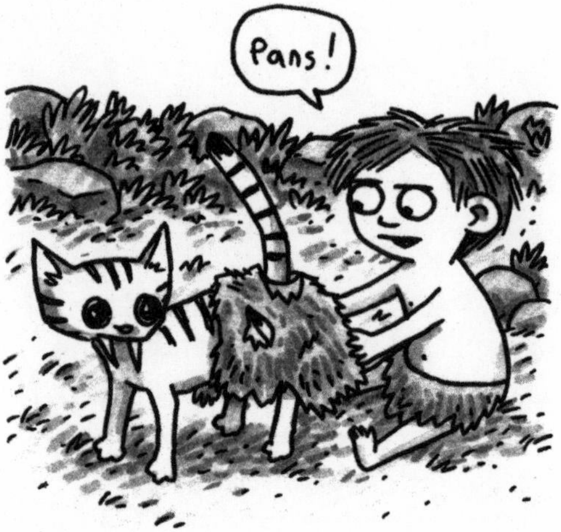
Pans!

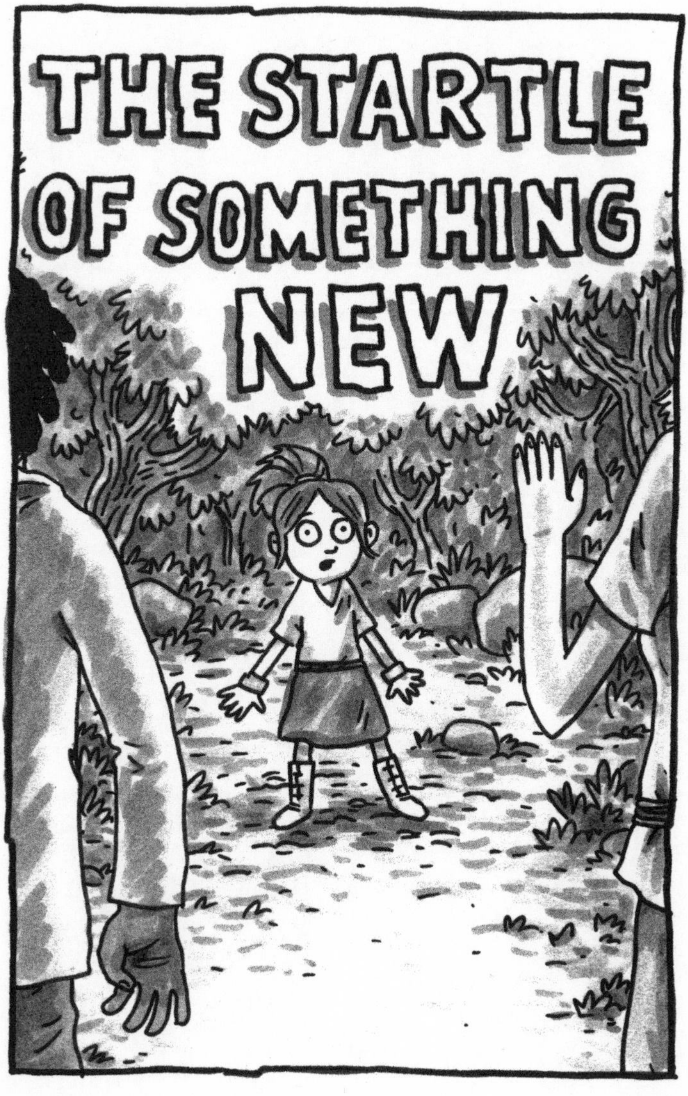
THE STARTLE OF SOMETHING NEW

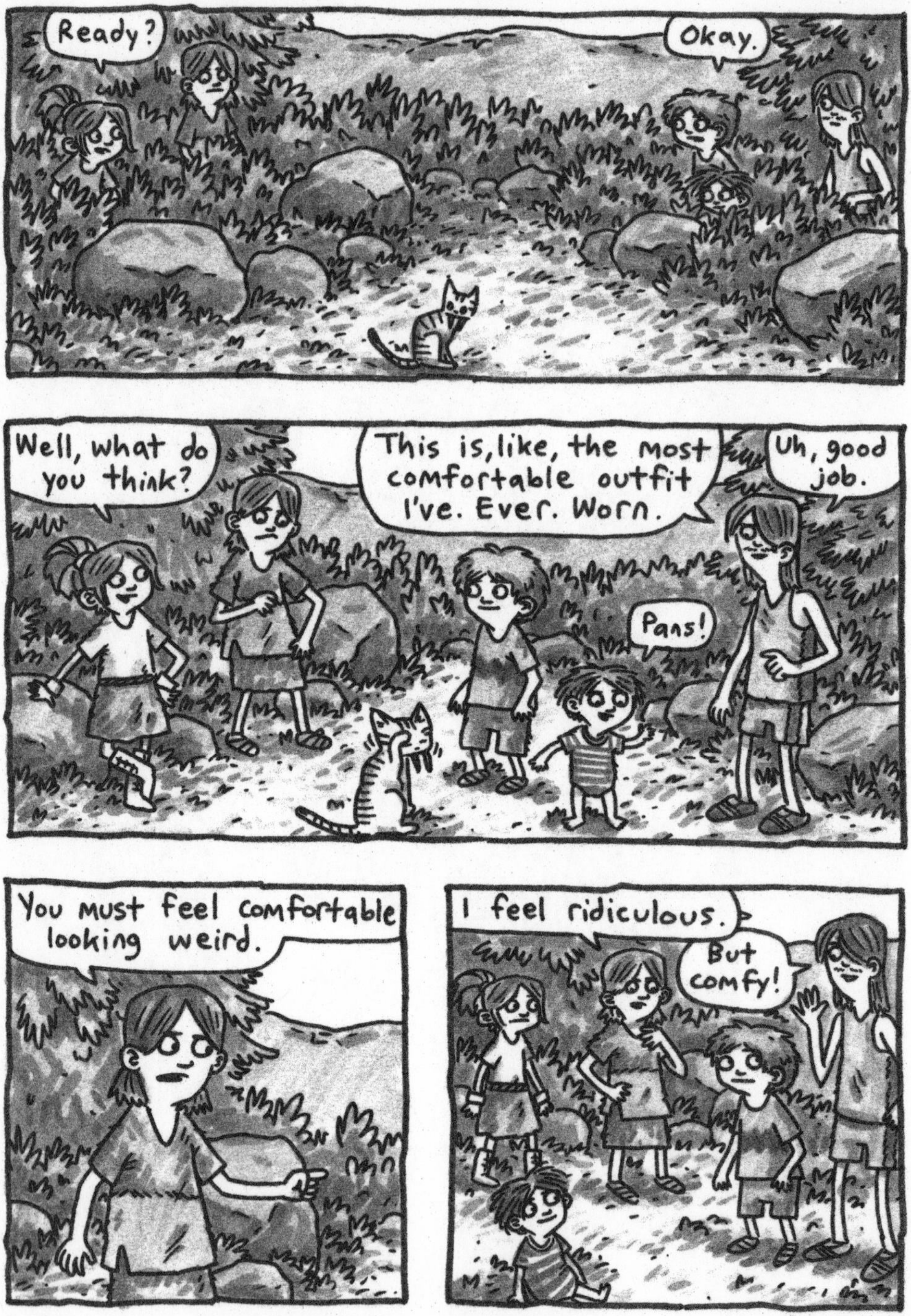
Ready?
Okay.
Well, what do you think?
This is, like, the most comfortable outfit I've. Ever. Worn.
Uh, good job.
Pans!
You must feel comfortable looking weird.
I feel ridiculous.
But comfy!

159

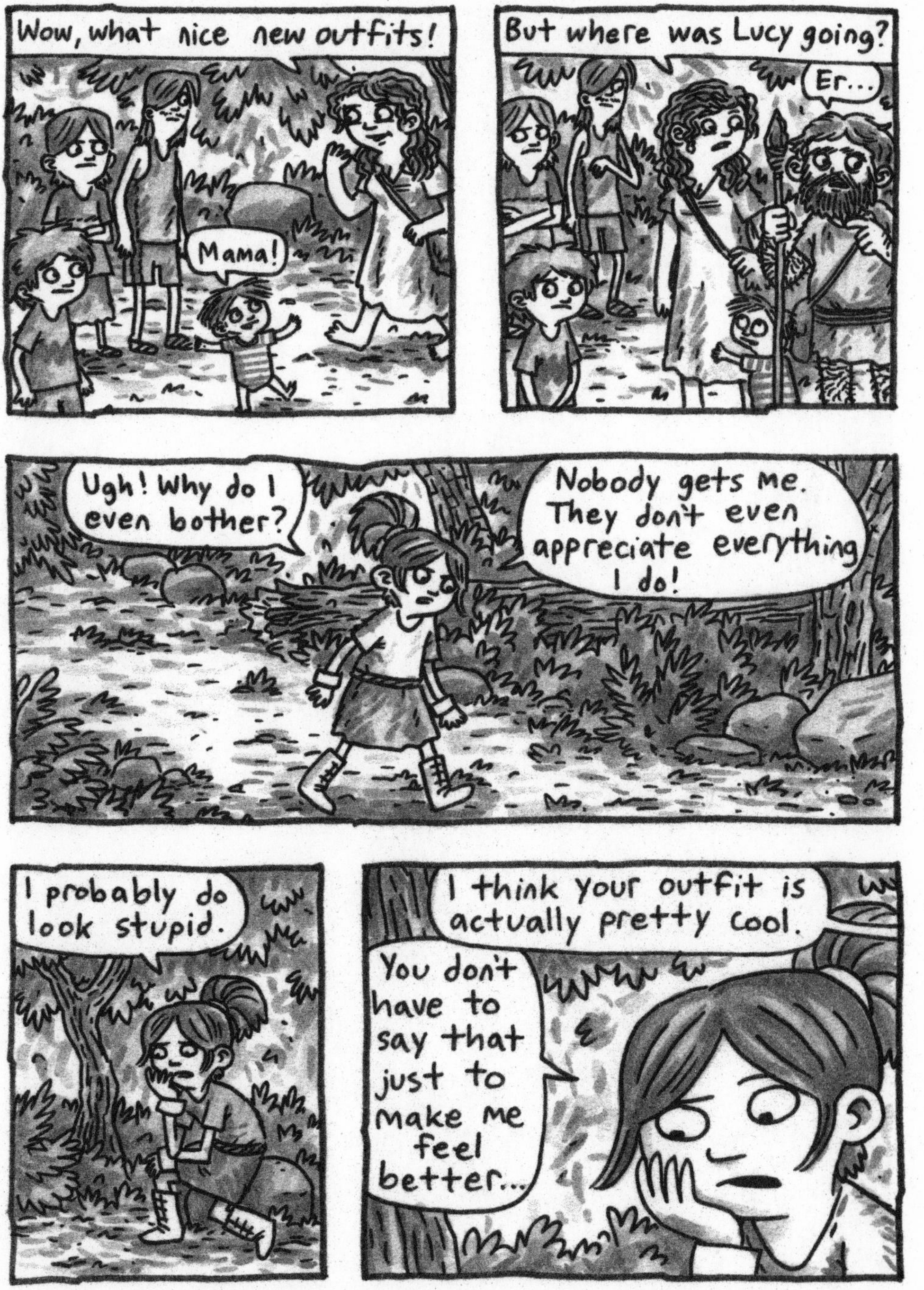
Wow, what nice new outfits!
Mama!
But where was Lucy going?
Er...
Ugh! Why do I even bother?
Nobody gets me. They don't even appreciate everything I do!
I probably do look stupid.
I think your outfit is actually pretty cool.
You don't have to say that just to make me feel better...

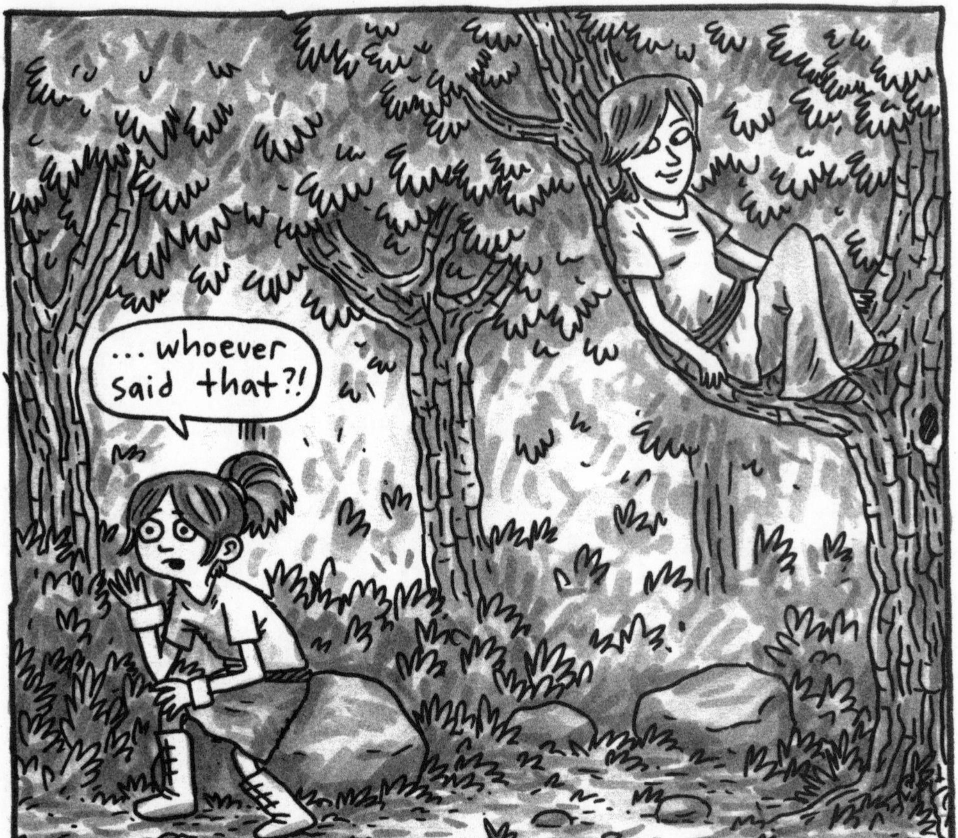
...whoever said that?!

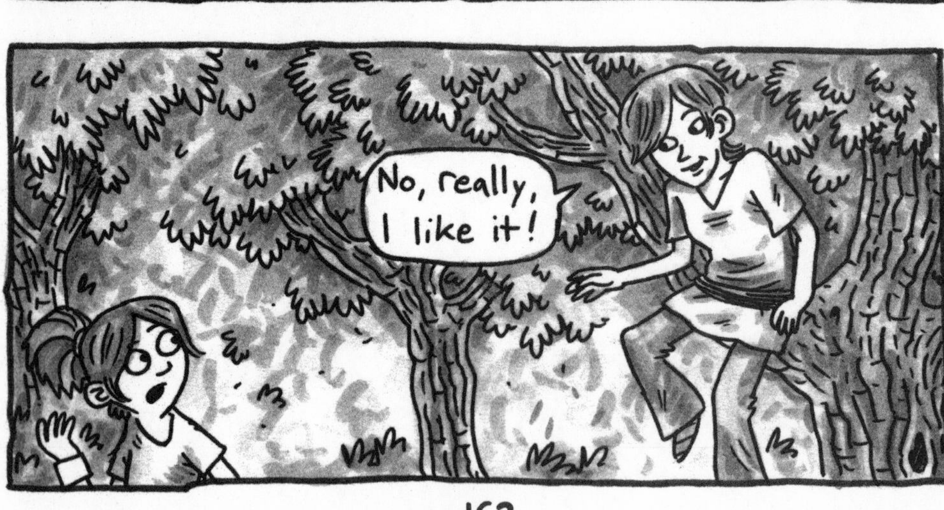
No, really, I like it!

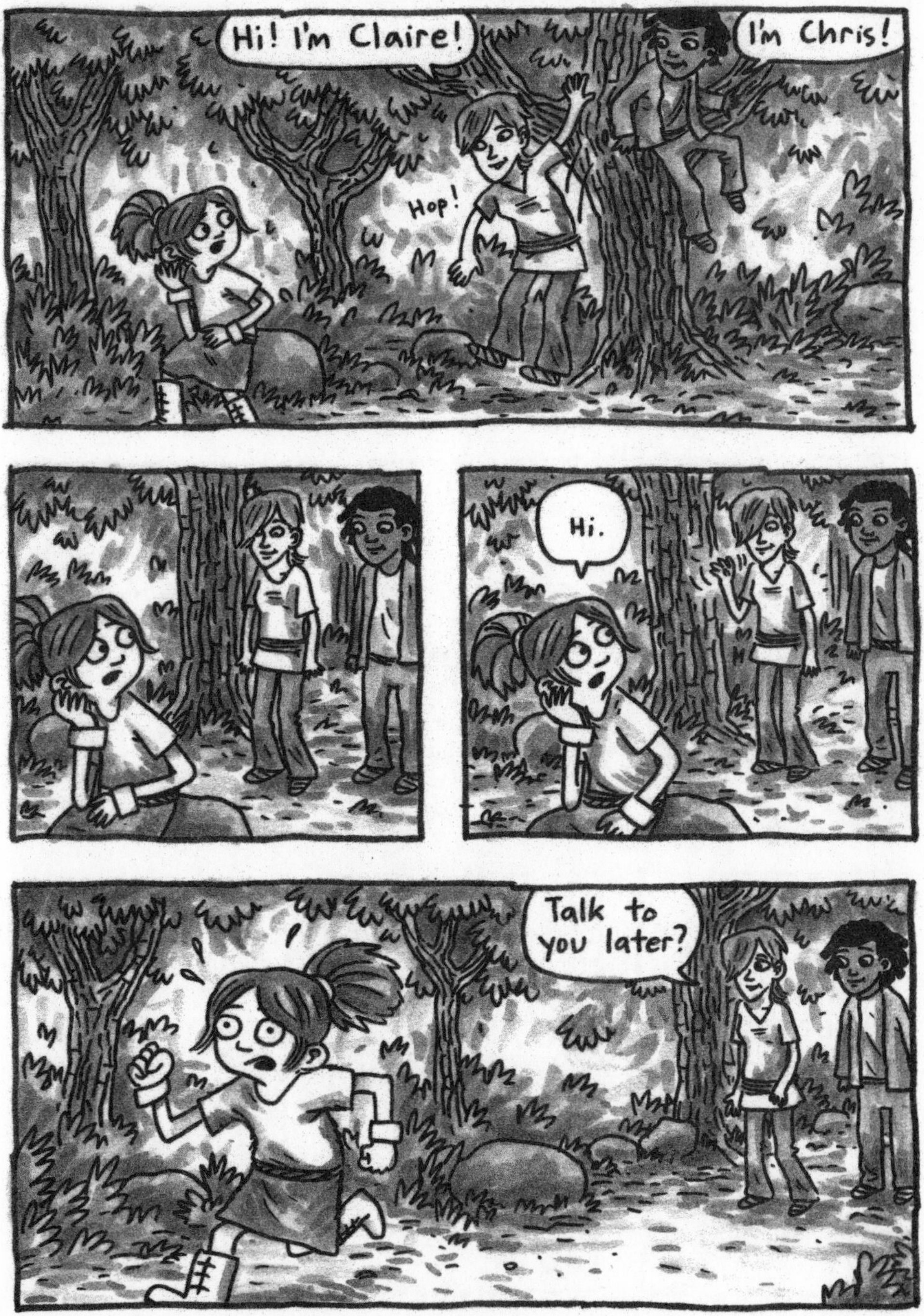
Hi! I'm Claire!
I'm Chris!
Hop!
Hi.
Talk to you later?

164

165

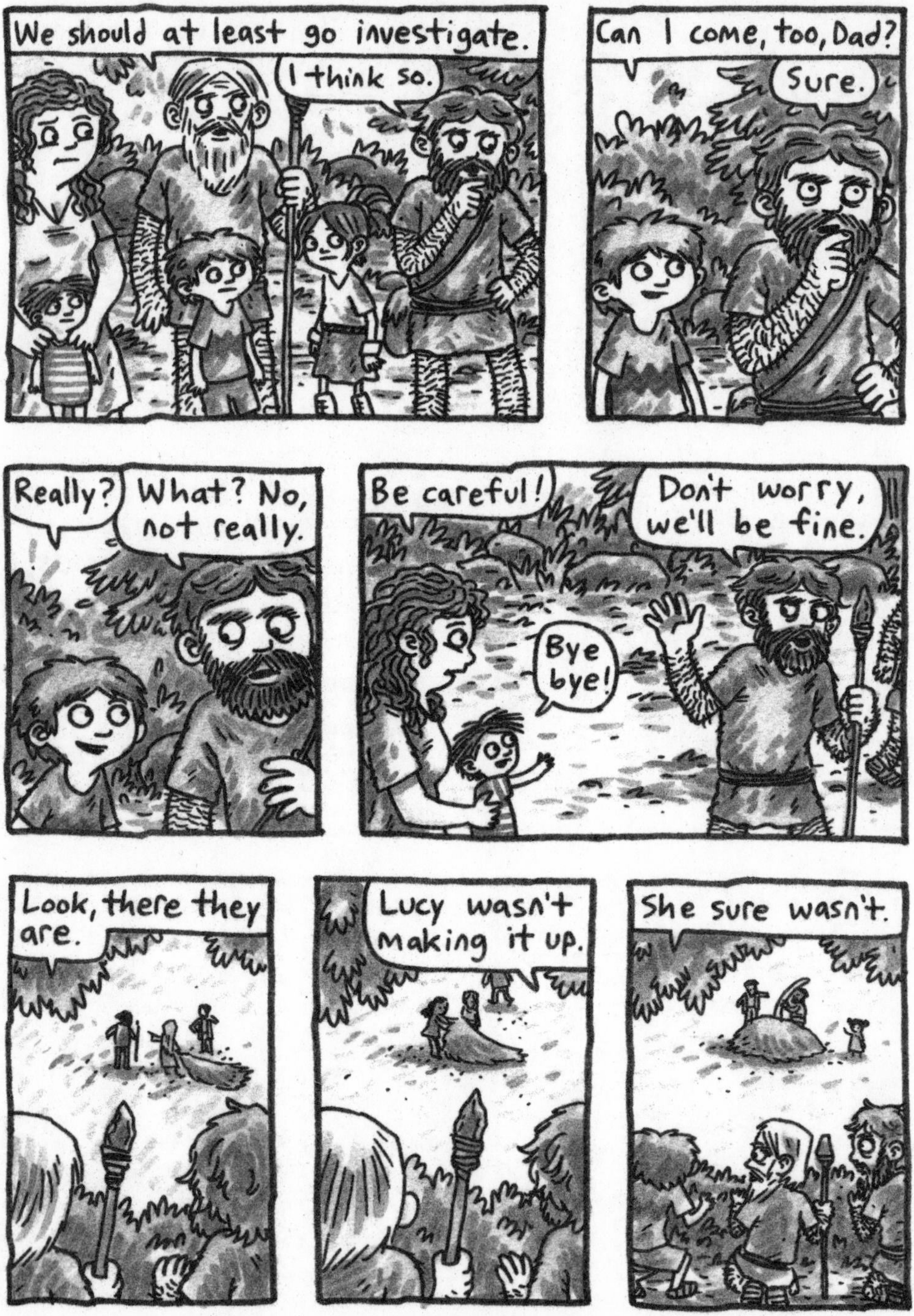
We should at least go investigate.
I think so.
Can I come, too, Dad?
Sure.
Really?
What? No, not really.
Be careful!
Don't worry, we'll be fine.
Bye bye!
Look, there they are.
Lucy wasn't making it up.
She sure wasn't.

The overall differences between early humans and Neanderthals were more pronounced than differences between any two humans today.

However, any single characteristic of Neanderthals — such as their brow ridge, lack of chin, or stout, thick limbs — can be found on different humans individually.

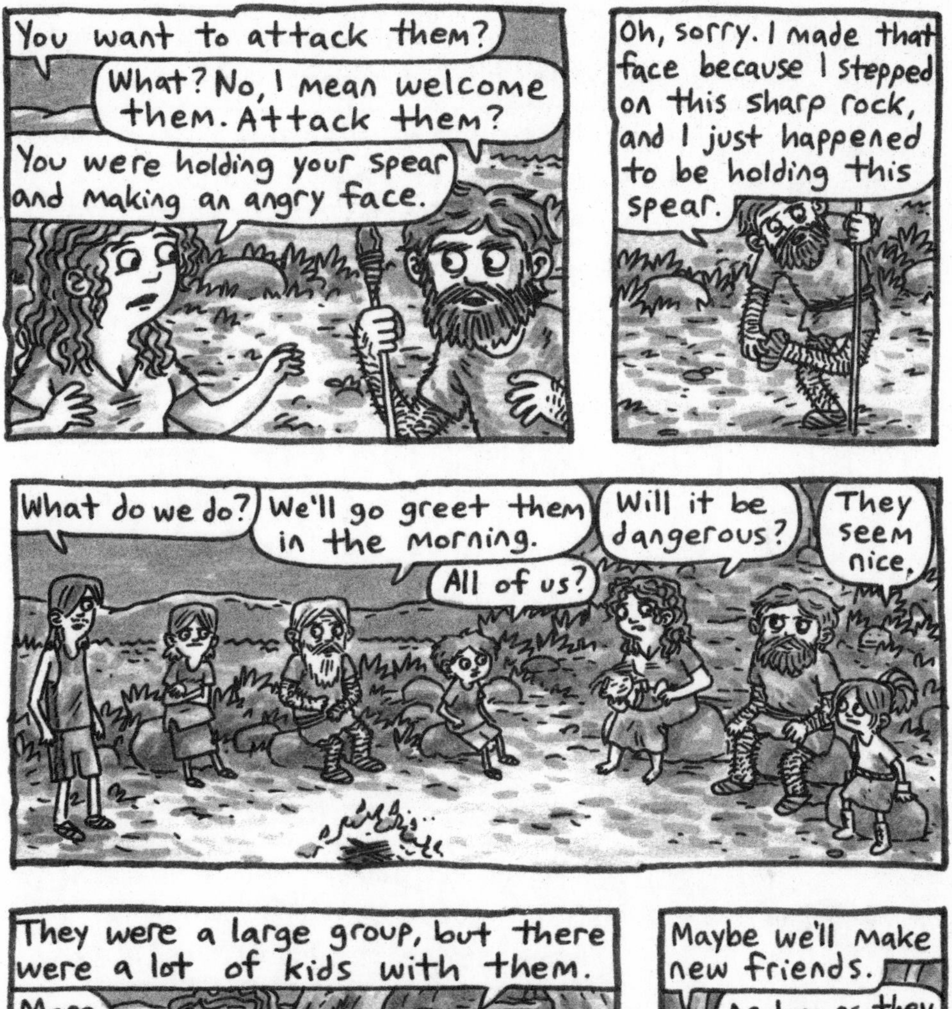
You want to attack them?
What? No, I mean welcome them. Attack them?
You were holding your spear and making an angry face.
Oh, sorry. I made that face because I stepped on this sharp rock, and I just happened to be holding this spear.
What do we do?
We'll go greet them in the morning.
All of us?
Will it be dangerous?
They seem nice.
They were a large group, but there were a lot of kids with them.
More kids?
Other kids?
Maybe we'll make new friends.
As long as they don't boss me around, too.

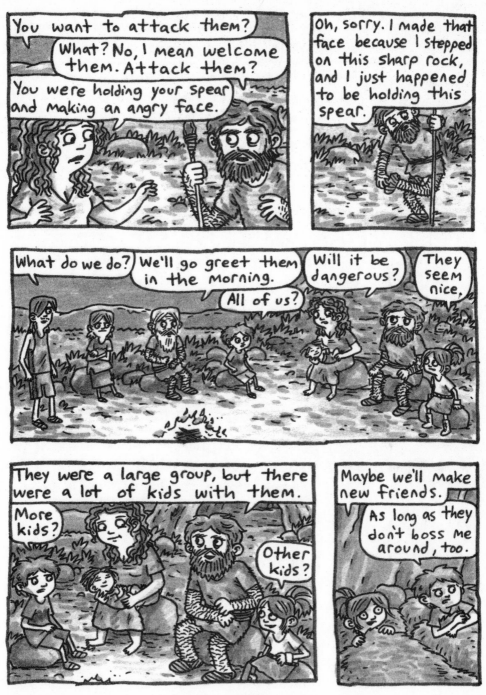

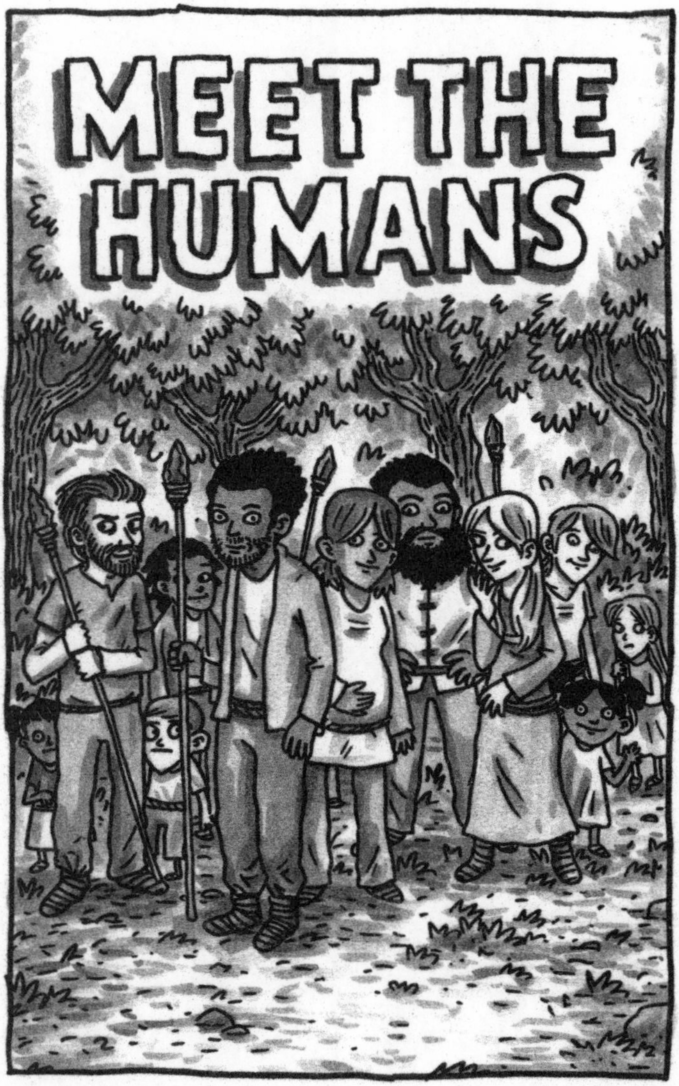
MEET THE HUMANS

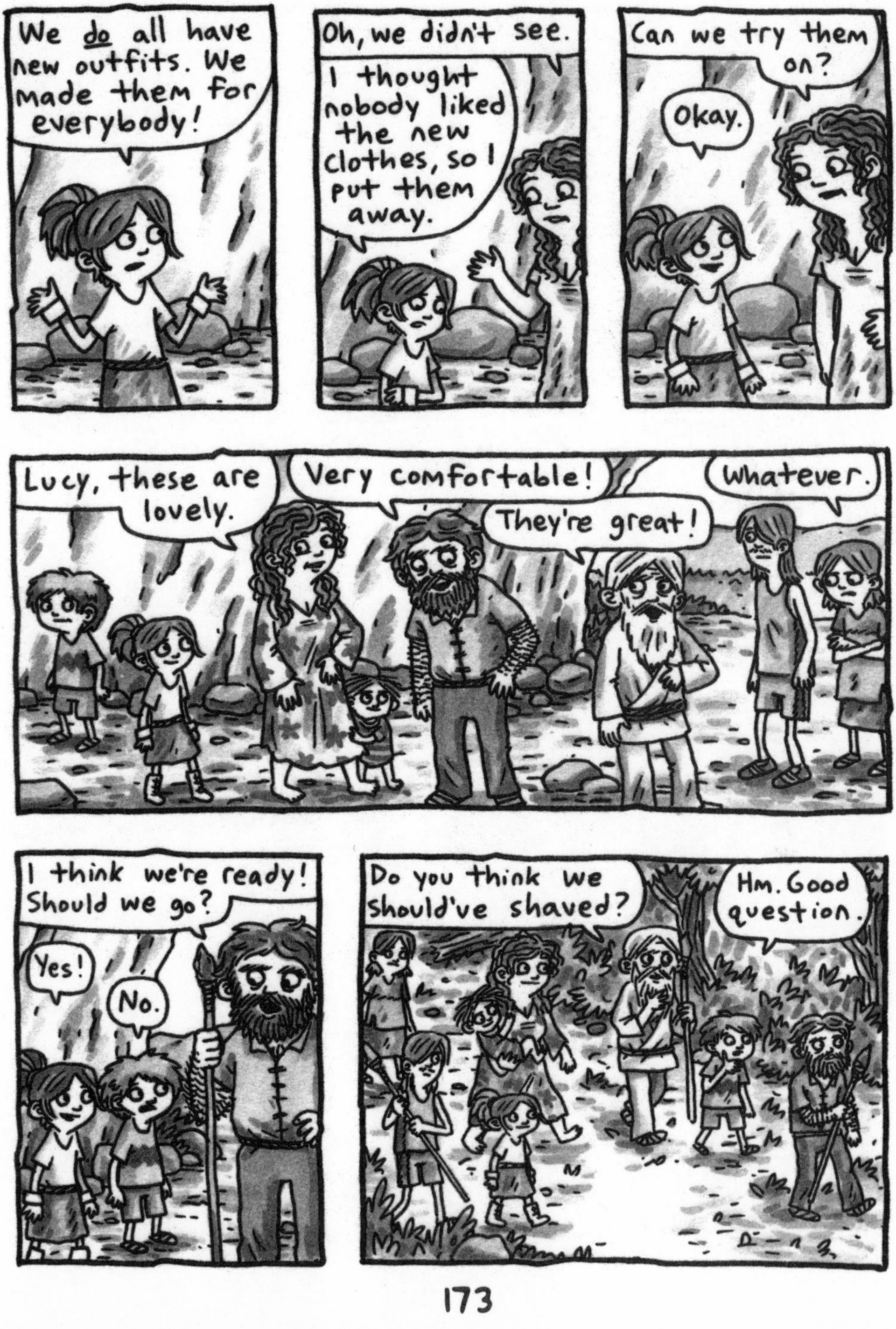
We do all have new outfits. We made them for everybody!
Oh, we didn't see.
I thought nobody liked the new clothes, so I put them away.
Can we try them on?
Okay.
Lucy, these are lovely.
Very comfortable!
They're great!
Whatever.
I think we're ready! Should we go?
Yes!
No.
Do you think we should've shaved?
Hm. Good question.

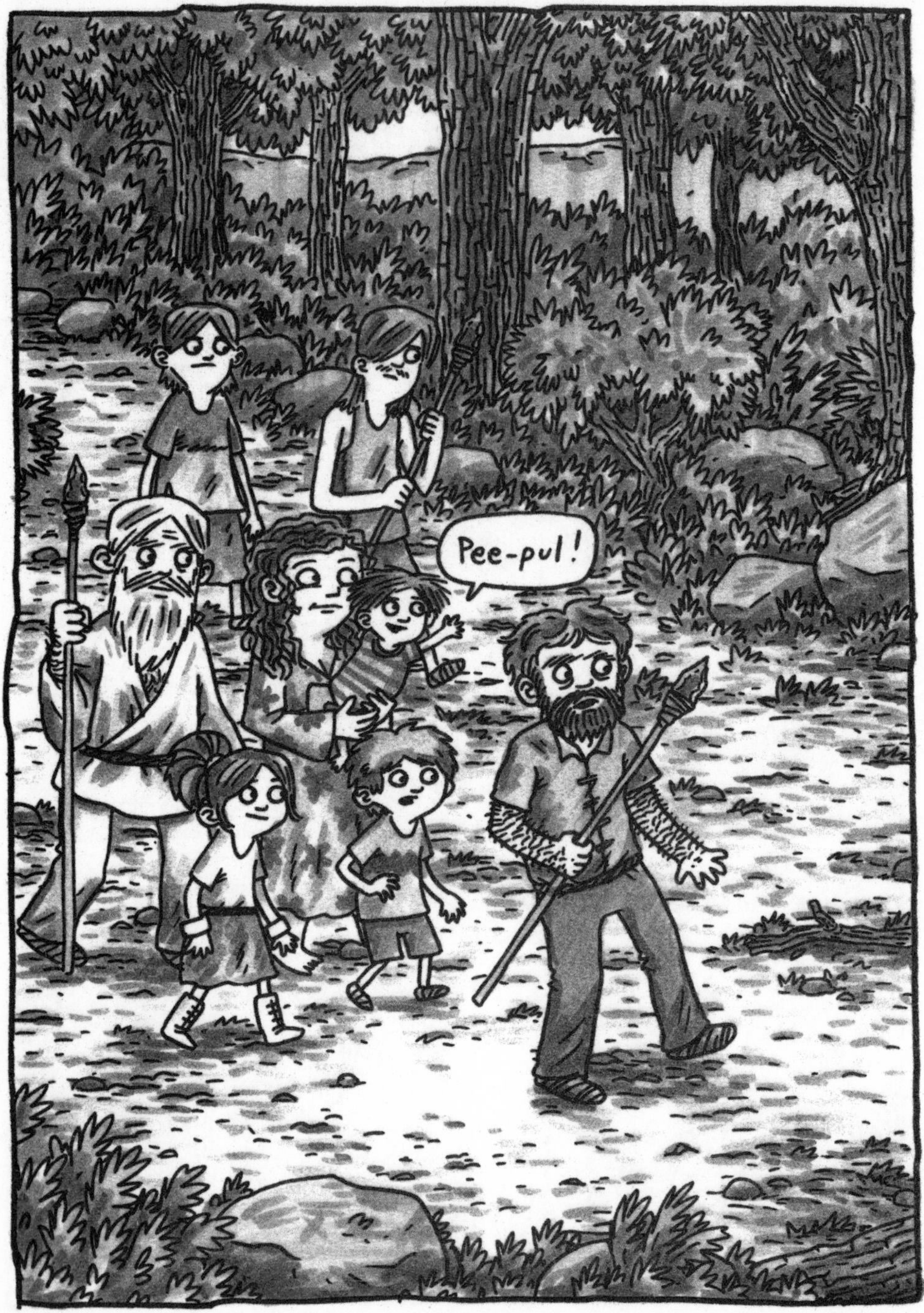
Pee-pul!

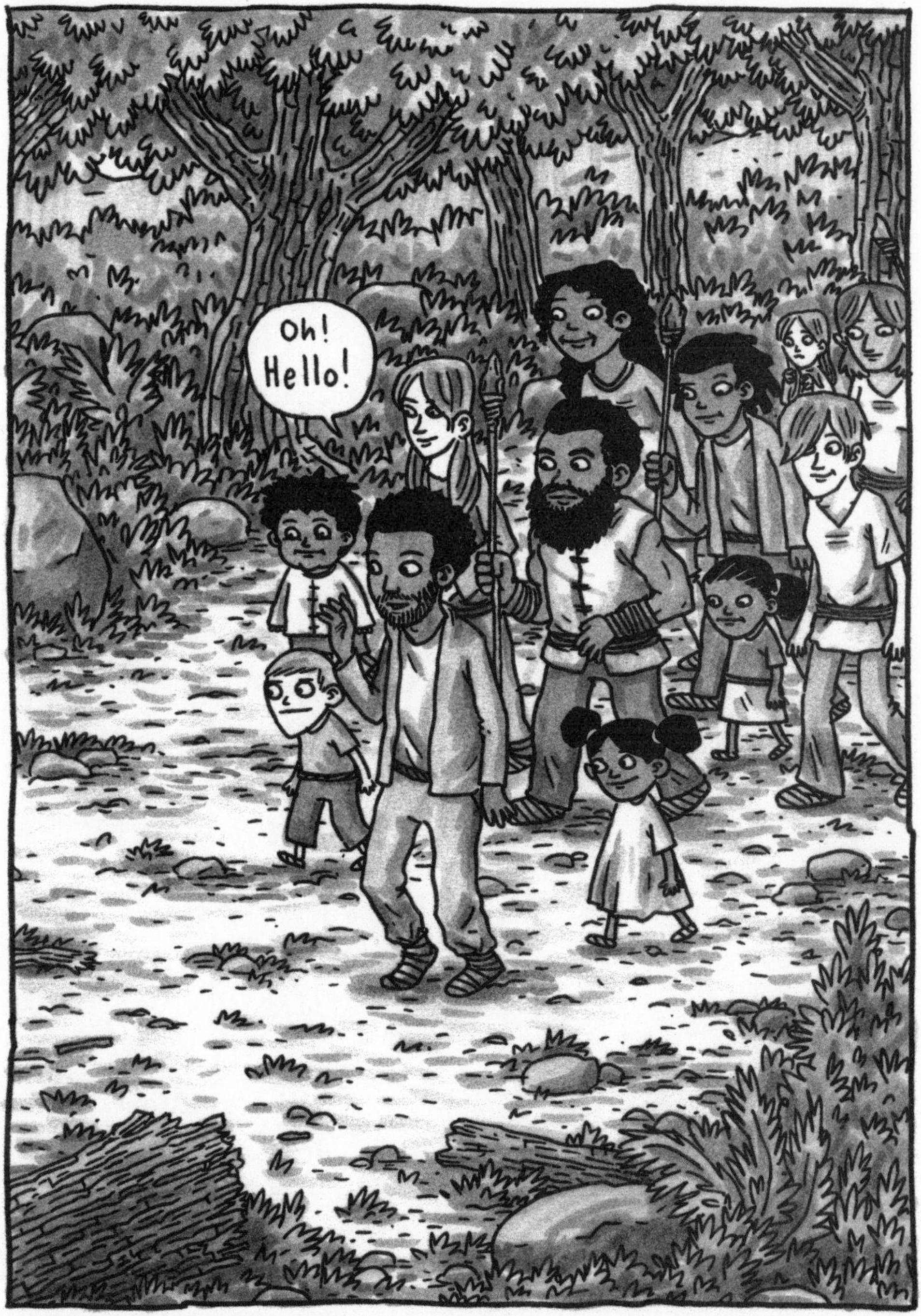
Oh! Hello!

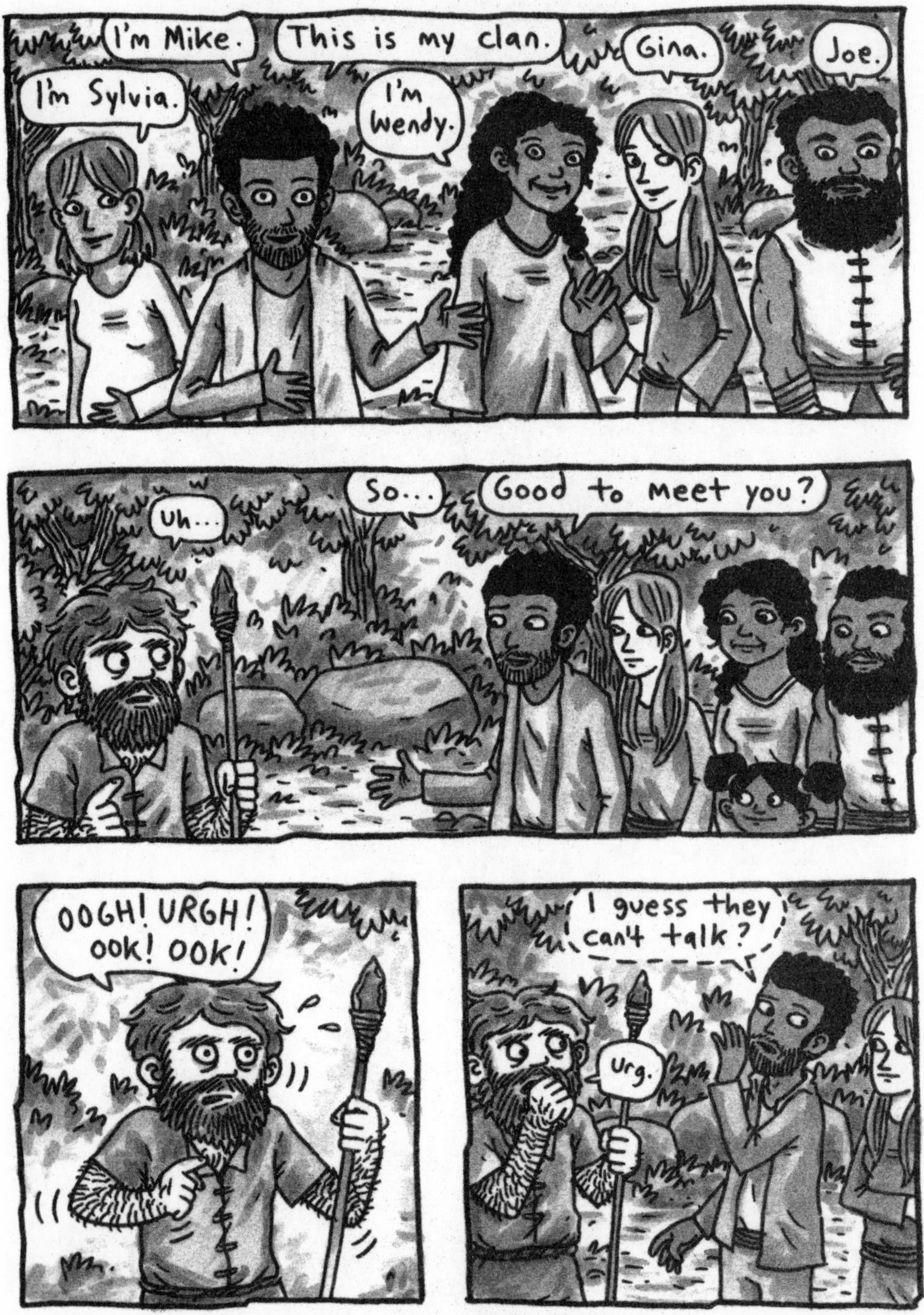
I'm Sylvia.
I'm Mike.
This is my clan.
I'm Wendy.
Gina.
Joe.
Uh...
So...
Good to meet you?
OOGH! URGH! OOK! OOK!
I guess they can't talk?
Urg.

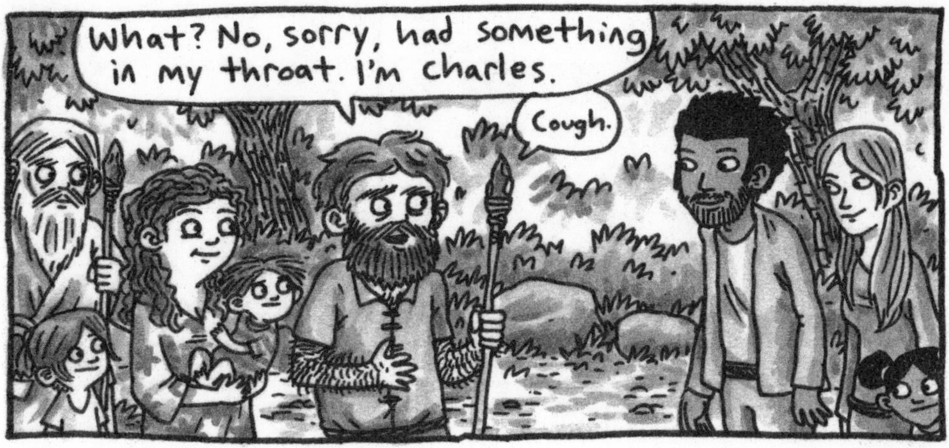
What? No, sorry, had something in my throat. I'm Charles.
Cough.

Humans have a hyoid bone – a small bone allowing the mouth and tongue to create complex sounds.

Scientists have discovered Neanderthals had a similar hyoid bone.

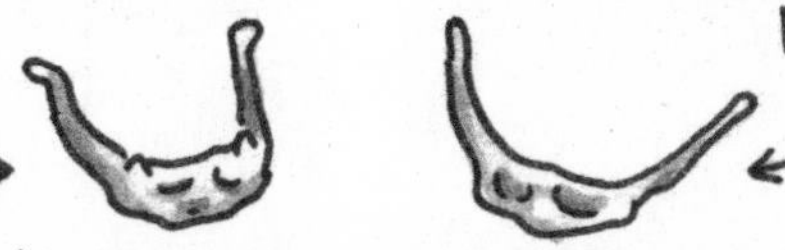

Neanderthals may not have been able to make the same range of sounds as humans, but they communicated with more than simple grunts and pointing!

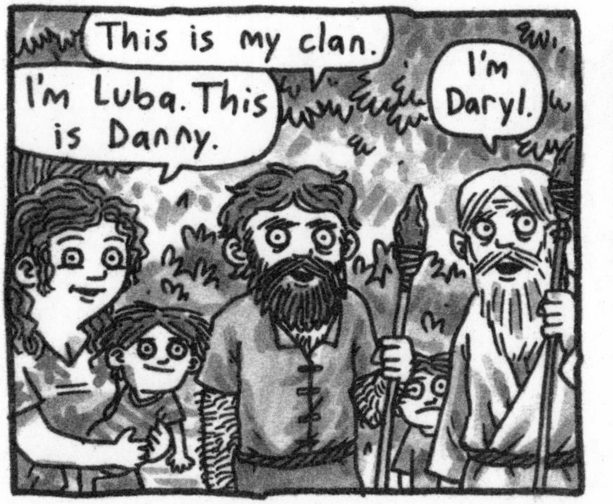
This is my clan.
I'm Luba. This is Danny.
I'm Daryl.

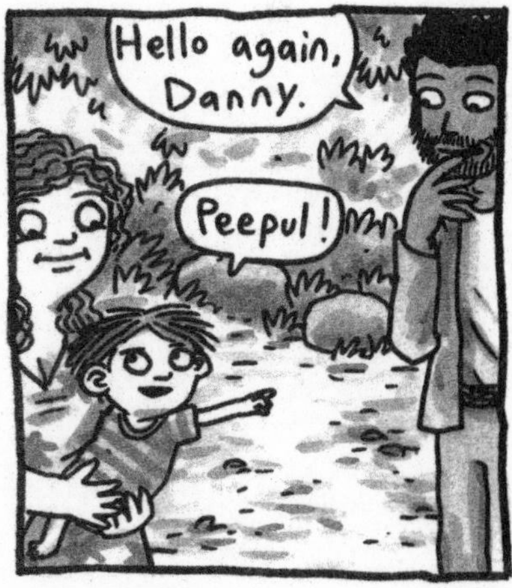
Hello again, Danny.
Peepul!

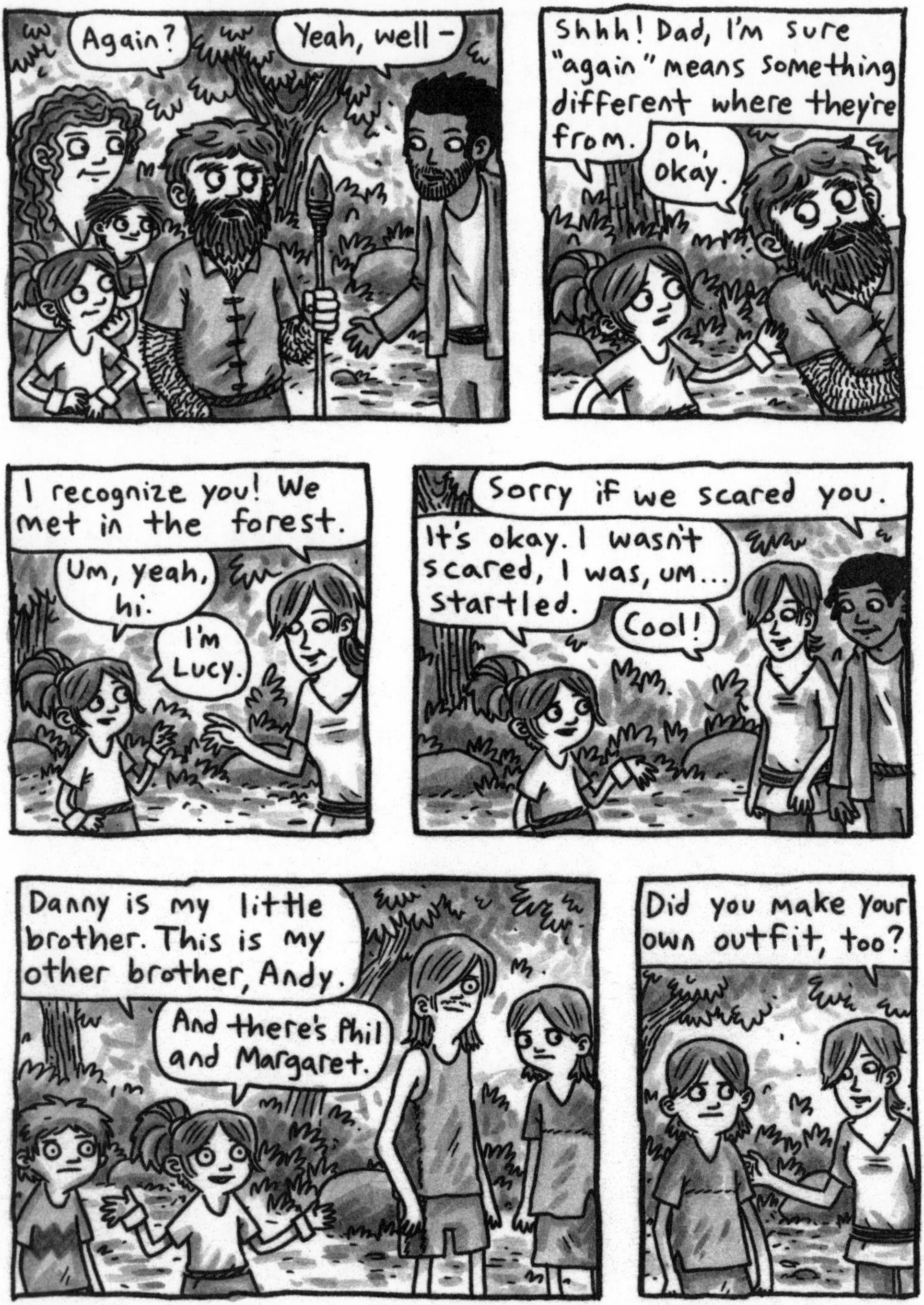

Again?
Yeah, well-
Shhh! Dad, I'm sure "again" means something different where they're from.
Oh, okay.
I recognize you! We met in the forest.
Um, yeah, hi.
I'm Lucy.
Sorry if we scared you.
It's okay. I wasn't scared, I was, um... startled.
Cool!
Danny is my little brother. This is my other brother, Andy.
And there's Phil and Margaret.
Did you make your own outfit, too?

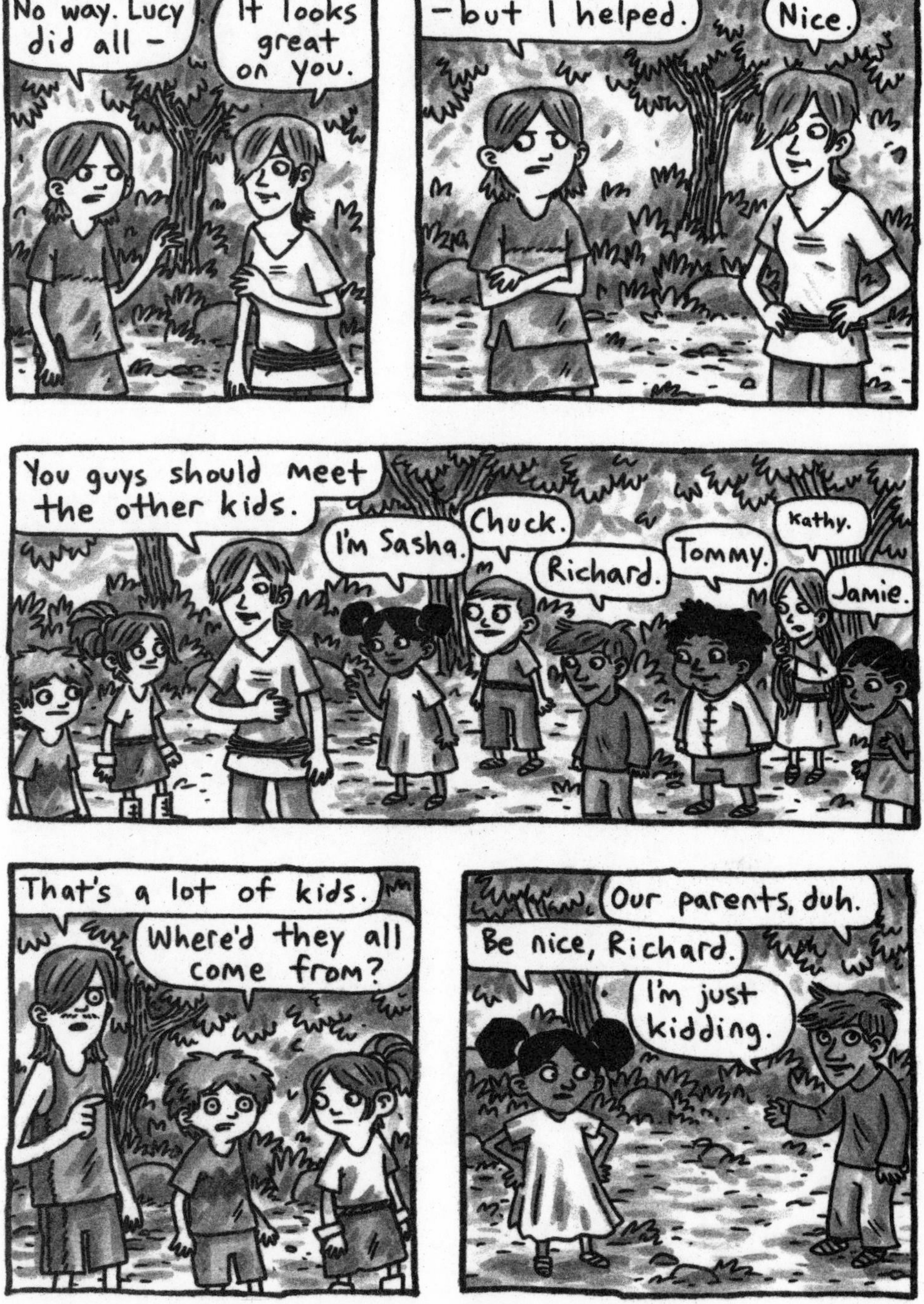
No way. Lucy did all -
It looks great on you.
-but I helped.
Nice.
You guys should meet the other kids.
I'm Sasha.
Chuck.
Richard.
Tommy.
Kathy.
Jamie.
That's a lot of kids.
Where'd they all come from?
Our parents, duh.
Be nice, Richard.
I'm just kidding.

Humans migrated north from Africa, through the Middle East, spreading out as their populations grew.

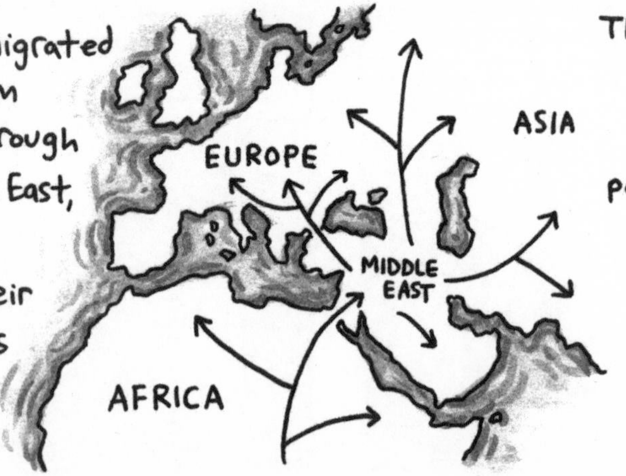

There were no cars or bikes — people didn't even ride horses yet. So it took thousands of years!

183

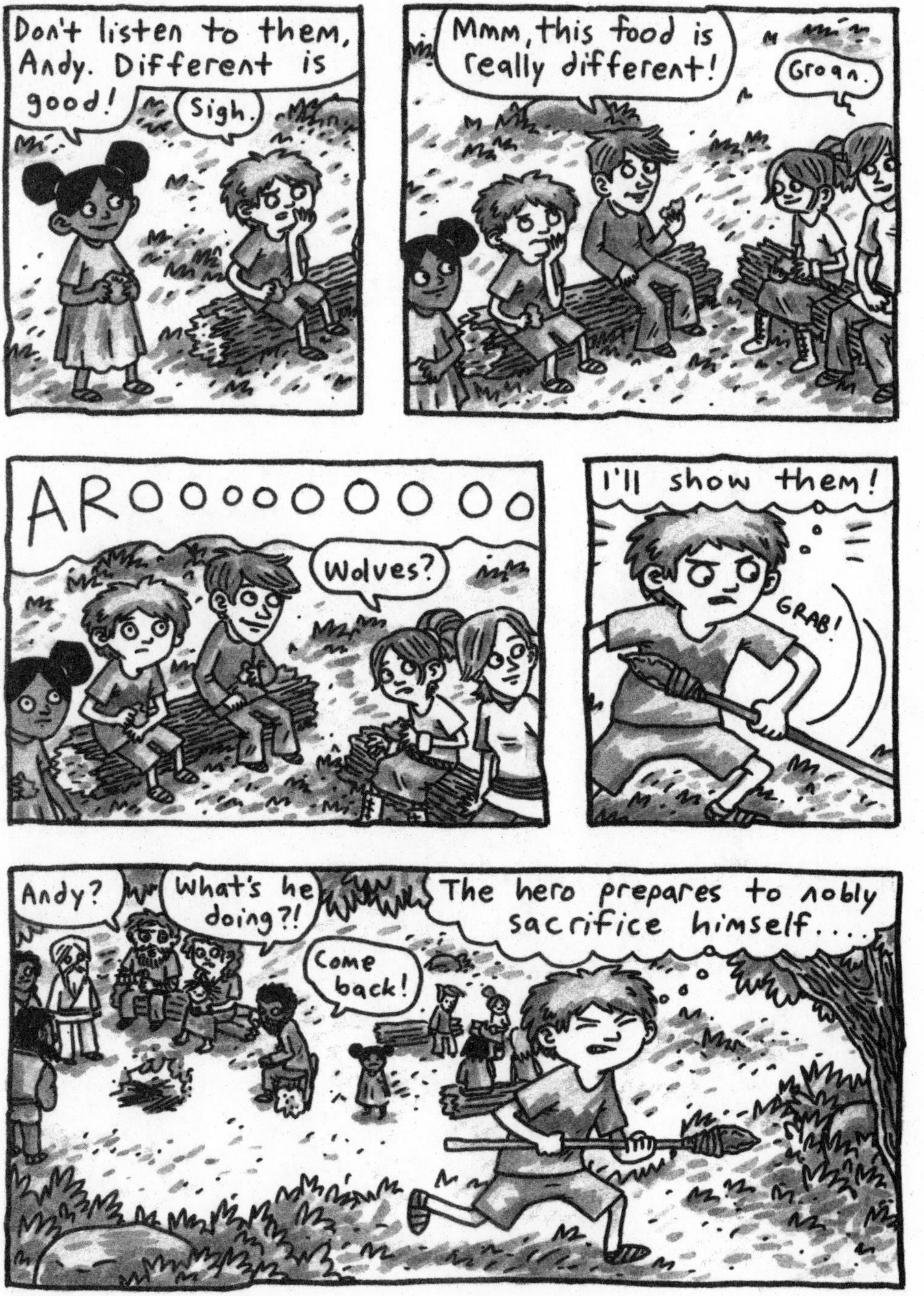
Don't listen to them, Andy. Different is good!
Sigh.
Mmm, this food is really different!
Groan.
AROOOOOOOOO
Wolves?
I'll show them!
GRAB!
Andy?
What's he doing?!
Come back!
The hero prepares to nobly sacrifice himself....

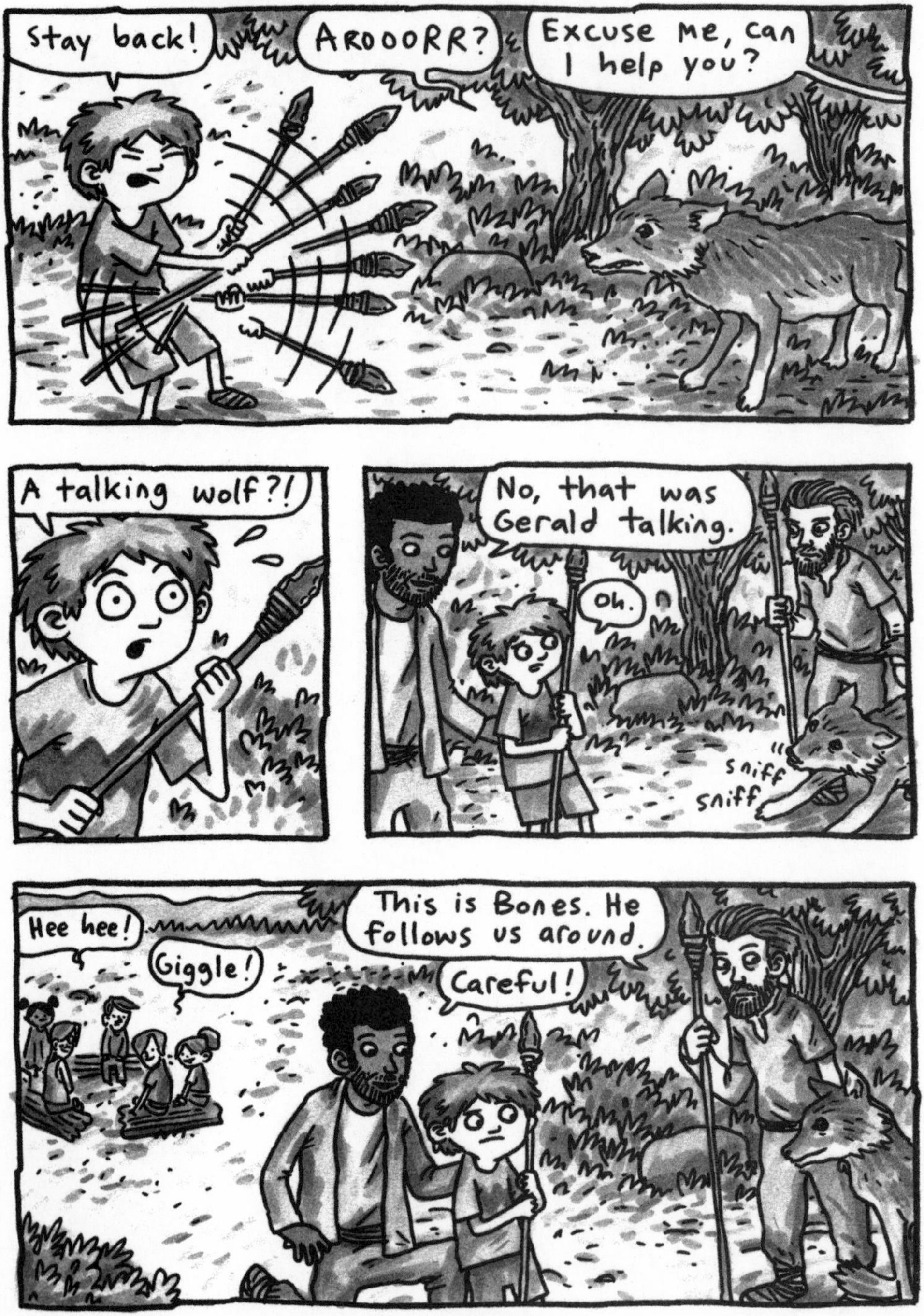
Stay back!
AROOORR?
Excuse me, can I help you?
A talking wolf?!
No, that was Gerald talking.
Oh.
sniff sniff
Hee hee!
Giggle!
This is Bones. He follows us around.
Careful!

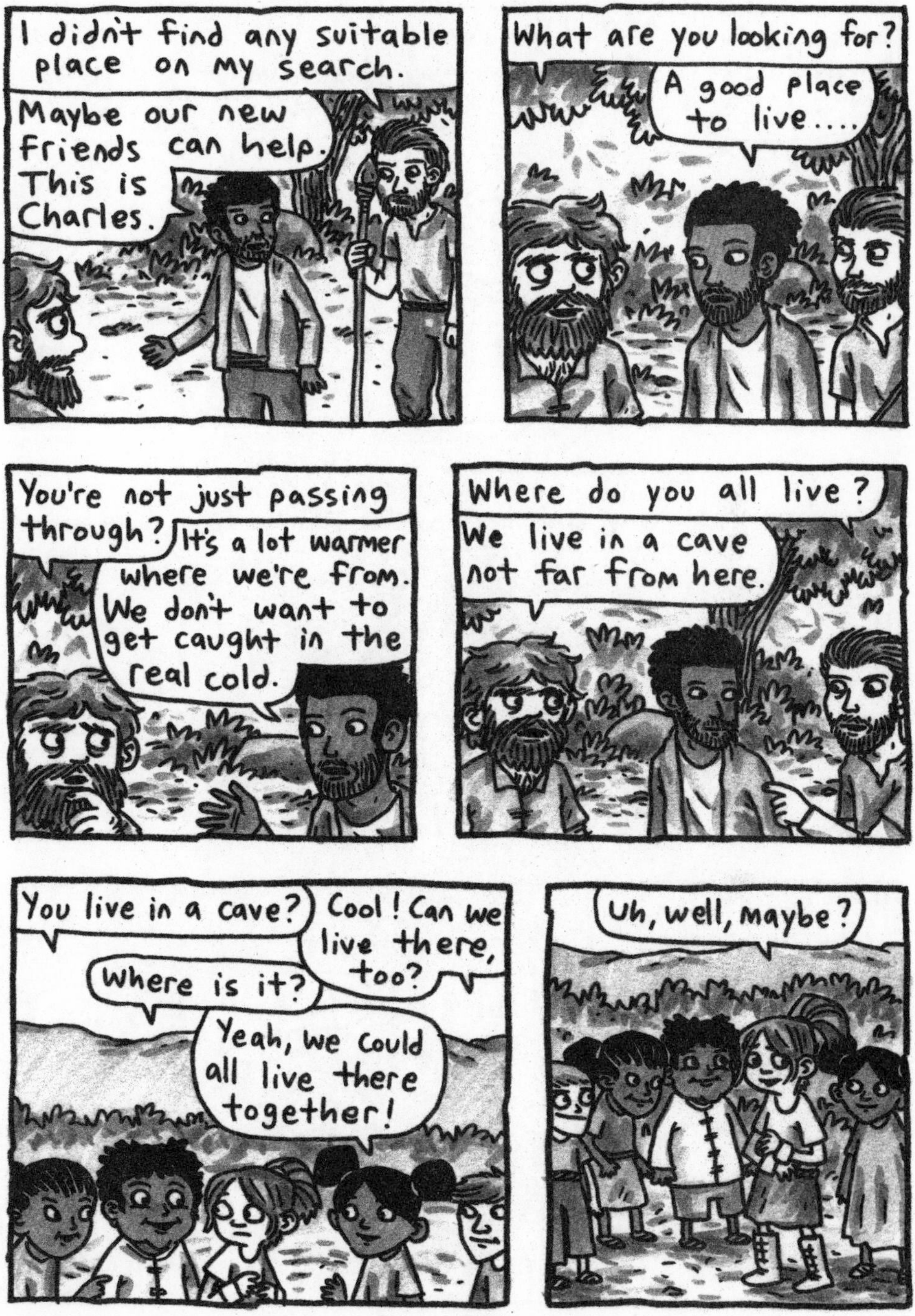
I didn't find any suitable place on my search.
Maybe our new friends can help. This is Charles.
What are you looking for?
A good place to live....
You're not just passing through?
It's a lot warmer where we're from. We don't want to get caught in the real cold.
Where do you all live?
We live in a cave not far from here.
You live in a cave?
Cool! Can we live there, too?
Where is it?
Yeah, we could all live there together!
Uh, well, maybe?

188

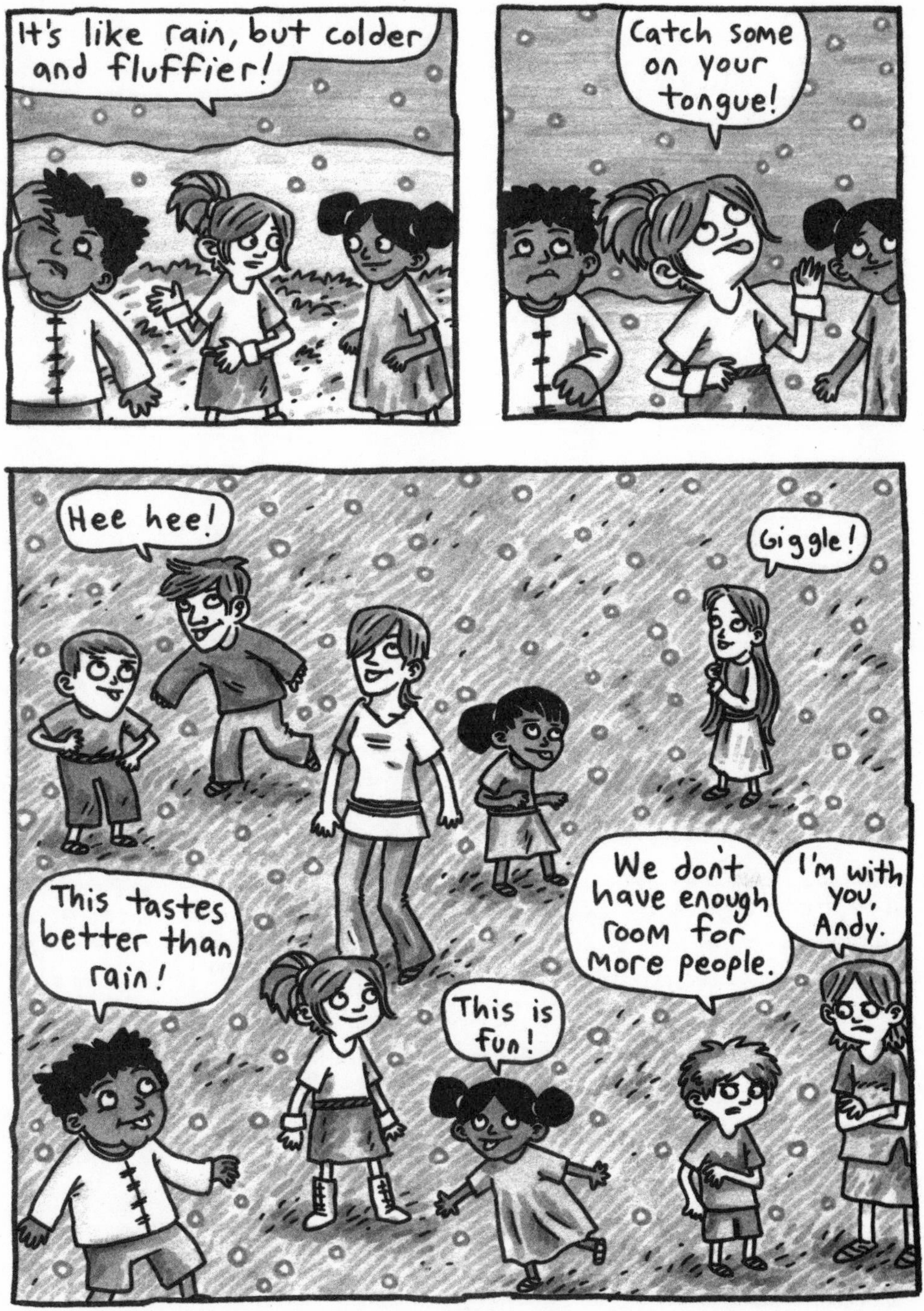
It's like rain, but colder and fluffier!
Catch some on your tongue!
Hee hee!
Giggle!
This tastes better than rain!
This is fun!
We don't have enough room for more people.
I'm with you, Andy.

191

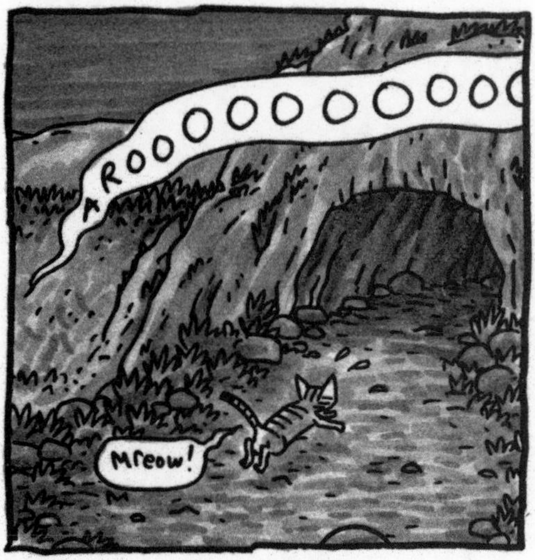
AROOOOOOOOOOOO
Mreow!

THE END

...OF THE NEANDERTHALS?!

FORTY THOUSAND YEARS LATER... (TODAY)

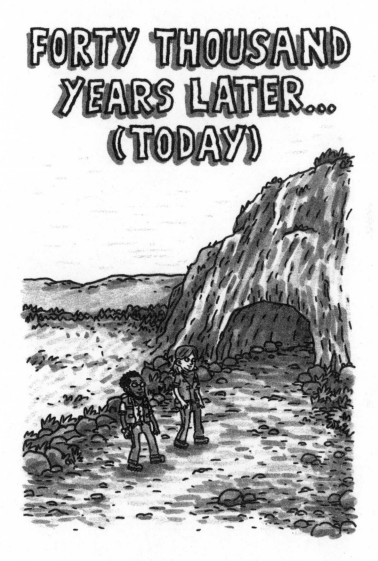

Some of the first Neanderthal fossils were found in Germany in 1856.

Workers digging in a limestone quarry

Caves were chosen based on a number of factors...

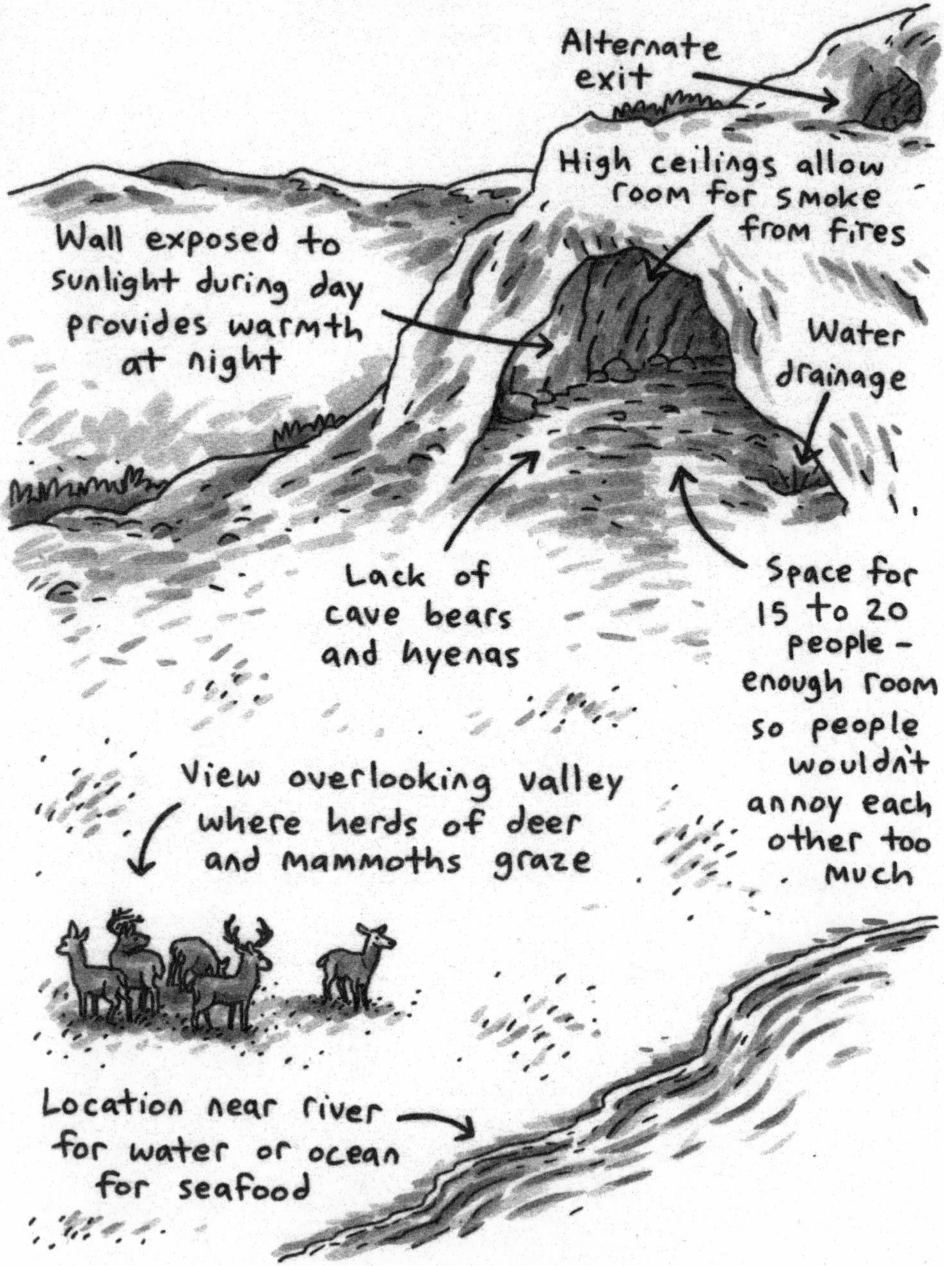
Alternate exit
High ceilings allow room for smoke from fires
Wall exposed to sunlight during day provides warmth at night
Water drainage
Lack of cave bears and hyenas
Space for 15 to 20 people - enough room so people wouldn't annoy each other too much
View overlooking valley where herds of deer and mammoths graze
Location near river for water or ocean for seafood

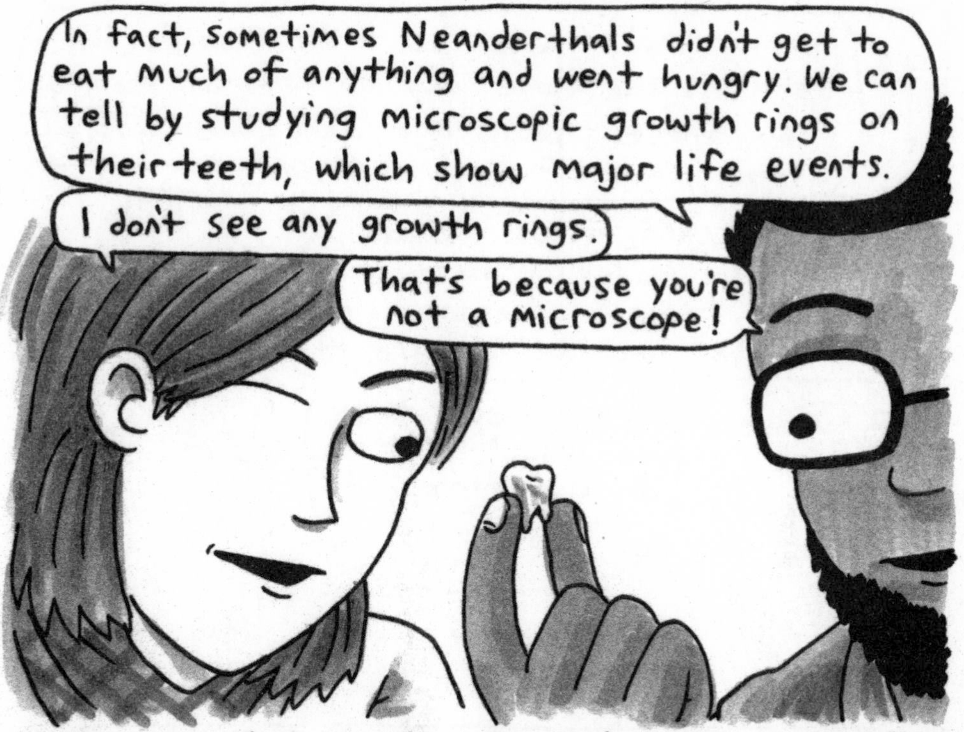
In fact, sometimes Neanderthals didn't get to eat much of anything and went hungry. We can tell by studying microscopic growth rings on their teeth, which show major life events.
I don't see any growth rings.
That's because you're not a microscope!

Dairy cows that provide milk didn't exist at the time, so Neanderthals got milk by nursing from their mothers.

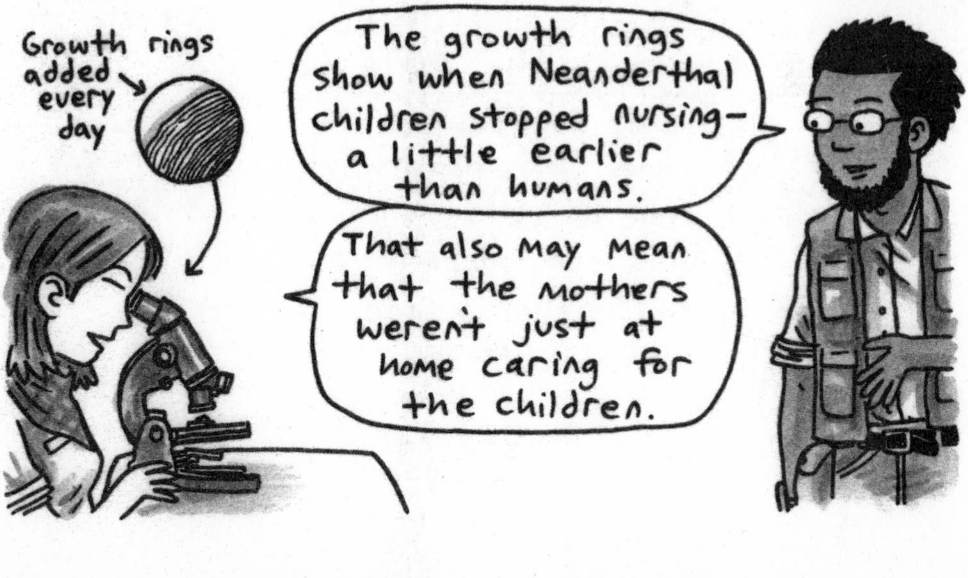
Growth rings added every day
The growth rings show when Neanderthal children stopped nursing– a little earlier than humans.
That also may mean that the mothers weren't just at home caring for the children.

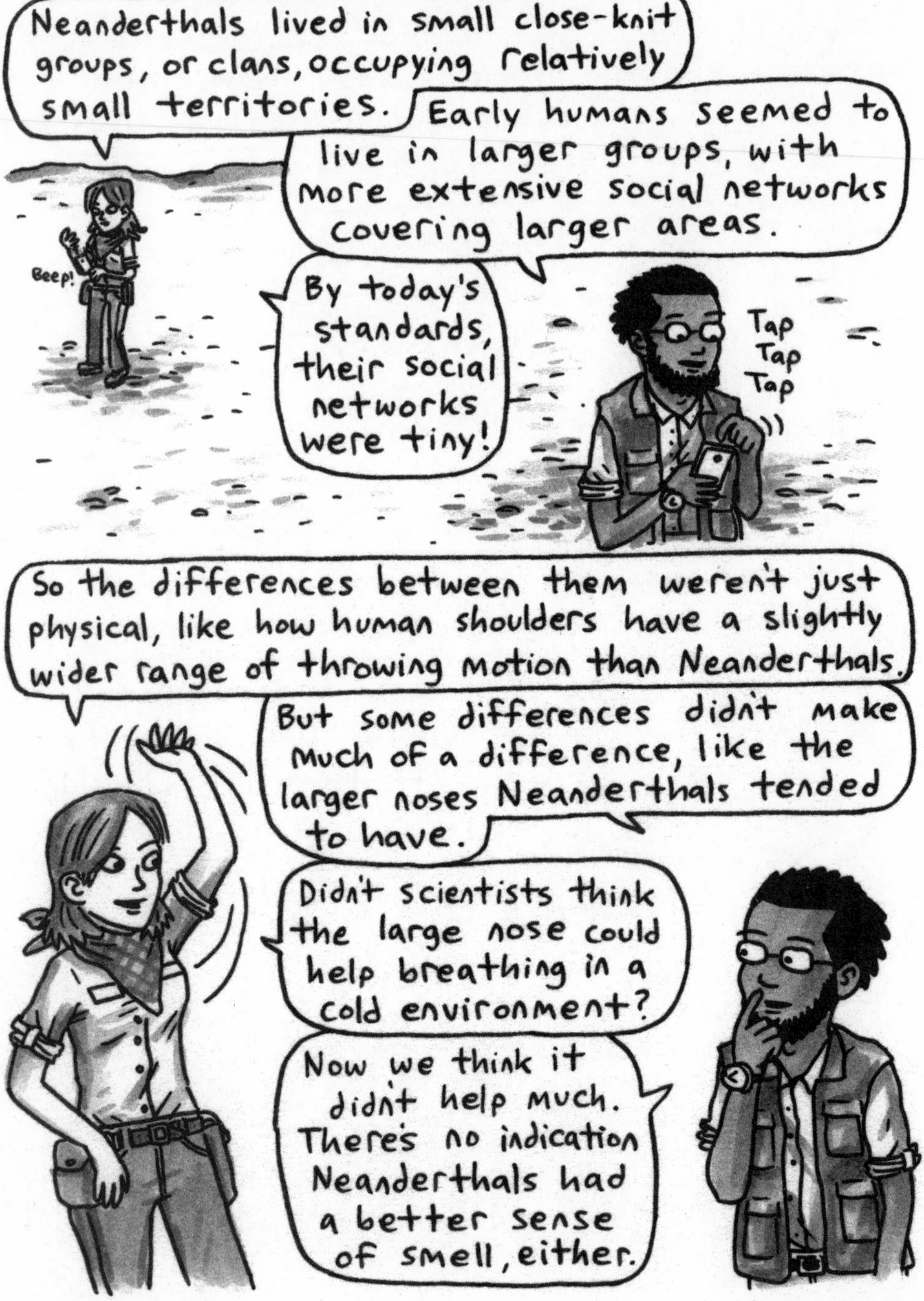
Neanderthals lived in small close-knit groups, or clans, occupying relatively small territories.
Early humans seemed to live in larger groups, with more extensive social networks covering larger areas.
Beep!
By today's standards, their social networks were tiny!
Tap Tap Tap
So the differences between them weren't just physical, like how human shoulders have a slightly wider range of throwing motion than Neanderthals.
But some differences didn't make much of a difference, like the larger noses Neanderthals tended to have.
Didn't scientists think the large nose could help breathing in a cold environment?
Now we think it didn't help much. There's no indication Neanderthals had a better sense of smell, either.

Humans may have had an advantage in sense of smell - through wolves that could track prey by scent. Wolves and humans could have helped each other hunt more successfully.
And defend against other predators. That would definitely have given humans an edge over Neanderthals, but they didn't have pet wolves, did they?!
The earliest signs of wolves being tamed are from about 40,000 years ago, just when early humans appeared in Neanderthal territory.
Wolves may have begun living closer to humans to scavenge campsites, over time becoming more and more comfortable with people.
Humans may have raised orphaned wolf pups, which became domesticated dogs many generations later.
I'm glad training my dog didn't take thousands of years!

A theory is an explanation of some aspect of the world, based on facts that have been confirmed by experiment and observation. Discovery of new evidence can lead to new explanations.

Some paleontologists work at museums. These are just a few museums you can visit to learn more about Neanderthals and early humans!

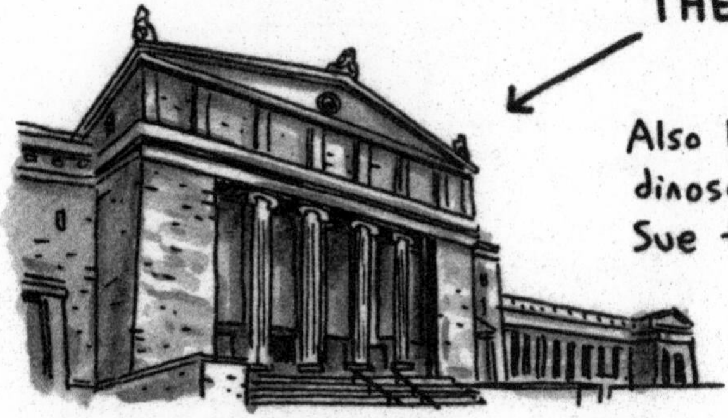

THE FIELD MUSEUM
Chicago, USA

Also has a great collection of dinosaur fossils - including Sue the T. rex!

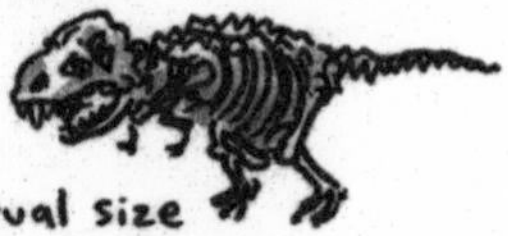

Not actual size

NEANDERTHAL MUSEUM
Mettmann, Germany

Located at the site where the first Neanderthal fossils were found and covers the evolution of humankind.

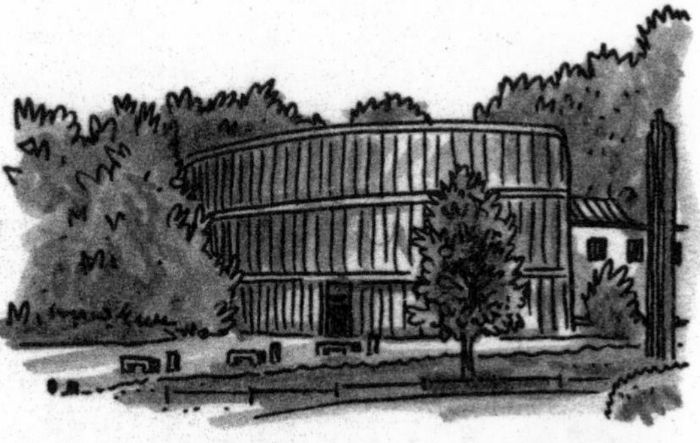

AMERICAN MUSEUM OF NATURAL HISTORY
New York City, USA

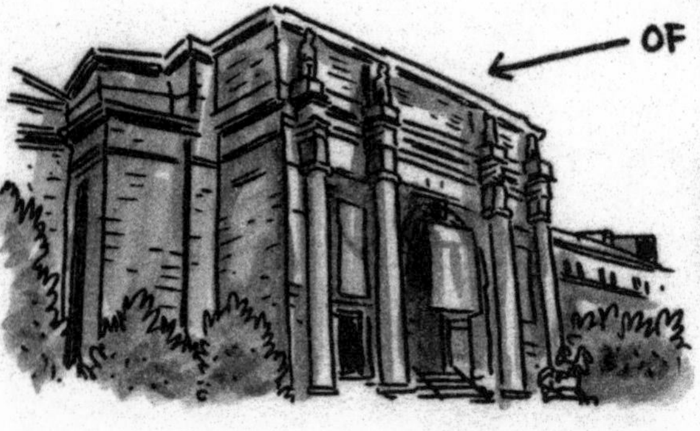

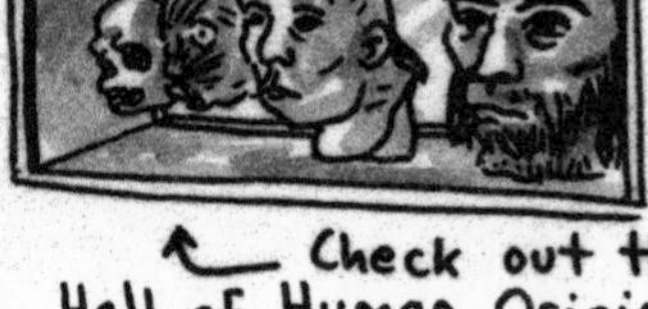

Check out the Hall of Human Origins!

A NEANDERTHAL TIMELINE*

*Dates subject to change, as new discoveries are made.

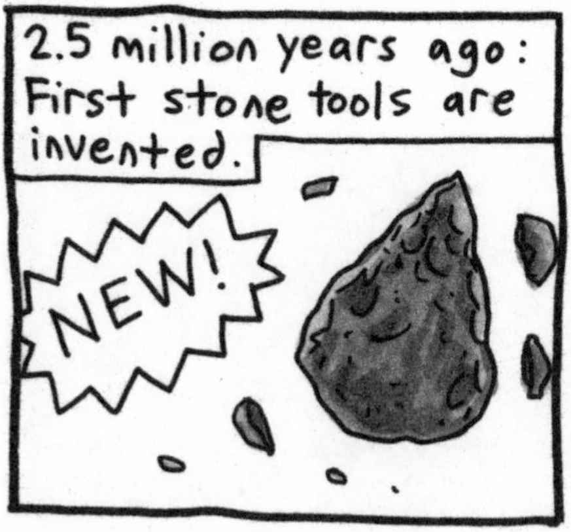
2.5 million years ago: First stone tools are invented.
NEW!

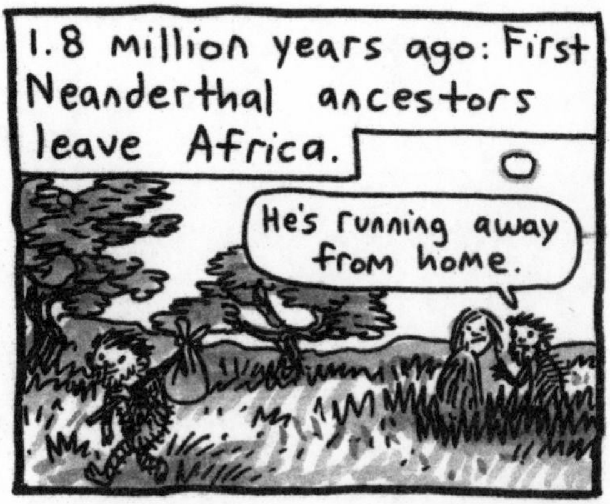
1.8 million years ago: First Neanderthal ancestors leave Africa.
He's running away from home.

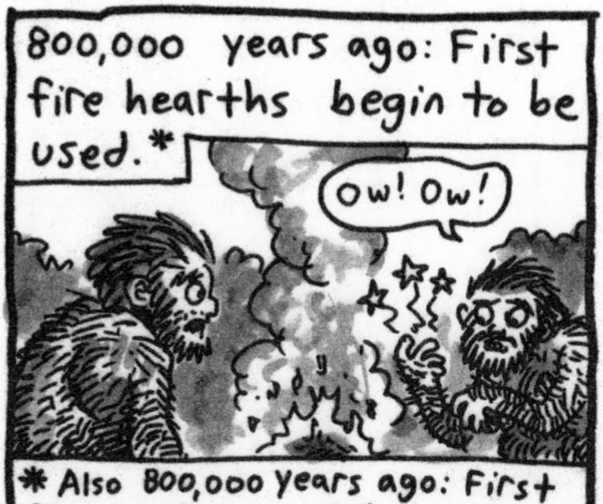
800,000 years ago: First fire hearths begin to be used.*
Ow! Ow!
* Also 800,000 years ago: First fingers burnt while cooking.

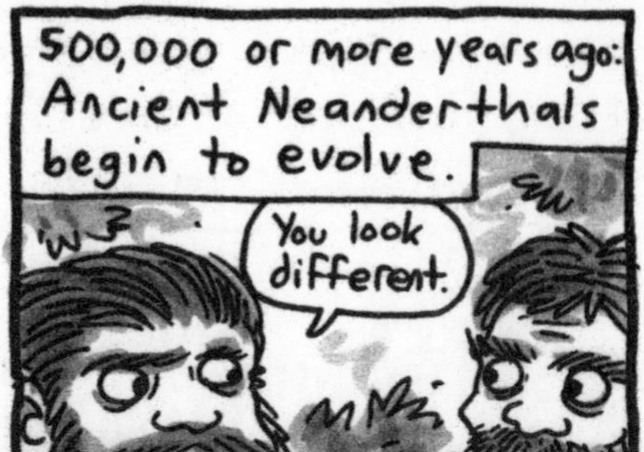
500,000 or more years ago: Ancient Neanderthals begin to evolve.
You look different.

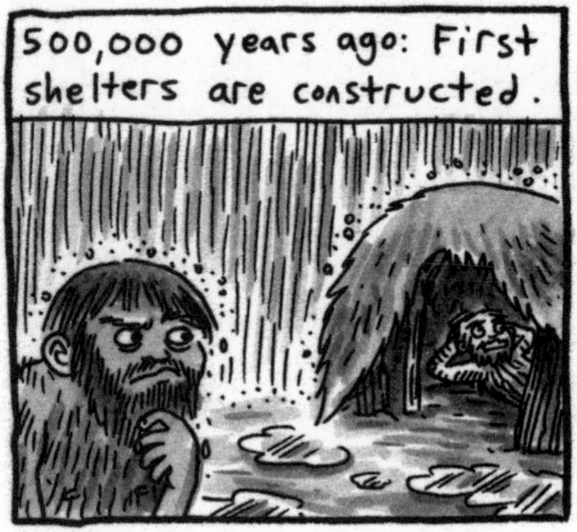
500,000 years ago: First shelters are constructed.

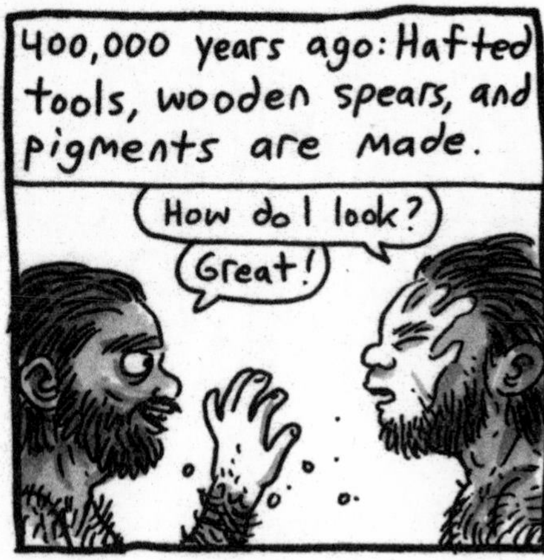
400,000 years ago: Hafted tools, wooden spears, and pigments are made.
How do I look?
Great!

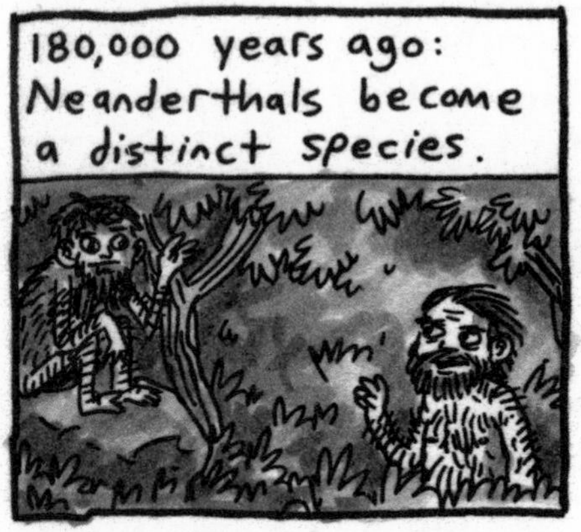
180,000 years ago: Neanderthals become a distinct species.

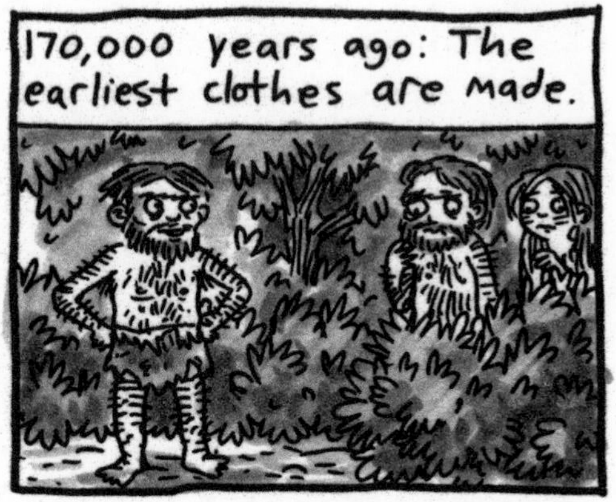
170,000 years ago: The earliest clothes are made.

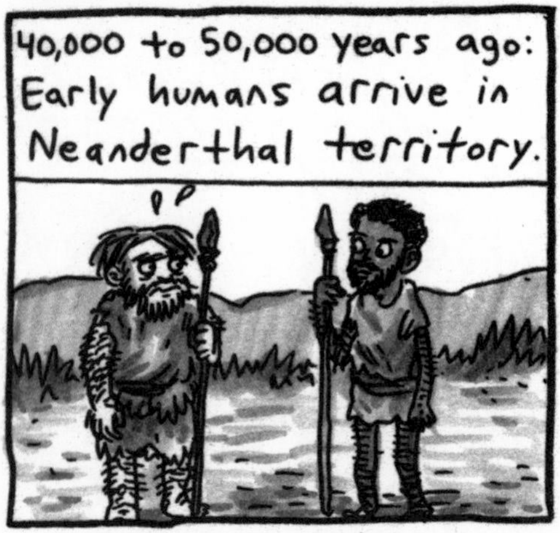
40,000 to 50,000 years ago: Early humans arrive in Neanderthal territory.

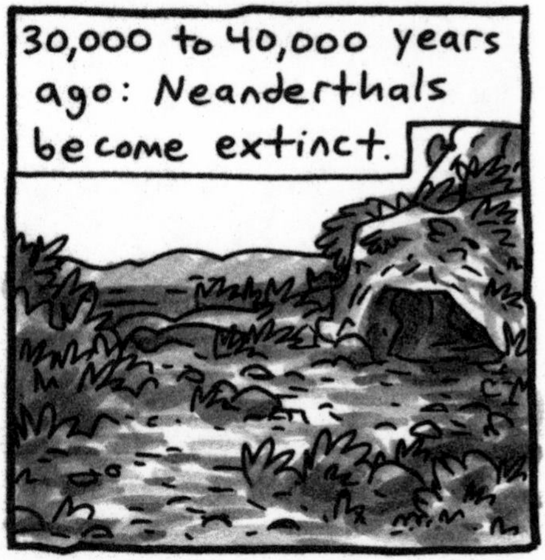
30,000 to 40,000 years ago: Neanderthals become extinct.

FACT VS. FICTION

While most of Lucy and Andy's story is based on the best of our knowledge about Neanderthals, there are some parts that might be stretching the truth....

DID NEANDERTHALS HAVE PET CATS? No, unfortunately not. Cats weren't pets until about 5,000 years ago. But cats are fun to draw and make funny characters!

DID NEANDERTHALS LIVE IN SUCH SMALL CLANS? Yes, but maybe not quite as small as Lucy and Andy's clan. Neanderthals probably lived in groups of 10 to 15, while early humans lived in groups of 25 to 30.

DID SOME NEANDERTHALS GET BAD ROCKS FOR TOOLMAKING? Yes, sometimes tool debris from poor-quality stones is found near debris from good stones. Neanderthals who were just learning probably practiced on the stones of lesser quality.

DID NEANDERTHALS EAT ACORNS? Remains found at cooking sites indicate that they did. Humans have a long history of eating acorns, and you can still eat them today, with the right recipe!

DID NEANDERTHAL WOMEN HUNT? Almost certainly. Scientists still debate whether men hunted more, but Neanderthal women at least participated in some, if not all, hunting.

DID NEANDERTHALS HAVE GOOD FASHION SENSE? Neanderthals didn't have time to worry about style, and their clothes were simple and useful, although they may have decorated them with pigment.

COULD NEANDERTHALS AND HUMANS TALK TO EACH OTHER? They didn't have the same language, but that wouldn't stop them from communicating. After all, people from different countries today still find ways to communicate with each other, even without knowing each other's words.

A BRIEF HISTORY OF CAVEMEN IN BOOKS & MOVIES

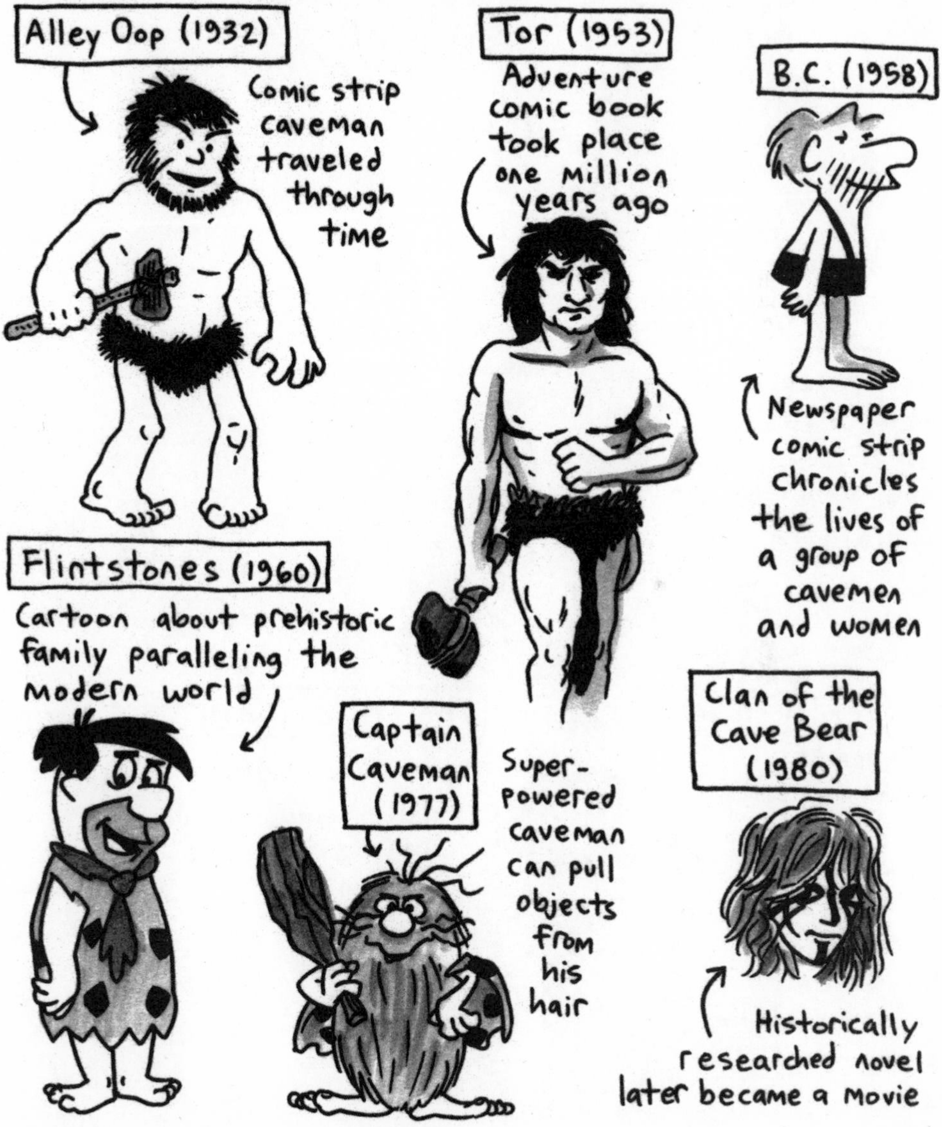

Alley Oop (1932)
Comic strip caveman traveled through time
Tor (1953)
Adventure comic book took place one million years ago
B.C. (1958)
Newspaper comic strip chronicles the lives of a group of cavemen and women
Flintstones (1960)
Cartoon about prehistoric family paralleling the modern world
Captain Caveman (1977)
Super-powered caveman can pull objects from his hair
Clan of the Cave Bear (1980)
Historically researched novel later became a movie

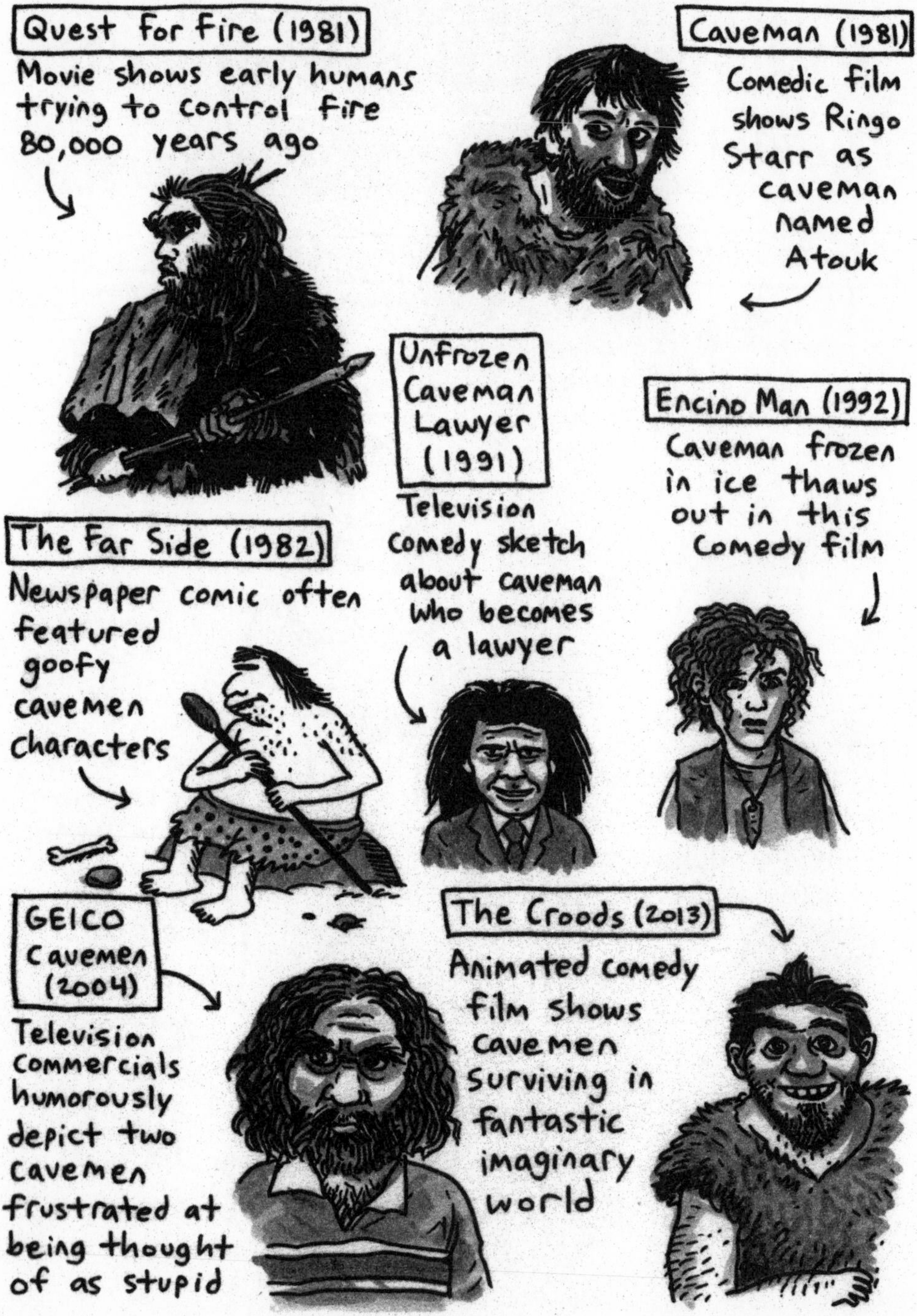
Quest for Fire (1981)
Movie shows early humans trying to control fire 80,000 years ago
Caveman (1981)
Comedic film shows Ringo Starr as caveman named Atouk
Unfrozen Caveman Lawyer (1991)
Television comedy sketch about caveman who becomes a lawyer
Encino Man (1992)
Caveman frozen in ice thaws out in this comedy film
The Far Side (1982)
Newspaper comic often featured goofy cavemen characters
GEICO Cavemen (2004)
Television commercials humorously depict two cavemen frustrated at being thought of as stupid
The Croods (2013)
Animated comedy film shows cavemen surviving in fantastic imaginary world

If Lucy & Andy want to survive the Ice Age,
they'll have to survive each another first!
Catch all the action in *LUCY & ANDY NEANDERTHAL: THE STONE COLD AGE!*

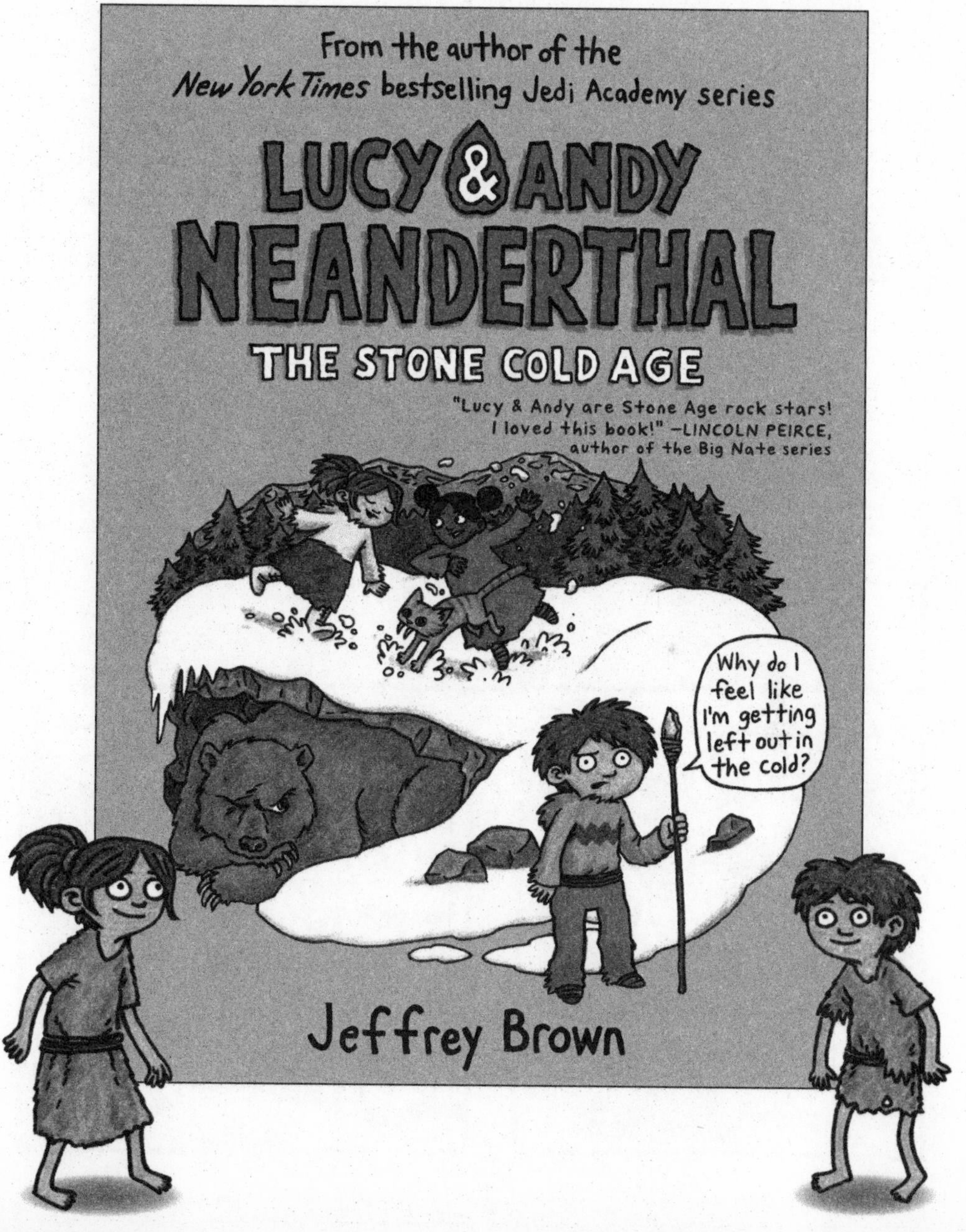
From the author of the
New York Times bestselling Jedi Academy series
LUCY & ANDY
NEANDERTHAL
THE STONE COLD AGE
"Lucy & Andy are Stone Age rock stars! I loved this book!" —LINCOLN PEIRCE, author of the Big Nate series
Why do I feel like I'm getting left out in the cold?
Jeffrey Brown

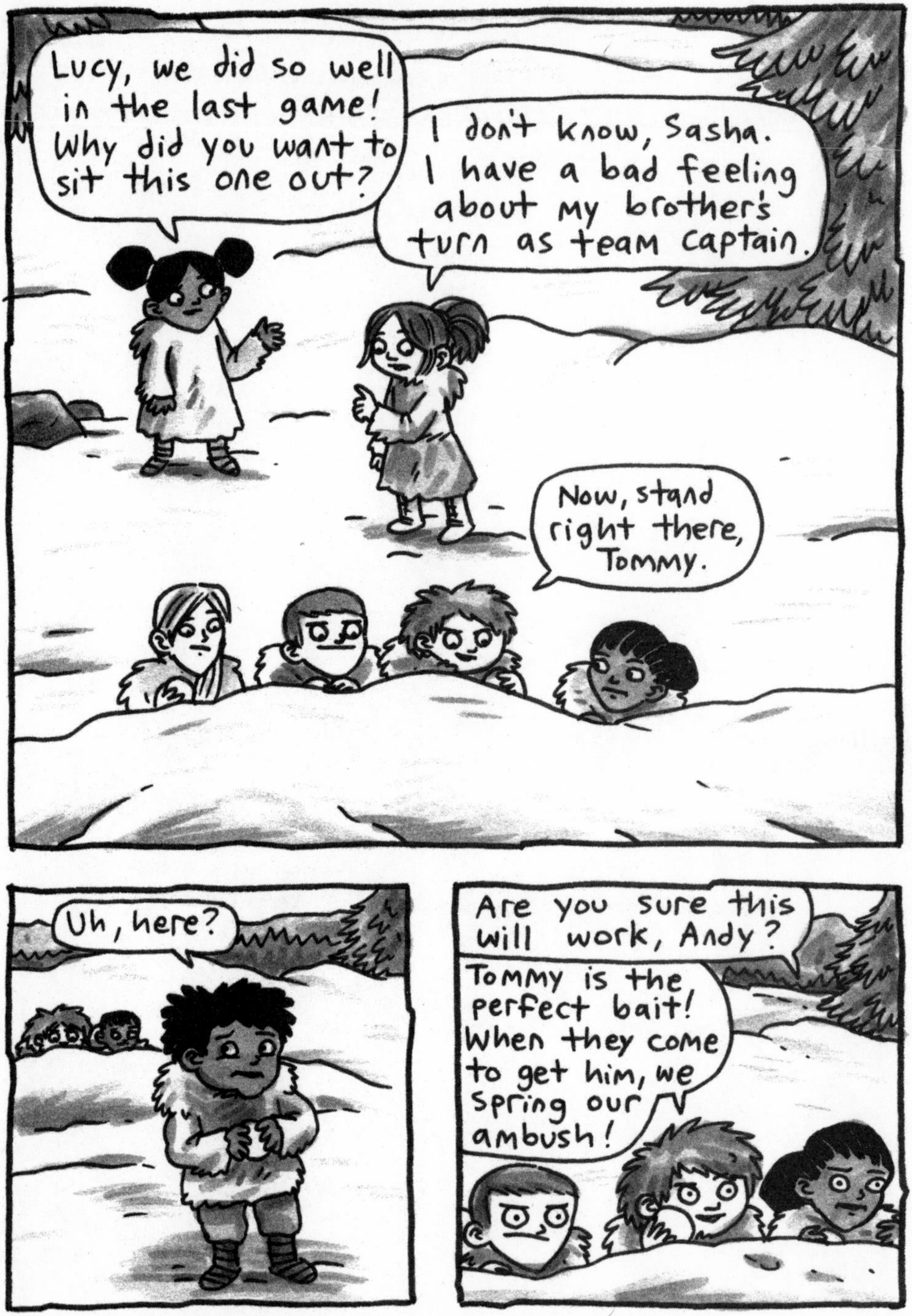
Lucy, we did so well in the last game! Why did you want to sit this one out?
I don't know, Sasha. I have a bad feeling about my brother's turn as team captain.
Now, stand right there, Tommy.
Uh, here?
Are you sure this will work, Andy?
Tommy is the perfect bait! When they come to get him, we spring our ambush!

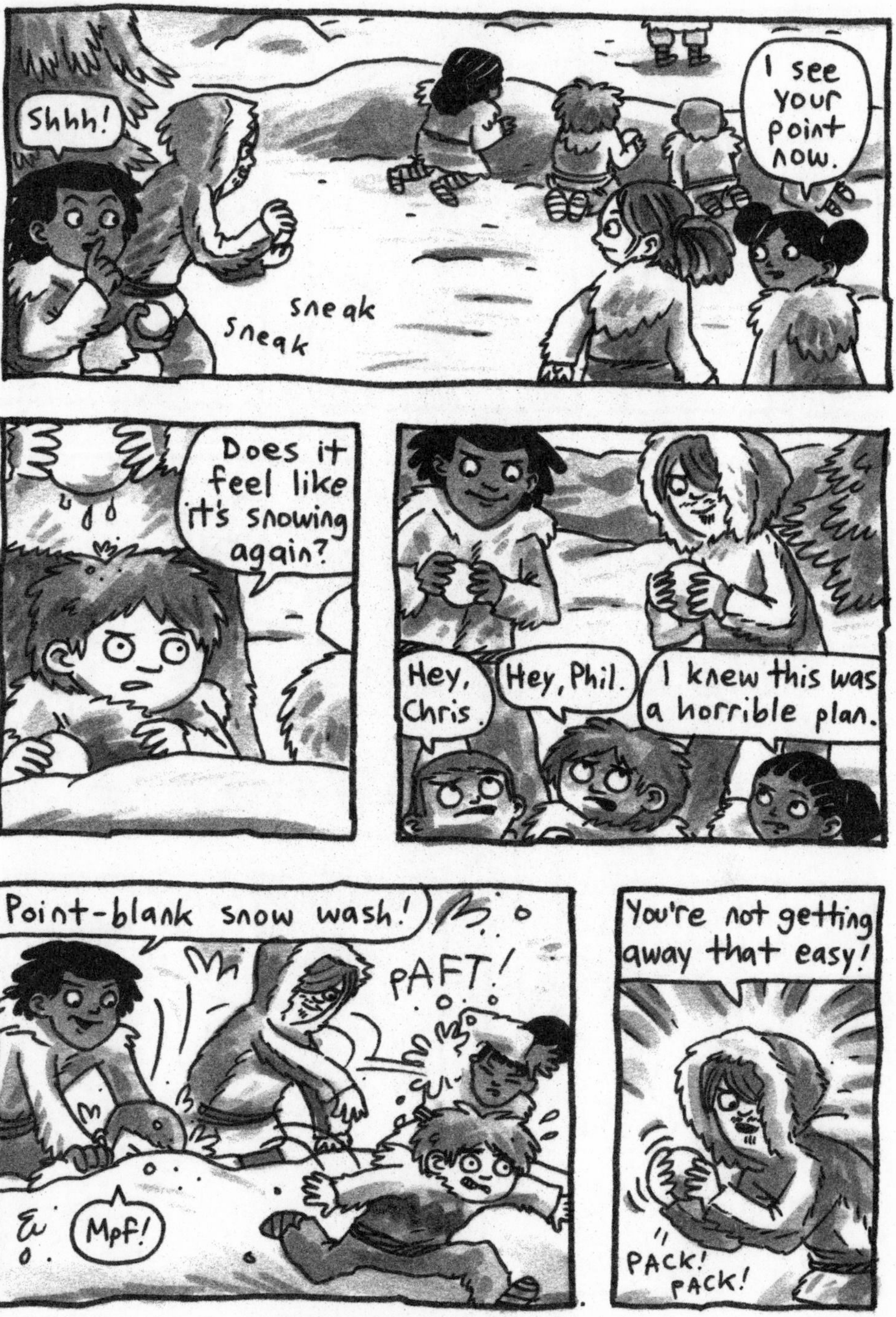
Shhh!
I see your point now.
sneak
sneak
Does it feel like it's snowing again?
Hey, Chris.
Hey, Phil.
I knew this was a horrible plan.
Point-blank snow wash!
PAFT!
Mpf!
You're not getting away that easy!
PACK!
PACK!

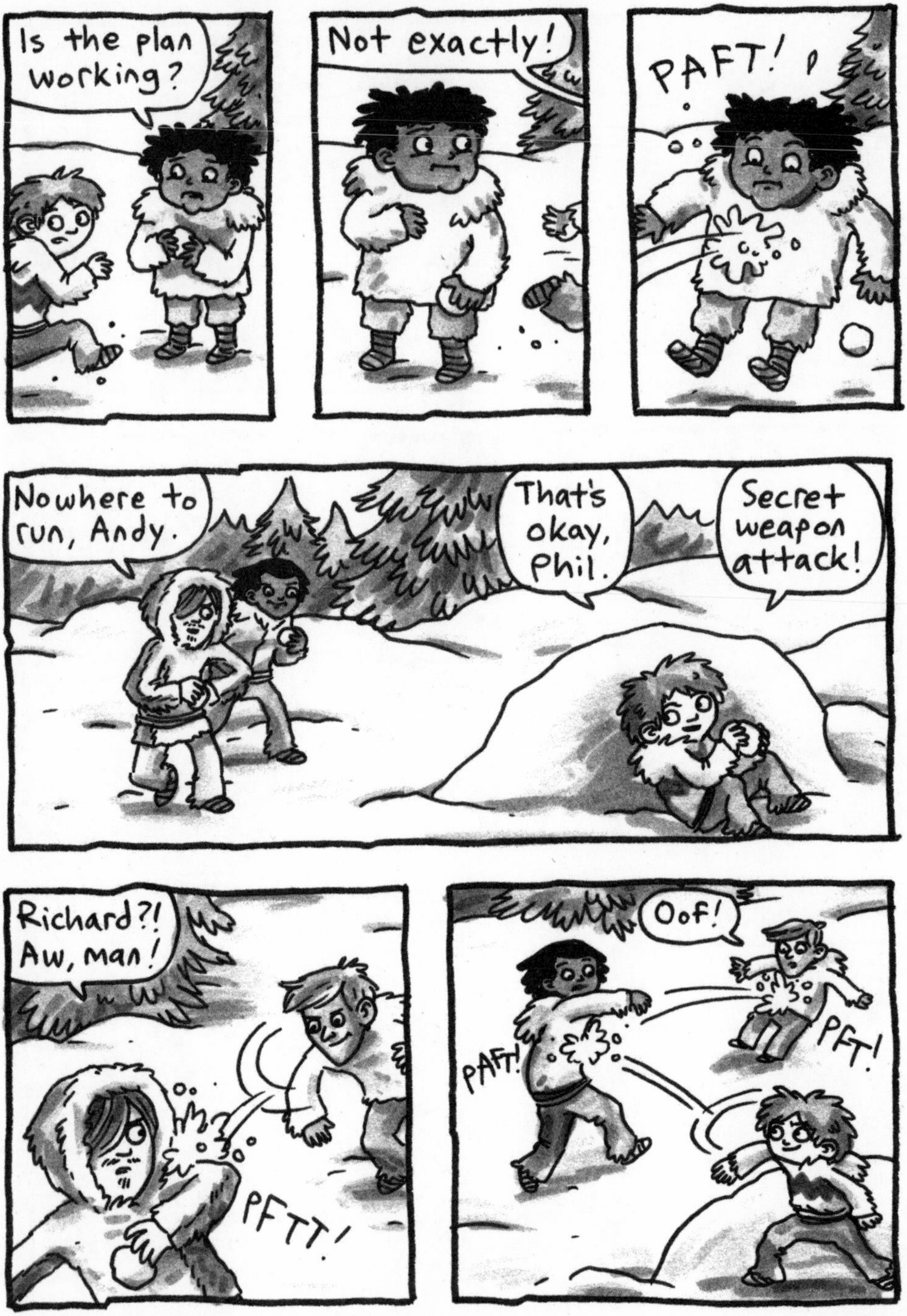
Is the plan working?
Not exactly!
PAFT!
Nowhere to run, Andy.
That's okay, Phil.
Secret weapon attack!
Richard?! Aw, man!
PFTT!
Oof!
PAFT!
PFT!

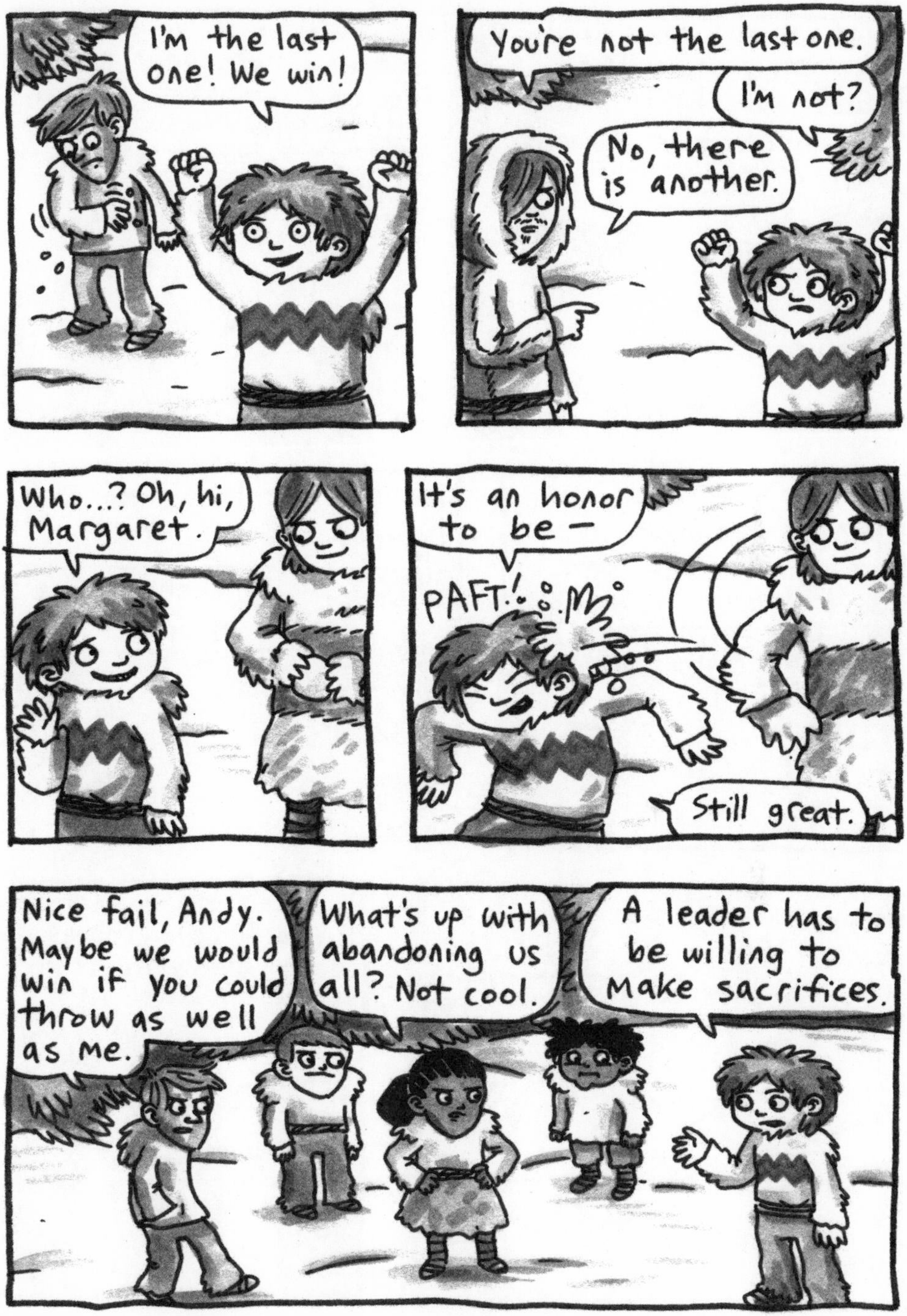
I'm the last one! We win!
You're not the last one.
I'm not?
No, there is another.
Who...? Oh, hi, Margaret.
It's an honor to be—
PAFT!
Still great.
Nice fail, Andy. Maybe we would win if you could throw as well as me.
What's up with abandoning us all? Not cool.
A leader has to be willing to make sacrifices.

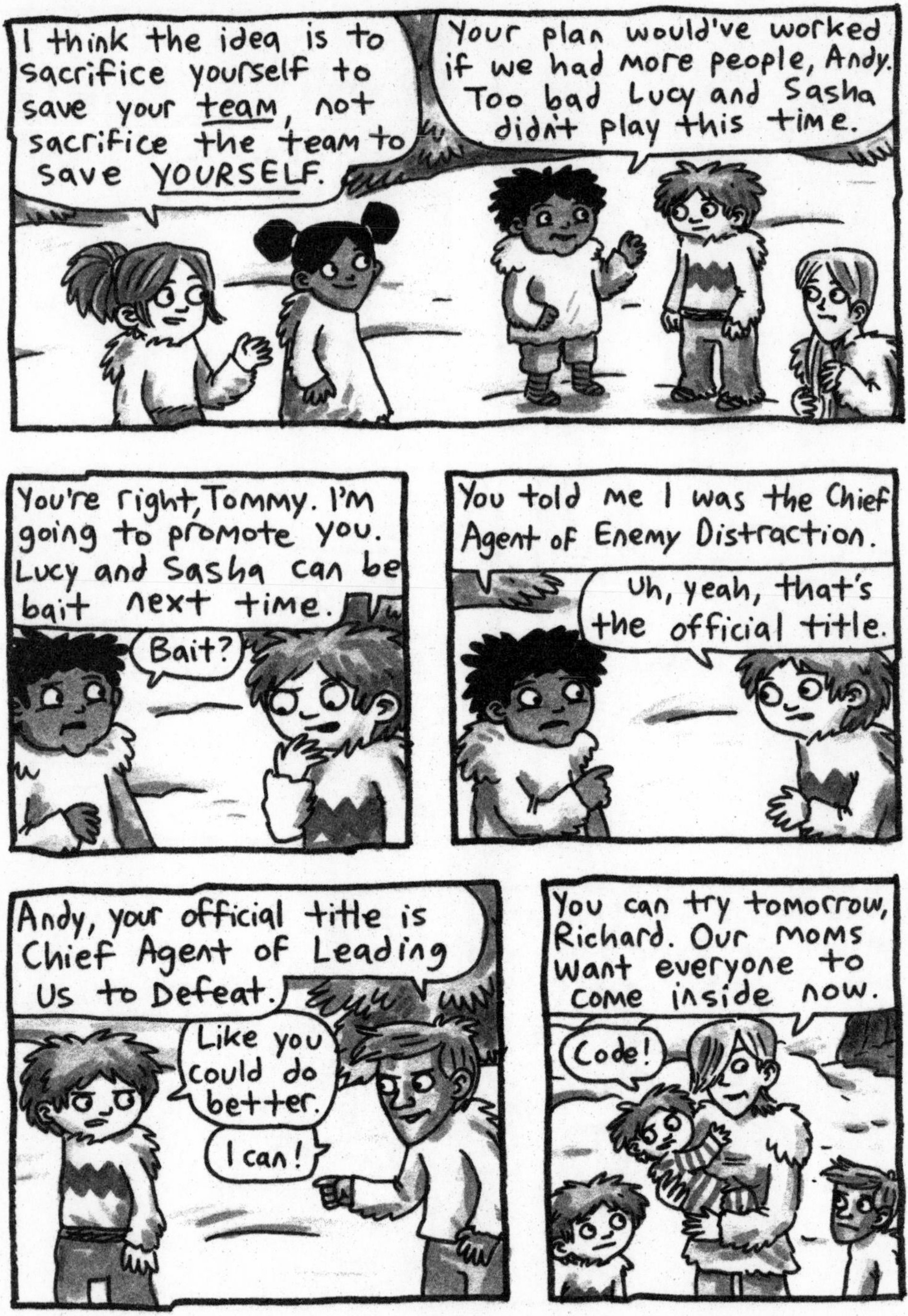
I think the idea is to sacrifice yourself to save your team, not sacrifice the team to save YOURSELF.
Your plan would've worked if we had more people, Andy. Too bad Lucy and Sasha didn't play this time.
You're right, Tommy. I'm going to promote you. Lucy and Sasha can be bait next time.
Bait?
You told me I was the Chief Agent of Enemy Distraction.
Uh, yeah, that's the official title.
Andy, your official title is Chief Agent of Leading Us to Defeat.
Like you could do better.
I can!
You can try tomorrow, Richard. Our moms want everyone to come inside now.
Code!

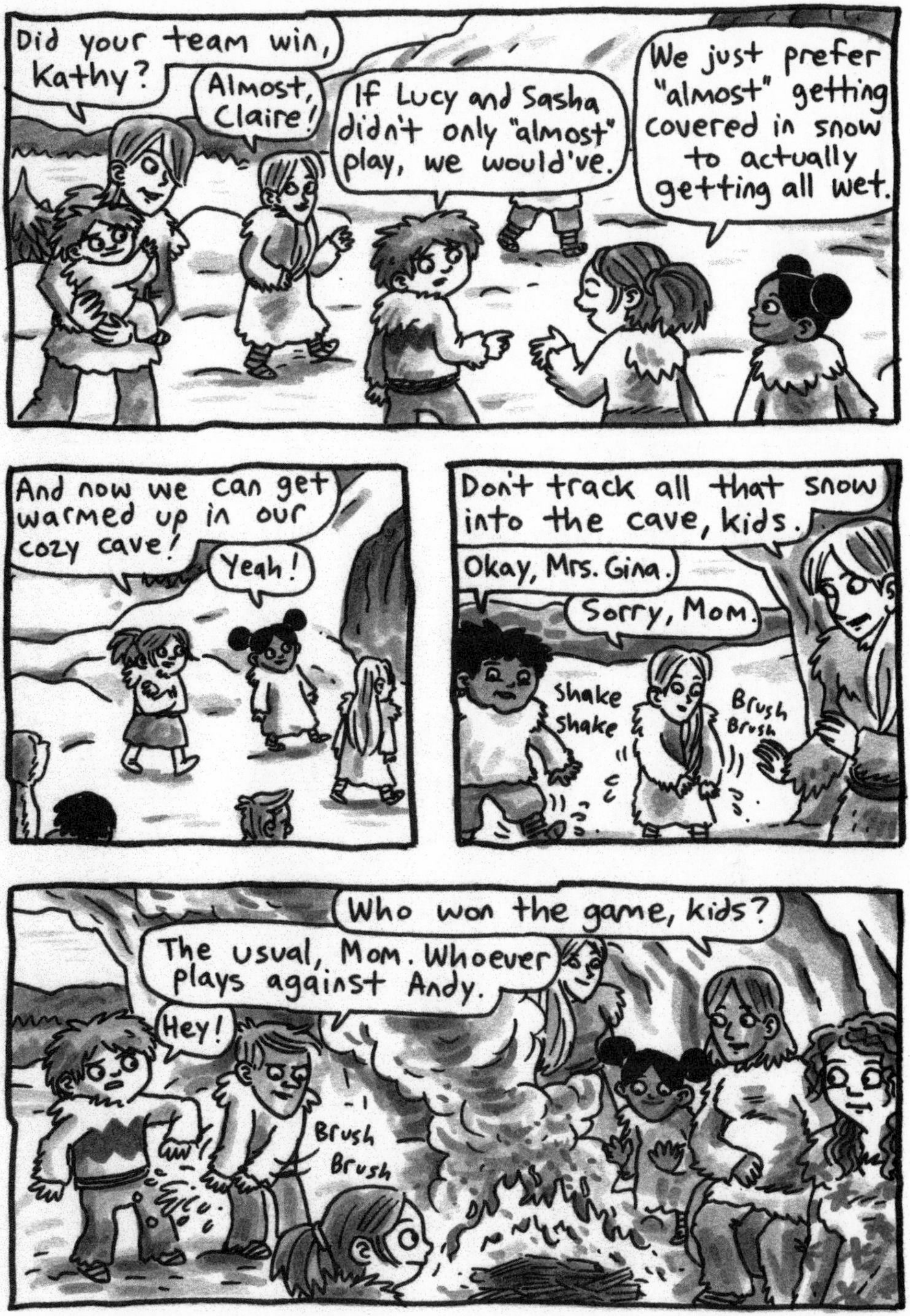
Did your team win, Kathy?
Almost, Claire!
If Lucy and Sasha didn't only "almost" play, we would've.
We just prefer "almost" getting covered in snow to actually getting all wet.
And now we can get warmed up in our cozy cave!
Yeah!
Don't track all that snow into the cave, kids.
Okay, Mrs. Gina.
Sorry, Mom.
Shake Shake
Brush Brush
Who won the game, kids?
The usual, Mom. Whoever plays against Andy.
Hey!
Brush Brush

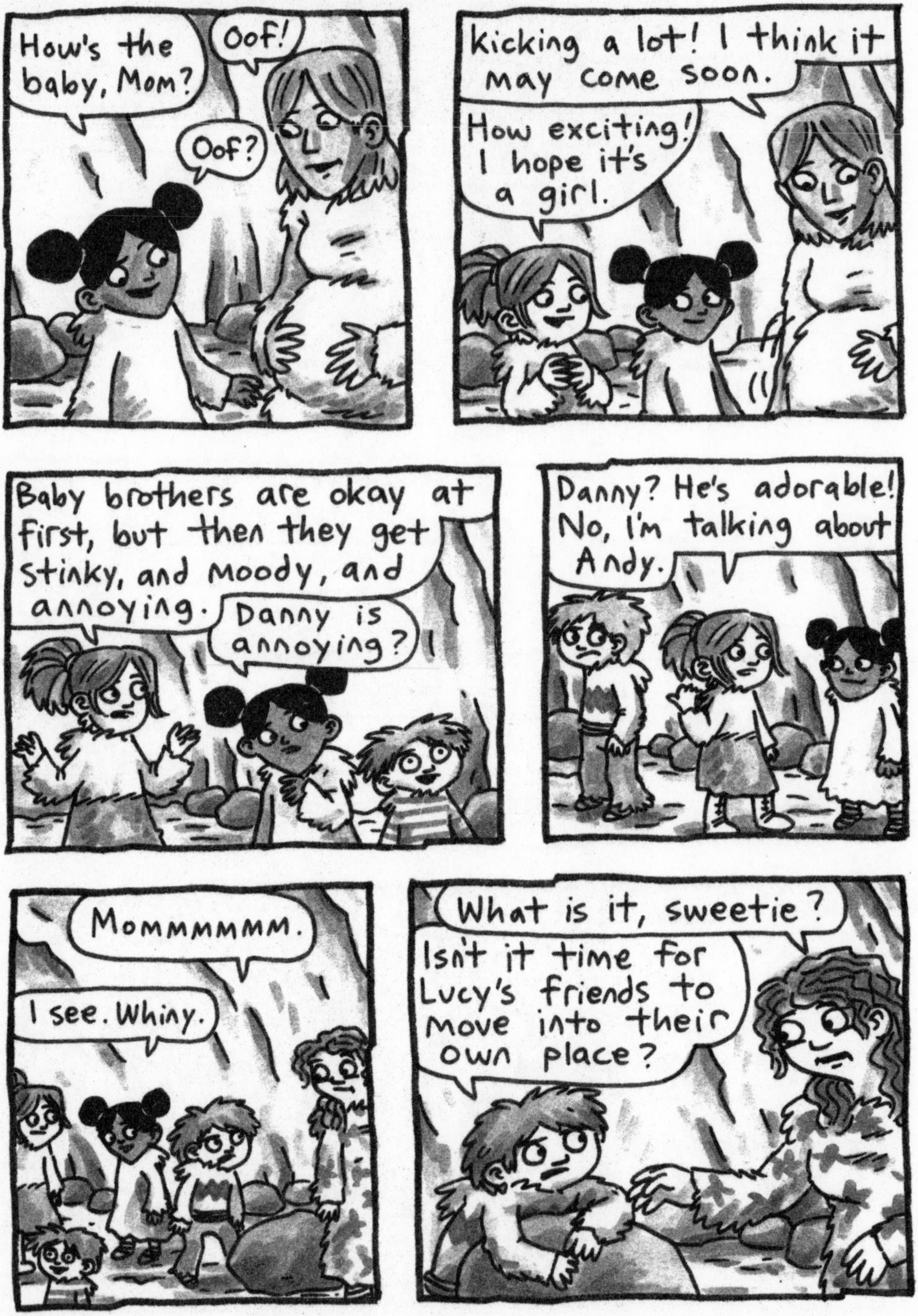
How's the baby, Mom?
Oof!
Oof?
Kicking a lot! I think it may come soon.
How exciting! I hope it's a girl.
Baby brothers are okay at first, but then they get stinky, and moody, and annoying.
Danny is annoying?
Danny? He's adorable! No, I'm talking about Andy.
MOMMMMMMM.
I see. Whiny.
What is it, sweetie?
Isn't it time for Lucy's friends to move into their own place?

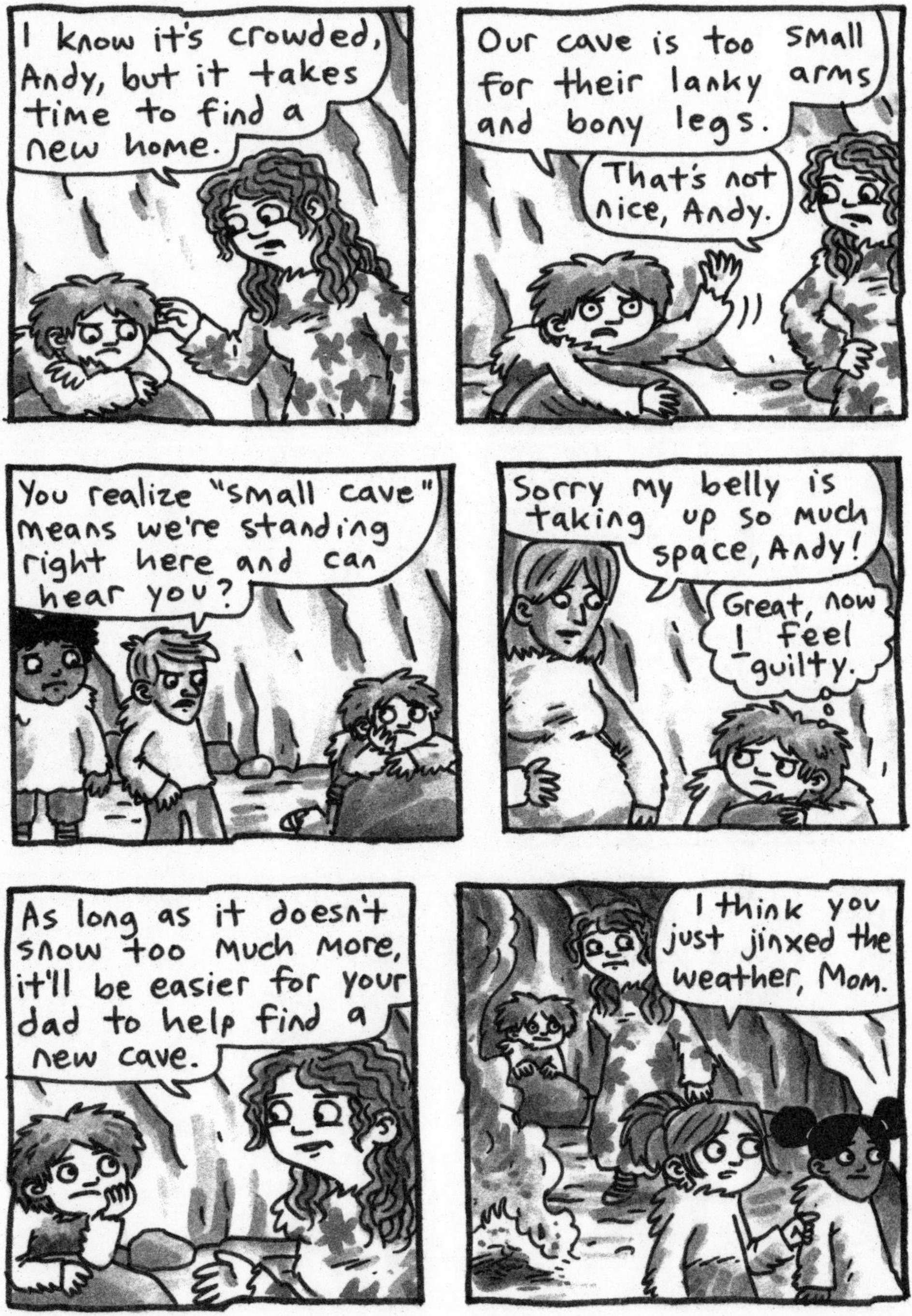
I know it's crowded, Andy, but it takes time to find a new home.
Our cave is too small for their lanky arms and bony legs.
That's not nice, Andy.
You realize "small cave" means we're standing right here and can hear you?
Sorry my belly is taking up so much space, Andy!
Great, now I feel guilty.
As long as it doesn't snow too much more, it'll be easier for your dad to help find a new cave.
I think you just jinxed the weather, Mom.

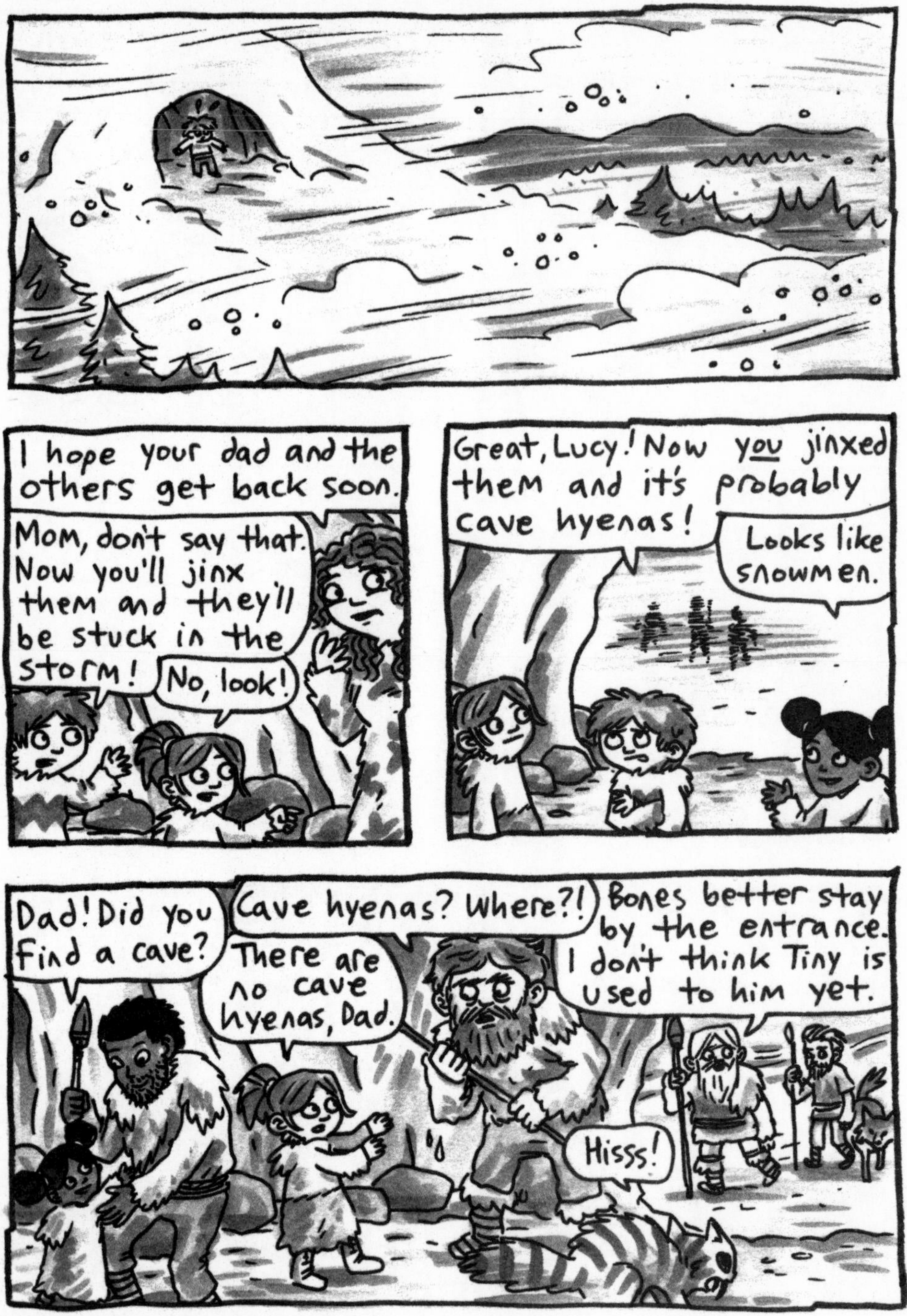
I hope your dad and the others get back soon.
Mom, don't say that. Now you'll jinx them and they'll be stuck in the storm!
No, look!
Great, Lucy! Now you jinxed them and it's probably cave hyenas!
Looks like snowmen.
Dad! Did you find a cave?
Cave hyenas? Where?!
There are no cave hyenas, Dad.
Bones better stay by the entrance. I don't think Tiny is used to him yet.
Hisss!

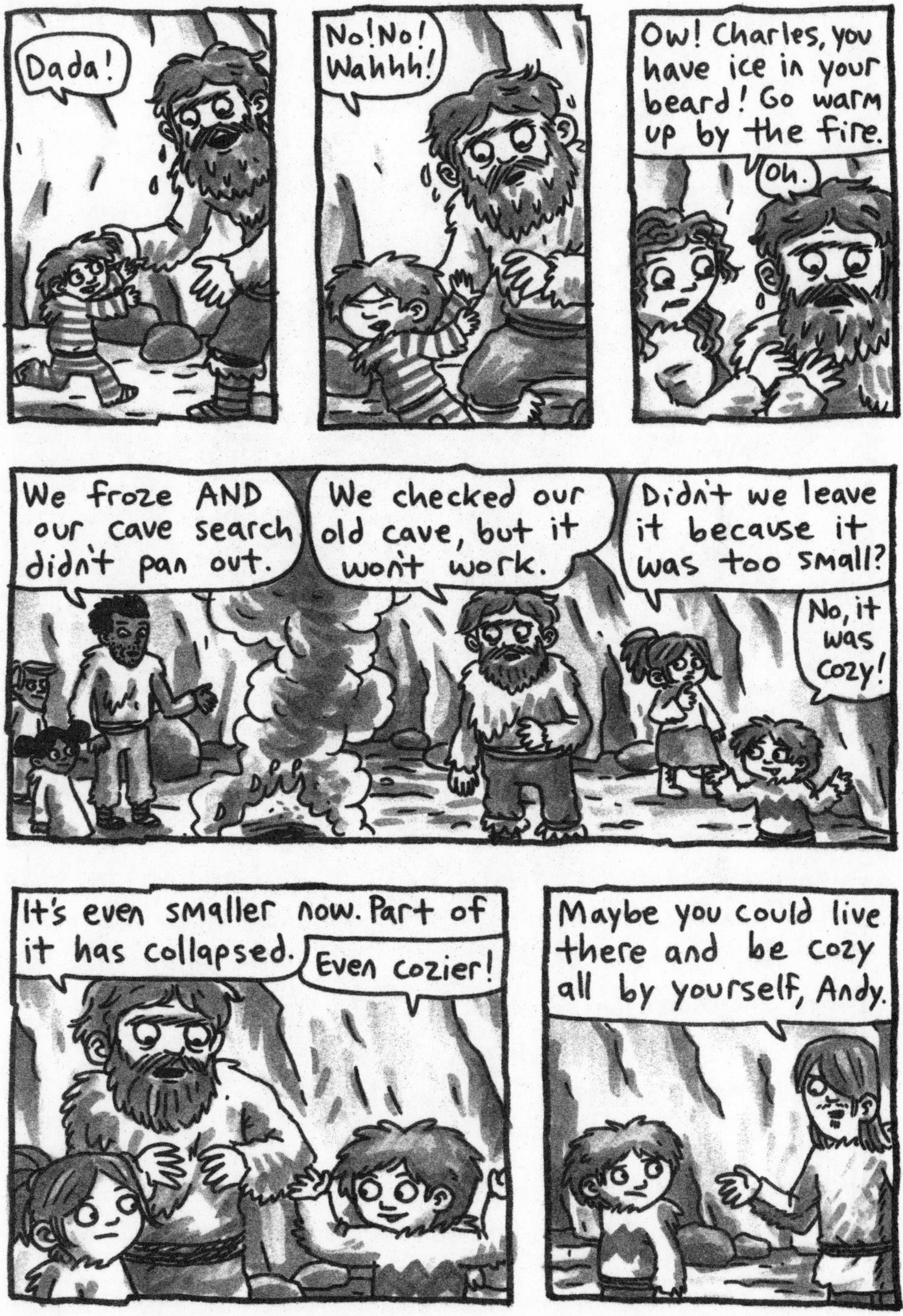
Dada!
No! No! Wahhh!
Ow! Charles, you have ice in your beard! Go warm up by the fire.
Oh.
We froze AND our cave search didn't pan out.
We checked our old cave, but it won't work.
Didn't we leave it because it was too small?
No, it was cozy!
It's even smaller now. Part of it has collapsed.
Even cozier!
Maybe you could live there and be cozy all by yourself, Andy.

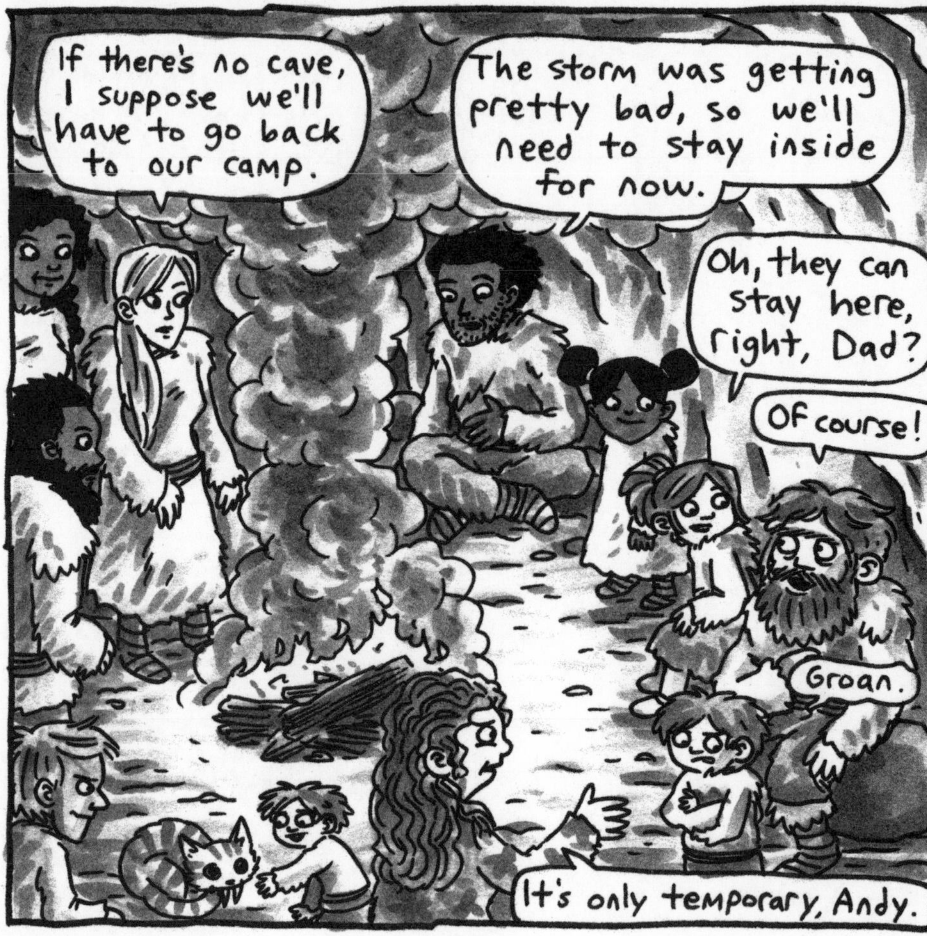
If there's no cave, I suppose we'll have to go back to our camp.
The storm was getting pretty bad, so we'll need to stay inside for now.
Oh, they can stay here, right, Dad?
Of course!
Groan.
It's only temporary, Andy.

Scientists have studied the soil of caves to learn that the smoke and residue from Neanderthal fires was the first man-made pollution!

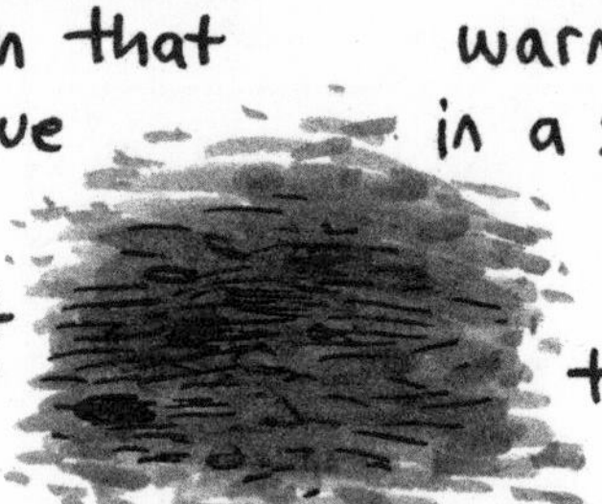

Needing to stay warm while living in a small, enclosed space made exposure to this pollution inevitable.

No warnings about the danger of secondhand smoke have been found in Neanderthal caves.

Don't miss another rockin' Lucy & Andy adventure.
The fun continues in *LUCY & ANDY: BAD TO THE BONES*!

From the author of the
New York Times bestselling Jedi Academy series
LUCY & ANDY
NEANDERTHAL
BAD TO THE BONES
Who says all the wildest creatures went extinct thousands of years ago?
Jeffrey Brown

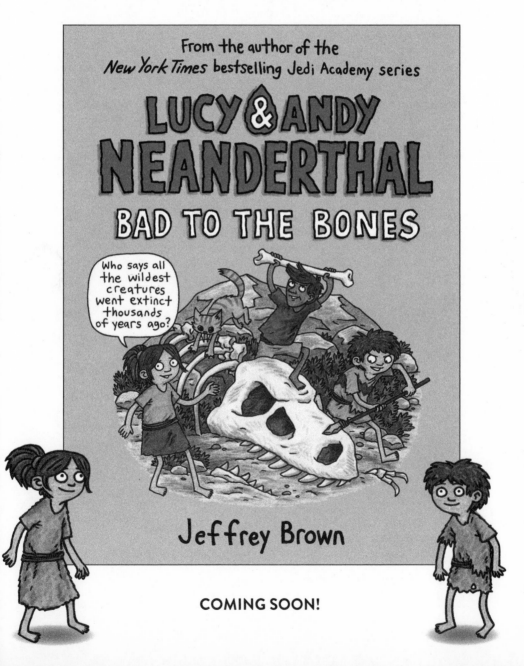

COMING SOON!

Jeffrey Brown is the author of numerous bestselling Star Wars books, including Darth Vader and Son and the middle-grade Jedi Academy series. He is not as old as ancient fossils yet, but he does have 2.2% Neanderthal DNA. He lives in Chicago with his wife and sons, who are not actually allowed to draw on the walls. Most of the time.

jeffreybrowncomics.com
P.O. Box 120, Deerfield, IL 60015-0120, USA

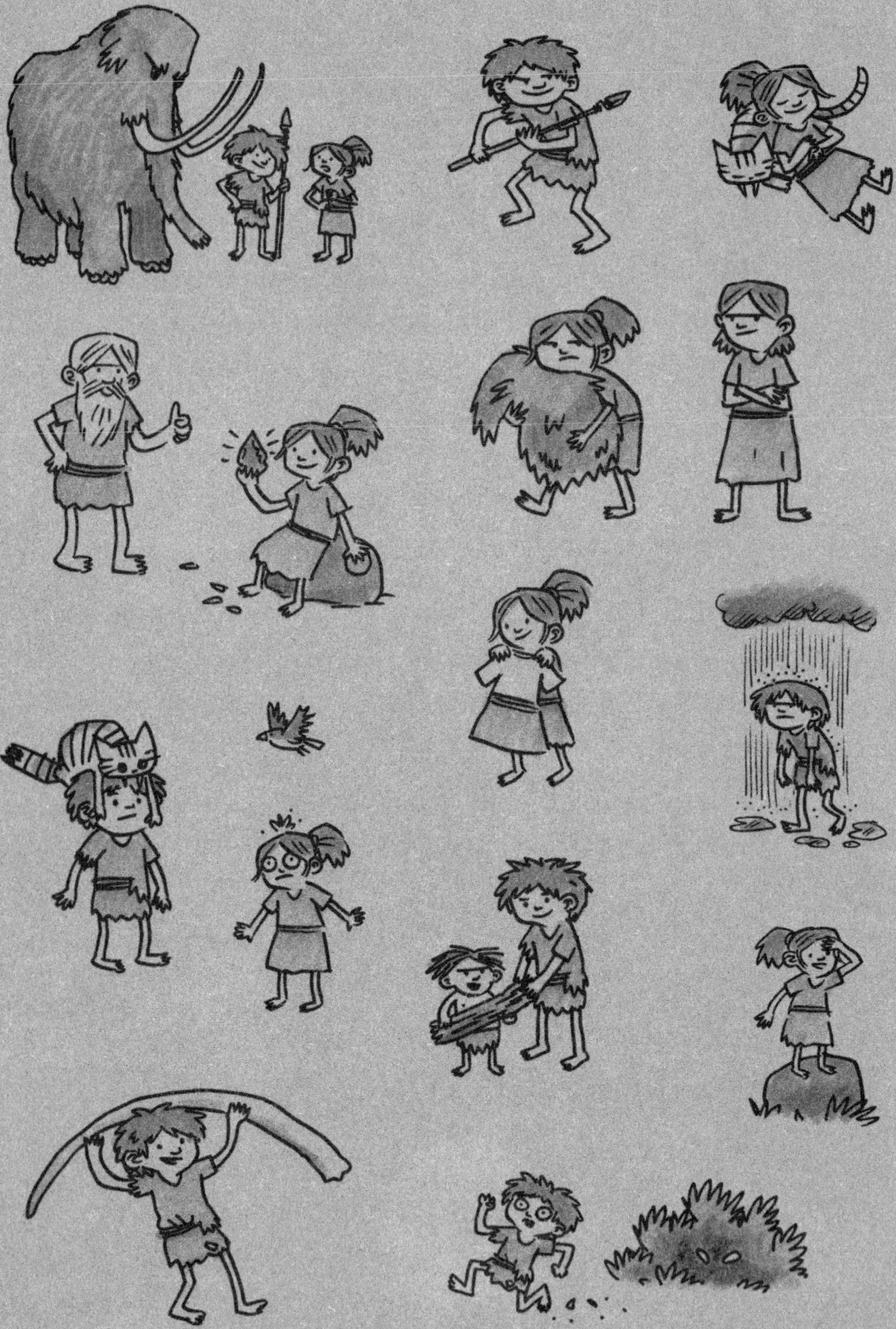